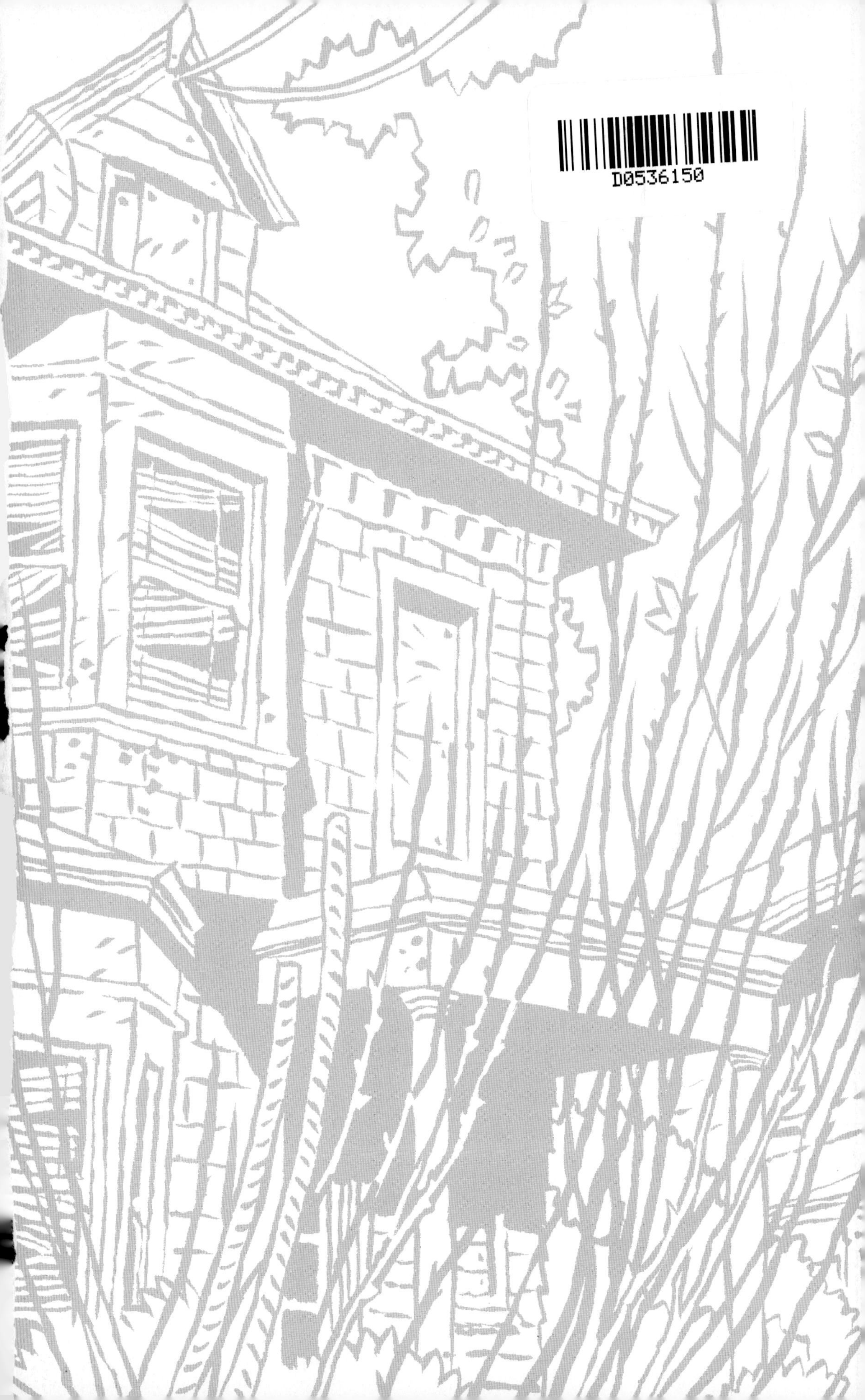

IMAGE COMICS, INC.

Robert Kirkman
CHIEF OPERATING OFFICER

Erik Larsen
CHIEF FINANCIAL OFFICER

Todd McFarlane
PRESIDENT

Marc Silvestri
CHIEF EXECUTIVE OFFICER

Jim Valentino
VICE-PRESIDENT

Eric Stephenson
PUBLISHER

Corey Murphy
DIRECTOR OF SALES

Jeff Boison
DIRECTOR OF PUBLISHING
PLANNING & BOOK TRADE SALES

Jeremy Sullivan
DIRECTOR OF DIGITAL SALES

Kat Salazar
DIRECTOR OF PR & MARKETING

Emily Miller
DIRECTOR OF OPERATIONS

Branwyn Bigglestone
SENIOR ACCOUNTS MANAGER

Sarah Mello
ACCOUNTS MANAGER

Drew Gill
ART DIRECTOR

Jonathan Chan
PRODUCTION MANAGER

Meredith Wallace
PRINT MANAGER

Briah Skelly
PUBLICITY ASSISTANT

Sasha Head
SALES & MARKETING
PRODUCTION DESIGNER

Randy Okamura
DIGITAL PRODUCTION
DESIGNER

David Brothers
BRANDING MANAGER

Ally Power
CONTENT MANAGER

Addison Duke
PRODUCTION ARTIST

Vincent Kukua
PRODUCTION ARTIST

Tricia Ramos
PRODUCTION ARTIST

Emilio Bautista
DIGITAL SALES ASSOCIATE

Jeff Stang
DIRECT MARKET SALES
REPRESENTATIVE

Leanna Caunter
ACCOUNTING ASSISTANT

Chloe Ramos-Peterson
ADMINISTRATIVE ASSISTANT

imagecomics.com

THEY'RE NOT ≠ LIKE US ™

VOLUME TWO

US AGAINST YOU

ERIC STEPHENSON
story

SIMON GANE
art

JORDIE BELLAIRE
color

FONOGRAFIKS
letters + design

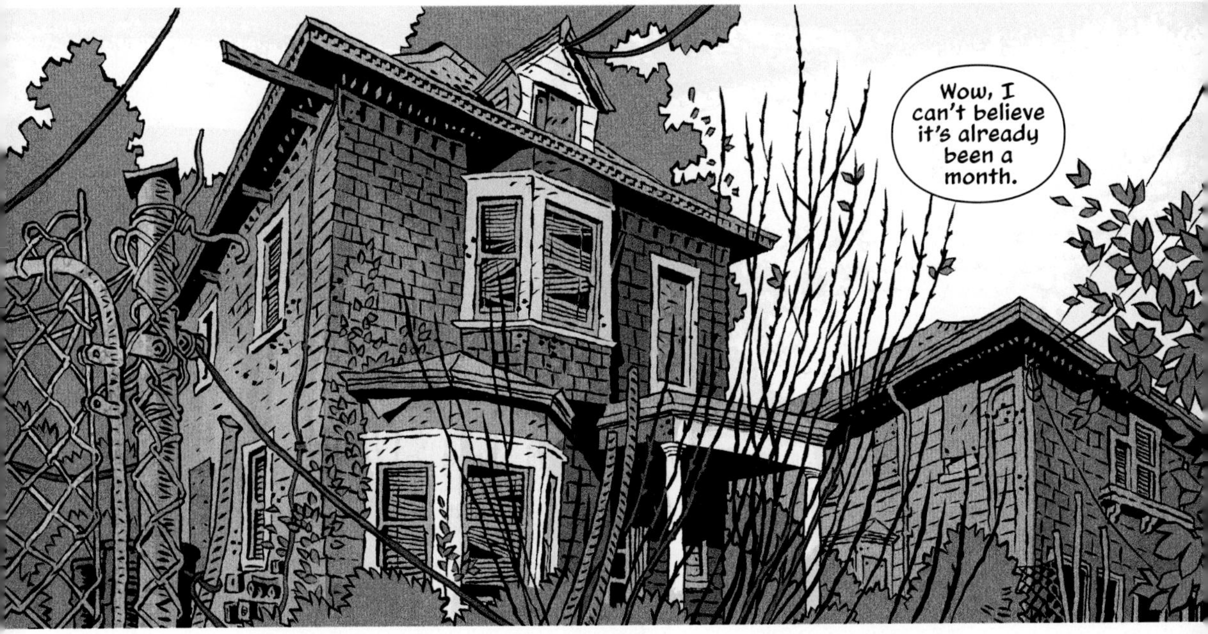
Wow, I can't believe it's already been a month.

7: STRIP IT DOWN

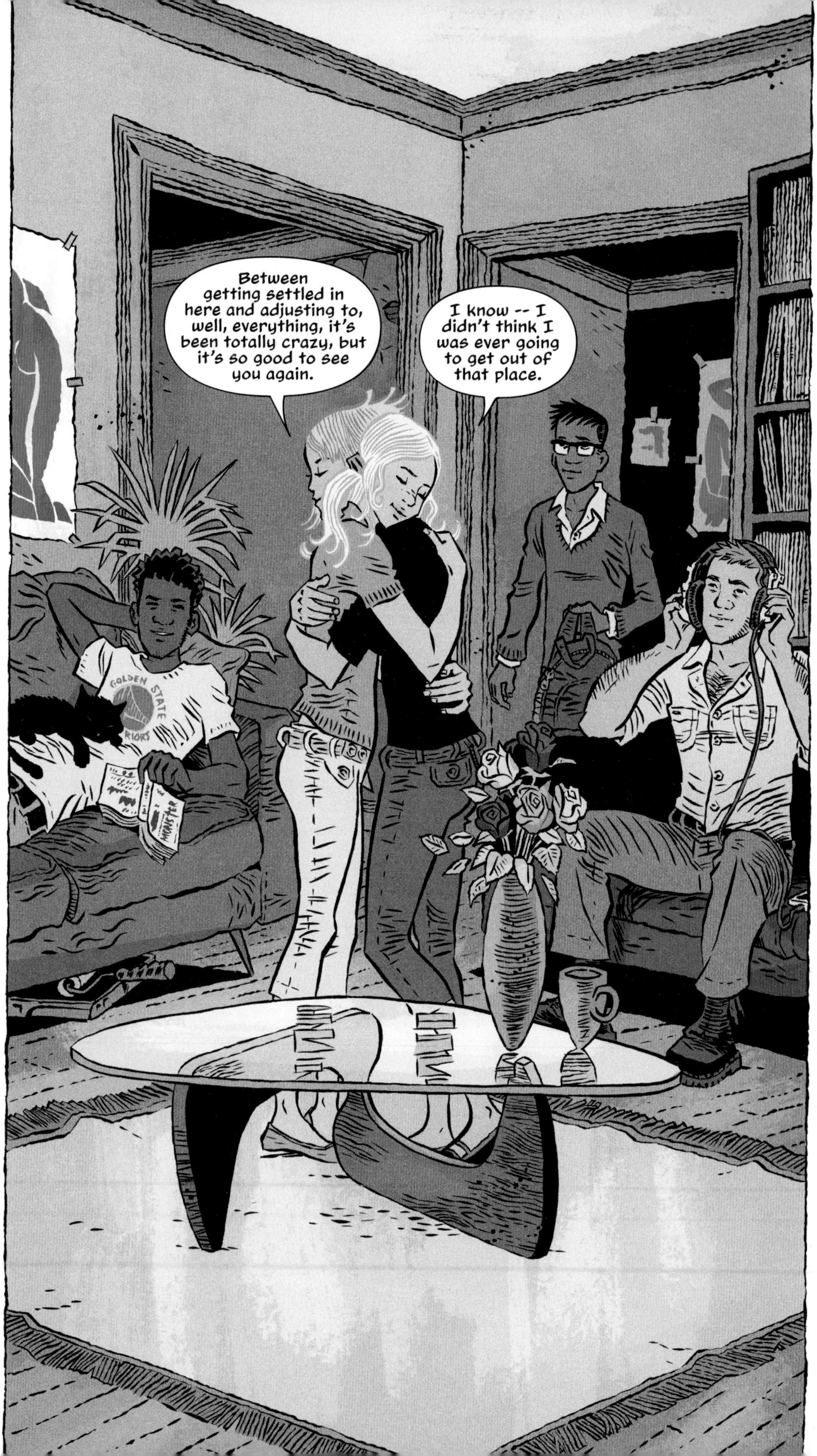
Between getting settled in here and adjusting to, well, everything, it's been totally crazy, but it's so good to see you again.
I know -- I didn't think I was ever going to get out of that place.
GOLDEN STATE
RIORS

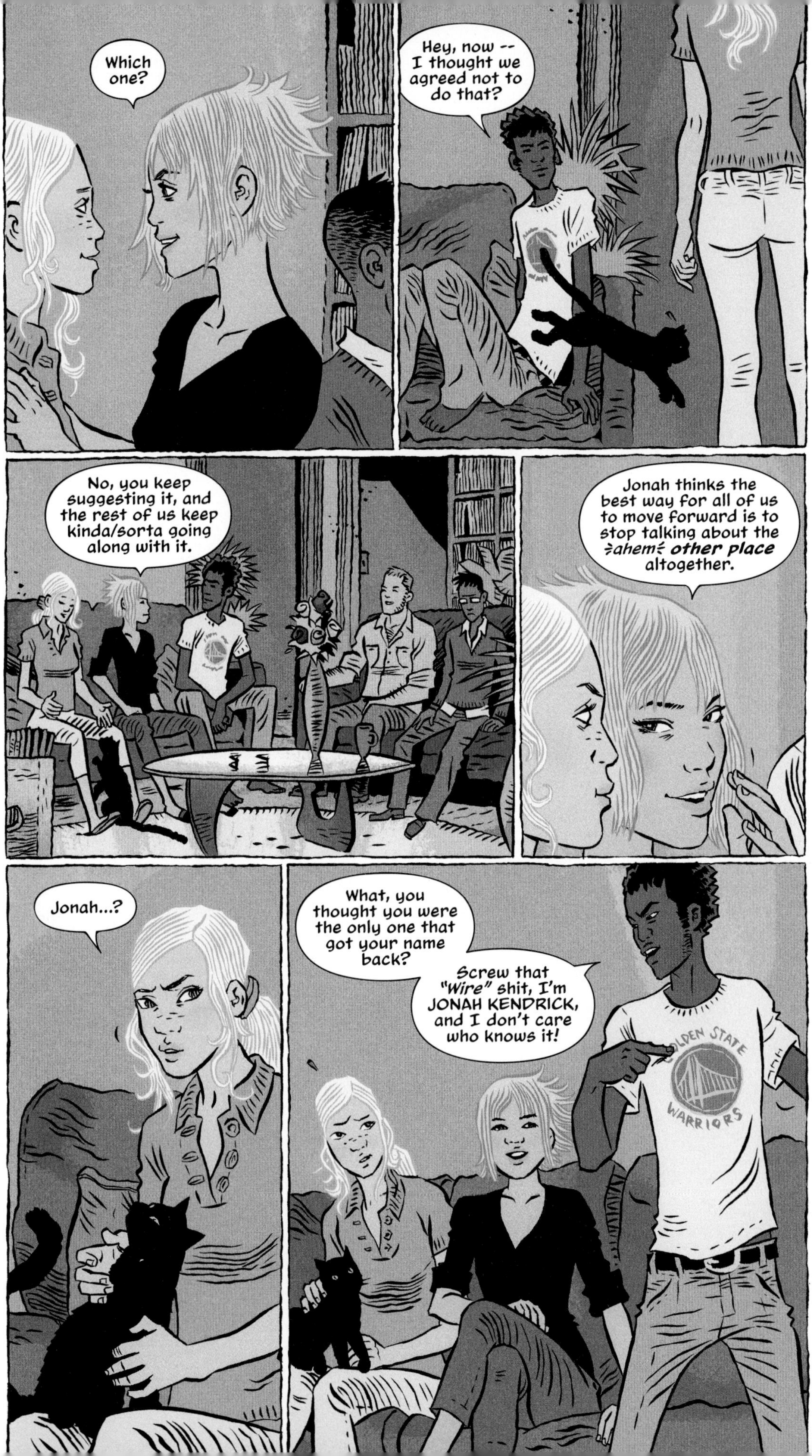
Which one?
Hey, now -- I thought we agreed not to do that?
No, you keep suggesting it, and the rest of us keep kinda/sorta going along with it.
Jonah thinks the best way for all of us to move forward is to stop talking about the *ahem* other place altogether.
Jonah...?
What, you thought you were the only one that got your name back?
Screw that "Wire" shit, I'm JONAH KENDRICK, and I don't care who knows it!
GOLDEN STATE WARRIORS

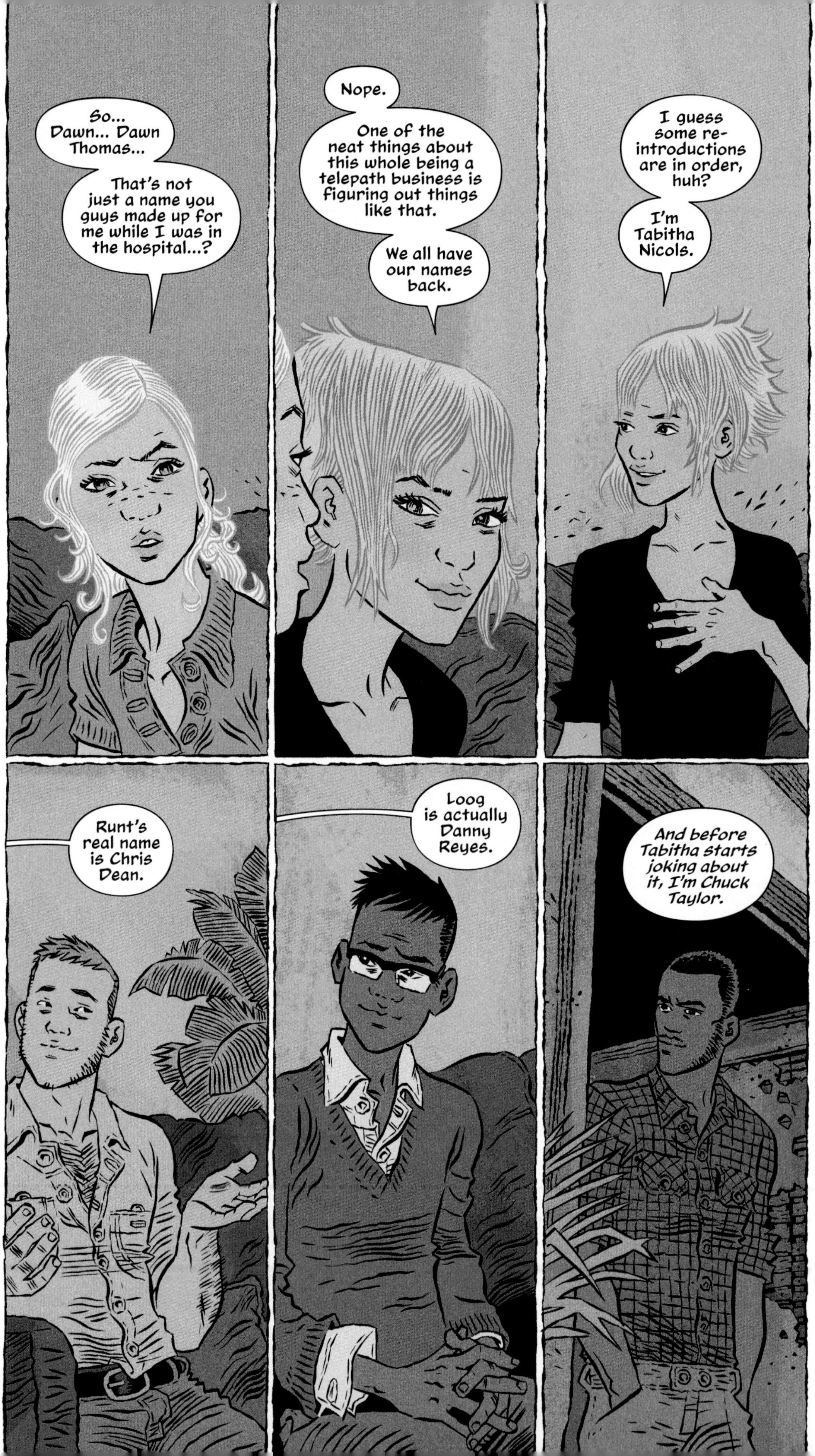
So... Dawn... Dawn Thomas...
That's not just a name you guys made up for me while I was in the hospital...?
Nope.
One of the neat things about this whole being a telepath business is figuring out things like that.
We all have our names back.
I guess some re-introductions are in order, huh?
I'm Tabitha Nicols.
Runt's real name is Chris Dean.
Loog is actually Danny Reyes.
And before Tabitha starts joking about it, I'm Chuck Taylor.

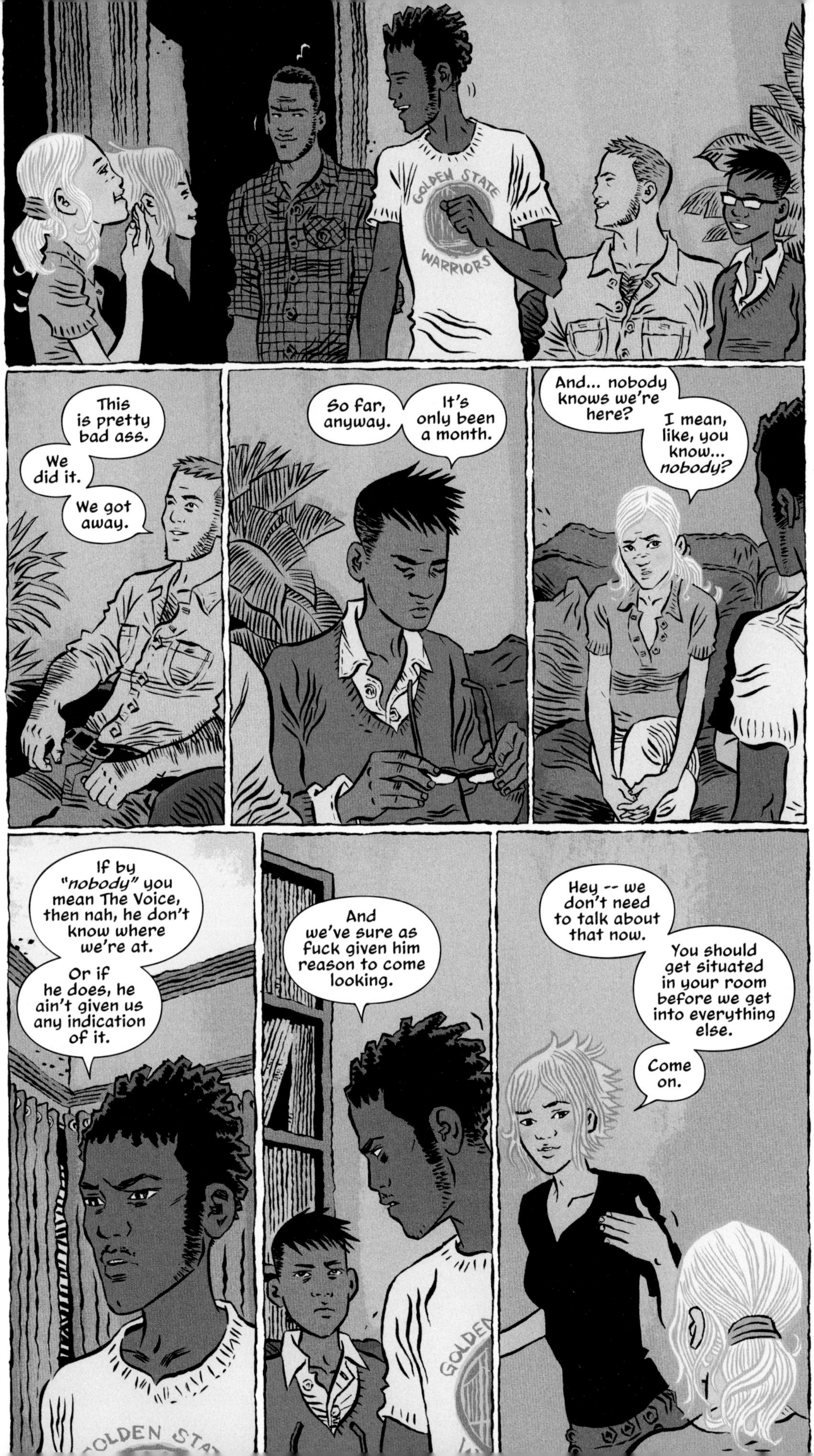
GOLDEN STATE WARRIORS
This is pretty bad ass.
We did it.
We got away.
So far, anyway.
It's only been a month.
And... nobody knows we're here?
I mean, like, you know... *nobody?*
If by "*nobody*" you mean The Voice, then nah, he don't know where we're at.
Or if he does, he ain't given us any indication of it.
And we've sure as fuck given him reason to come looking.
Hey -- we don't need to talk about that now.
You should get situated in your room before we get into everything else.
Come on.

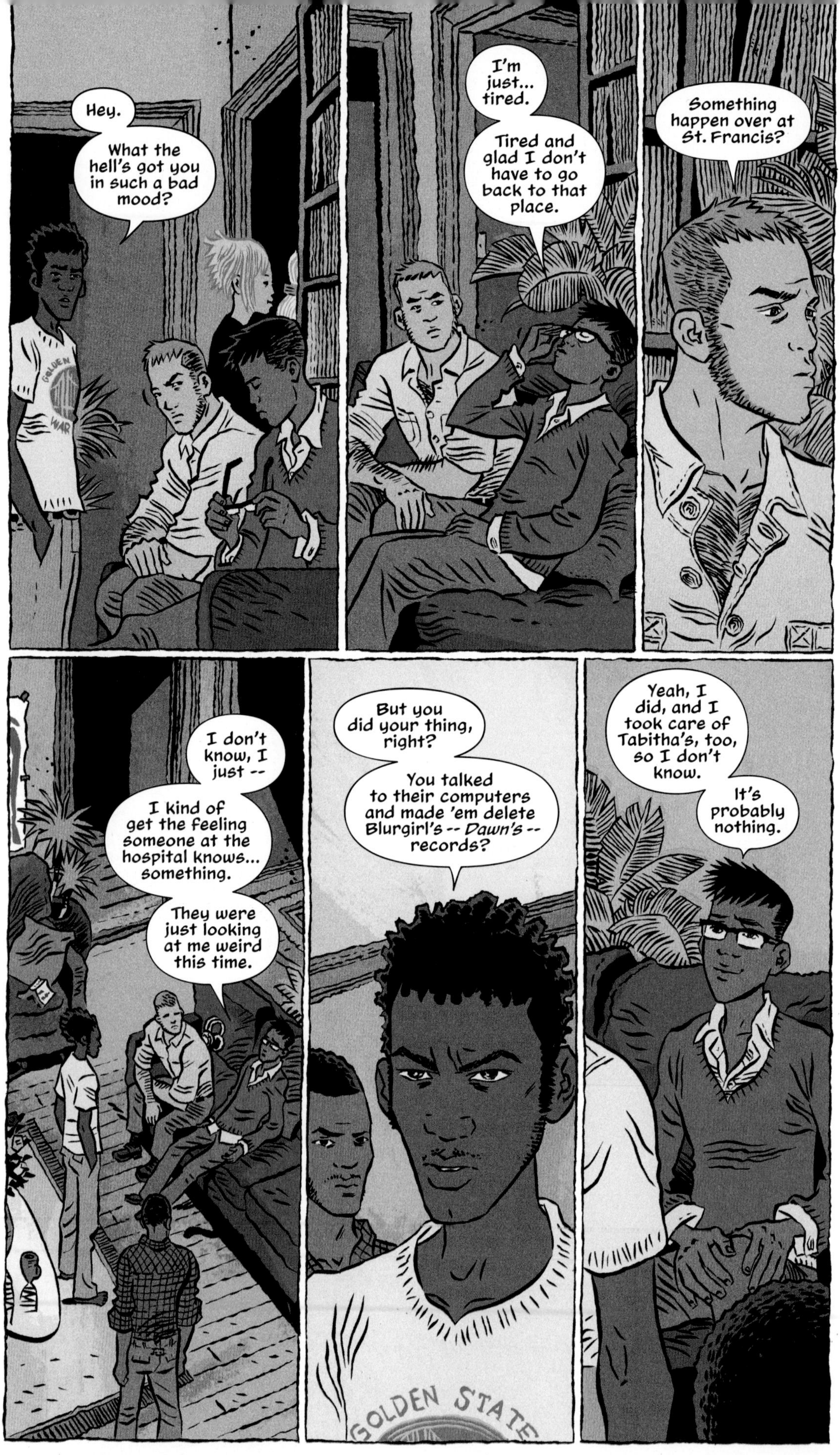
Hey.
What the hell's got you in such a bad mood?
I'm just... tired.
Tired and glad I don't have to go back to that place.
Something happen over at St. Francis?
I don't know, I just --
I kind of get the feeling someone at the hospital knows... something.
They were just looking at me weird this time.
But you did your thing, right?
You talked to their computers and made 'em delete Blurgirl's -- *Dawn's* -- records?
Yeah, I did, and I took care of Tabitha's, too, so I don't know.
It's probably nothing.
GOLDEN STATE

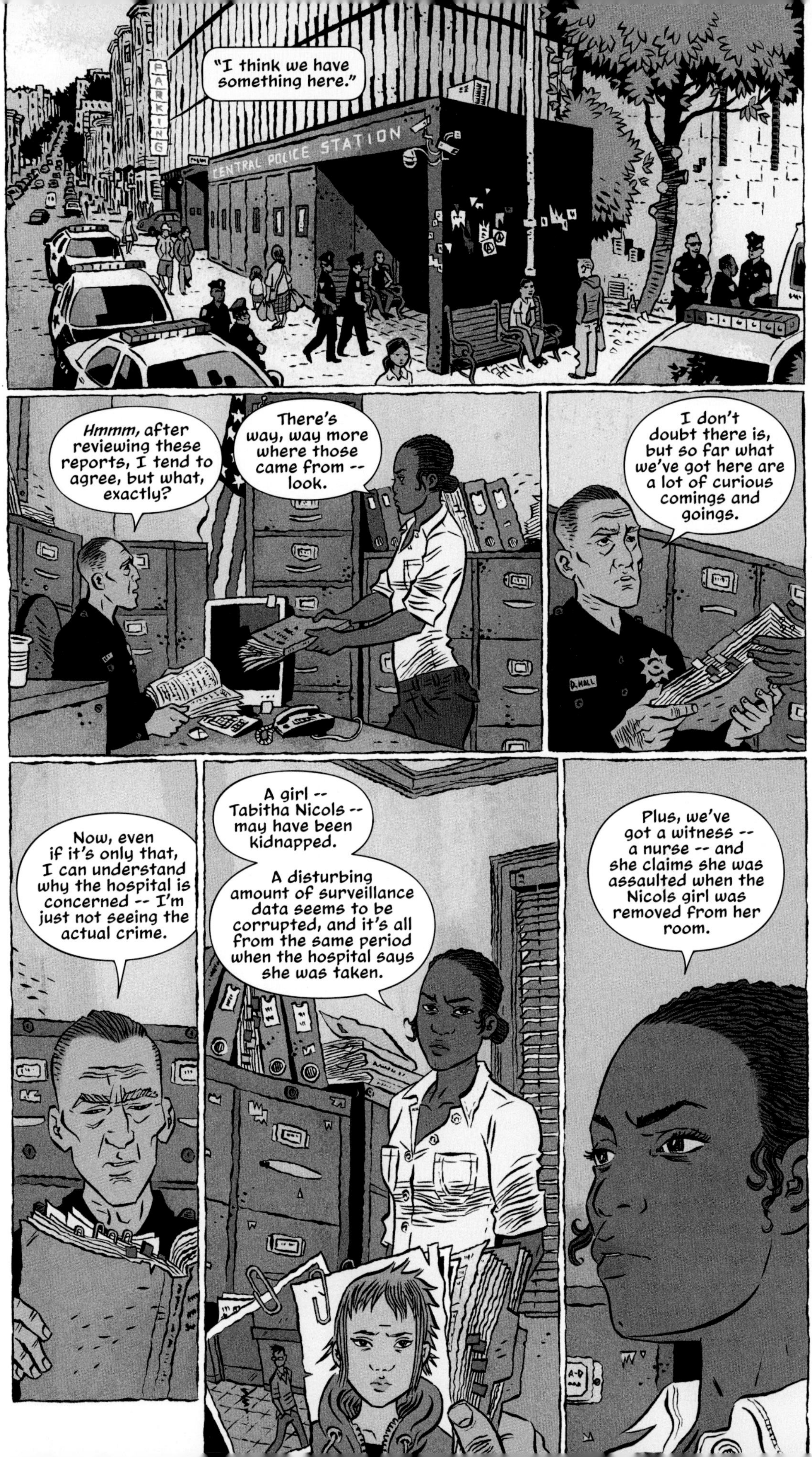
"I think we have something here."
PARKING
CENTRAL POLICE STATION
Hmmm, after reviewing these reports, I tend to agree, but what, exactly?
There's way, way more where those came from -- look.
I don't doubt there is, but so far what we've got here are a lot of curious comings and goings.
D. HALL
Now, even if it's only that, I can understand why the hospital is concerned -- I'm just not seeing the actual crime.
A girl -- Tabitha Nicols -- may have been kidnapped.
A disturbing amount of surveillance data seems to be corrupted, and it's all from the same period when the hospital says she was taken.
Plus, we've got a witness -- a nurse -- and she claims she was assaulted when the Nicols girl was removed from her room.

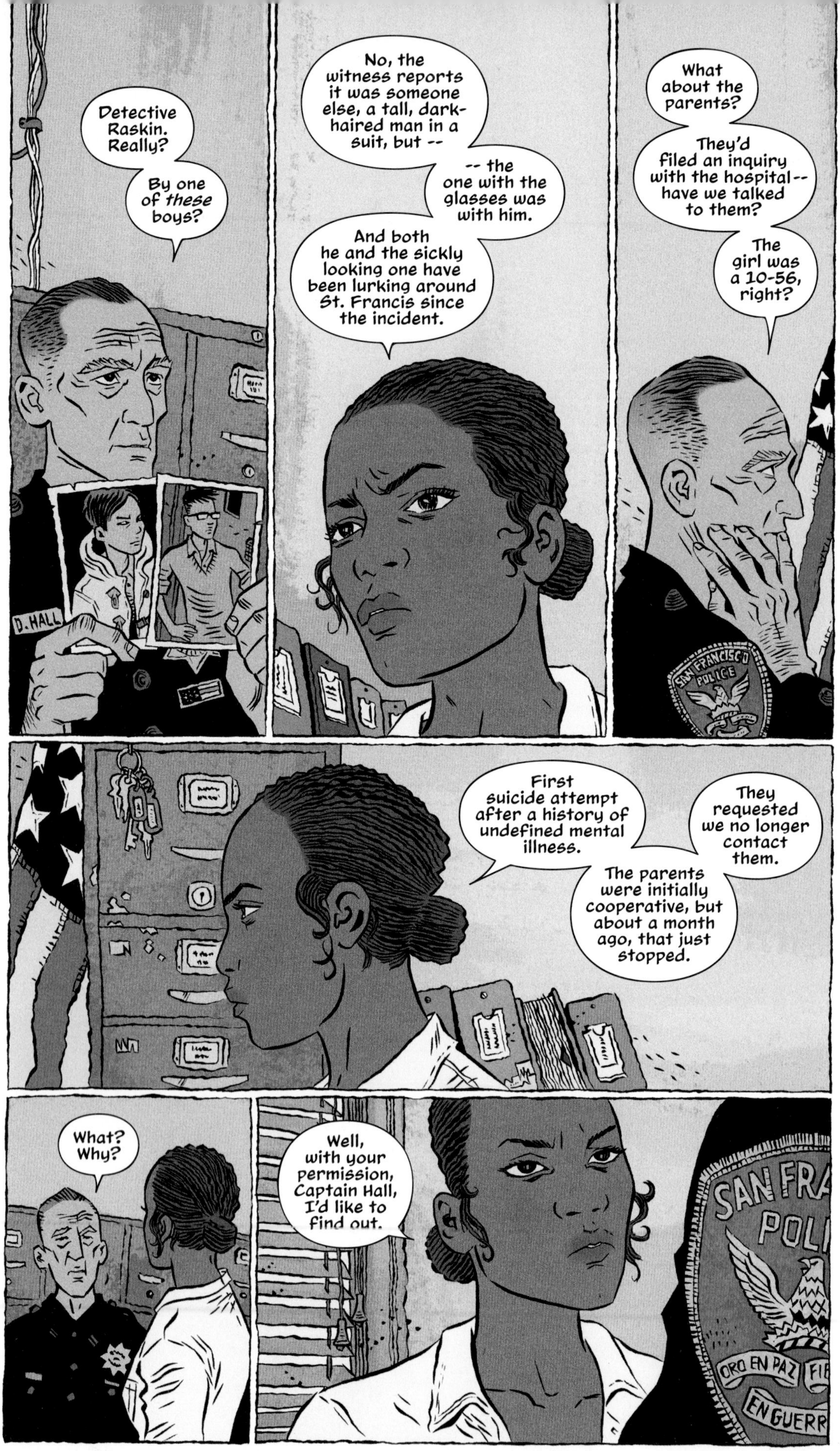
Detective Raskin. Really?
By one of *these* boys?
D. HALL
No, the witness reports it was someone else, a tall, dark-haired man in a suit, but --
-- the one with the glasses was with him.
And both he and the sickly looking one have been lurking around St. Francis since the incident.
What about the parents?
They'd filed an inquiry with the hospital -- have we talked to them?
The girl was a 10-56, right?
SAN FRANCISCO POLICE
First suicide attempt after a history of undefined mental illness.
The parents were initially cooperative, but about a month ago, that just stopped.
They requested we no longer contact them.
What? Why?
Well, with your permission, Captain Hall, I'd like to find out.
SAN FRA
POLI
ORO EN PAZ FI
EN GUERR

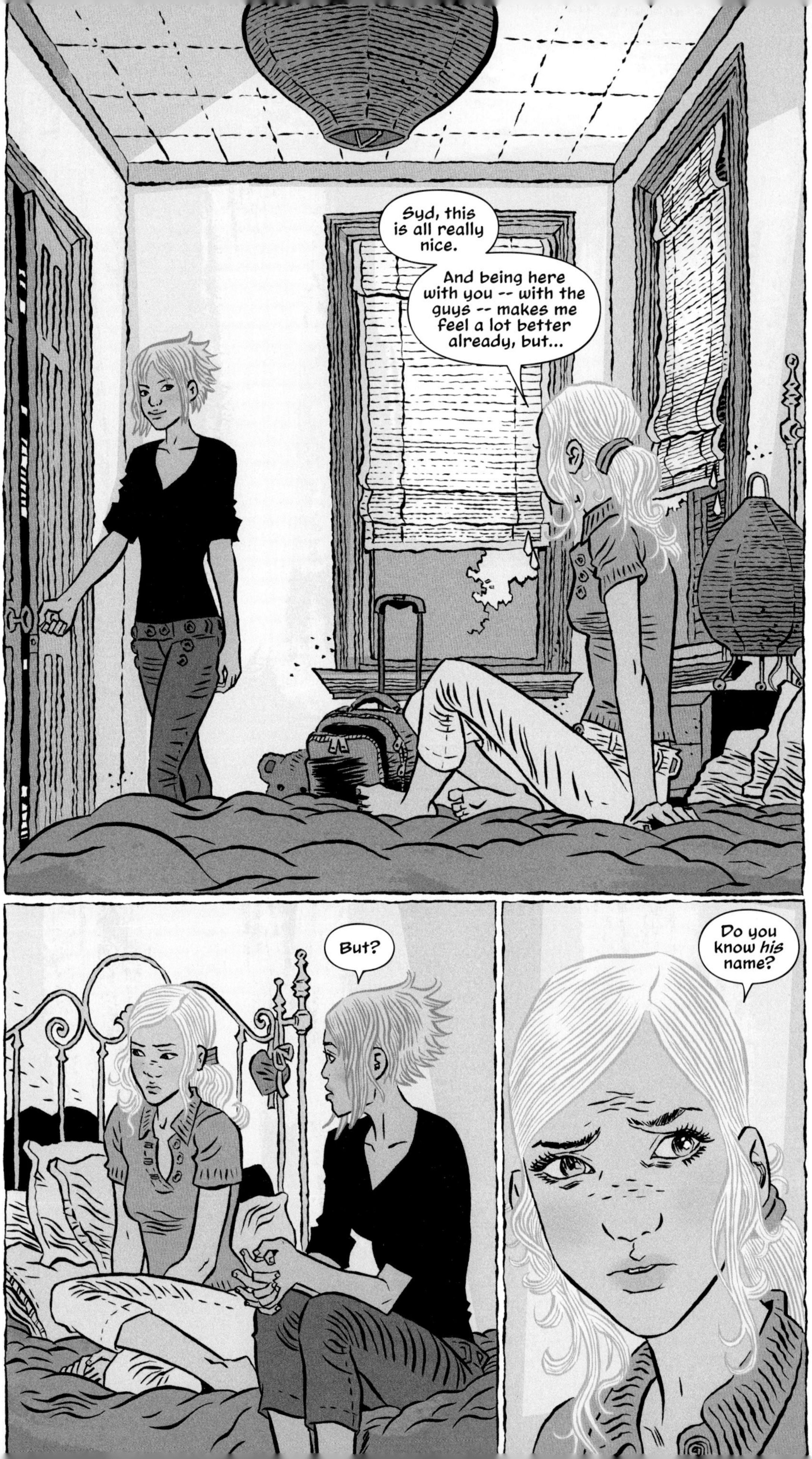
Syd, this is all really nice.
And being here with you -- with the guys -- makes me feel a lot better already, but...
But?
Do you know *his* name?

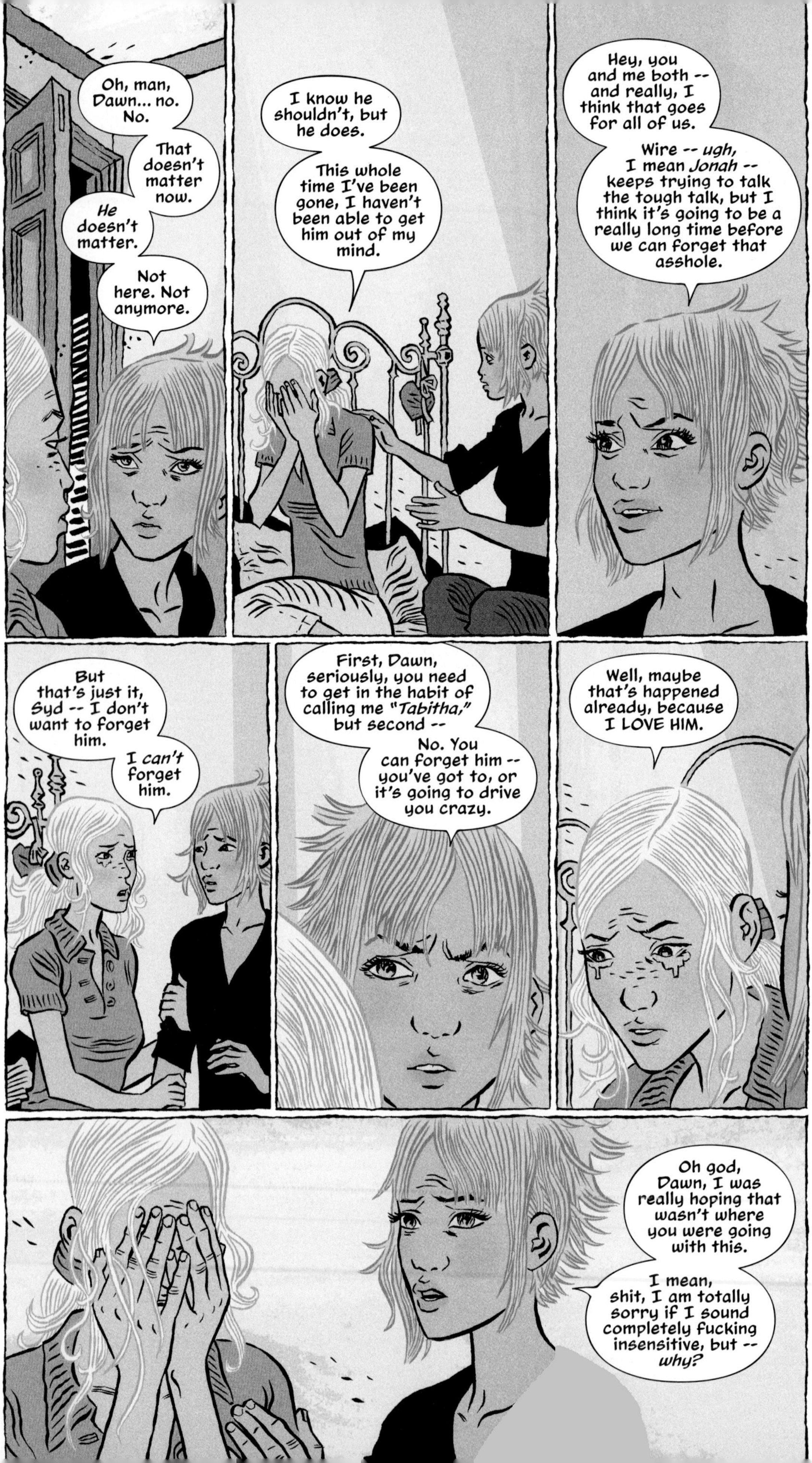

Oh, man, Dawn... no. No.
That doesn't matter now.
He doesn't matter.
Not here. Not anymore.
I know he shouldn't, but he does.
This whole time I've been gone, I haven't been able to get him out of my mind.
Hey, you and me both -- and really, I think that goes for all of us.
Wire -- ugh, I mean Jonah -- keeps trying to talk the tough talk, but I think it's going to be a really long time before we can forget that asshole.
But that's just it, Syd -- I don't want to forget him.
I can't forget him.
First, Dawn, seriously, you need to get in the habit of calling me "Tabitha," but second --
No. You can forget him -- you've got to, or it's going to drive you crazy.
Well, maybe that's happened already, because I LOVE HIM.
Oh god, Dawn, I was really hoping that wasn't where you were going with this.
I mean, shit, I am totally sorry if I sound completely fucking insensitive, but -- why?

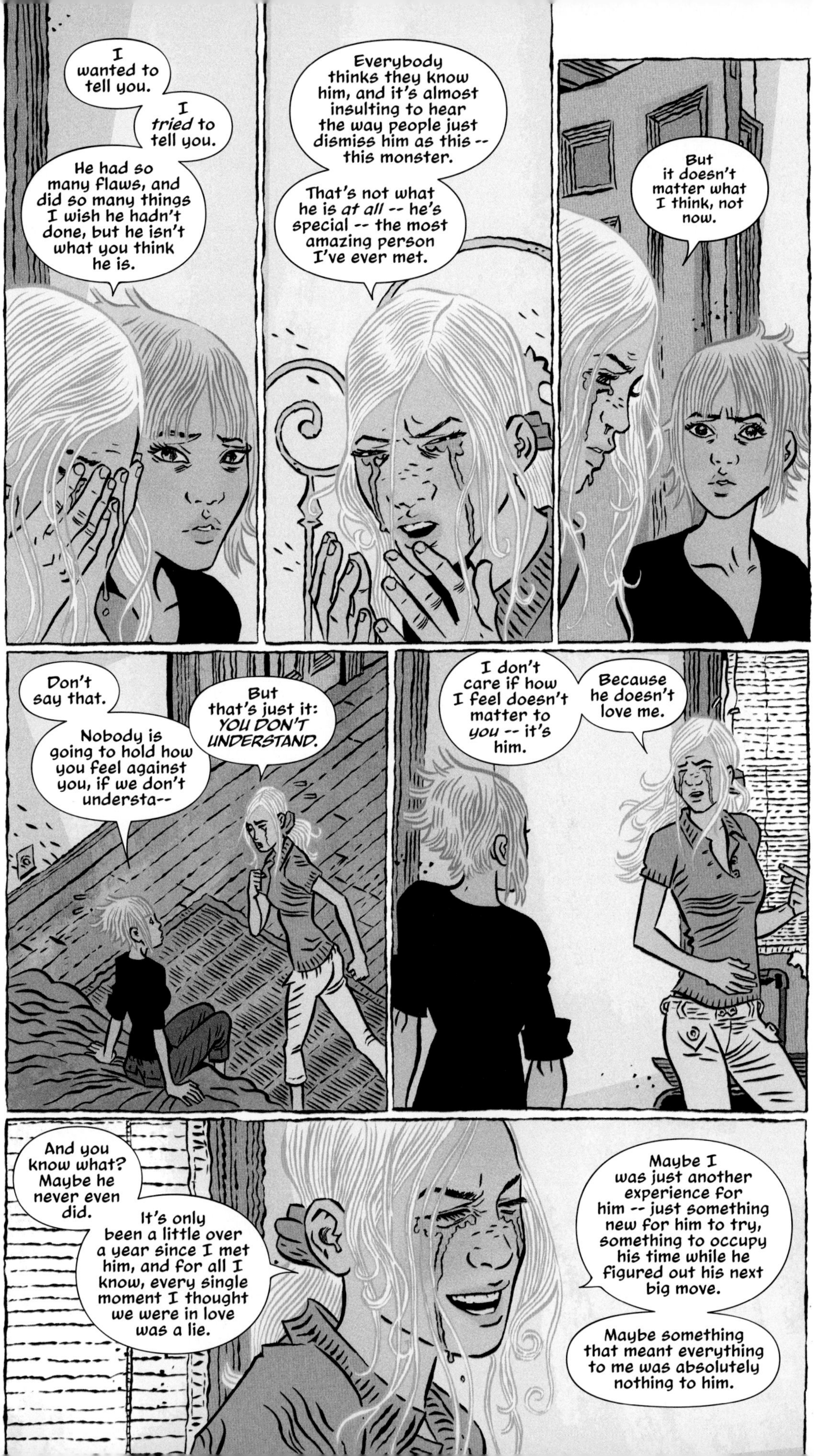
I wanted to tell you.
I *tried* to tell you.
He had so many flaws, and did so many things I wish he hadn't done, but he isn't what you think he is.
Everybody thinks they know him, and it's almost insulting to hear the way people just dismiss him as this -- this monster.
That's not what he is *at all* -- he's special -- the most amazing person I've ever met.
But it doesn't matter what I think, not now.
Don't say that.
Nobody is going to hold how you feel against you, if we don't understa--
But that's just it: *YOU DON'T UNDERSTAND.*
I don't care if how I feel doesn't matter to *you* -- it's him.
Because he doesn't love me.
And you know what? Maybe he never even did.
It's only been a little over a year since I met him, and for all I know, every single moment I thought we were in love was a lie.
Maybe I was just another experience for him -- just something new for him to try, something to occupy his time while he figured out his next big move.
Maybe something that meant everything to me was absolutely nothing to him.

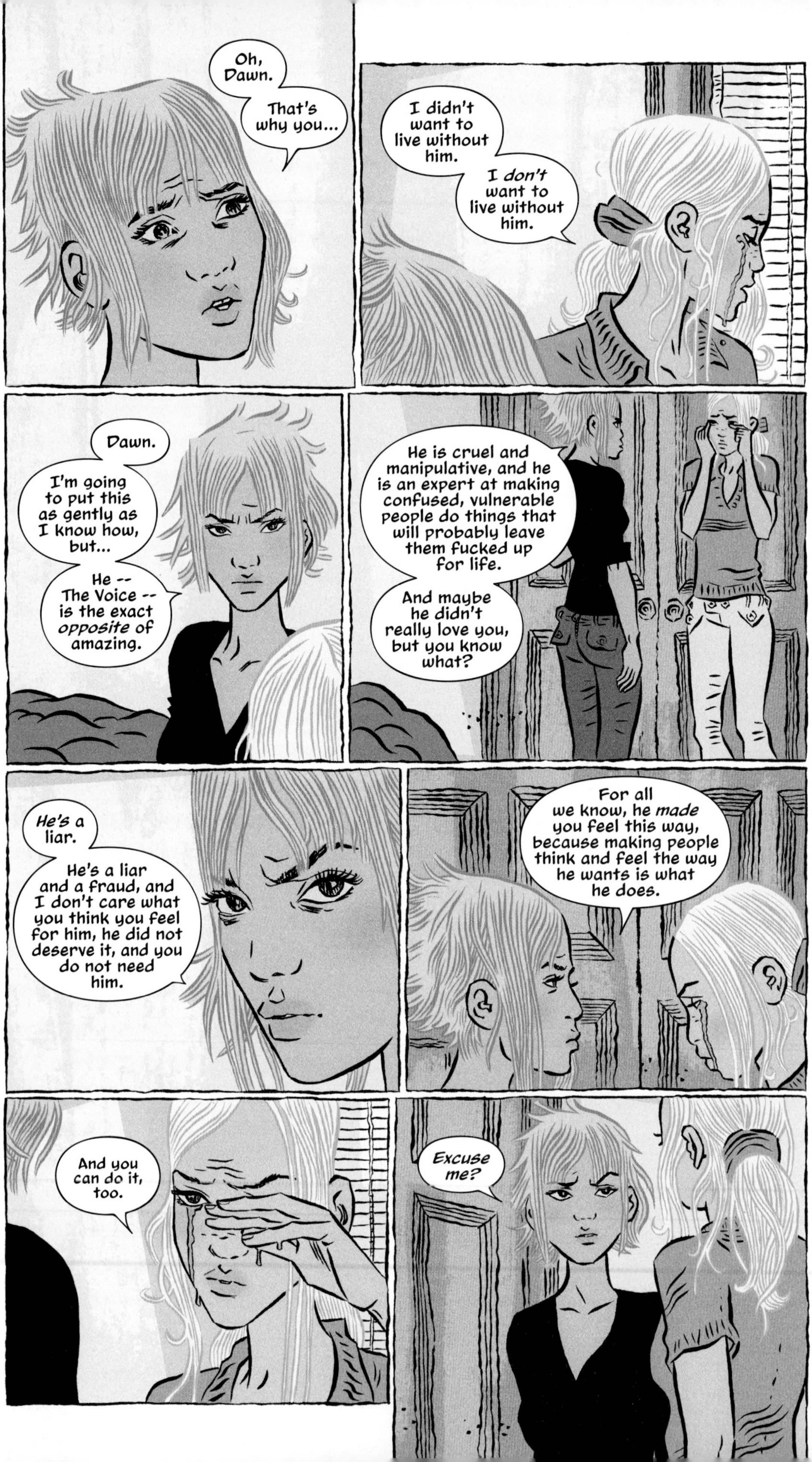
Oh, Dawn.
That's why you...
I didn't want to live without him.
I *don't* want to live without him.
Dawn.
I'm going to put this as gently as I know how, but...
He -- The Voice -- is the exact *opposite* of amazing.
He is cruel and manipulative, and he is an expert at making confused, vulnerable people do things that will probably leave them fucked up for life.
And maybe he didn't really love you, but you know what?
He's a liar.
He's a liar and a fraud, and I don't care what you think you feel for him, he did not deserve it, and you do not need him.
For all we know, he *made* you feel this way, because making people think and feel the way he wants is what he does.
And you can do it, too.
Excuse me?

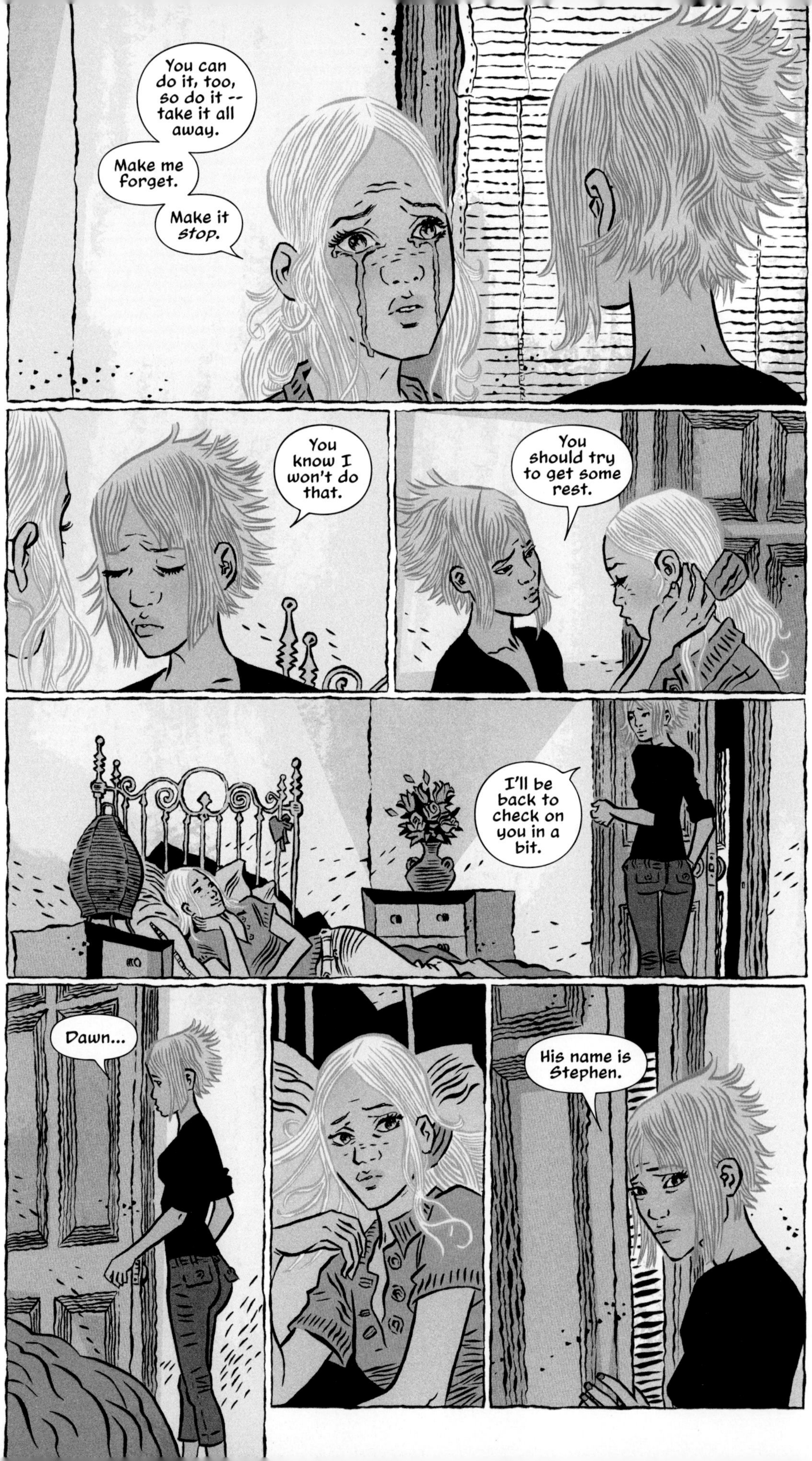
You can do it, too, so do it -- take it all away.
Make me forget.
Make it *stop.*
You know I won't do that.
You should try to get some rest.
I'll be back to check on you in a bit.
Dawn...
His name is Stephen.

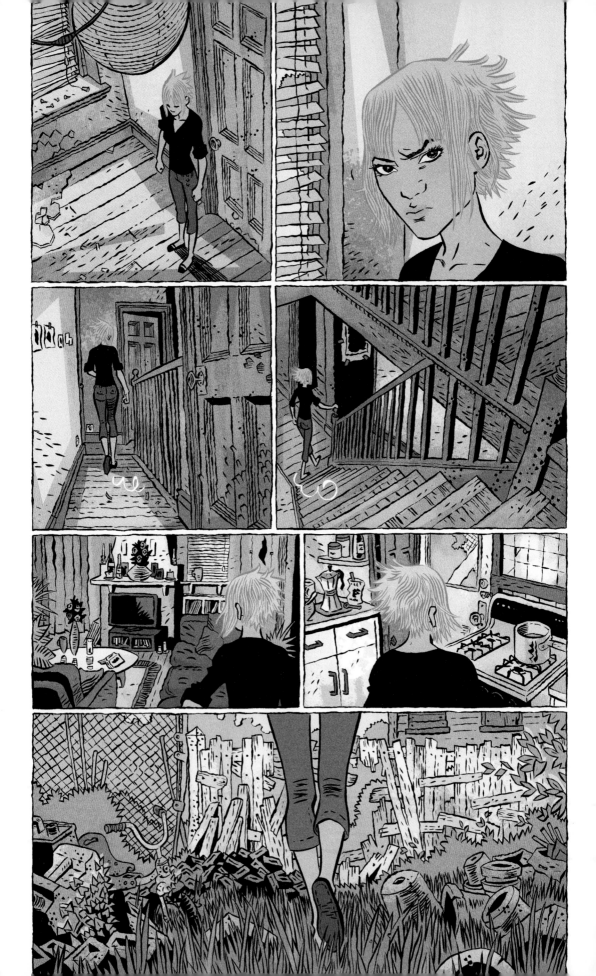

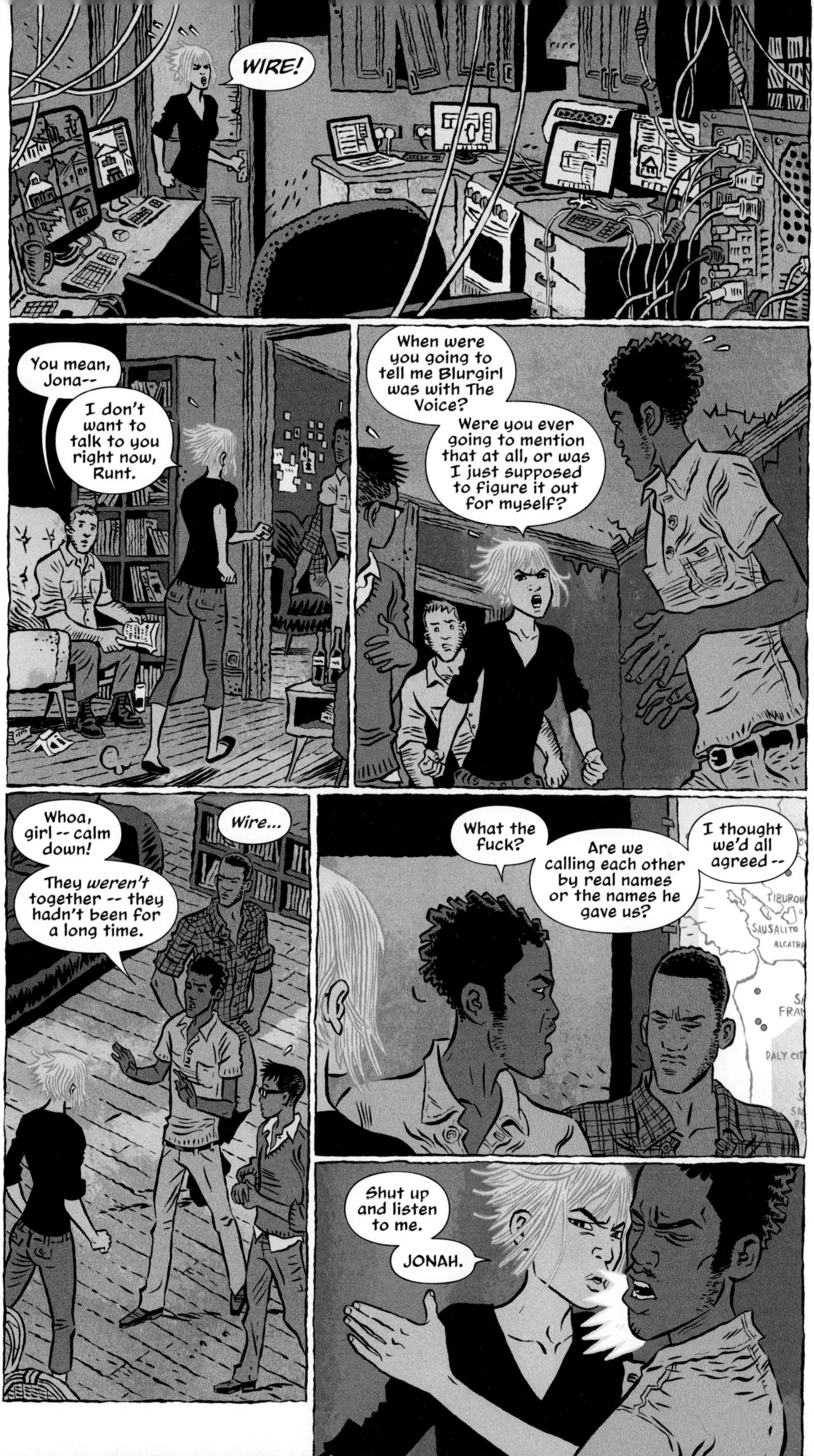
WIRE!
You mean, Jona--
I don't want to talk to you right now, Runt.
When were you going to tell me Blurgirl was with The Voice?
Were you ever going to mention that at all, or was I just supposed to figure it out for myself?
Whoa, girl -- calm down!
Wire...
They *weren't* together -- they hadn't been for a long time.
What the fuck?
Are we calling each other by real names or the names he gave us?
I thought we'd all agreed --
TIBURON
SAUSALITO
Shut up and listen to me.
JONAH.

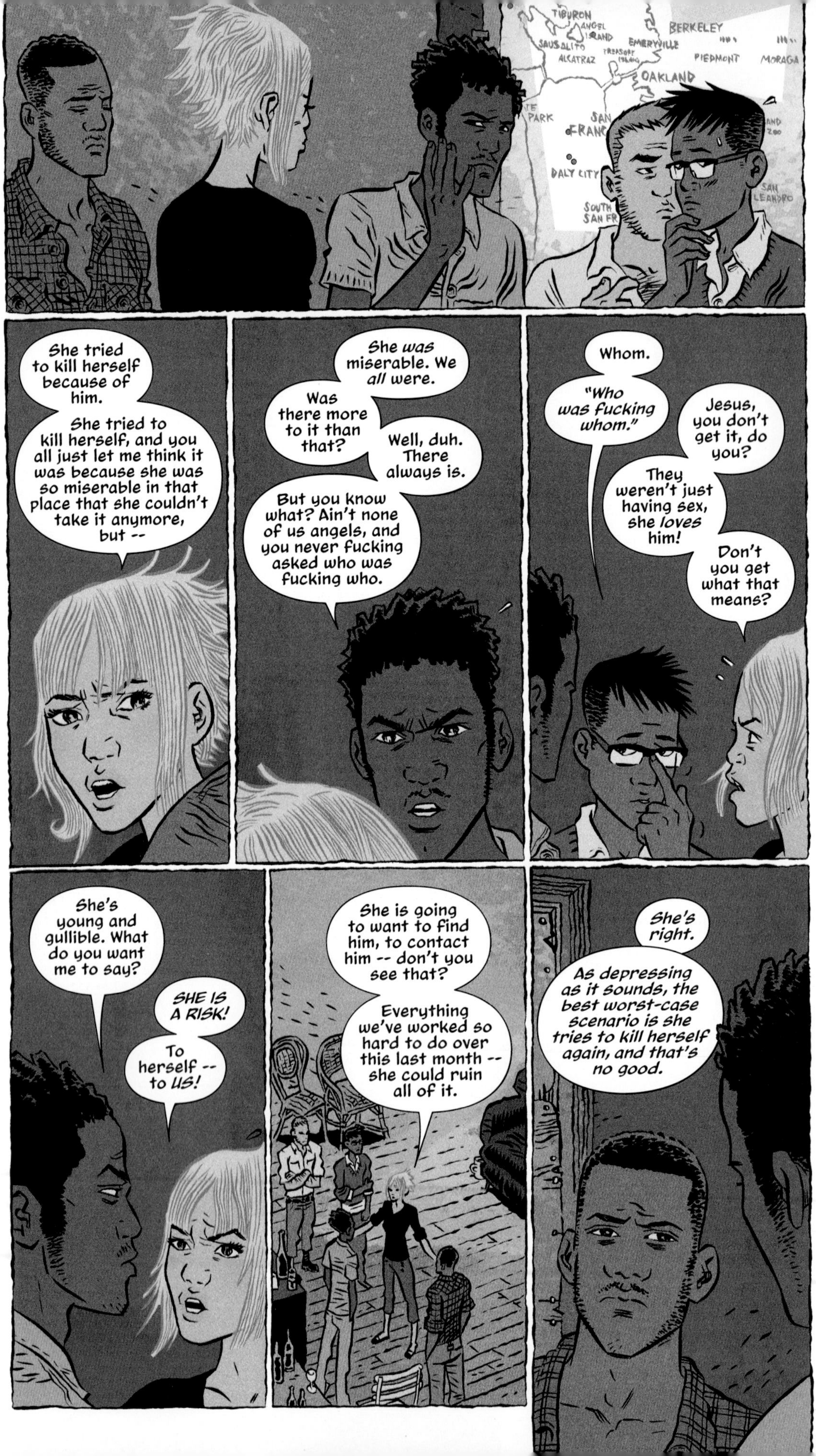
TIBURON
BERKELEY
EMERYVILLE
ALCATRAZ
PIEDMONT
MORAGA
OAKLAND
DALY CITY
SAN LEANDRO
She tried to kill herself because of him.
She tried to kill herself, and you all just let me think it was because she was so miserable in that place that she couldn't take it anymore, but --
She *was* miserable. We *all* were.
Was there more to it than that?
Well, duh. There always is.
But you know what? Ain't none of us angels, and you never fucking asked who was fucking who.
Whom.
"Who was fucking whom."
Jesus, you don't get it, do you?
They weren't just having sex, she *loves* him!
Don't you get what that means?
She's young and gullible. What do you want me to say?
SHE IS A RISK!
To herself -- to *US!*
She is going to want to find him, to contact him -- don't you see that?
Everything we've worked so hard to do over this last month -- she could ruin all of it.
She's right.
As depressing as it sounds, the best worst-case scenario is she tries to kill herself again, and that's no good.

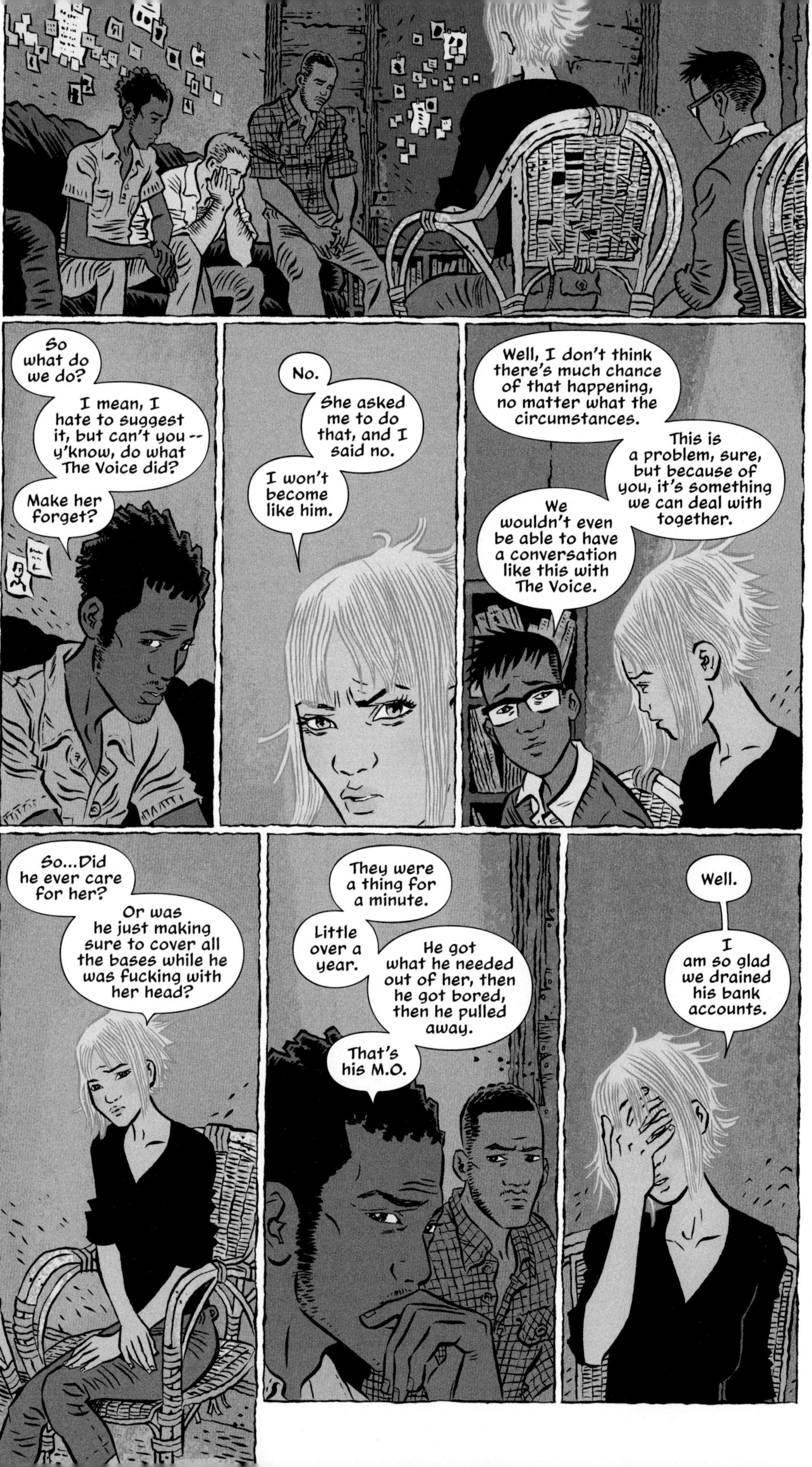
So what do we do?
I mean, I hate to suggest it, but can't you -- y'know, do what The Voice did?
Make her forget?
No.
She asked me to do that, and I said no.
I won't become like him.
Well, I don't think there's much chance of that happening, no matter what the circumstances.
This is a problem, sure, but because of you, it's something we can deal with together.
We wouldn't even be able to have a conversation like this with The Voice.
So...Did he ever care for her?
Or was he just making sure to cover all the bases while he was fucking with her head?
They were a thing for a minute.
Little over a year.
He got what he needed out of her, then he got bored, then he pulled away.
That's his M.O.
Well.
I am so glad we drained his bank accounts.

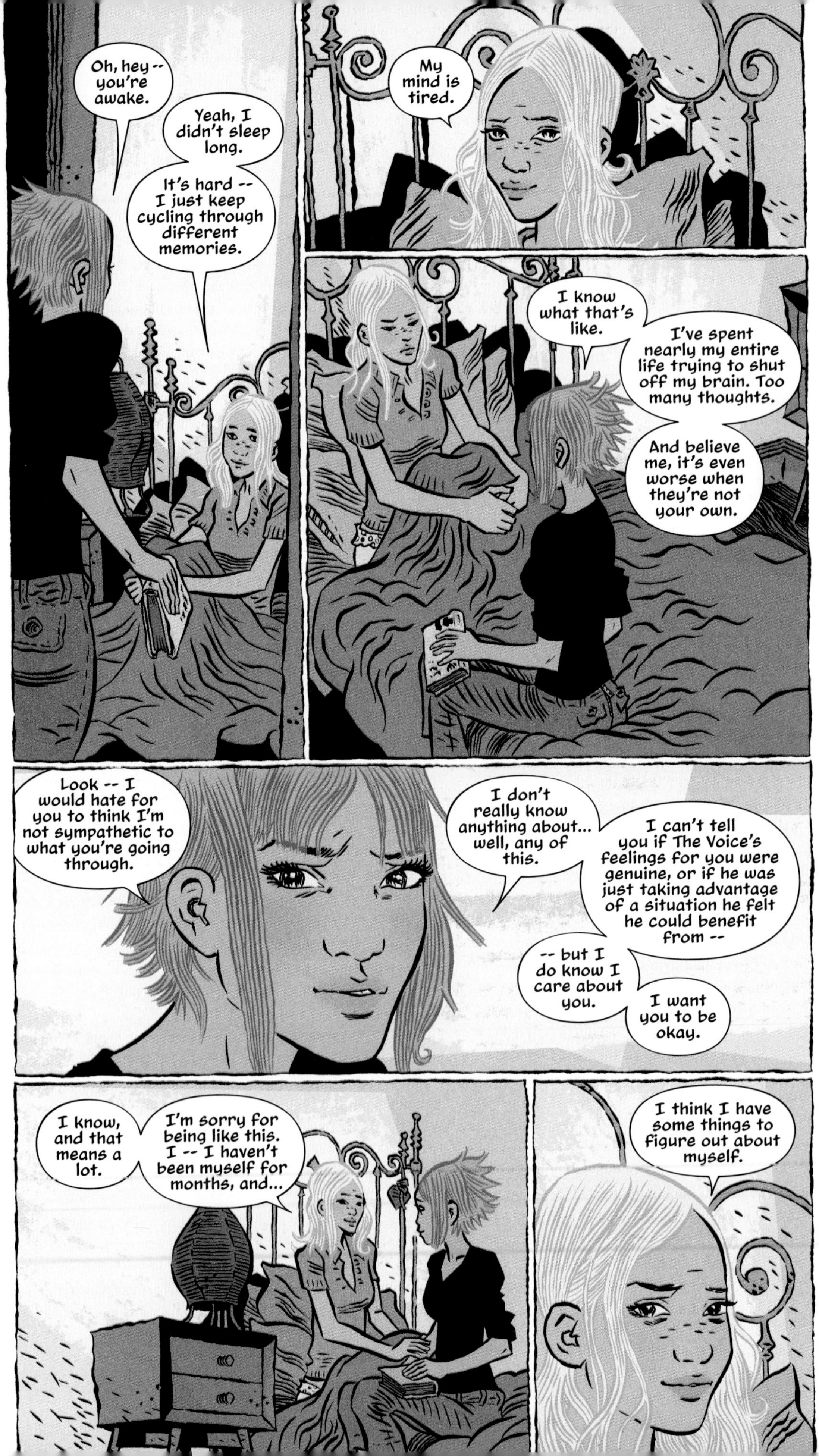
Oh, hey -- you're awake.
Yeah, I didn't sleep long.
It's hard -- I just keep cycling through different memories.
My mind is tired.
I know what that's like.
I've spent nearly my entire life trying to shut off my brain. Too many thoughts.
And believe me, it's even worse when they're not your own.
Look -- I would hate for you to think I'm not sympathetic to what you're going through.
I don't really know anything about... well, any of this.
I can't tell you if The Voice's feelings for you were genuine, or if he was just taking advantage of a situation he felt he could benefit from --
-- but I do know I care about you.
I want you to be okay.
I know, and that means a lot.
I'm sorry for being like this. I -- I haven't been myself for months, and...
I think I have some things to figure out about myself.

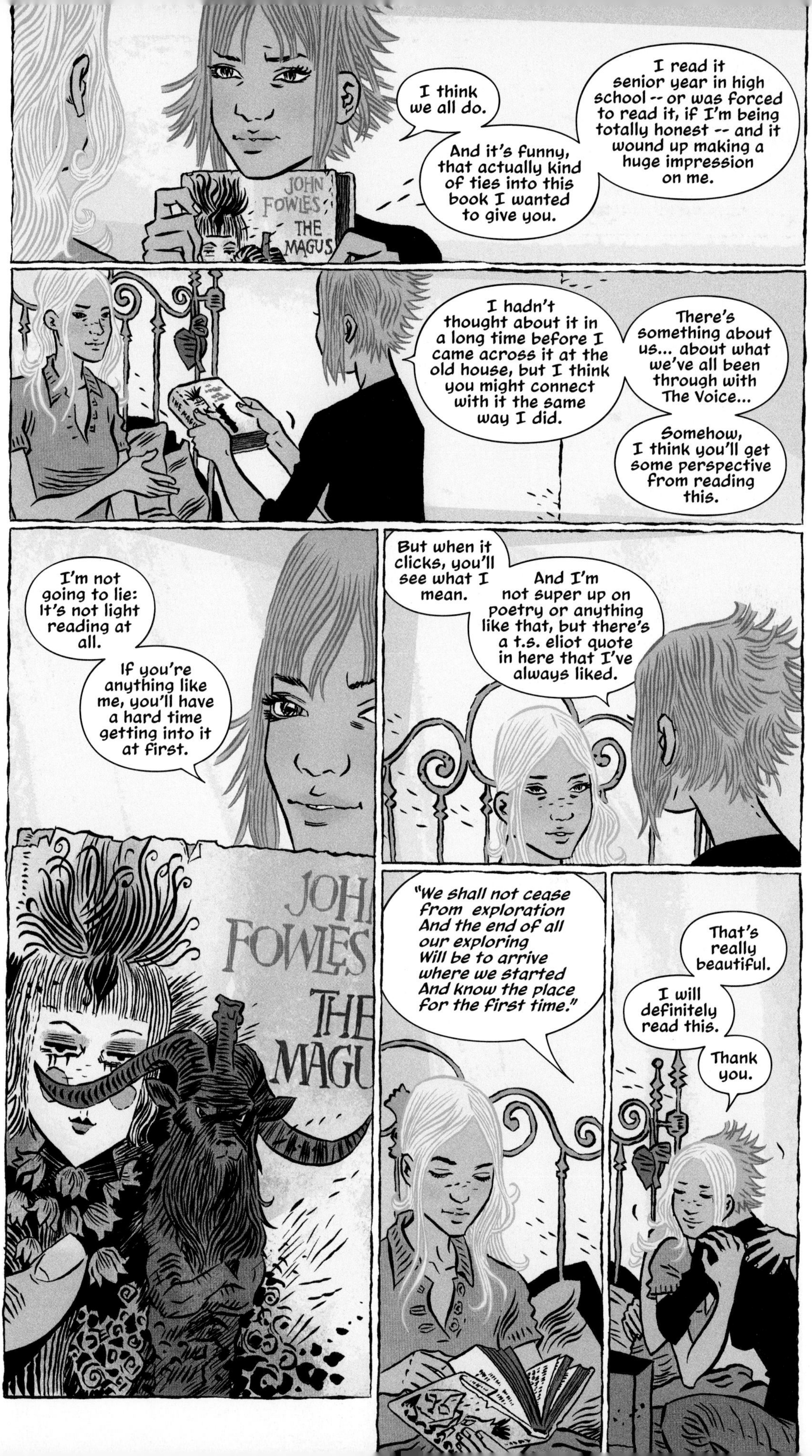
JOHN FOWLES THE MAGUS
I read it senior year in high school -- or was forced to read it, if I'm being totally honest -- and it wound up making a huge impression on me.
I think we all do.
And it's funny, that actually kind of ties into this book I wanted to give you.
I hadn't thought about it in a long time before I came across it at the old house, but I think you might connect with it the same way I did.
There's something about us... about what we've all been through with The Voice...
Somehow, I think you'll get some perspective from reading this.
I'm not going to lie: It's not light reading at all.
If you're anything like me, you'll have a hard time getting into it at first.
But when it clicks, you'll see what I mean.
And I'm not super up on poetry or anything like that, but there's a t.s. eliot quote in here that I've always liked.
JOHN FOWLES THE MAGUS
"We shall not cease from exploration And the end of all our exploring Will be to arrive where we started And know the place for the first time."
That's really beautiful.
I will definitely read this.
Thank you.

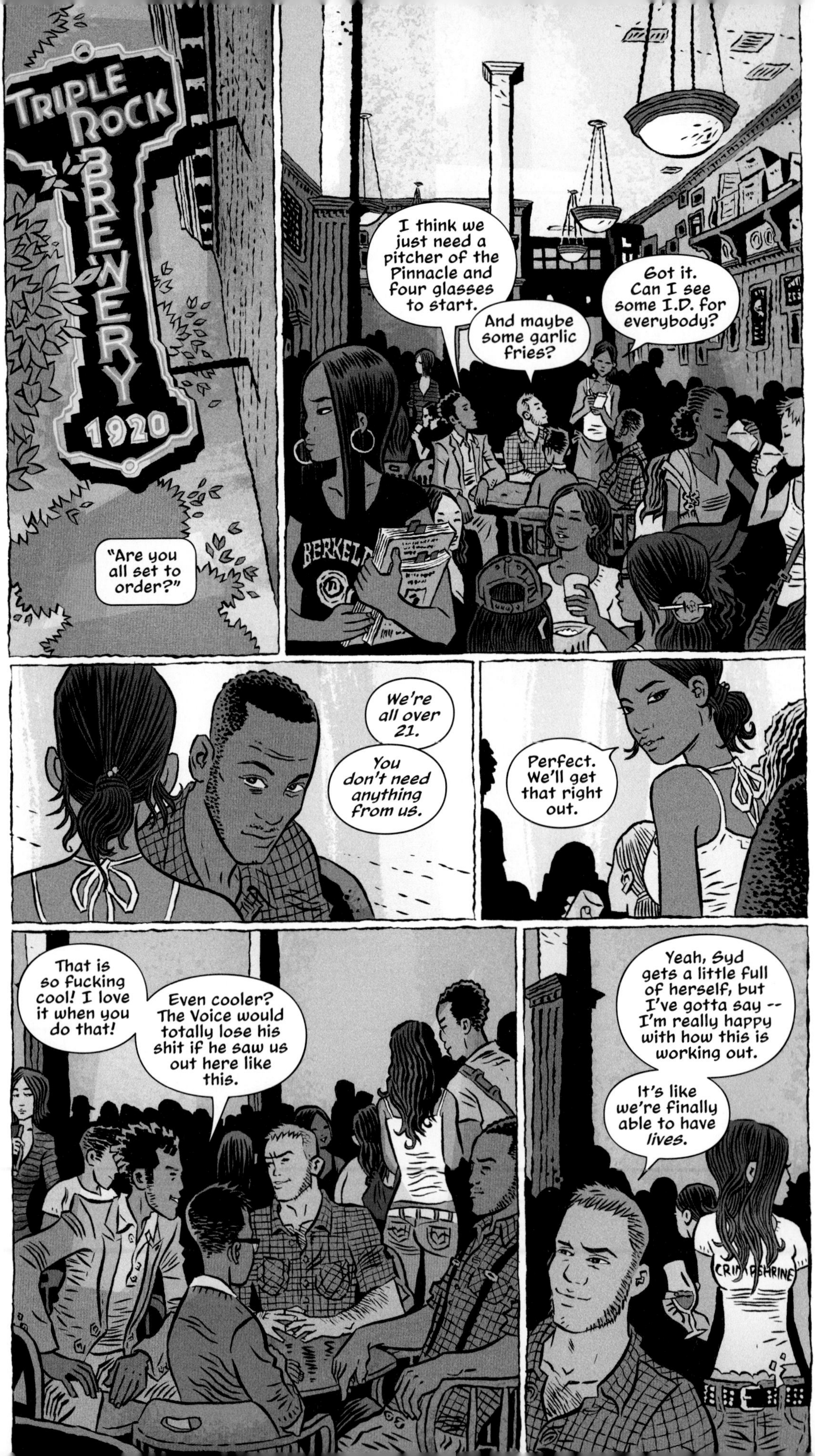
TRIPLE ROCK BREWERY 1920
"Are you all set to order?"
I think we just need a pitcher of the Pinnacle and four glasses to start.
And maybe some garlic fries?
Got it. Can I see some I.D. for everybody?
BERKELEY
We're all over 21.
You don't need anything from us.
Perfect. We'll get that right out.
That is so fucking cool! I love it when you do that!
Even cooler? The Voice would totally lose his shit if he saw us out here like this.
Yeah, Syd gets a little full of herself, but I've gotta say -- I'm really happy with how this is working out.
It's like we're finally able to have lives.
CRIMPSHRINE

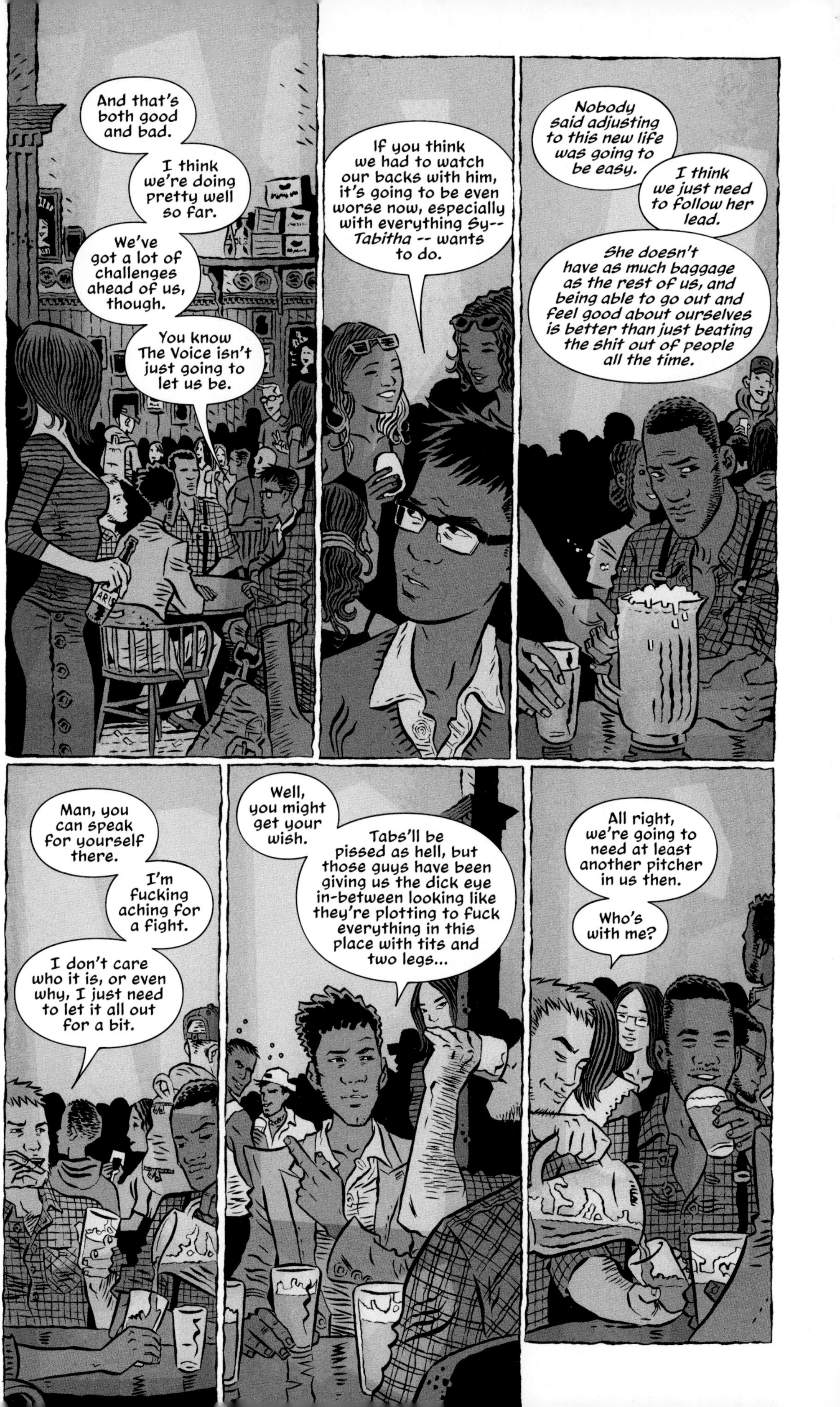
And that's both good and bad.
I think we're doing pretty well so far.
We've got a lot of challenges ahead of us, though.
You know The Voice isn't just going to let us be.
If you think we had to watch our backs with him, it's going to be even worse now, especially with everything Sy-- *Tabitha* -- wants to do.
Nobody said adjusting to this new life was going to be easy.
I think we just need to follow her lead.
She doesn't have as much baggage as the rest of us, and being able to go out and feel good about ourselves is better than just beating the shit out of people all the time.
Man, you can speak for yourself there.
I'm fucking aching for a fight.
I don't care who it is, or even why, I just need to let it all out for a bit.
Well, you might get your wish.
Tabs'll be pissed as hell, but those guys have been giving us the dick eye in-between looking like they're plotting to fuck everything in this place with tits and two legs...
All right, we're going to need at least another pitcher in us then.
Who's with me?

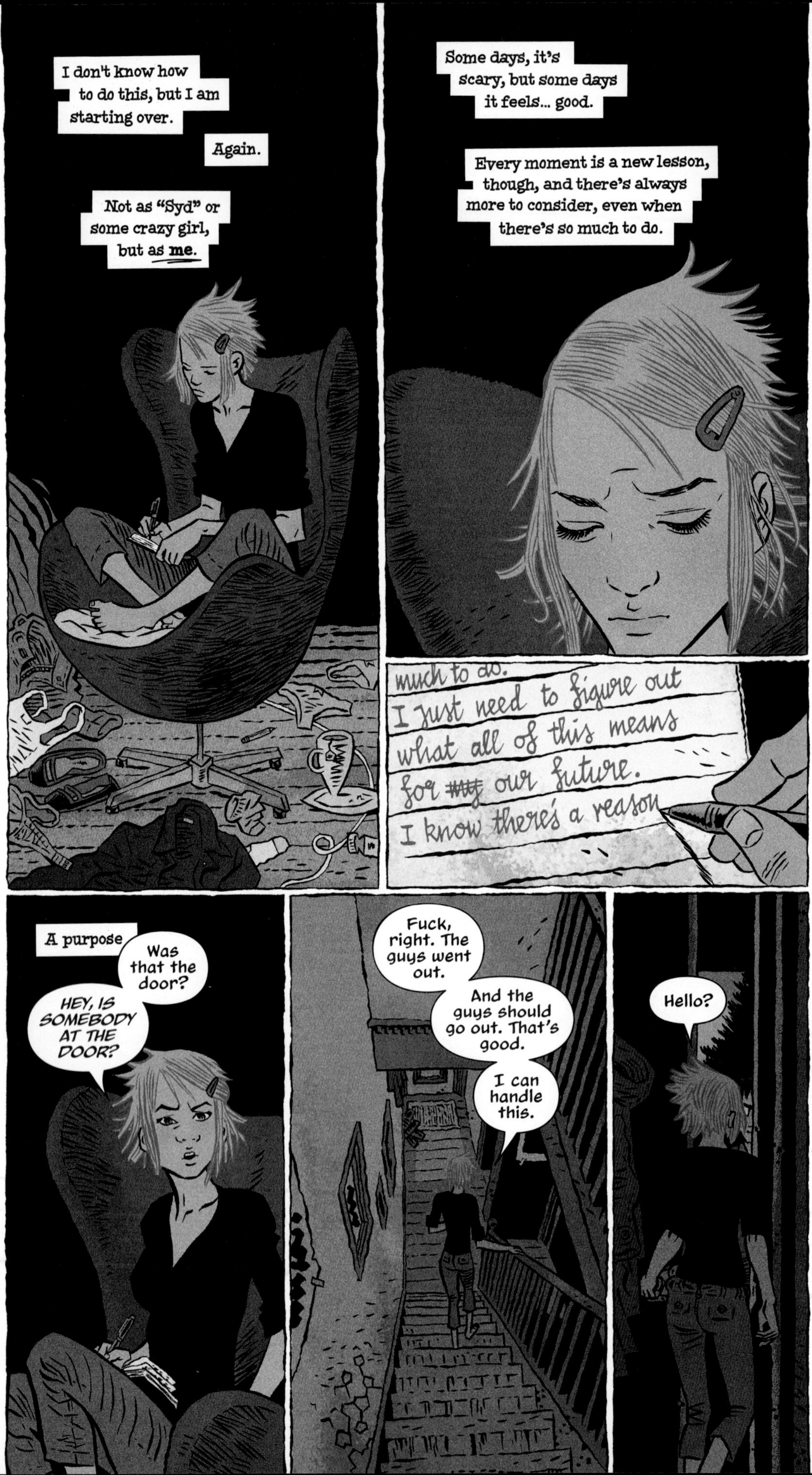
I don't know how to do this, but I am starting over.
Again.
Not as "Syd" or some crazy girl, but as me.
Some days, it's scary, but some days it feels... good.
Every moment is a new lesson, though, and there's always more to consider, even when there's so much to do.
much to do.
I just need to figure out what all of this means for ~~my~~ our future.
I know there's a reason
A purpose
Was that the door?
HEY, IS SOMEBODY AT THE DOOR?
Fuck, right. The guys went out.
And the guys should go out. That's good.
I can handle this.
Hello?

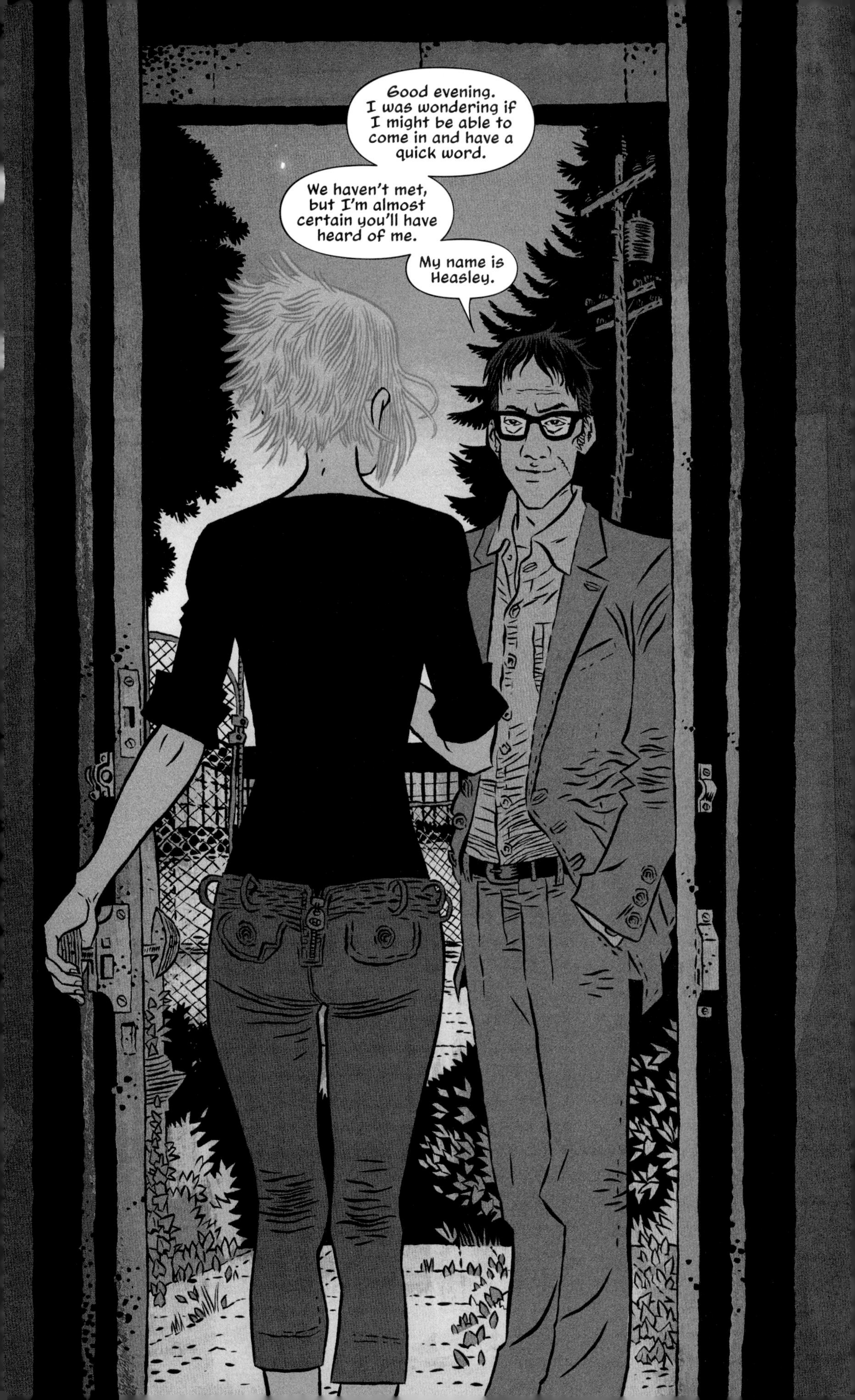
Good evening. I was wondering if I might be able to come in and have a quick word.
We haven't met, but I'm almost certain you'll have heard of me.
My name is Heasley.

TO BE
YOURSELF,
YOUR TRUE
SELF, IS THE
HARDEST
THING TO
DO AND TO
DO RIGHT.

STEPHEN DUFFY

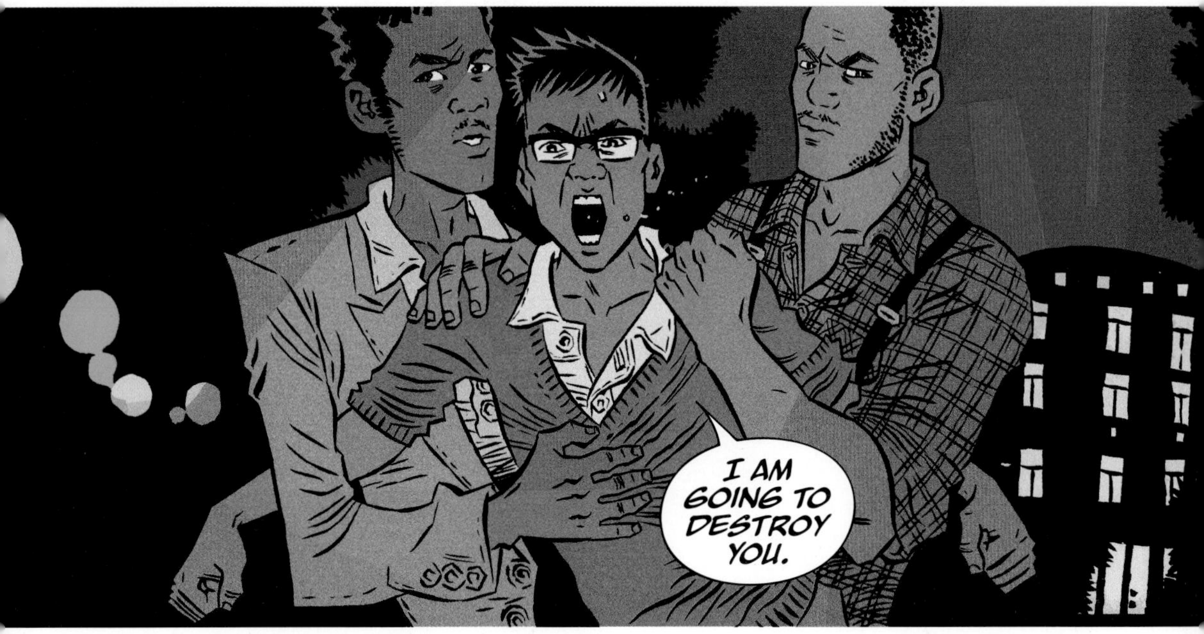
I AM GOING TO DESTROY YOU.

8: TABITHA'S ISLAND

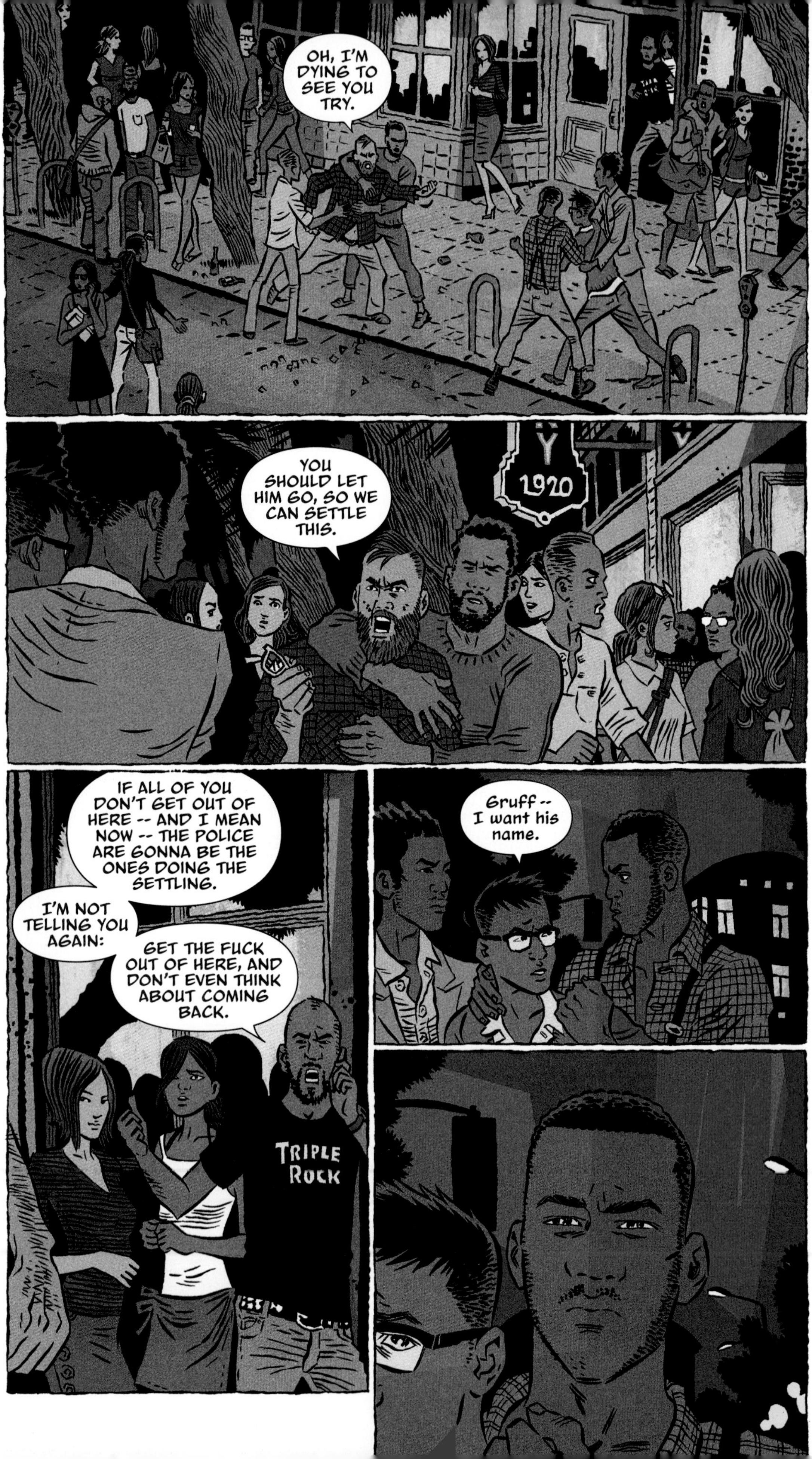
OH, I'M DYING TO SEE YOU TRY.
TRIPLE ROCK
YOU SHOULD LET HIM GO, SO WE CAN SETTLE THIS.
1920
IF ALL OF YOU DON'T GET OUT OF HERE -- AND I MEAN NOW -- THE POLICE ARE GONNA BE THE ONES DOING THE SETTLING.
I'M NOT TELLING YOU AGAIN:
GET THE FUCK OUT OF HERE, AND DON'T EVEN THINK ABOUT COMING BACK.
TRIPLE ROCK
Gruff -- I want his name.

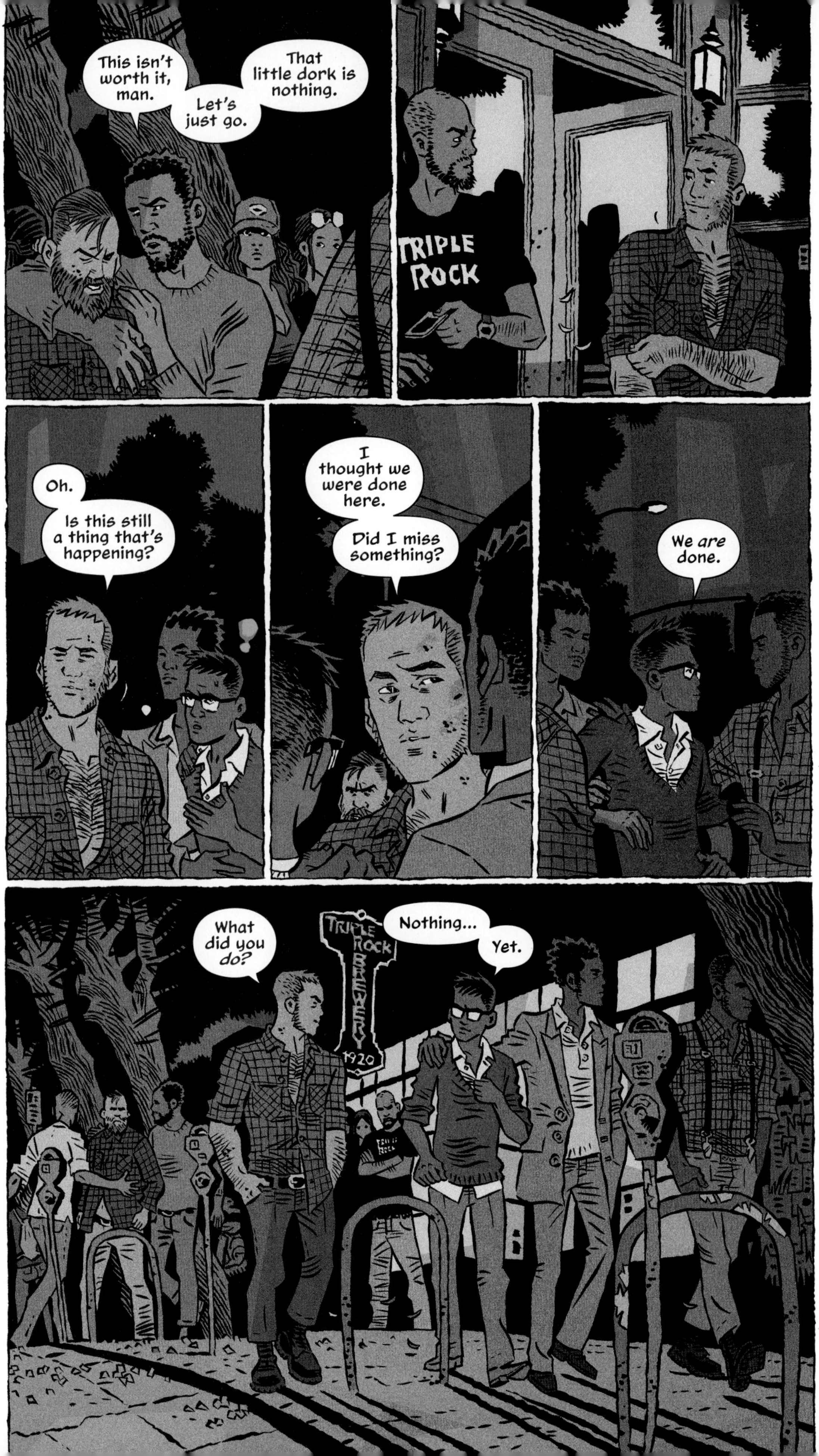
This isn't worth it, man.
Let's just go.
That little dork is nothing.
TRIPLE ROCK
Oh.
Is this still a thing that's happening?
I thought we were done here.
Did I miss something?
We are done.
What did you do?
TRIPLE ROCK BREWERY 1920
Nothing...
Yet.

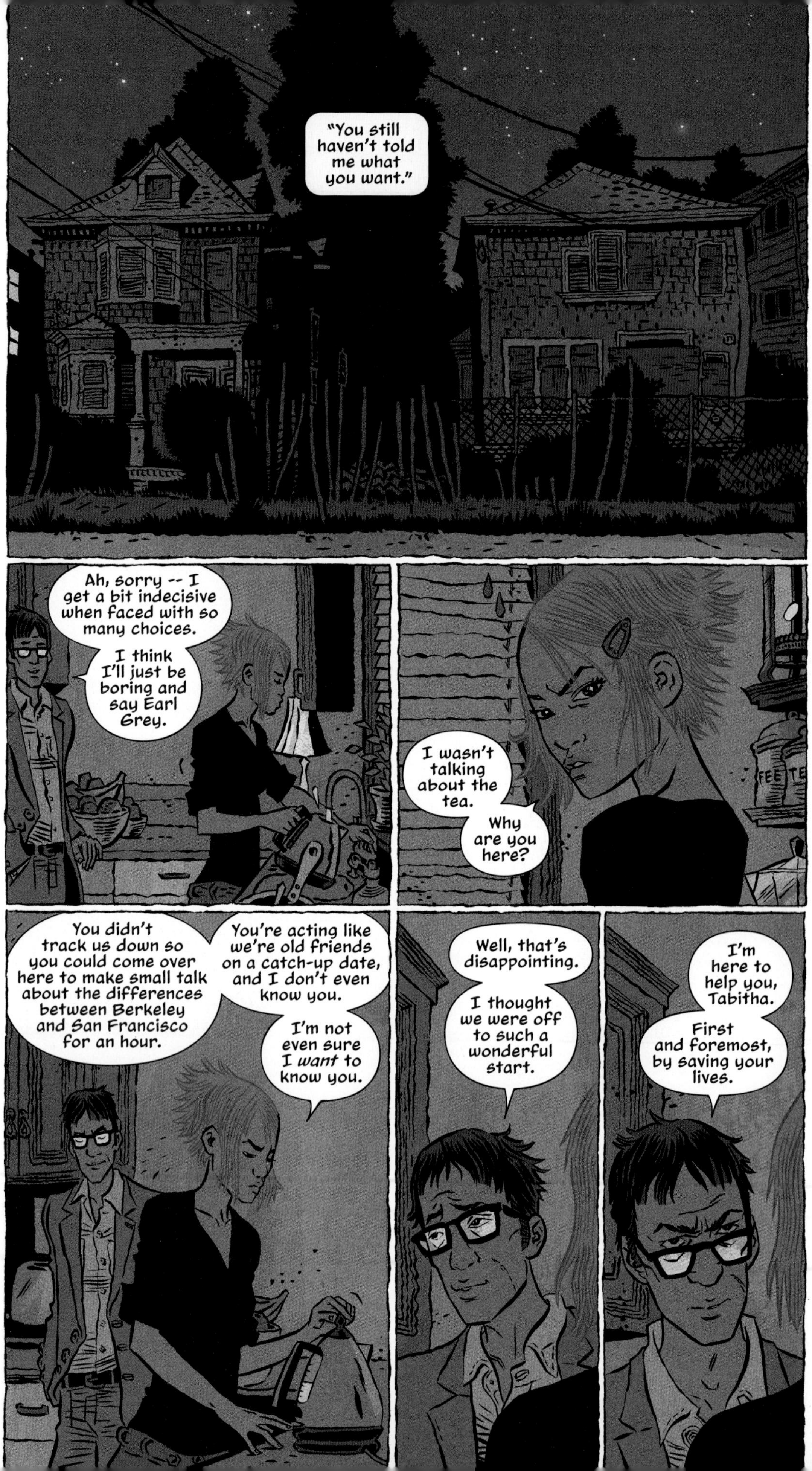
"You still haven't told me what you want."
Ah, sorry -- I get a bit indecisive when faced with so many choices.
I think I'll just be boring and say Earl Grey.
I wasn't talking about the tea.
Why are you here?
You didn't track us down so you could come over here to make small talk about the differences between Berkeley and San Francisco for an hour.
You're acting like we're old friends on a catch-up date, and I don't even know you.
I'm not even sure I *want* to know you.
Well, that's disappointing.
I thought we were off to such a wonderful start.
I'm here to help you, Tabitha.
First and foremost, by saving your lives.

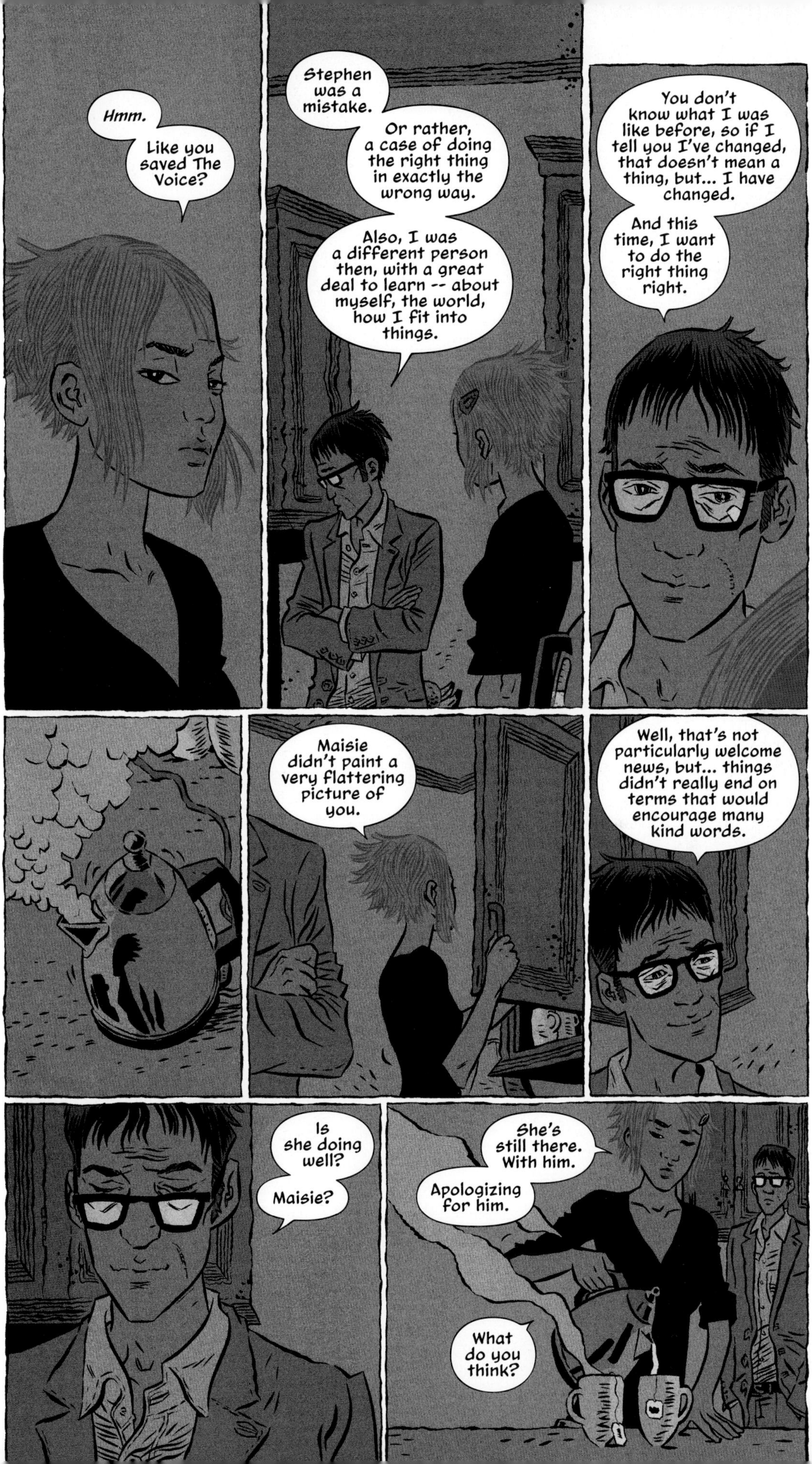

Hmm.
Like you saved The Voice?
Stephen was a mistake.
Or rather, a case of doing the right thing in exactly the wrong way.
Also, I was a different person then, with a great deal to learn -- about myself, the world, how I fit into things.
You don't know what I was like before, so if I tell you I've changed, that doesn't mean a thing, but... I have changed.
And this time, I want to do the right thing right.
Maisie didn't paint a very flattering picture of you.
Well, that's not particularly welcome news, but... things didn't really end on terms that would encourage many kind words.
Is she doing well?
Maisie?
She's still there. With him.
Apologizing for him.
What do you think?

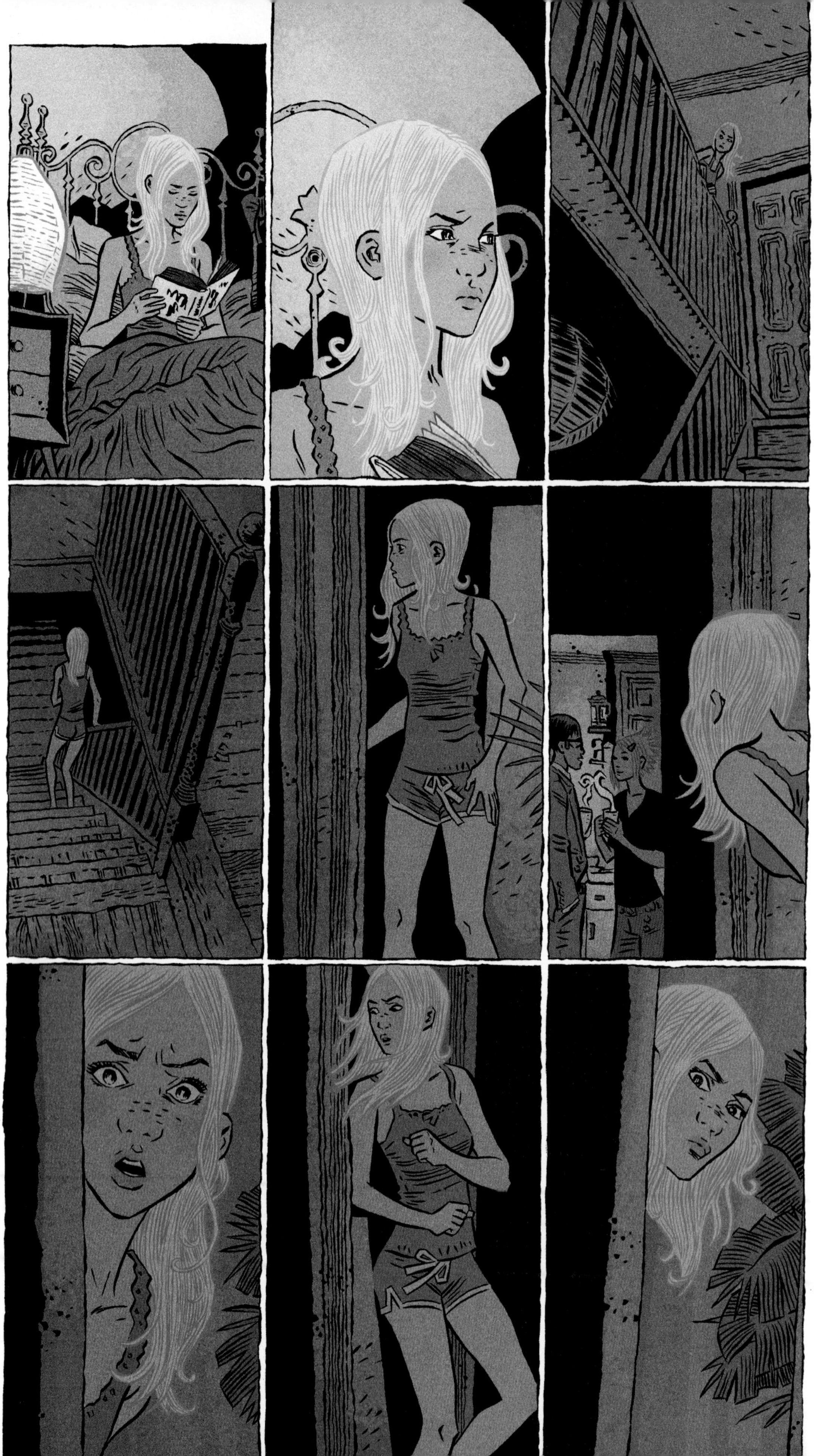

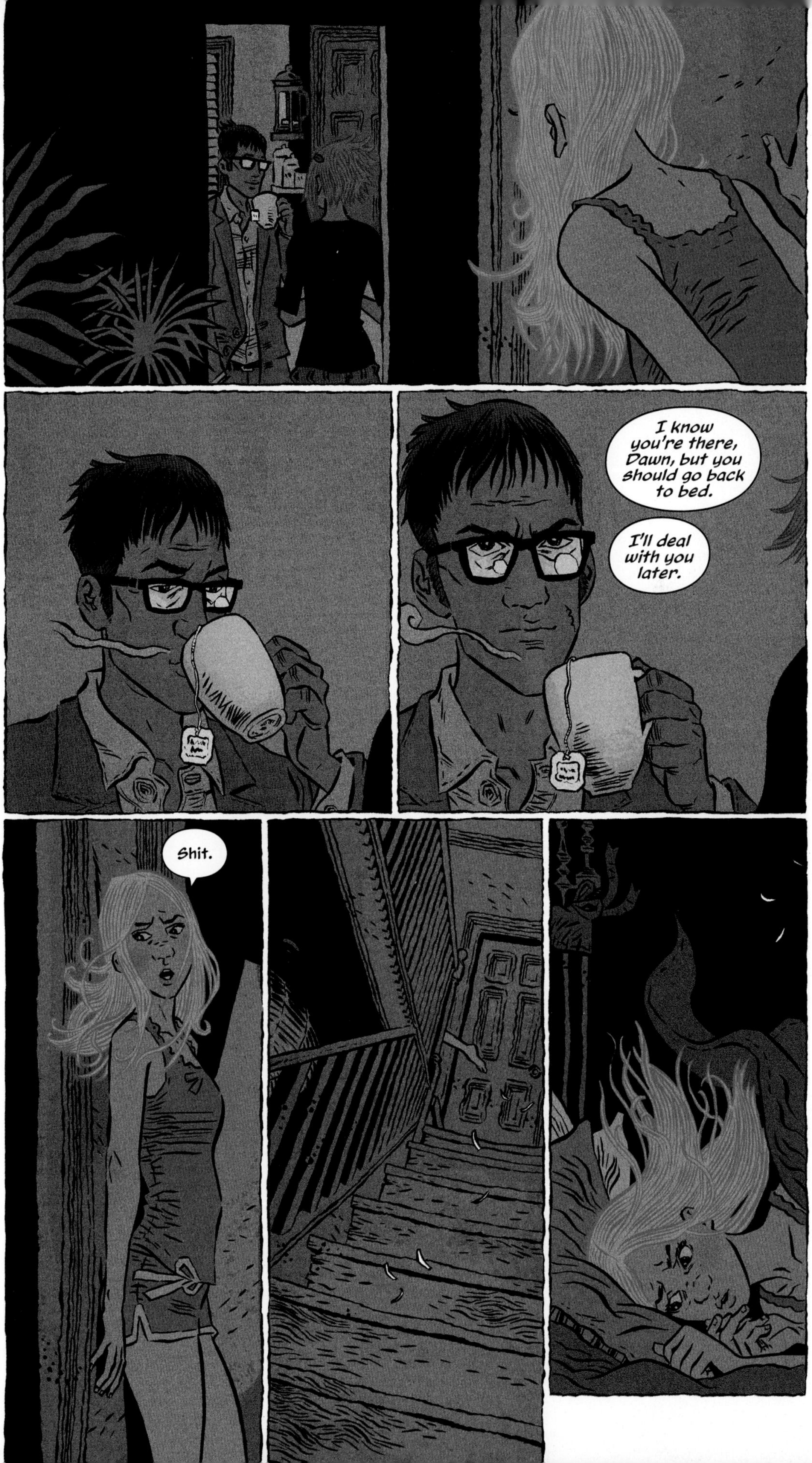
I know you're there, Dawn, but you should go back to bed.
I'll deal with you later.
Shit.

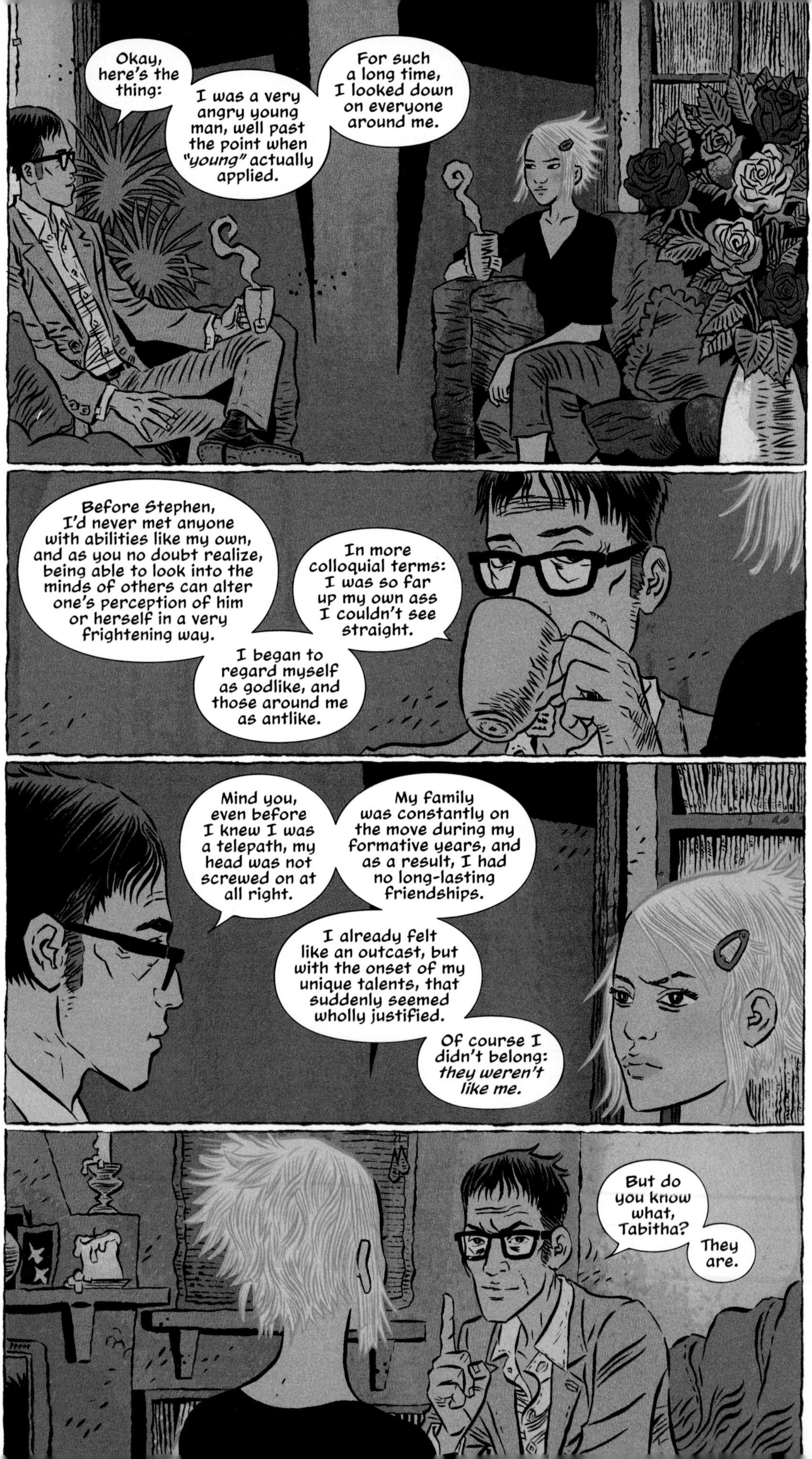
Okay, here's the thing:
I was a very angry young man, well past the point when *"young"* actually applied.
For such a long time, I looked down on everyone around me.
Before Stephen, I'd never met anyone with abilities like my own, and as you no doubt realize, being able to look into the minds of others can alter one's perception of him or herself in a very frightening way.
In more colloquial terms: I was so far up my own ass I couldn't see straight.
I began to regard myself as godlike, and those around me as antlike.
Mind you, even before I knew I was a telepath, my head was not screwed on at all right.
My family was constantly on the move during my formative years, and as a result, I had no long-lasting friendships.
I already felt like an outcast, but with the onset of my unique talents, that suddenly seemed wholly justified.
Of course I didn't belong: *they weren't like me.*
But do you know what, Tabitha?
They are.

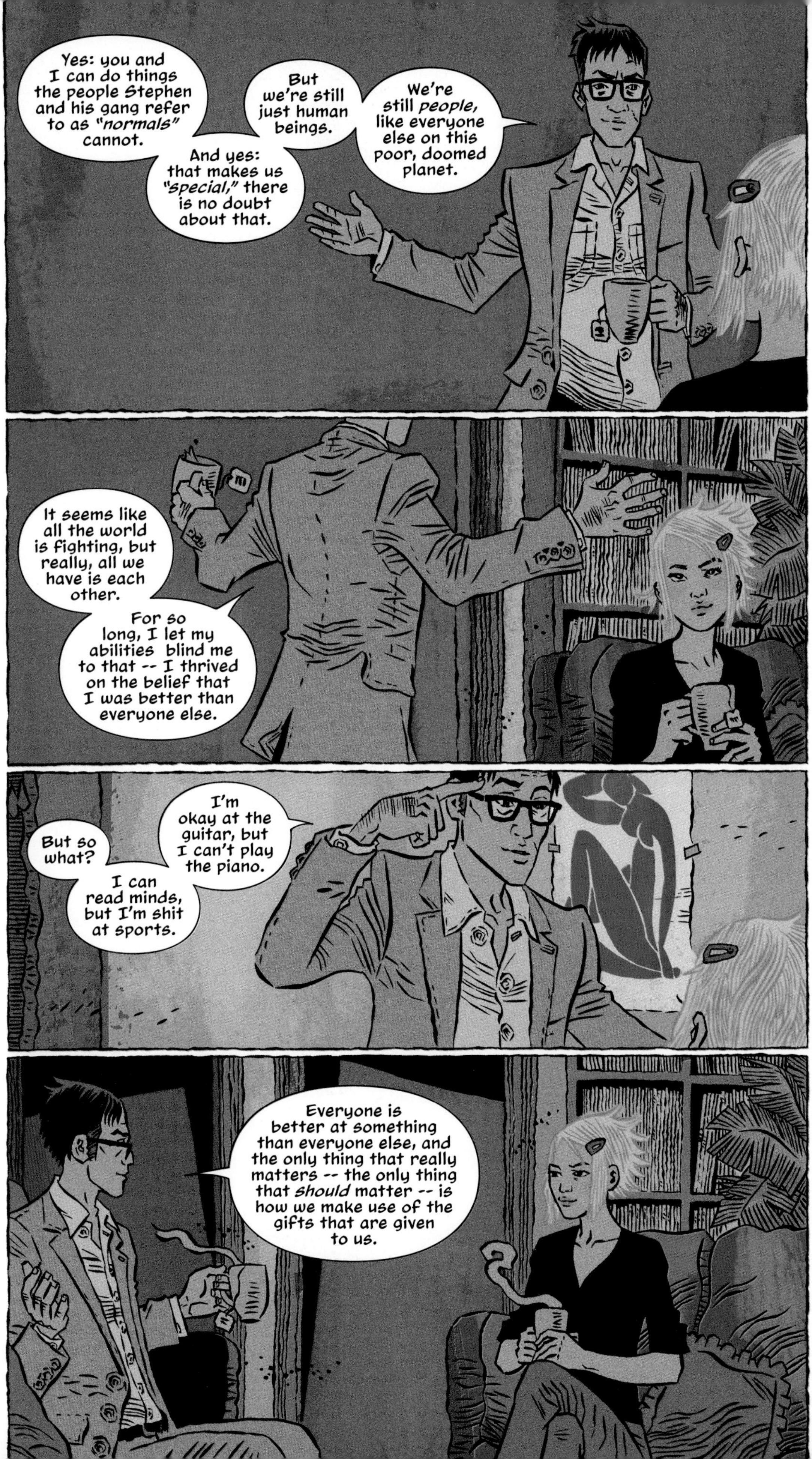
Yes: you and I can do things the people Stephen and his gang refer to as "normals" cannot.
And yes: that makes us "special," there is no doubt about that.
But we're still just human beings.
We're still people, like everyone else on this poor, doomed planet.
It seems like all the world is fighting, but really, all we have is each other.
For so long, I let my abilities blind me to that -- I thrived on the belief that I was better than everyone else.
But so what?
I can read minds, but I'm shit at sports.
I'm okay at the guitar, but I can't play the piano.
Everyone is better at something than everyone else, and the only thing that really matters -- the only thing that should matter -- is how we make use of the gifts that are given to us.

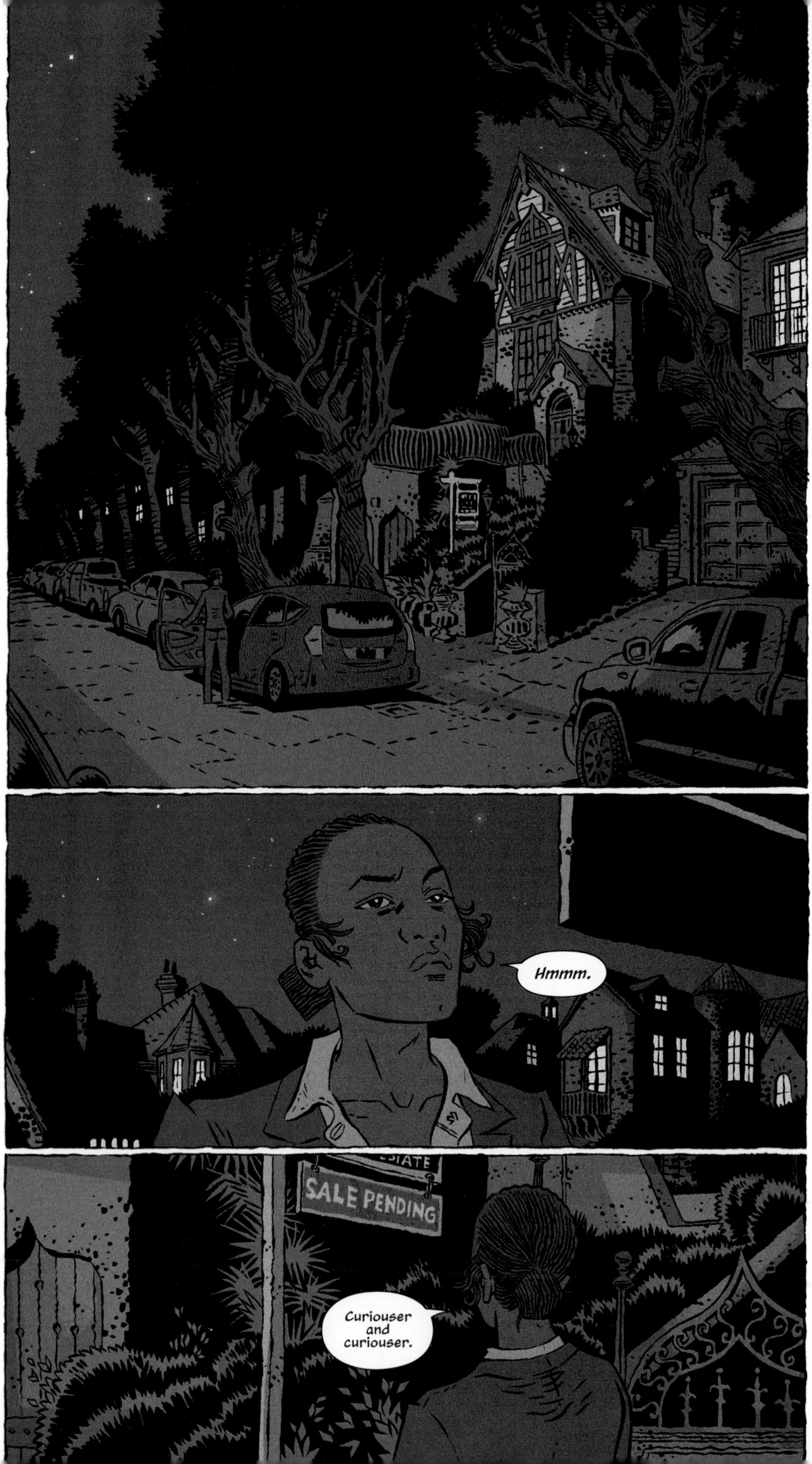
Hmmm.
SALE PENDING
Curiouser
and
curiouser.

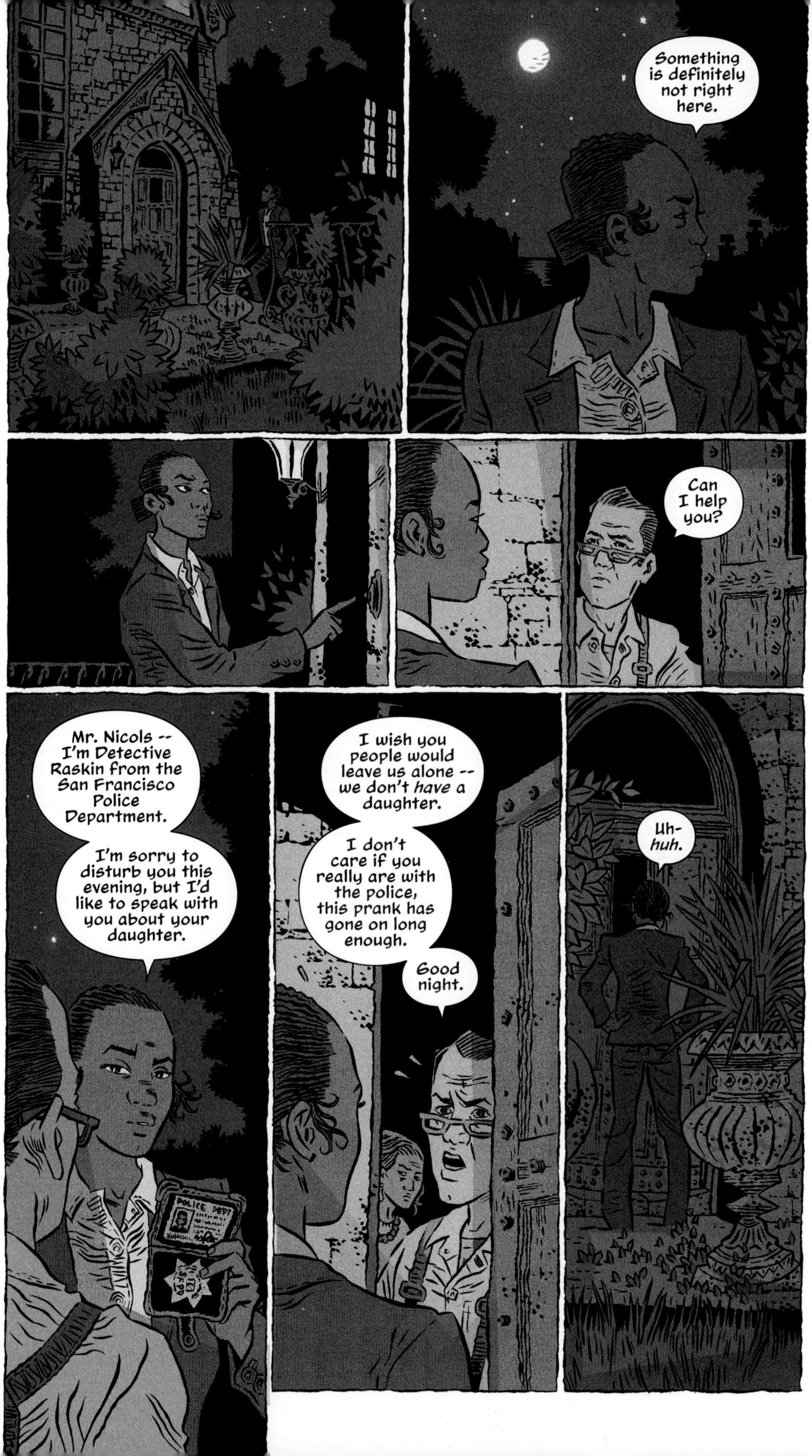
Something is definitely not right here.
Can I help you?
Mr. Nicols -- I'm Detective Raskin from the San Francisco Police Department.
I'm sorry to disturb you this evening, but I'd like to speak with you about your daughter.
POLICE DEPT
I wish you people would leave us alone -- we don't *have* a daughter.
I don't care if you really are with the police, this prank has gone on long enough.
Good night.
Uh-*huh.*

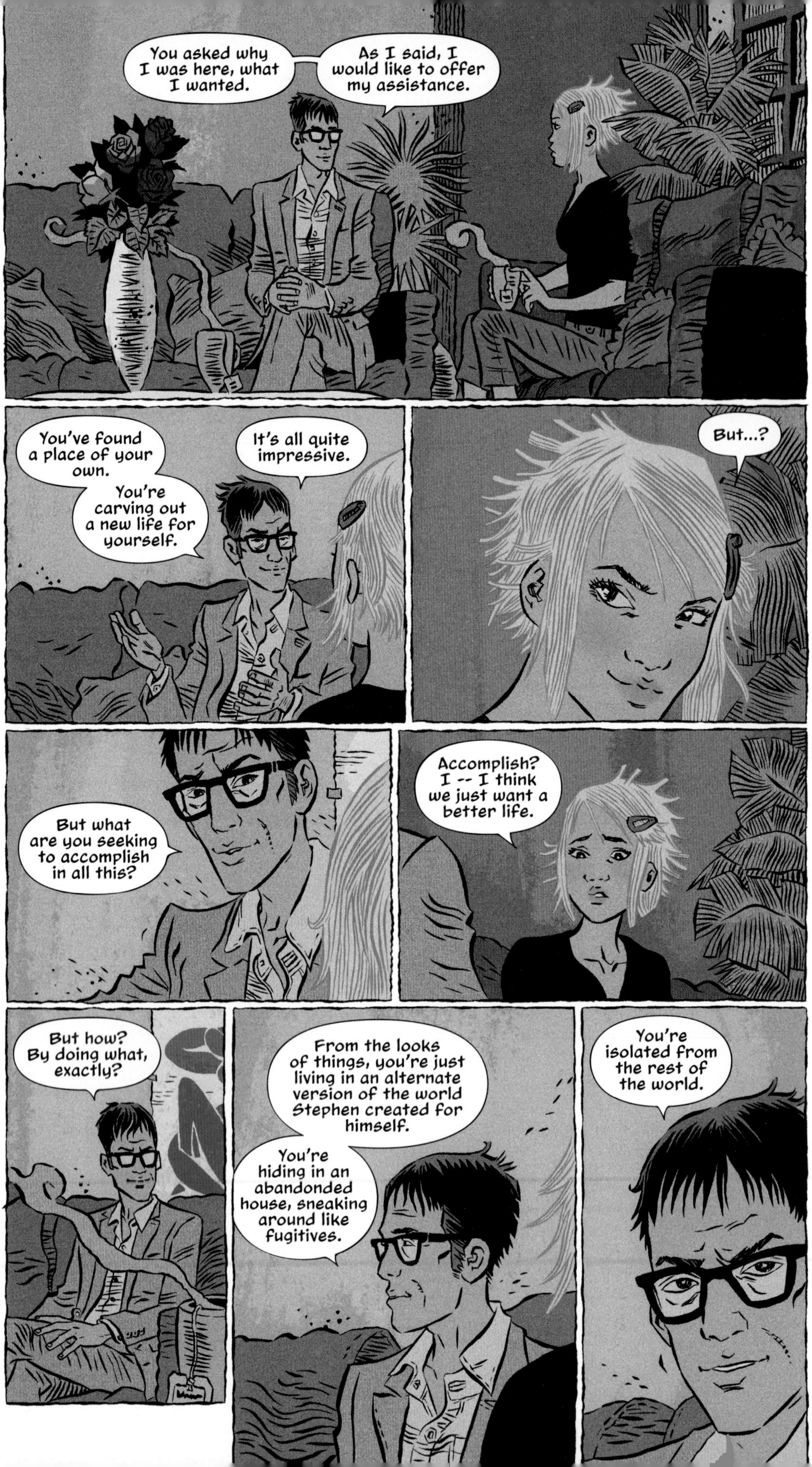
You asked why I was here, what I wanted.
As I said, I would like to offer my assistance.
You've found a place of your own.
You're carving out a new life for yourself.
It's all quite impressive.
But...?
But what are you seeking to accomplish in all this?
Accomplish? I -- I think we just want a better life.
But how? By doing what, exactly?
From the looks of things, you're just living in an alternate version of the world Stephen created for himself.
You're hiding in an abandoned house, sneaking around like fugitives.
You're isolated from the rest of the world.

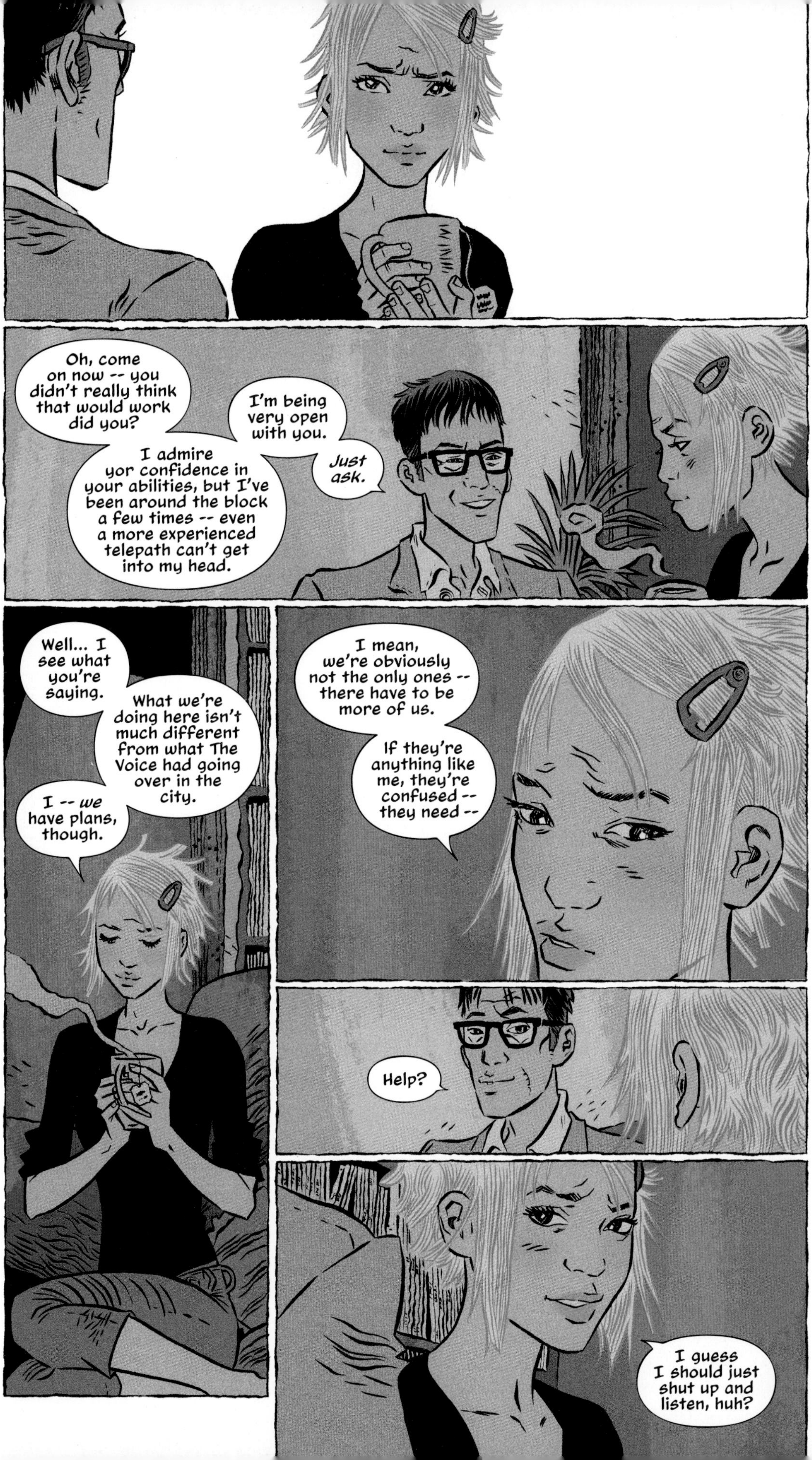
Oh, come on now -- you didn't really think that would work did you?
I admire yor confidence in your abilities, but I've been around the block a few times -- even a more experienced telepath can't get into my head.
I'm being very open with you.
Just ask.
Well... I see what you're saying.
What we're doing here isn't much different from what The Voice had going over in the city.
I -- *we* have plans, though.
I mean, we're obviously not the only ones -- there have to be more of us.
If they're anything like me, they're confused -- they need --
Help?
I guess I should just shut up and listen, huh?

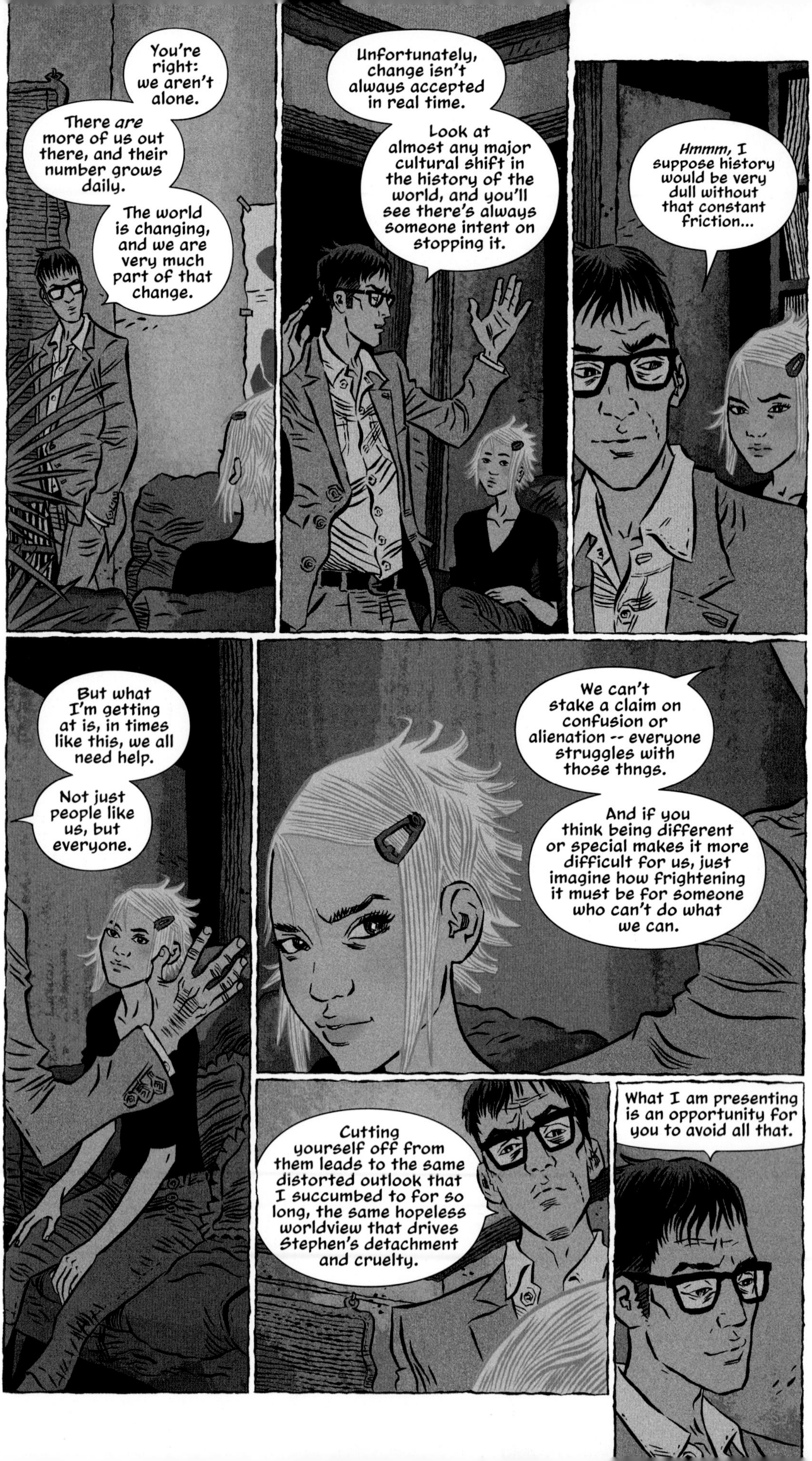
You're right: we aren't alone.
There *are* more of us out there, and their number grows daily.
The world is changing, and we are very much part of that change.
Unfortunately, change isn't always accepted in real time.
Look at almost any major cultural shift in the history of the world, and you'll see there's always someone intent on stopping it.
Hmmm, I suppose history would be very dull without that constant friction...
But what I'm getting at is, in times like this, we all need help.
Not just people like us, but everyone.
We can't stake a claim on confusion or alienation -- everyone struggles with those thngs.
And if you think being different or special makes it more difficult for us, just imagine how frightening it must be for someone who can't do what we can.
Cutting yourself off from them leads to the same distorted outlook that I succumbed to for so long, the same hopeless worldview that drives Stephen's detachment and cruelty.
What I am presenting is an opportunity for you to avoid all that.

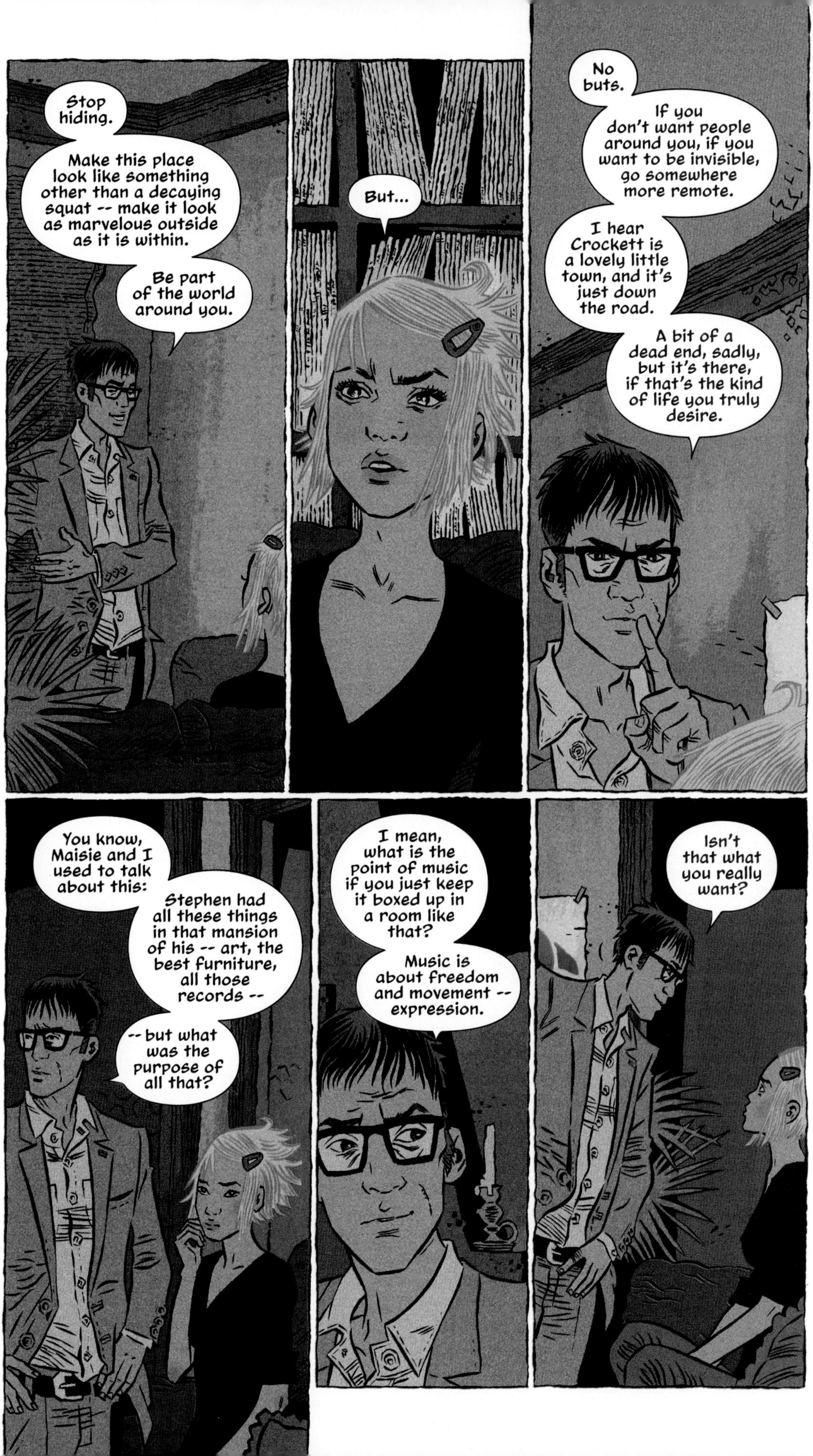
Stop hiding.
Make this place look like something other than a decaying squat -- make it look as marvelous outside as it is within.
Be part of the world around you.
But...
No buts.
If you don't want people around you, if you want to be invisible, go somewhere more remote.
I hear Crockett is a lovely little town, and it's just down the road.
A bit of a dead end, sadly, but it's there, if that's the kind of life you truly desire.
You know, Maisie and I used to talk about this:
Stephen had all these things in that mansion of his -- art, the best furniture, all those records --
-- but what was the purpose of all that?
I mean, what is the point of music if you just keep it boxed up in a room like that?
Music is about freedom and movement -- expression.
Isn't that what you really want?

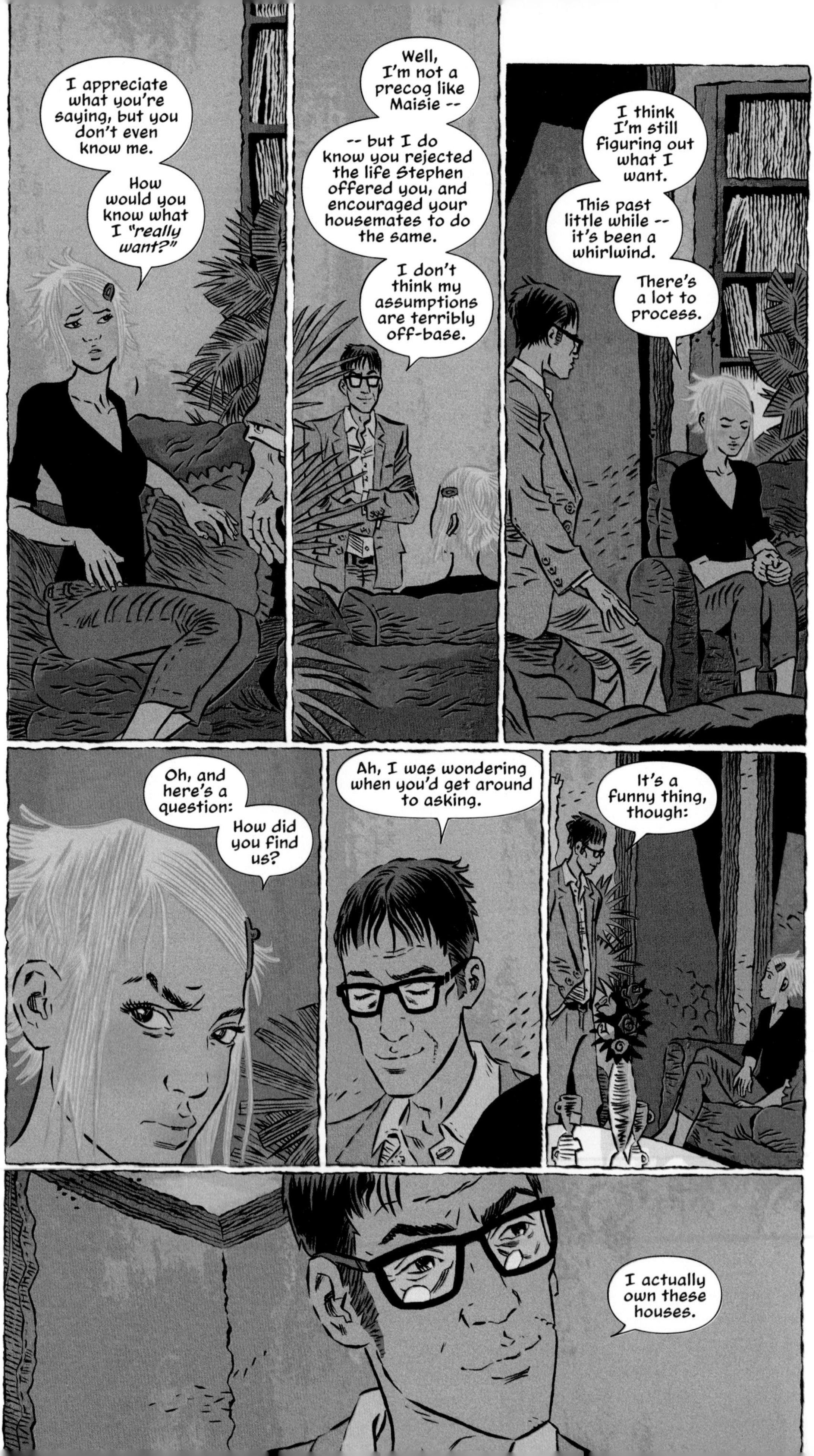
I appreciate what you're saying, but you don't even know me.
How would you know what I *"really want?"*
Well, I'm not a precog like Maisie --
-- but I do know you rejected the life Stephen offered you, and encouraged your housemates to do the same.
I don't think my assumptions are terribly off-base.
I think I'm still figuring out what I want.
This past little while -- it's been a whirlwind.
There's a lot to process.
Oh, and here's a question:
How did you find us?
Ah, I was wondering when you'd get around to asking.
It's a funny thing, though:
I actually own these houses.

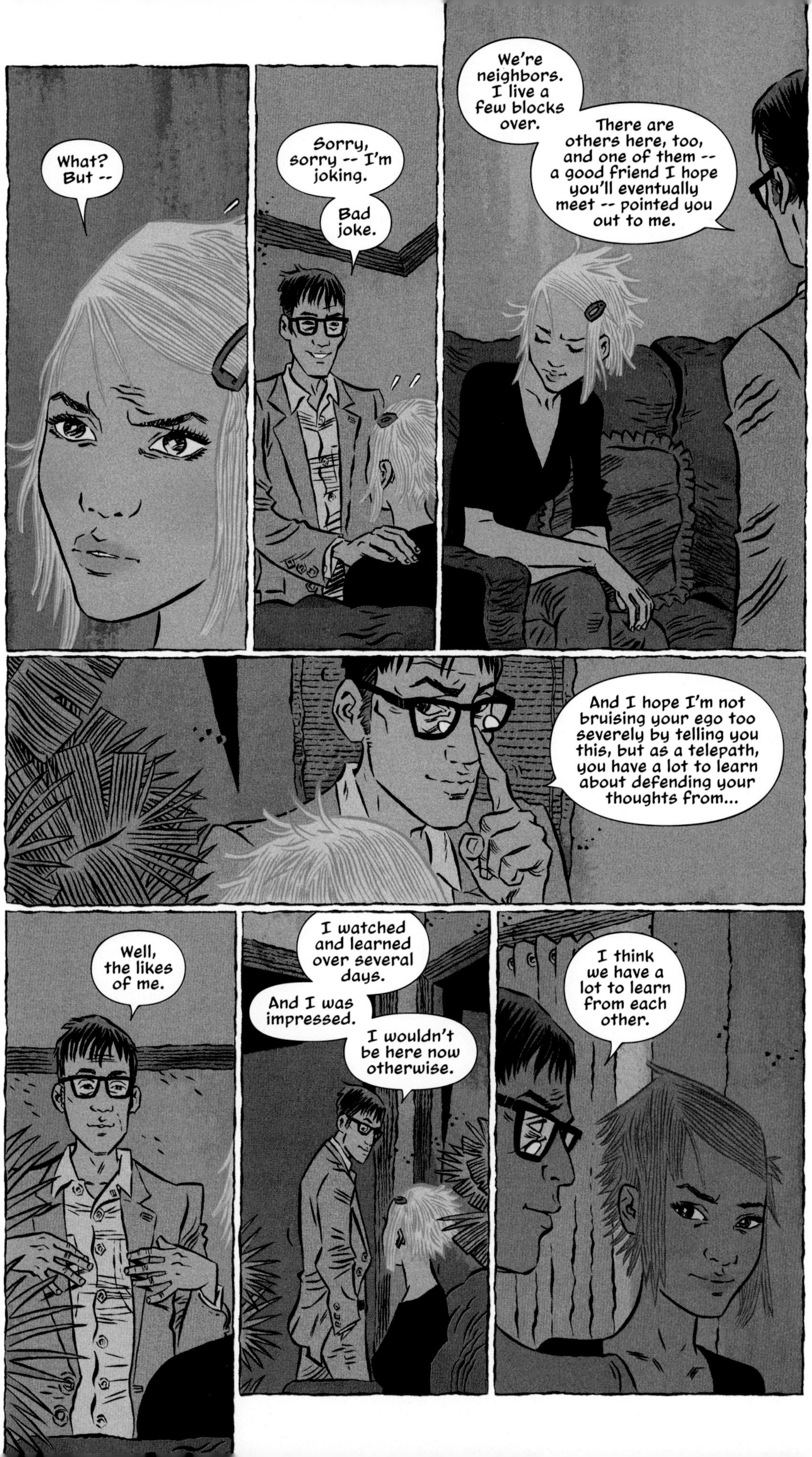
What? But --
Sorry, sorry -- I'm joking.
Bad joke.
We're neighbors. I live a few blocks over.
There are others here, too, and one of them -- a good friend I hope you'll eventually meet -- pointed you out to me.
And I hope I'm not bruising your ego too severely by telling you this, but as a telepath, you have a lot to learn about defending your thoughts from...
Well, the likes of me.
I watched and learned over several days.
And I was impressed.
I wouldn't be here now otherwise.
I think we have a lot to learn from each other.

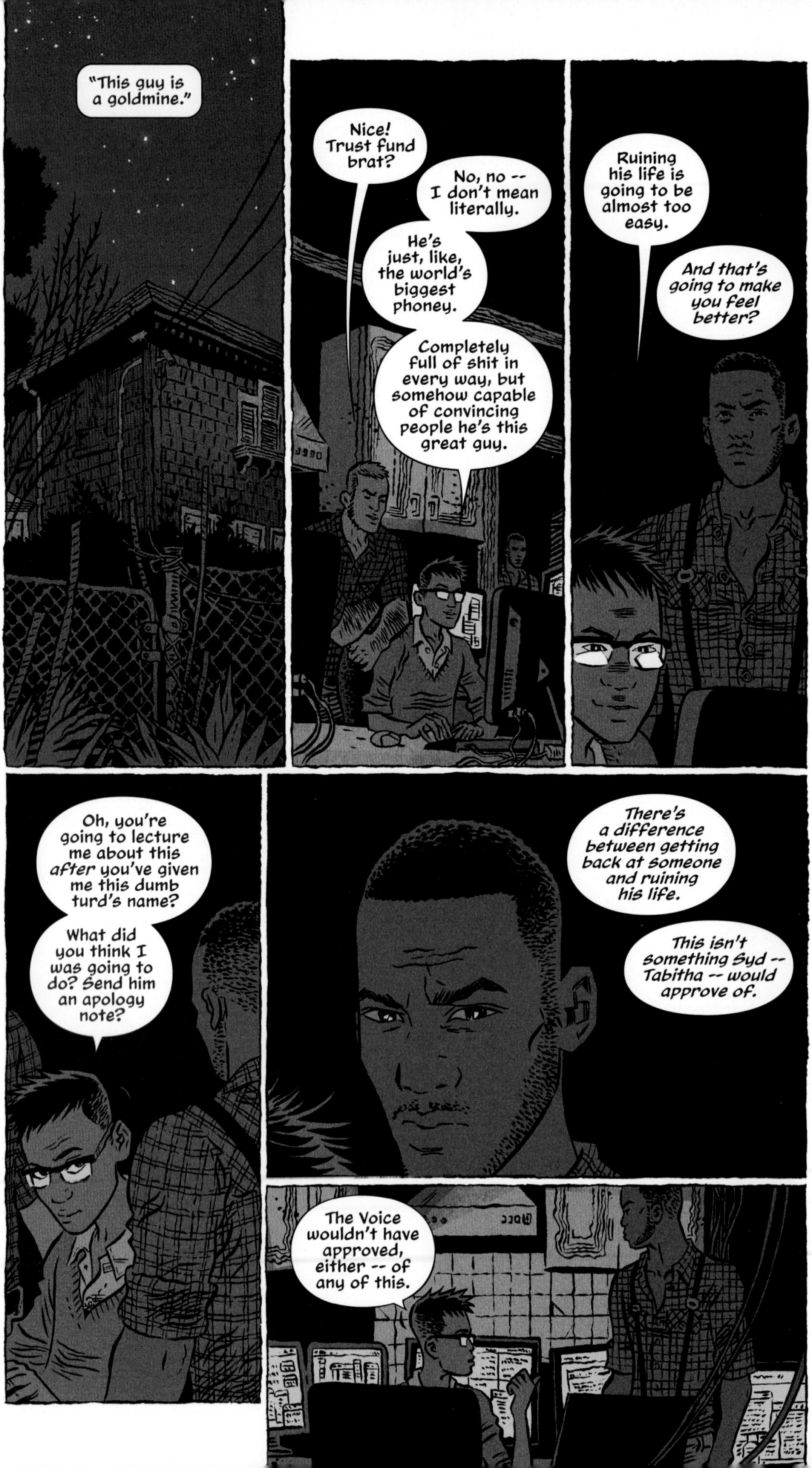
"This guy is a goldmine."
Nice! Trust fund brat?
No, no -- I don't mean literally.
He's just, like, the world's biggest phoney.
Completely full of shit in every way, but somehow capable of convincing people he's this great guy.
Ruining his life is going to be almost too easy.
And that's going to make you feel better?
Oh, you're going to lecture me about this *after* you've given me this dumb turd's name?
What did you think I was going to do? Send him an apology note?
There's a difference between getting back at someone and ruining his life.
This isn't something Syd -- Tabitha -- would approve of.
The Voice wouldn't have approved, either -- of any of this.

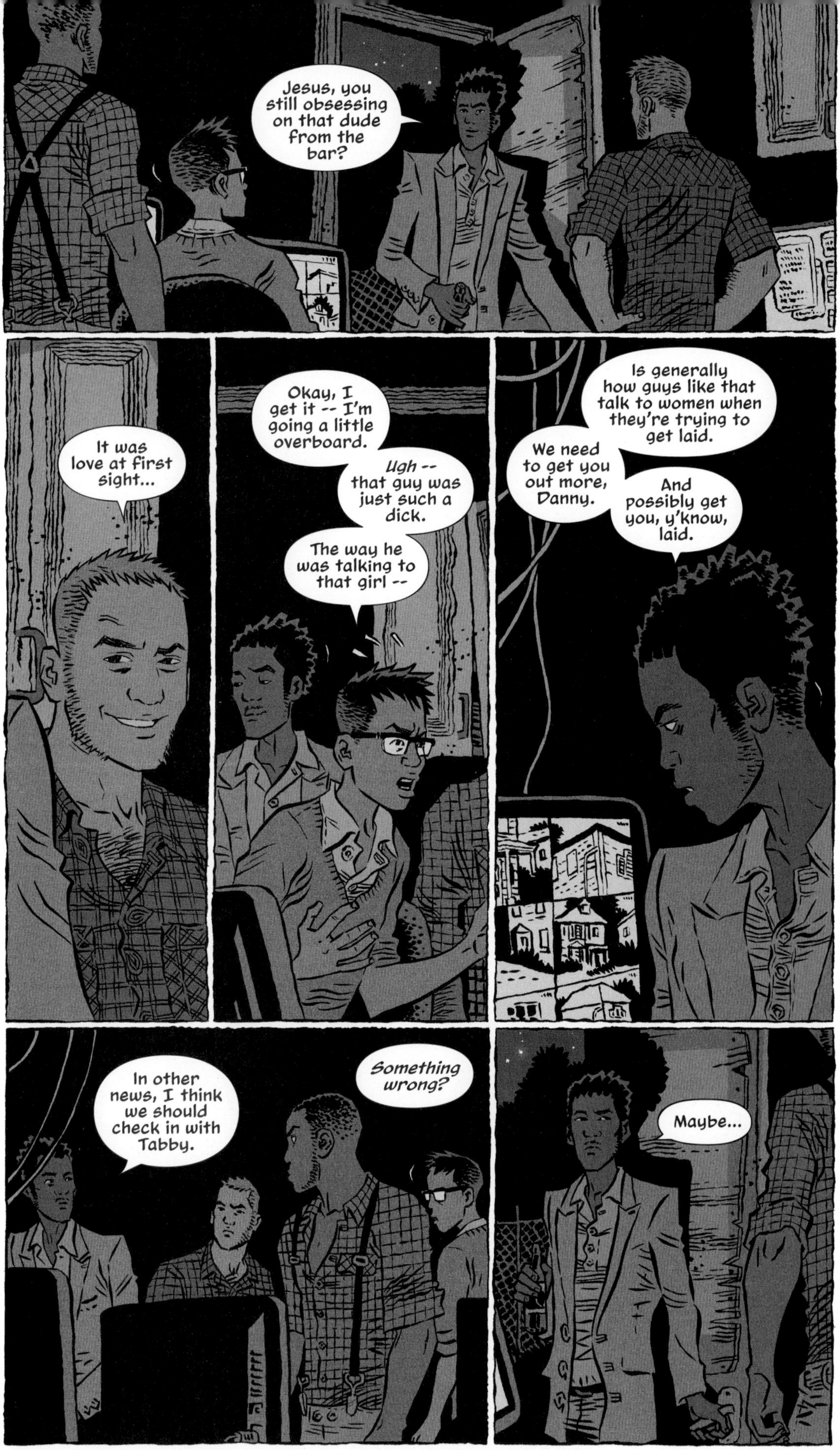
Jesus, you still obsessing on that dude from the bar?
It was love at first sight...
Okay, I get it -- I'm going a little overboard.
Ugh -- that guy was just such a dick.
The way he was talking to that girl --
Is generally how guys like that talk to women when they're trying to get laid.
We need to get you out more, Danny.
And possibly get you, y'know, laid.
In other news, I think we should check in with Tabby.
Something wrong?
Maybe...

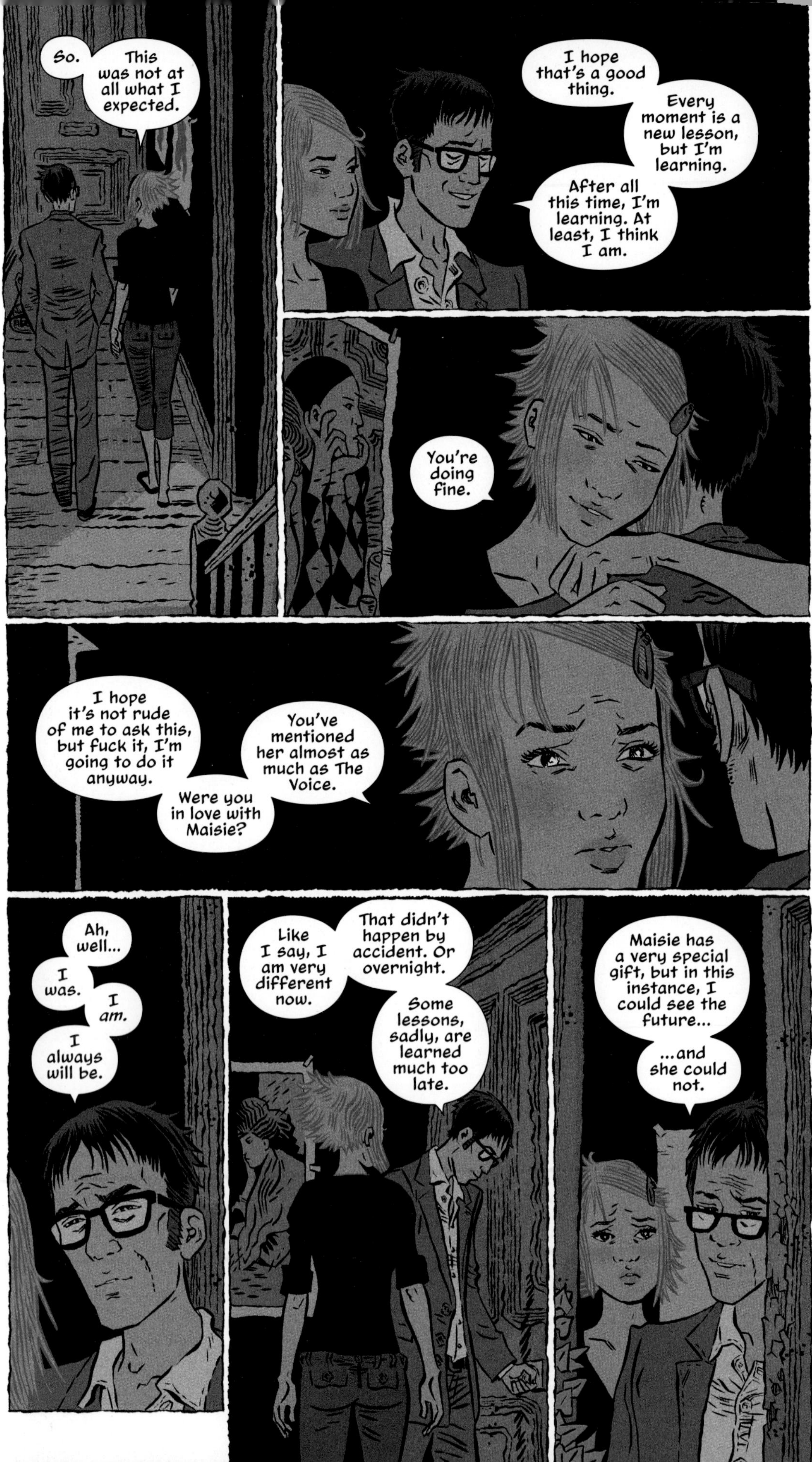
So.
This was not at all what I expected.
I hope that's a good thing.
Every moment is a new lesson, but I'm learning.
After all this time, I'm learning. At least, I think I am.
You're doing fine.
I hope it's not rude of me to ask this, but fuck it, I'm going to do it anyway.
Were you in love with Maisie?
You've mentioned her almost as much as The Voice.
Ah, well...
I was.
I *am*.
I always will be.
Like I say, I am very different now.
That didn't happen by accident. Or overnight.
Some lessons, sadly, are learned much too late.
Maisie has a very special gift, but in this instance, I could see the future...
...and she could not.

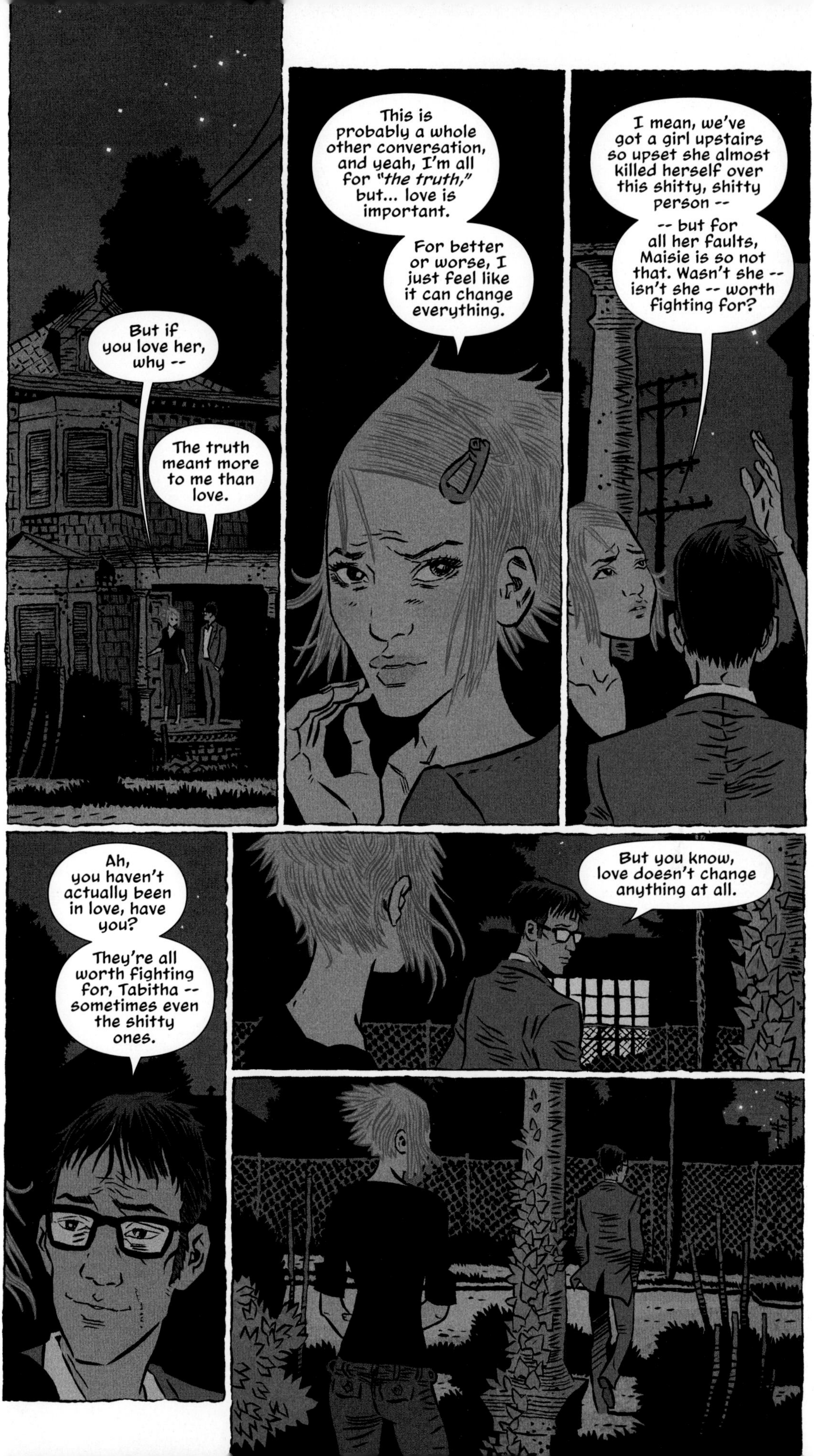

But if you love her, why --
The truth meant more to me than love.
This is probably a whole other conversation, and yeah, I'm all for *"the truth,"* but... love is important.
For better or worse, I just feel like it can change everything.
I mean, we've got a girl upstairs so upset she almost killed herself over this shitty, shitty person --
-- but for all her faults, Maisie is so not that. Wasn't she -- isn't she -- worth fighting for?
Ah, you haven't actually been in love, have you?
They're all worth fighting for, Tabitha -- sometimes even the shitty ones.
But you know, love doesn't change anything at all.

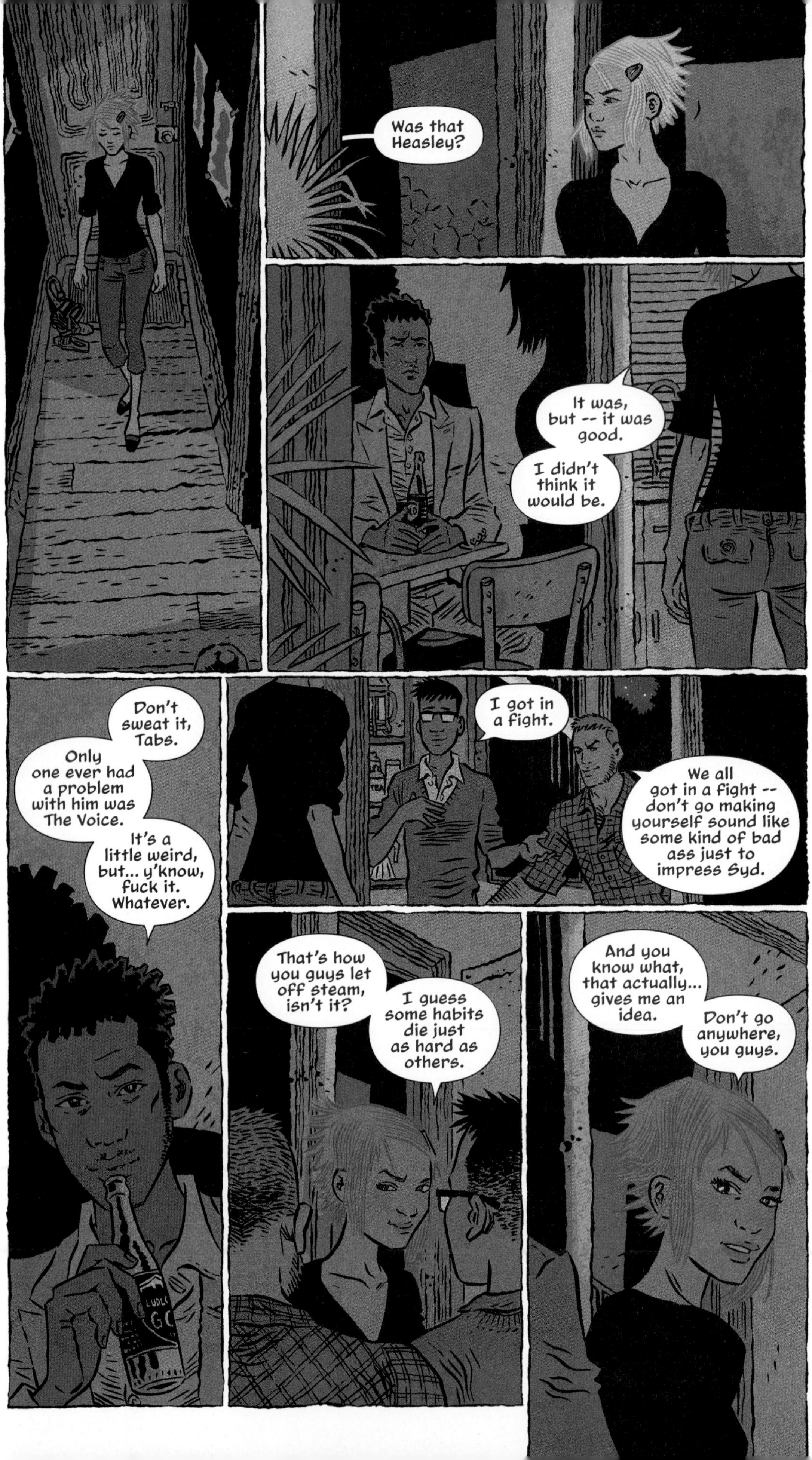
Was that Heasley?
It was, but -- it was good.
I didn't think it would be.
Don't sweat it, Tabs.
Only one ever had a problem with him was The Voice.
It's a little weird, but... y'know, fuck it. Whatever.
I got in a fight.
We all got in a fight -- don't go making yourself sound like some kind of bad ass just to impress Syd.
That's how you guys let off steam, isn't it?
I guess some habits die just as hard as others.
And you know what, that actually... gives me an idea.
Don't go anywhere, you guys.

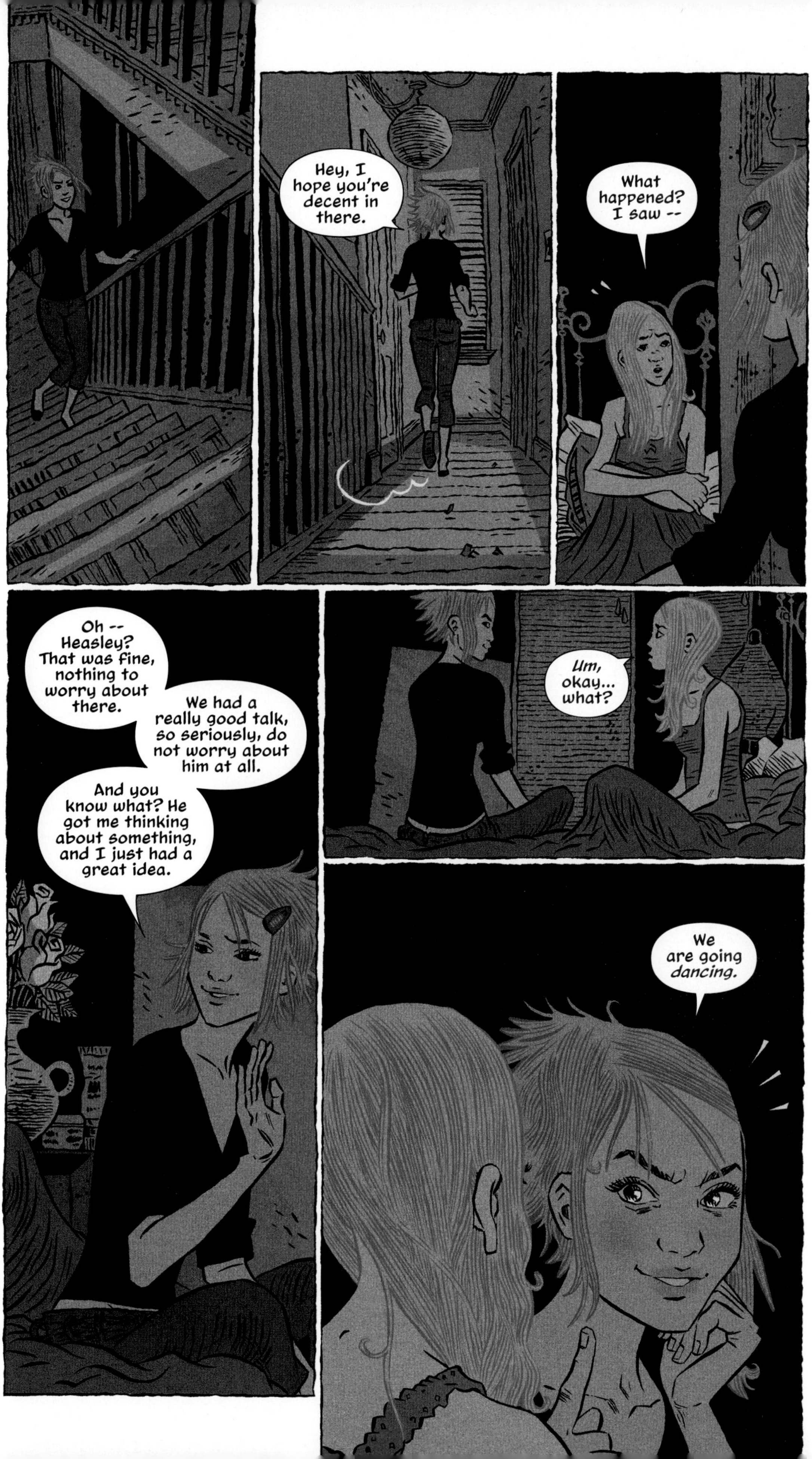
Hey, I hope you're decent in there.
What happened? I saw --
Oh -- Heasley? That was fine, nothing to worry about there.
We had a really good talk, so seriously, do not worry about him at all.
And you know what? He got me thinking about something, and I just had a great idea.
Um, okay... what?
We are going *dancing.*

SURVIVAL'S AS NATURAL AS SORROW

RICHARD JAMES EDWARDS

9: THE PARTY LINE

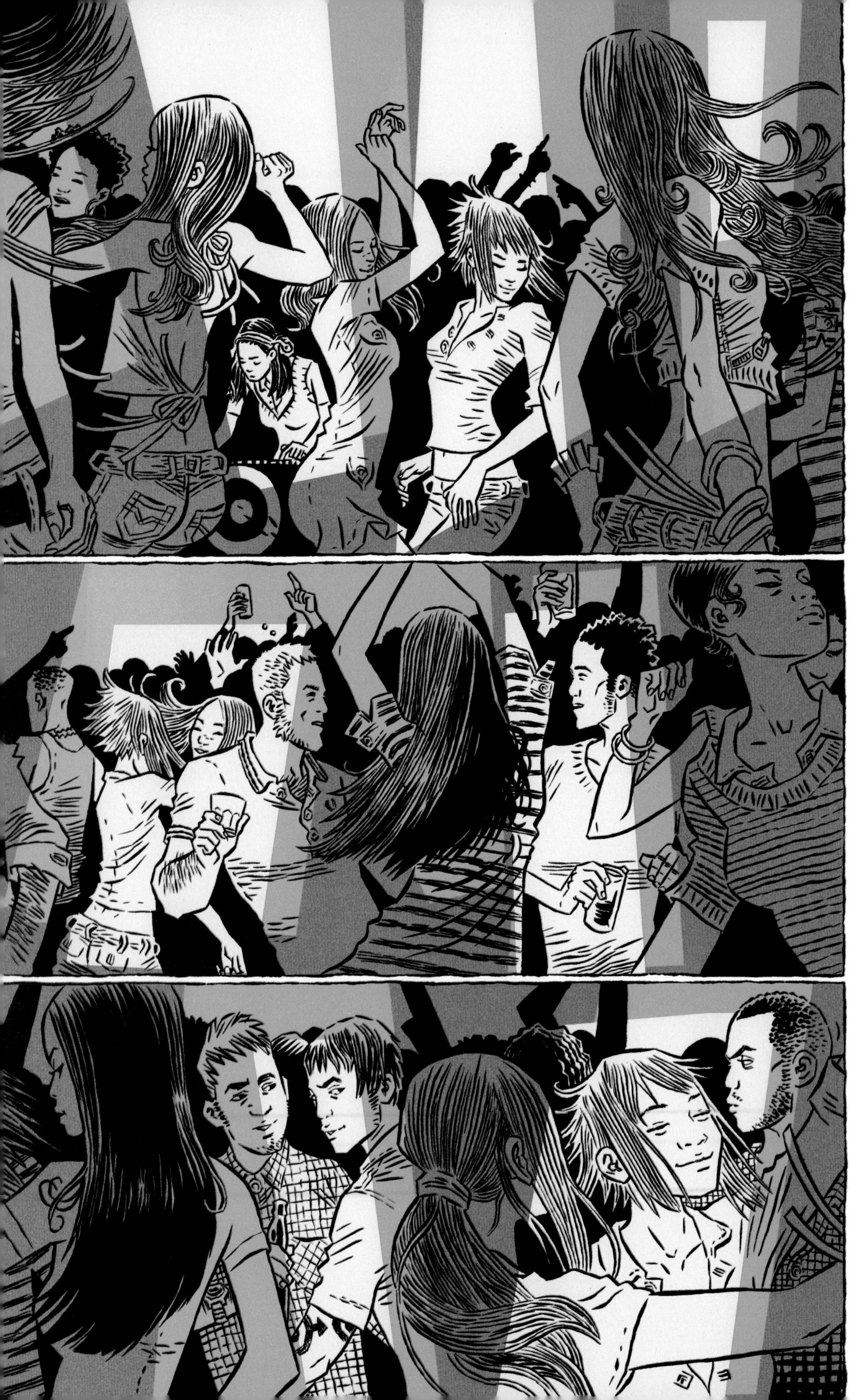

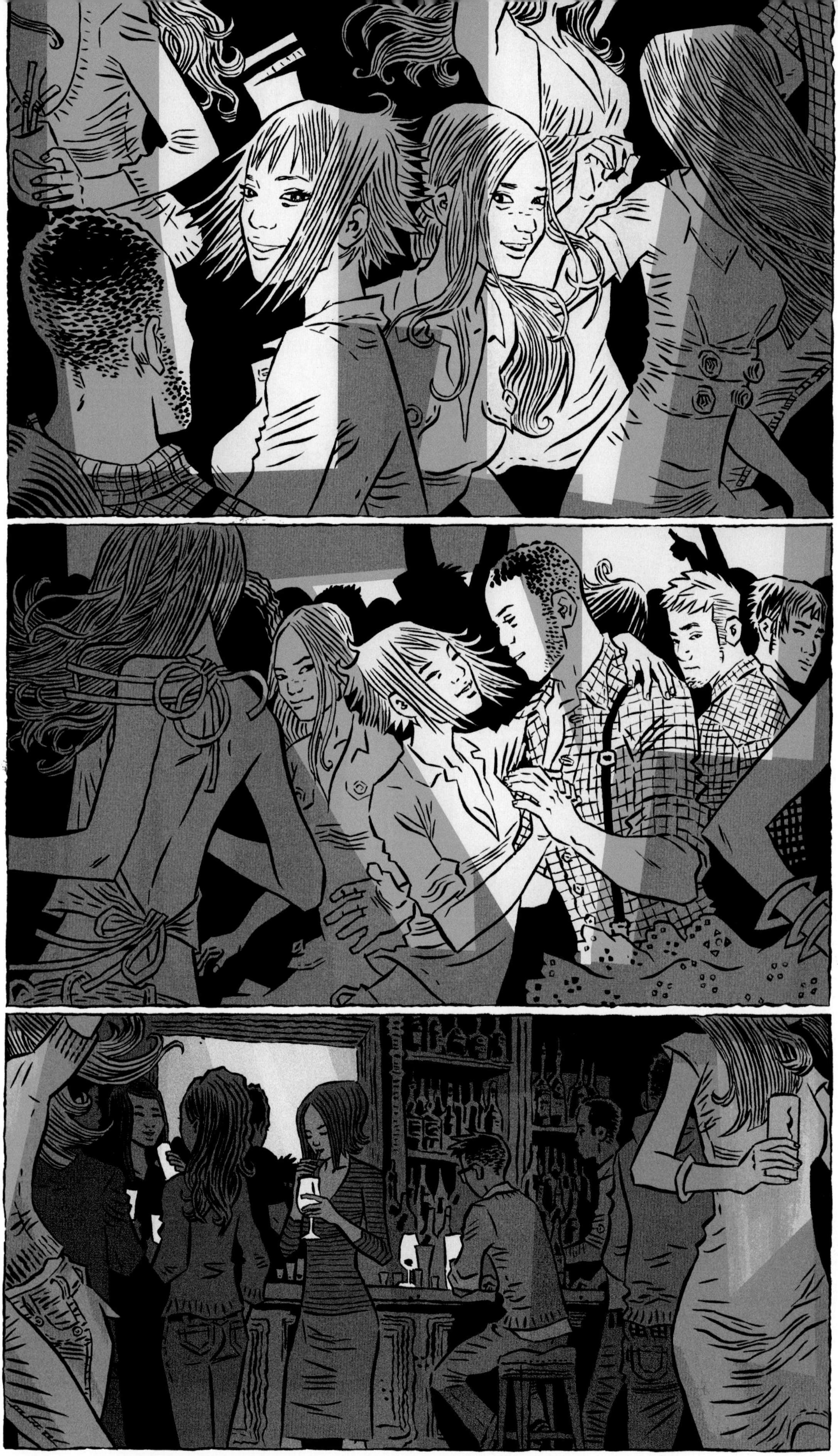

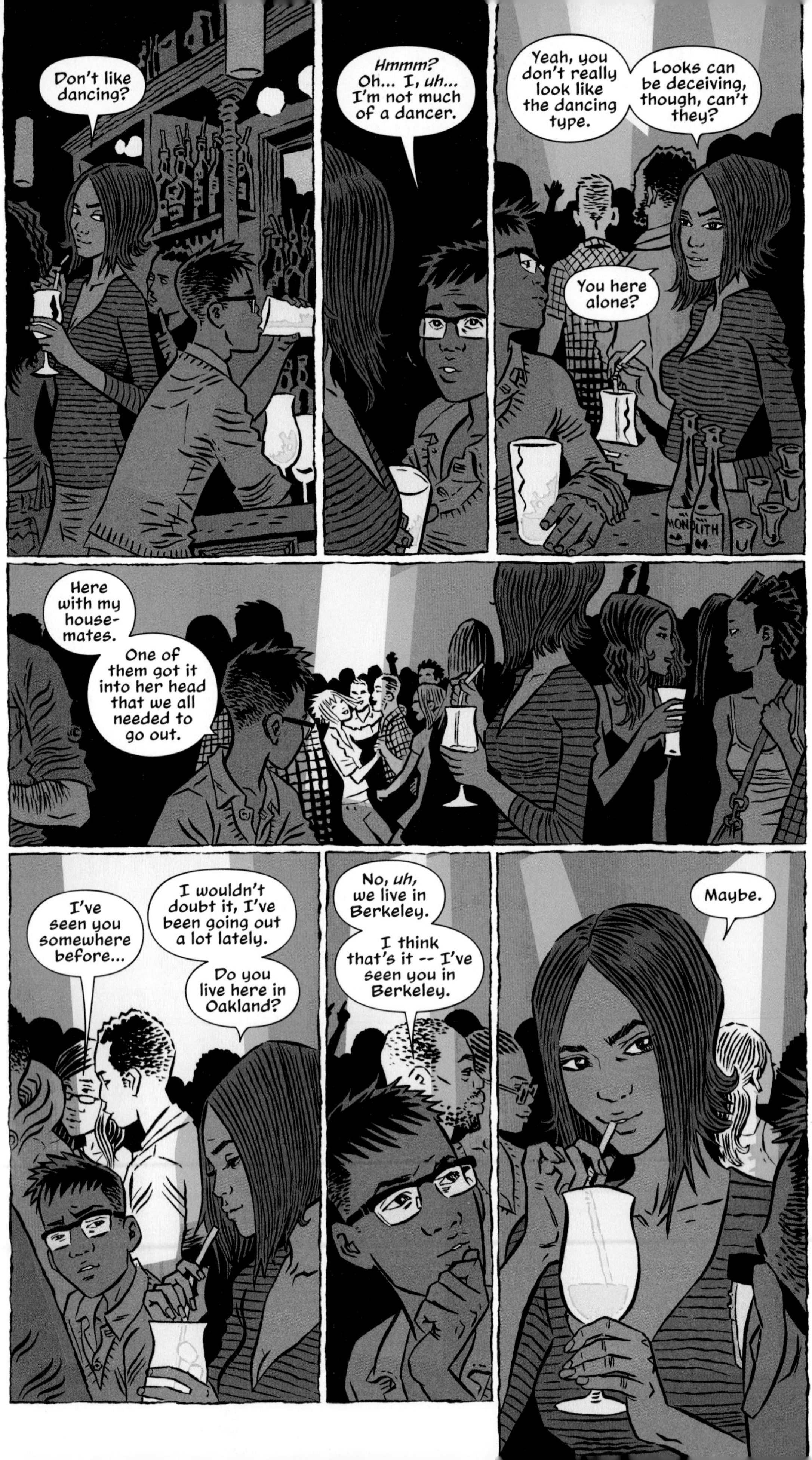
Don't like dancing?
Hmmm? Oh... I, *uh*... I'm not much of a dancer.
Yeah, you don't really look like the dancing type.
Looks can be deceiving, though, can't they?
You here alone?
MONOLITH
Here with my house-mates.
One of them got it into her head that we all needed to go out.
I've seen you somewhere before...
I wouldn't doubt it, I've been going out a lot lately.
Do you live here in Oakland?
No, *uh*, we live in Berkeley.
I think that's it -- I've seen you in Berkeley.
Maybe.

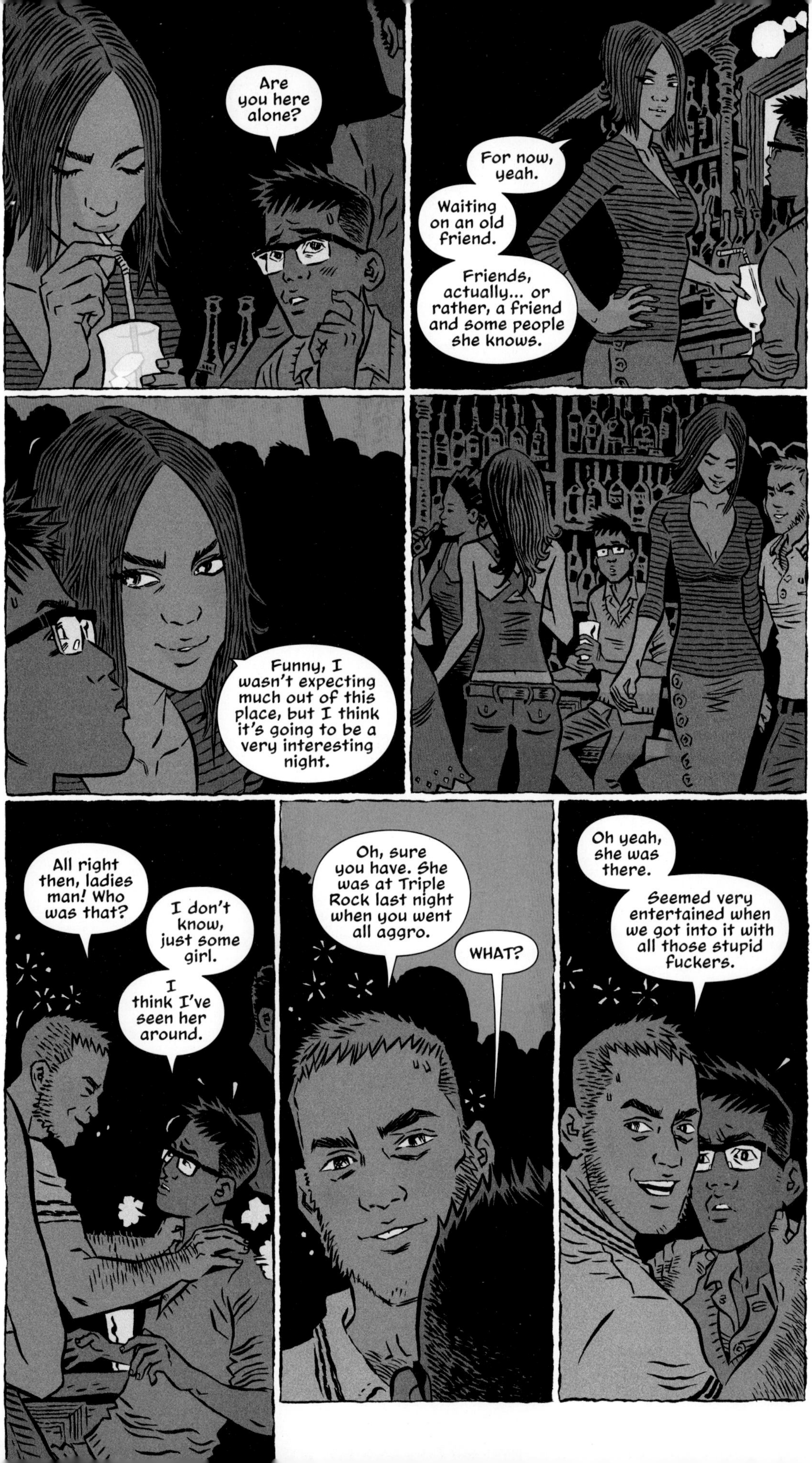
Are you here alone?
For now, yeah.
Waiting on an old friend.
Friends, actually... or rather, a friend and some people she knows.
Funny, I wasn't expecting much out of this place, but I think it's going to be a very interesting night.
All right then, ladies man! Who was that?
I don't know, just some girl.
I think I've seen her around.
Oh, sure you have. She was at Triple Rock last night when you went all aggro.
WHAT?
Oh yeah, she was there.
Seemed very entertained when we got into it with all those stupid fuckers.

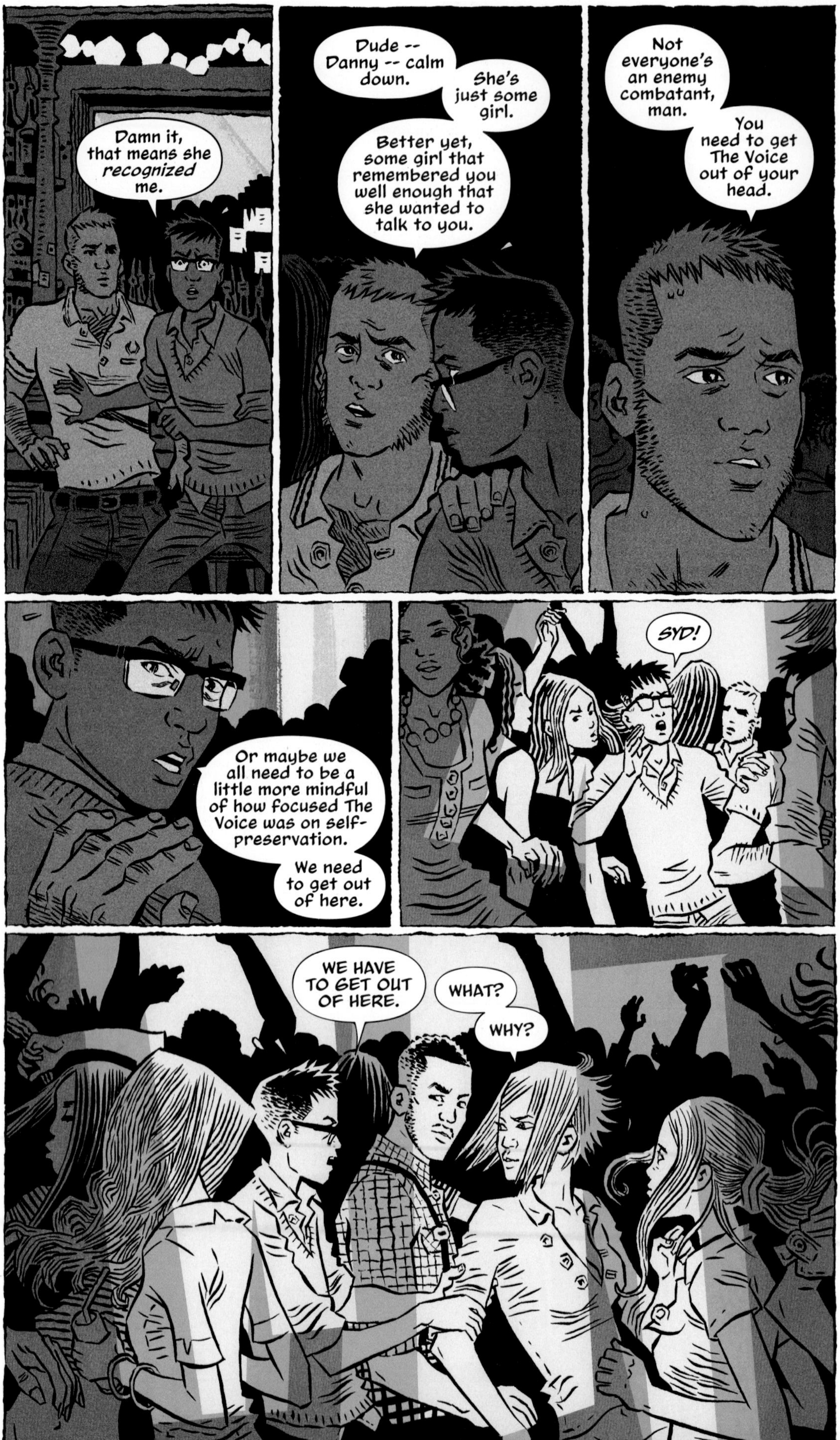

Damn it, that means she *recognized* me.
Dude -- Danny -- calm down.
She's just some girl.
Better yet, some girl that remembered you well enough that she wanted to talk to you.
Not everyone's an enemy combatant, man.
You need to get The Voice out of your head.
Or maybe we all need to be a little more mindful of how focused The Voice was on self-preservation.
We need to get out of here.
SYD!
WE HAVE TO GET OUT OF HERE.
WHAT?
WHY?

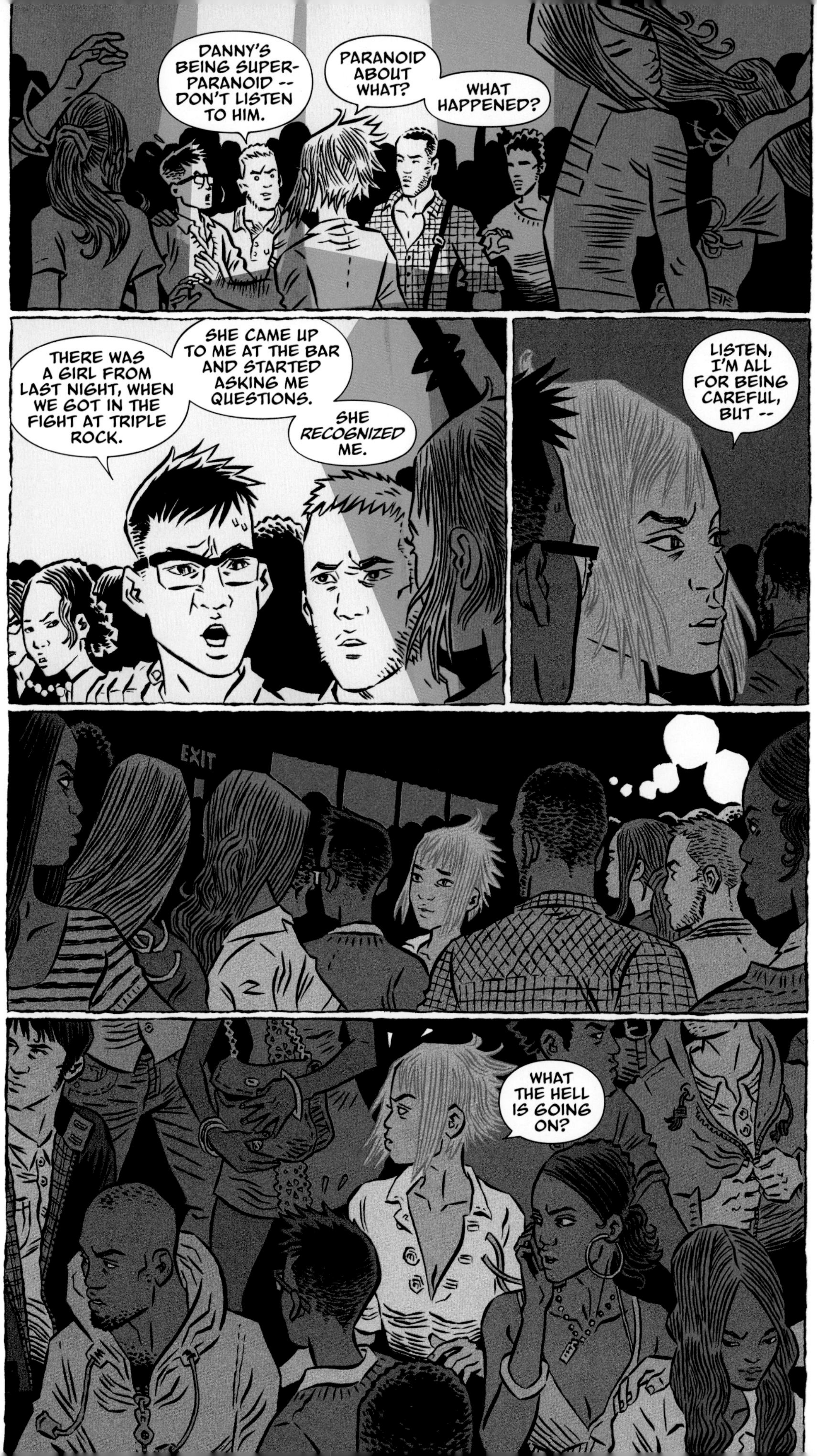
DANNY'S BEING SUPER-PARANOID -- DON'T LISTEN TO HIM.
PARANOID ABOUT WHAT?
WHAT HAPPENED?
THERE WAS A GIRL FROM LAST NIGHT, WHEN WE GOT IN THE FIGHT AT TRIPLE ROCK.
SHE CAME UP TO ME AT THE BAR AND STARTED ASKING ME QUESTIONS.
SHE *RECOGNIZED* ME.
LISTEN, I'M ALL FOR BEING CAREFUL, BUT --
EXIT
WHAT THE HELL IS GOING ON?

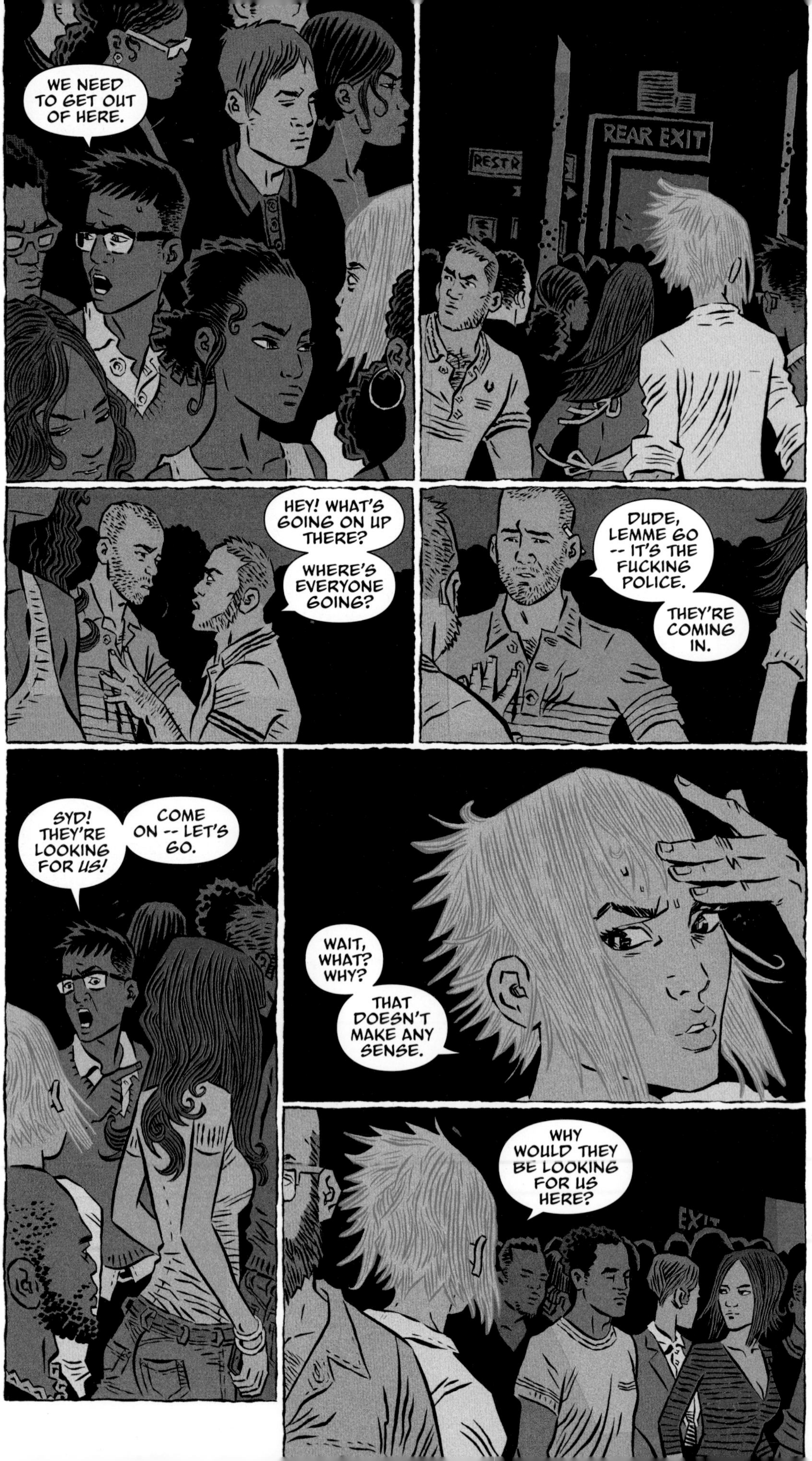
WE NEED TO GET OUT OF HERE.
REAR EXIT
HEY! WHAT'S GOING ON UP THERE?
WHERE'S EVERYONE GOING?
DUDE, LEMME GO -- IT'S THE FUCKING POLICE.
THEY'RE COMING IN.
SYD! THEY'RE LOOKING FOR US!
COME ON -- LET'S GO.
WAIT, WHAT? WHY?
THAT DOESN'T MAKE ANY SENSE.
WHY WOULD THEY BE LOOKING FOR US HERE?
EXIT

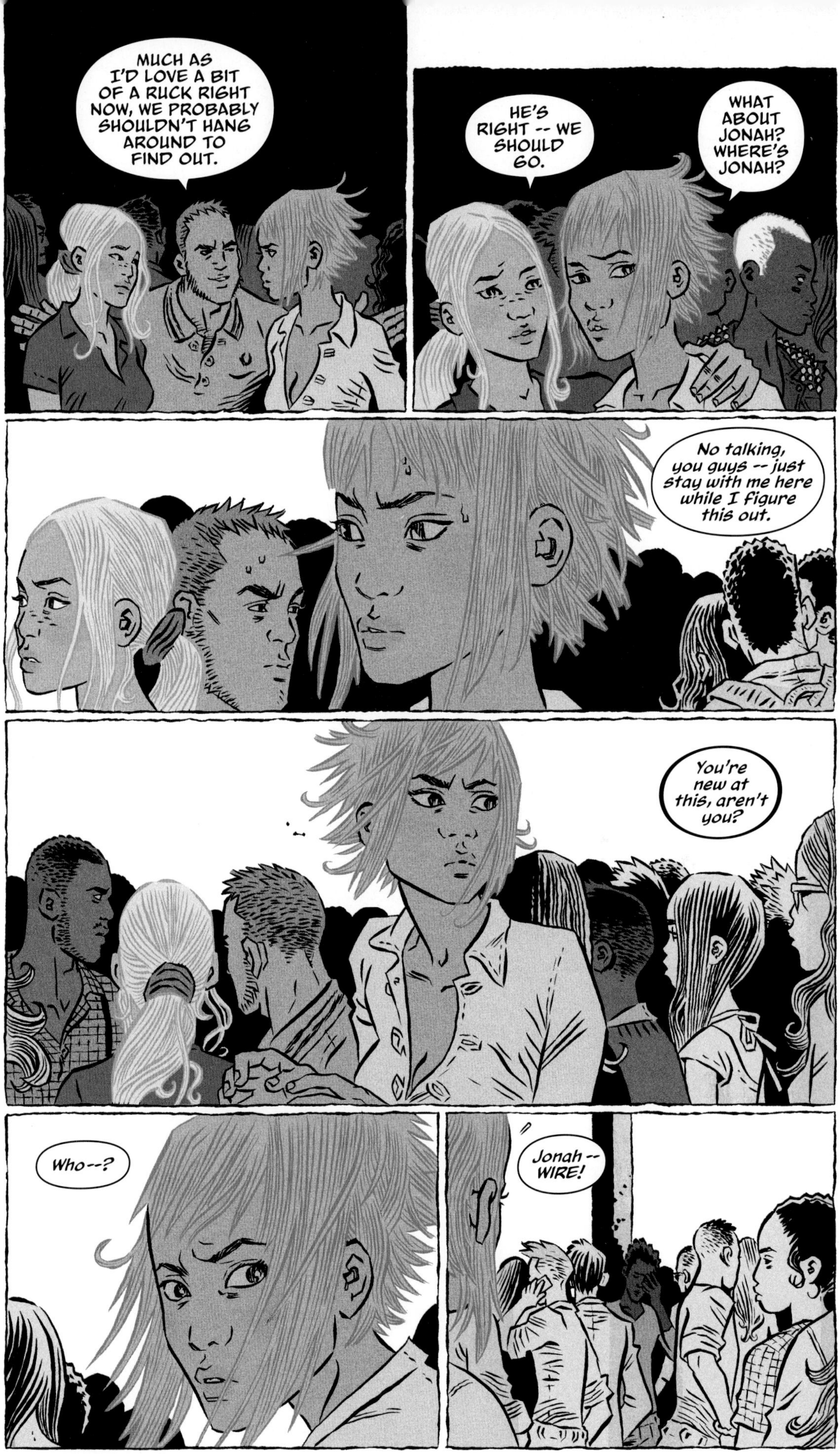
MUCH AS I'D LOVE A BIT OF A RUCK RIGHT NOW, WE PROBABLY SHOULDN'T HANG AROUND TO FIND OUT.
HE'S RIGHT -- WE SHOULD GO.
WHAT ABOUT JONAH? WHERE'S JONAH?
No talking, you guys -- just stay with me here while I figure this out.
You're new at this, aren't you?
Who--?
Jonah -- WIRE!

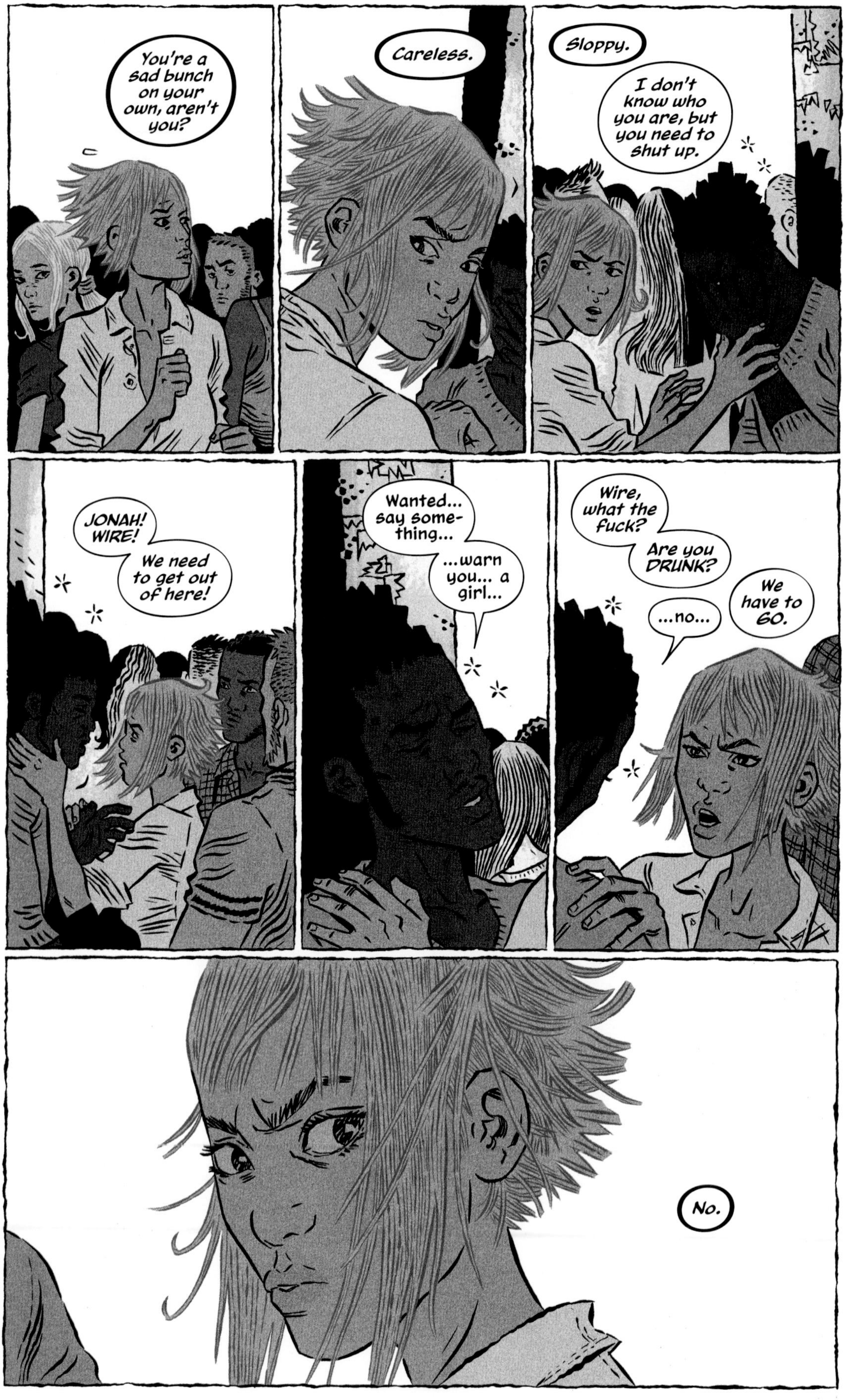
You're a sad bunch on your own, aren't you?
Careless.
Sloppy.
I don't know who you are, but you need to shut up.
JONAH! WIRE!
We need to get out of here!
Wanted... say some-thing...
...warn you... a girl...
Wire, what the fuck?
Are you DRUNK?
...no...
We have to GO.
No.

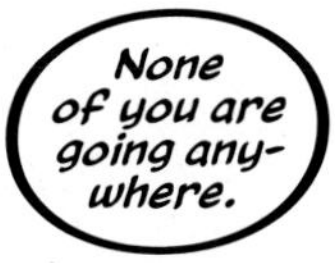
None of you are going any-where.

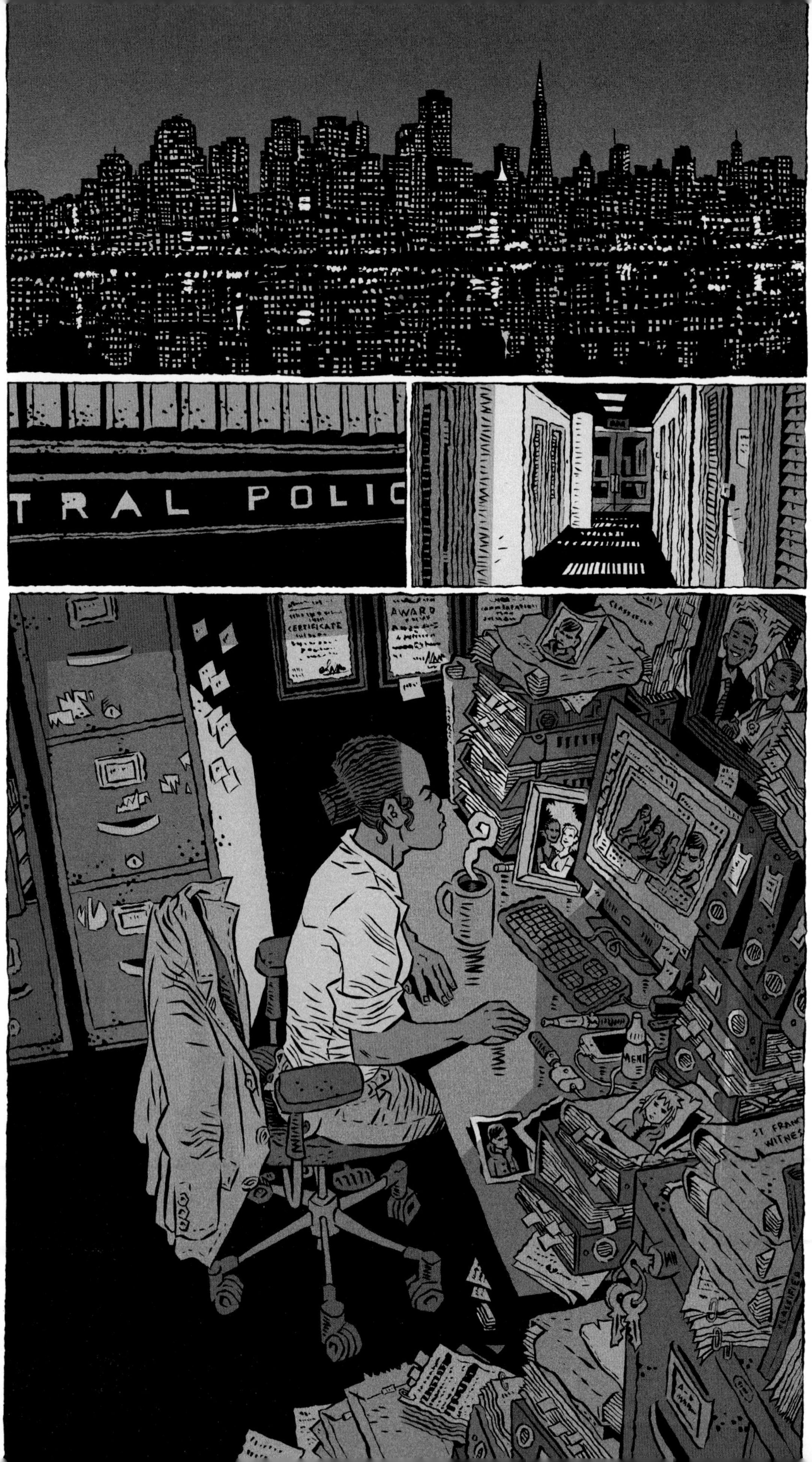
TRAL POLIC
AWARD
CERTIFICATE

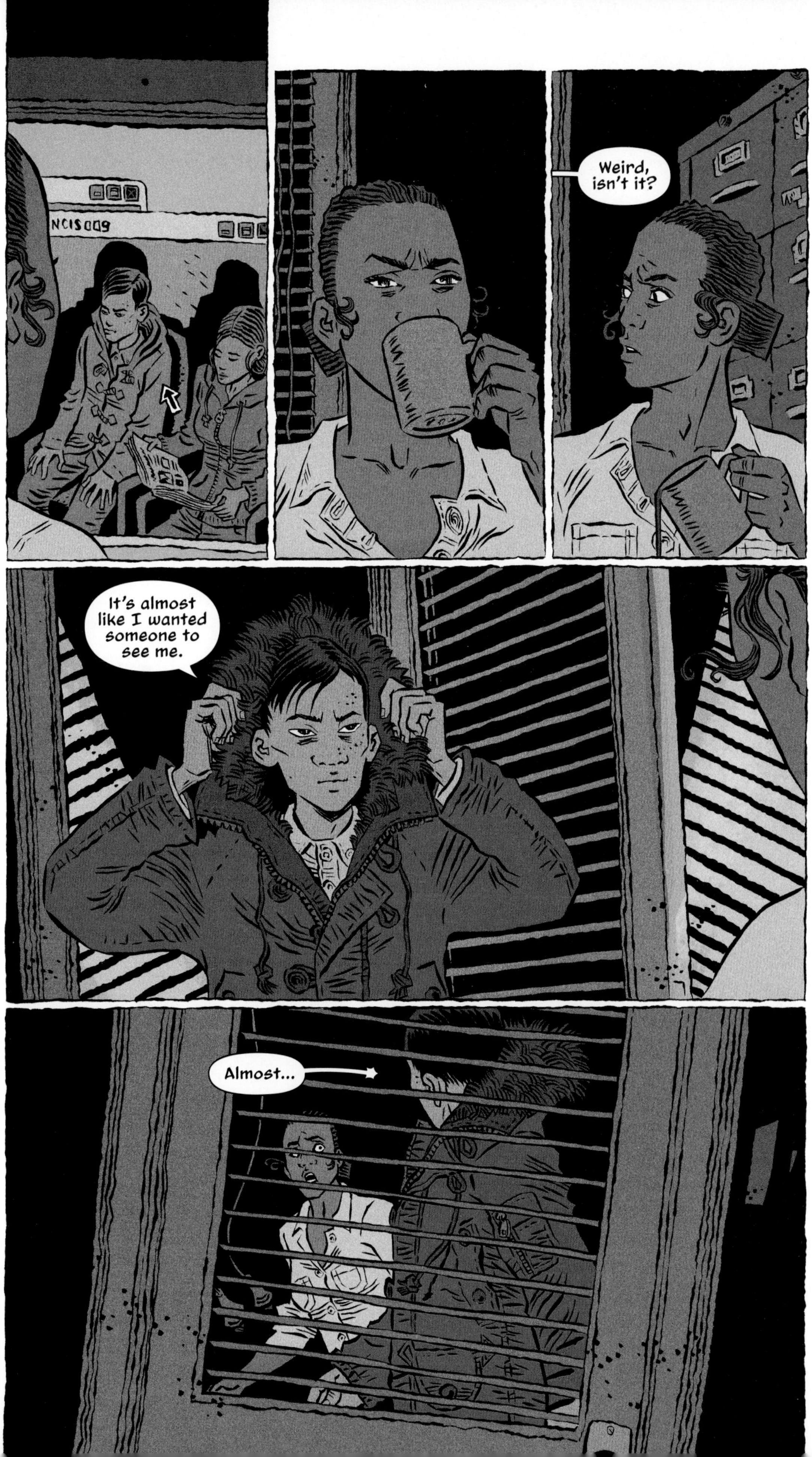
NCIS009
Weird, isn't it?
It's almost like I wanted someone to see me.
Almost...

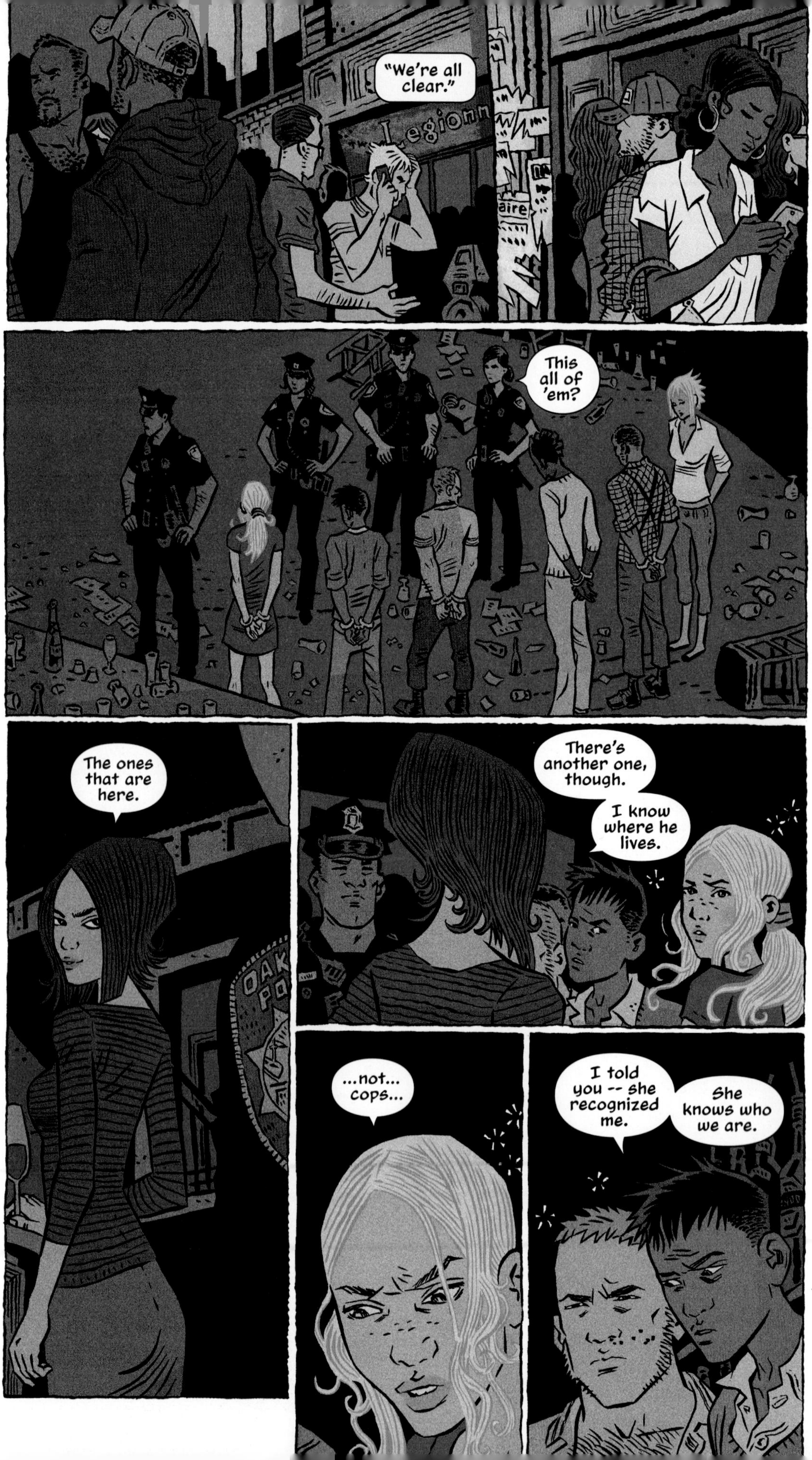
"We're all clear."
Legionn
aire
This all of 'em?
The ones that are here.
There's another one, though.
I know where he lives.
...not... cops...
I told you -- she recognized me.
She knows who we are.

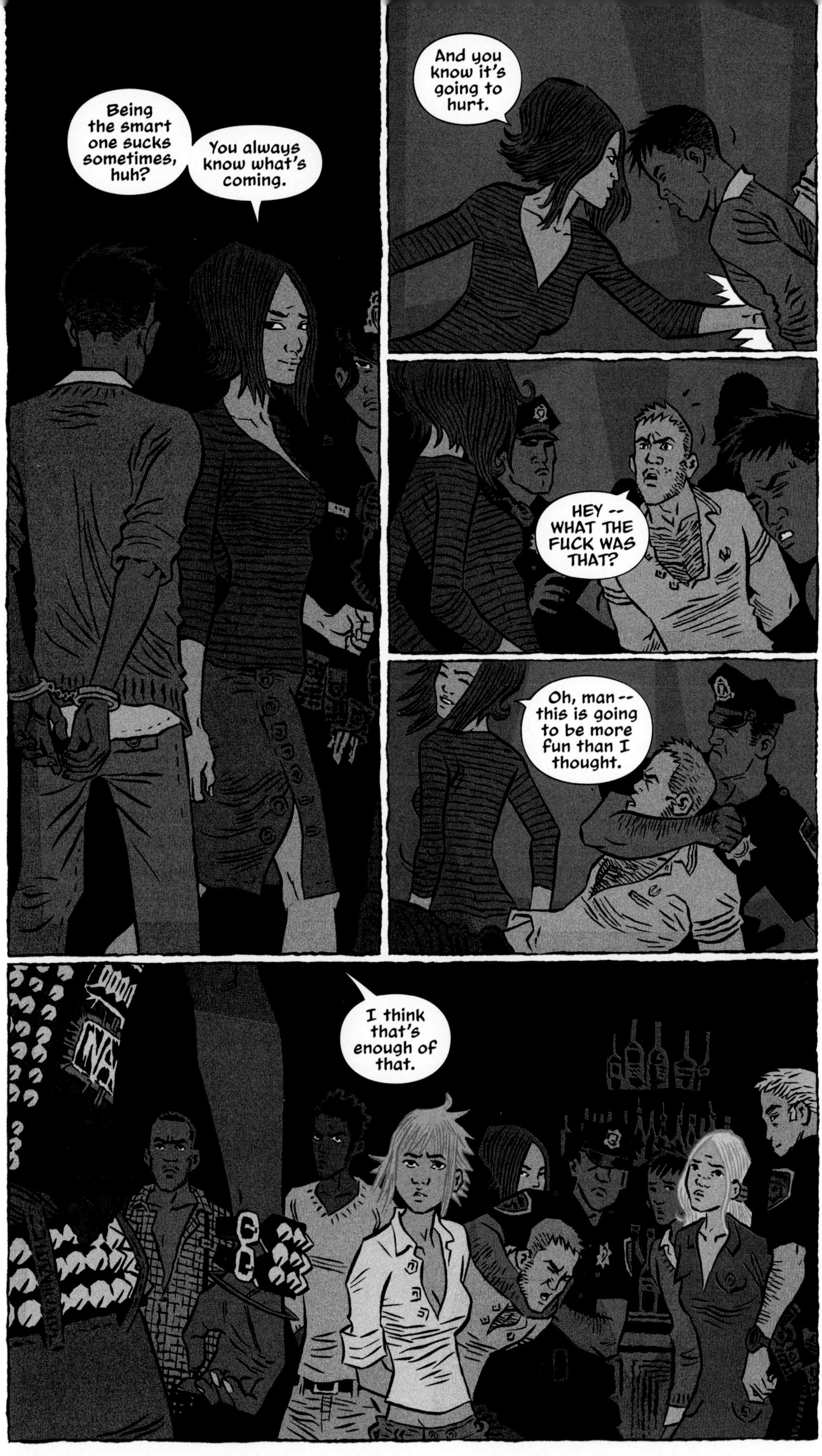
Being the smart one sucks sometimes, huh?
You always know what's coming.
And you know it's going to hurt.
HEY -- WHAT THE FUCK WAS THAT?
Oh, man -- this is going to be more fun than I thought.
I think that's enough of that.

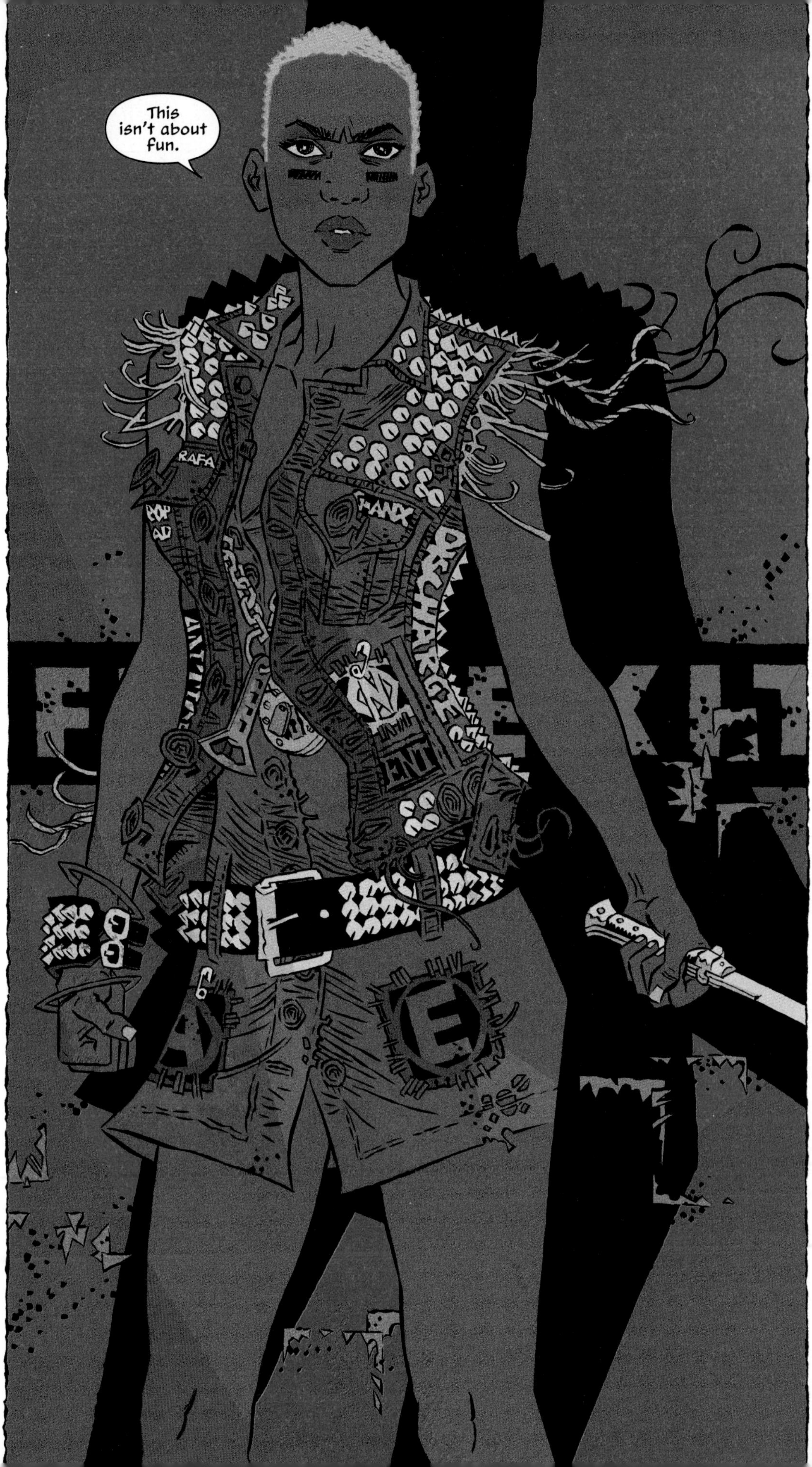
This isn't about fun.
RAFA
DISCHARGE

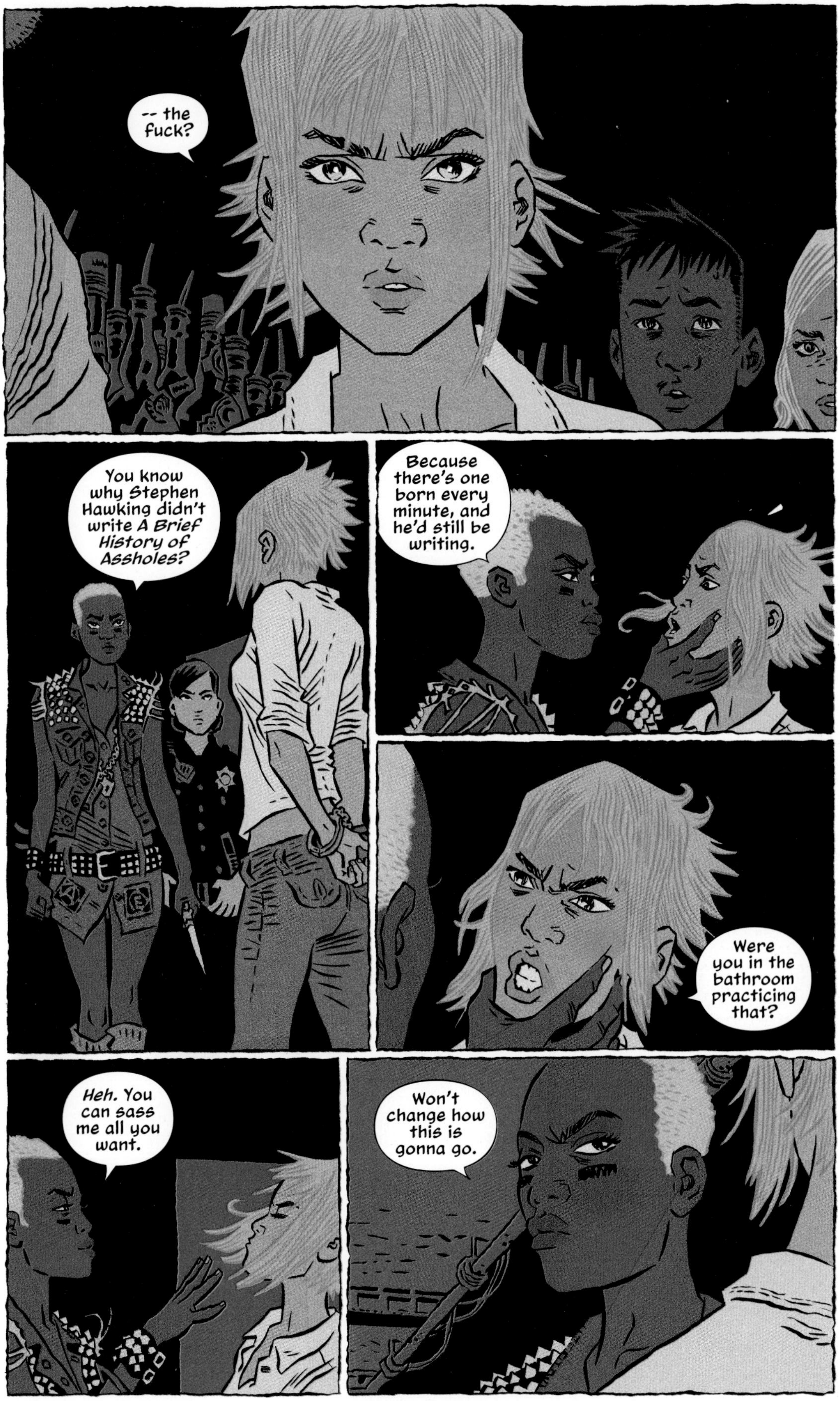
-- the fuck?
You know why Stephen Hawking didn't write *A Brief History of Assholes*?
Because there's one born every minute, and he'd still be writing.
Were you in the bathroom practicing that?
Heh. You can sass me all you want.
Won't change how this is gonna go.

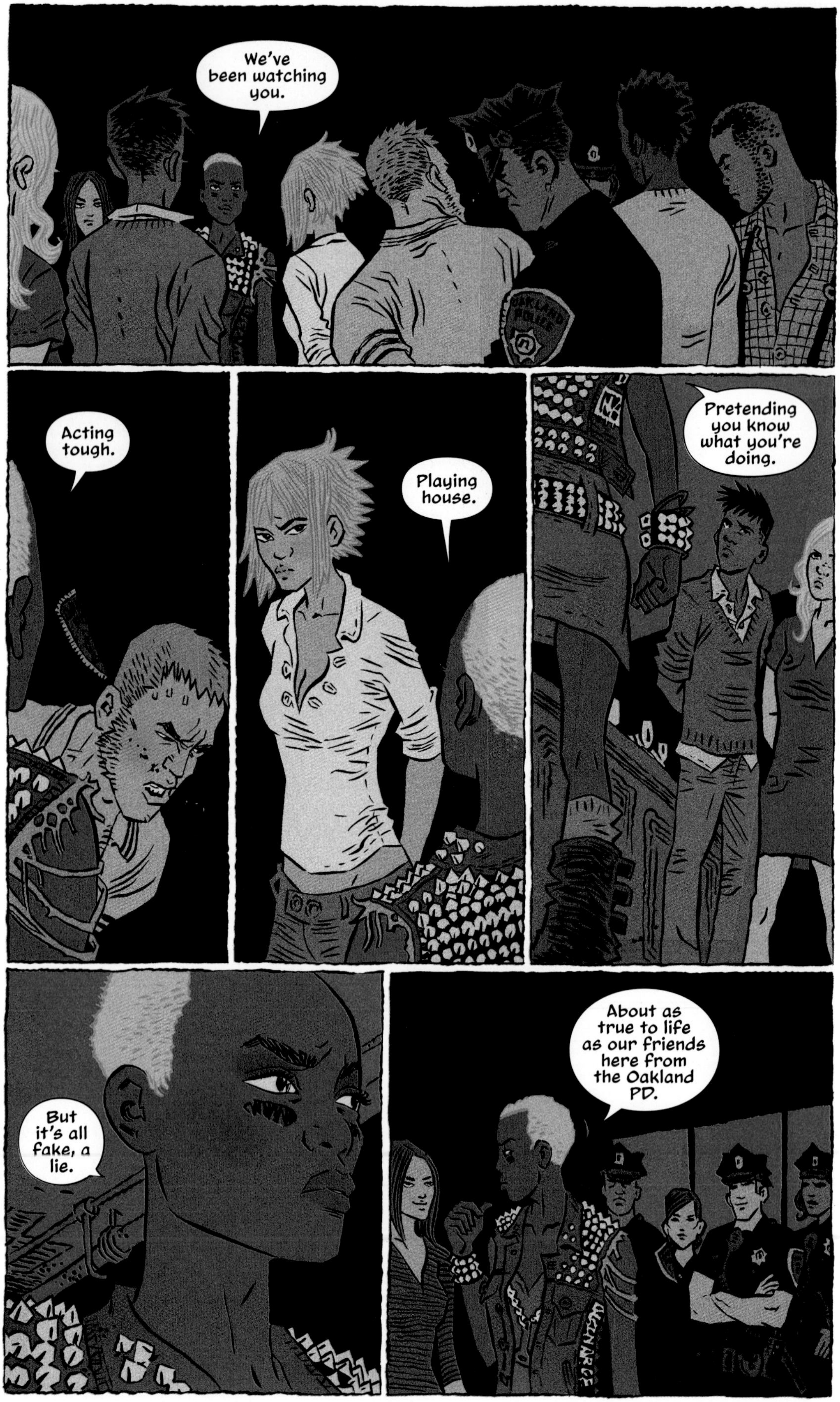
We've been watching you.
Acting tough.
Playing house.
Pretending you know what you're doing.
But it's all fake, a lie.
About as true to life as our friends here from the Oakland PD.
OAKLAND POLICE

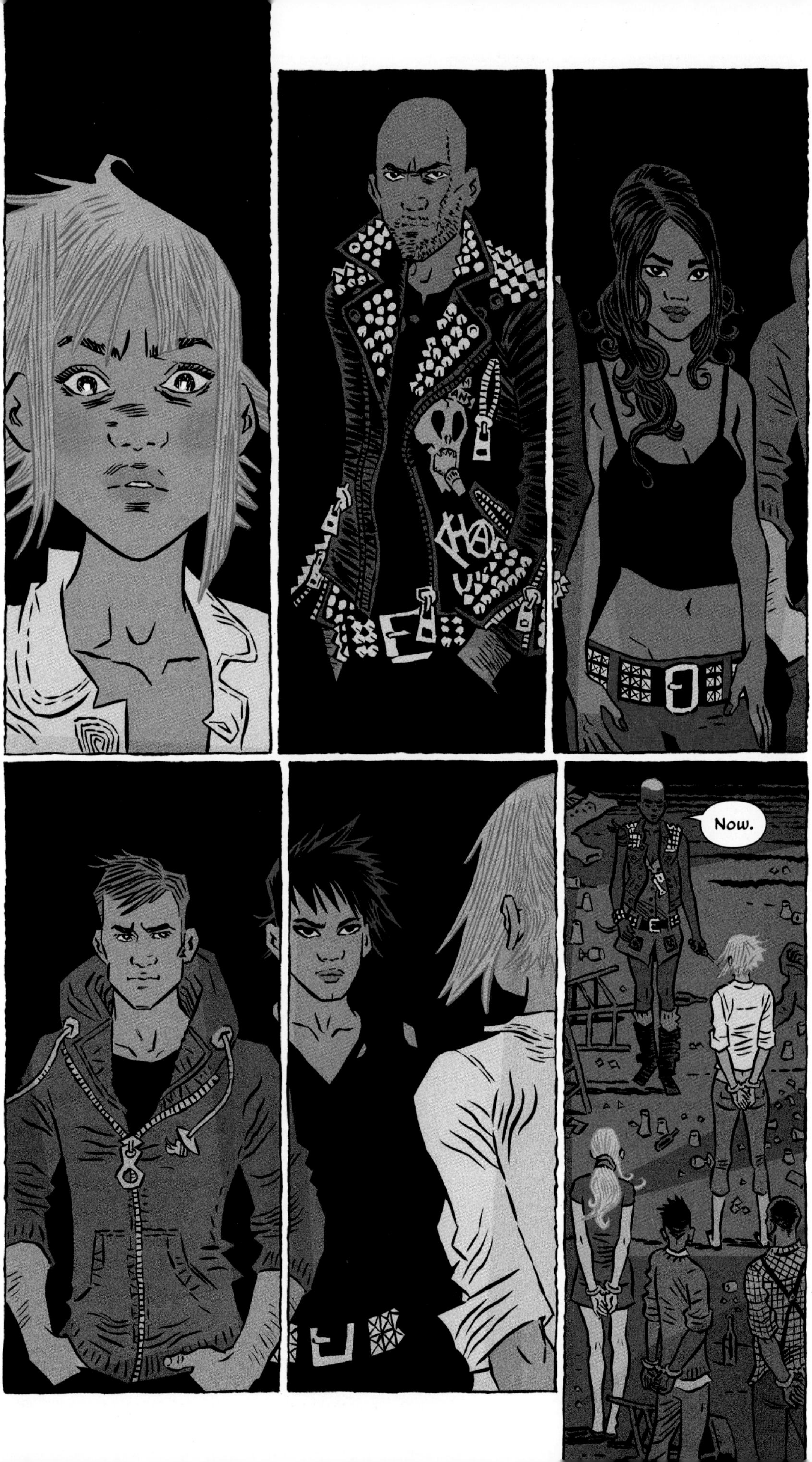
Now.

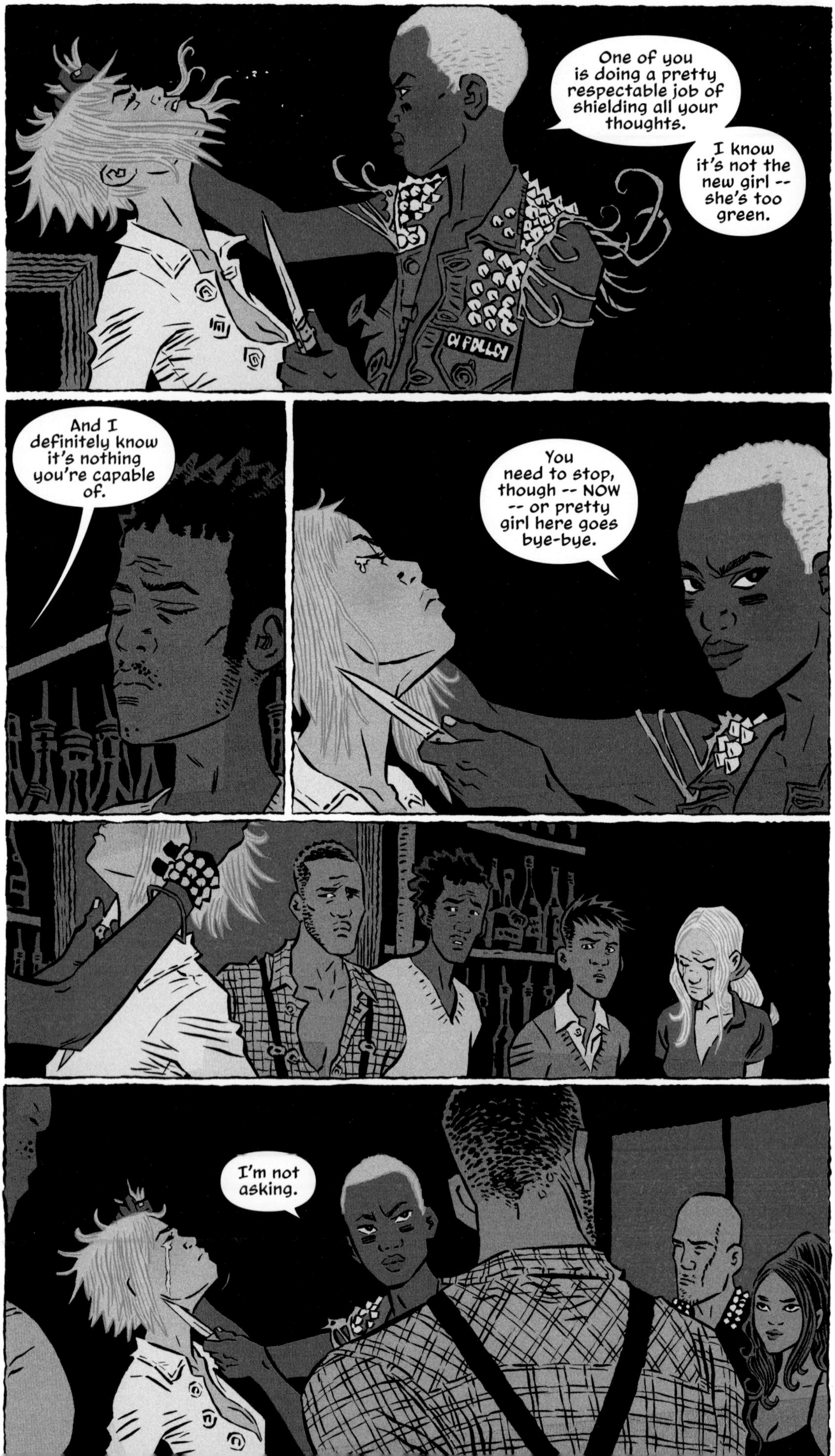
One of you is doing a pretty respectable job of shielding all your thoughts.
I know it's not the new girl -- she's too green.
OI POLLOI
And I definitely know it's nothing you're capable of.
You need to stop, though -- NOW -- or pretty girl here goes bye-bye.
I'm not asking.

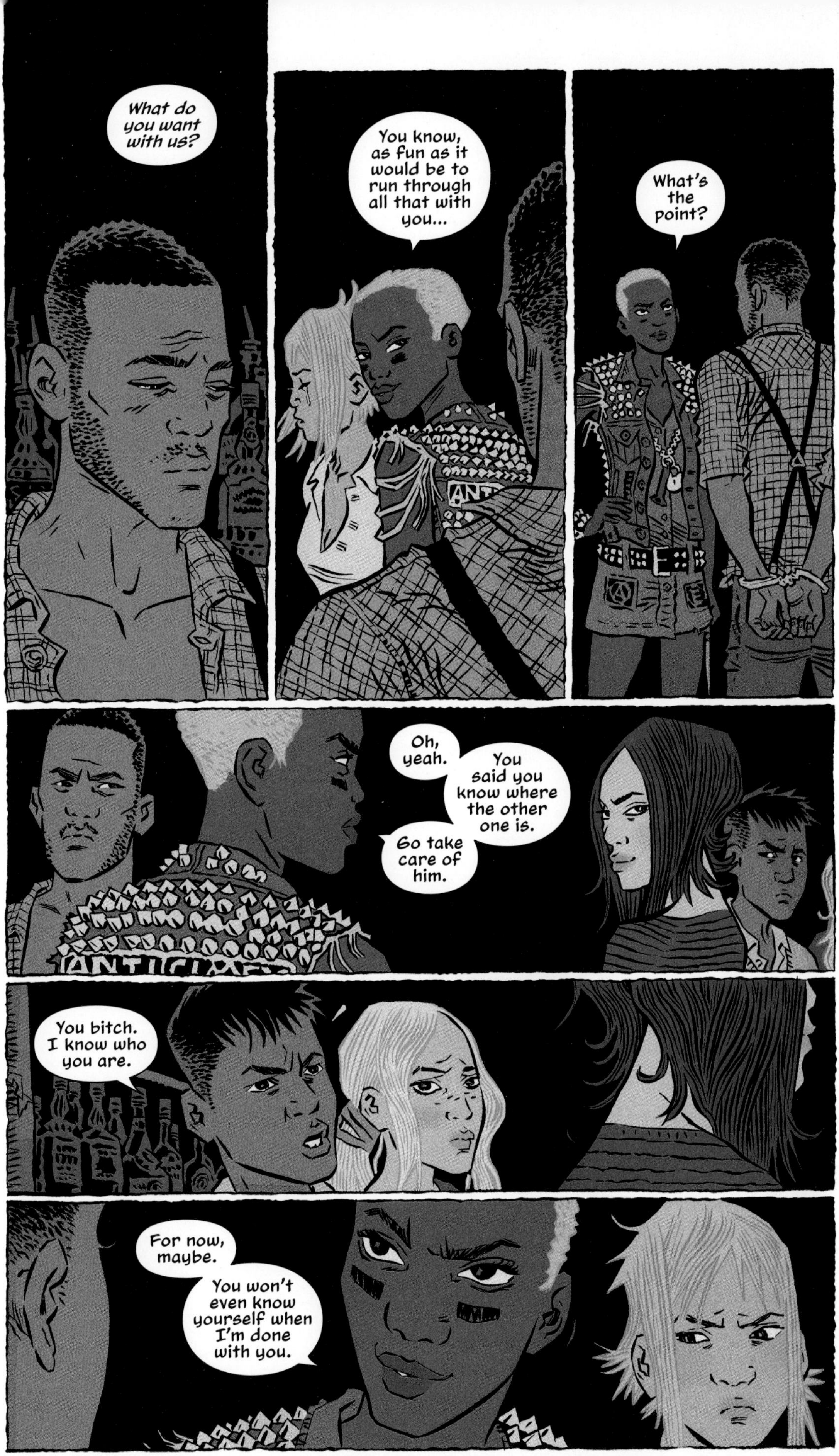
What do you want with us?
You know, as fun as it would be to run through all that with you...
What's the point?
Oh, yeah.
You said you know where the other one is.
Go take care of him.
You bitch. I know who you are.
For now, maybe.
You won't even know yourself when I'm done with you.

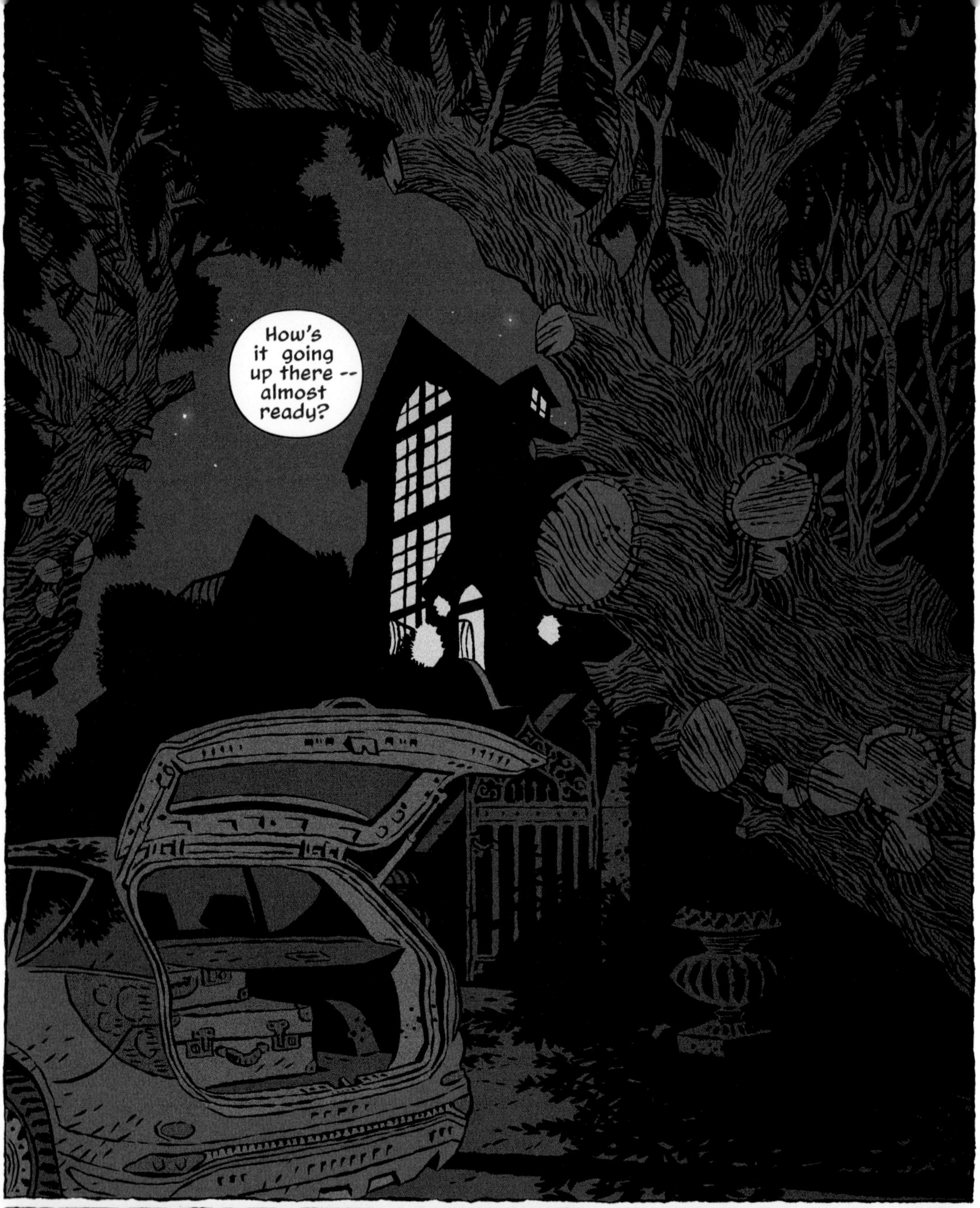
How's it going up there -- almost ready?

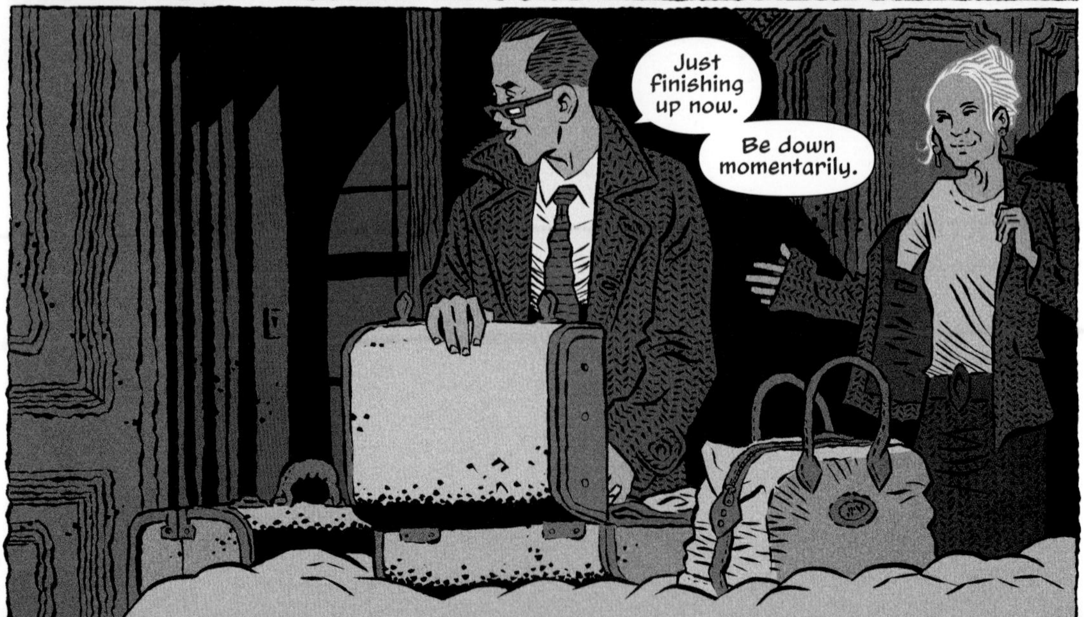
Just finishing up now.
Be down momentarily.

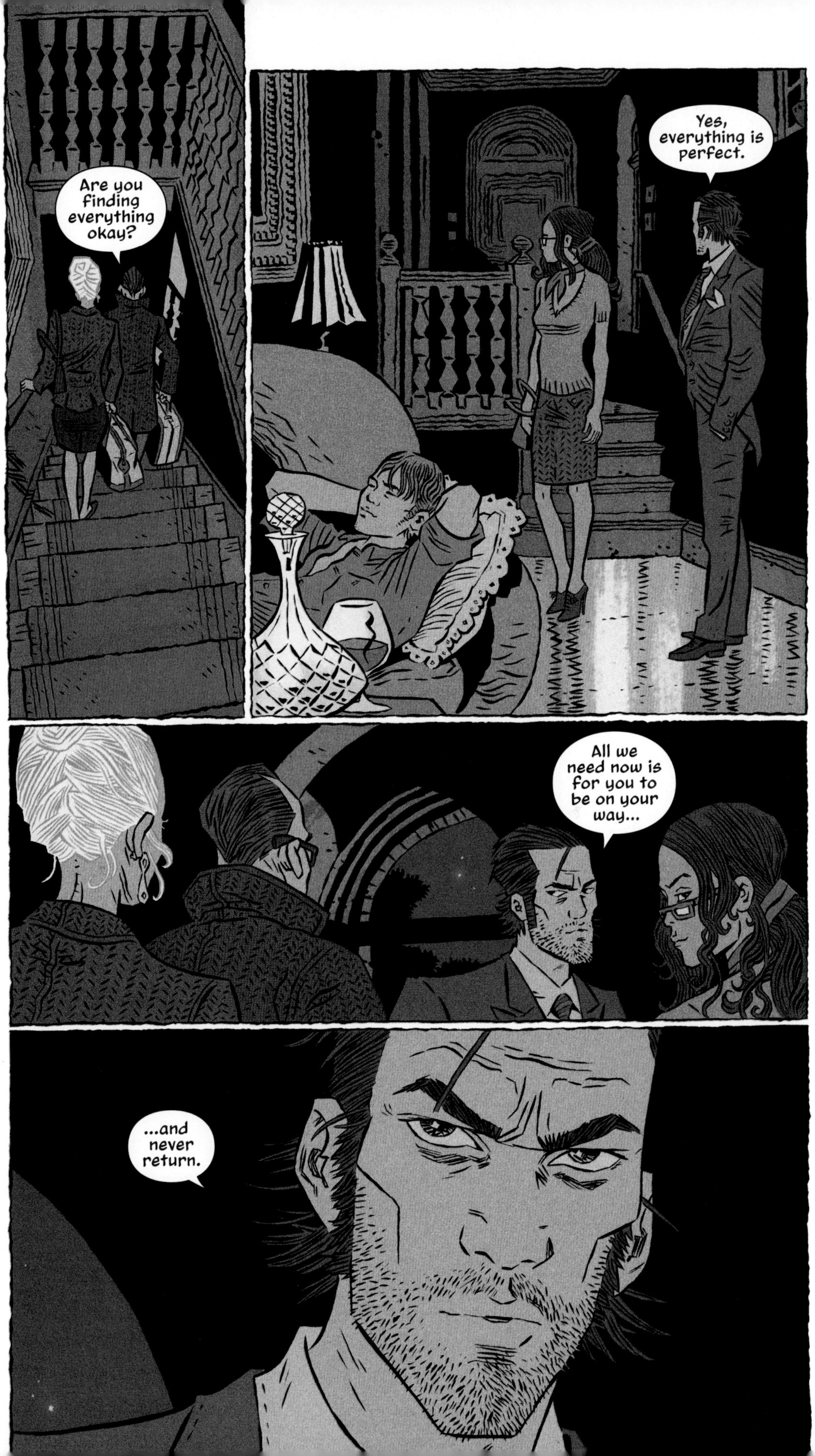
Are you finding everything okay?
Yes, everything is perfect.
All we need now is for you to be on your way...
...and never return.

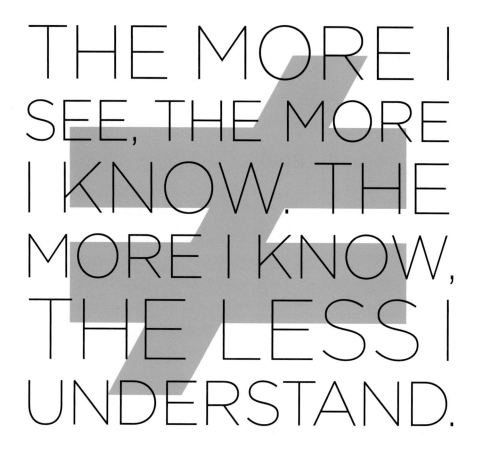

THE MORE I
SEE, THE MORE
I KNOW. THE
MORE I KNOW,
THE LESS I
UNDERSTAND.

PAUL WELLER

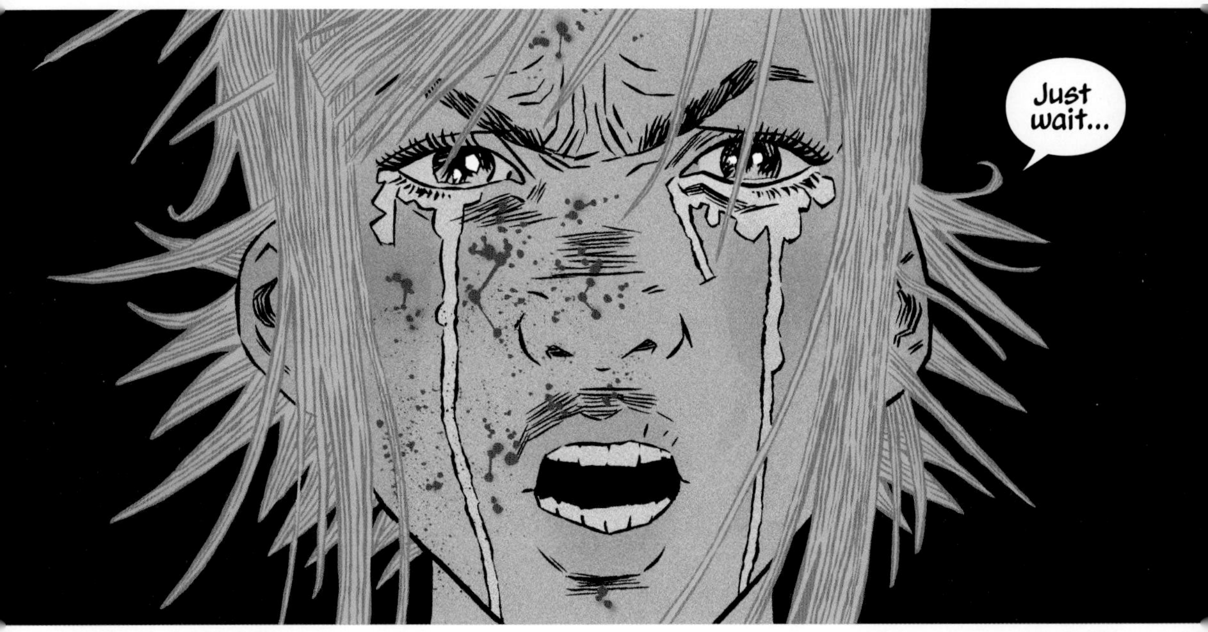
Just wait...

10: THIS IS WHAT SHE'S LIKE

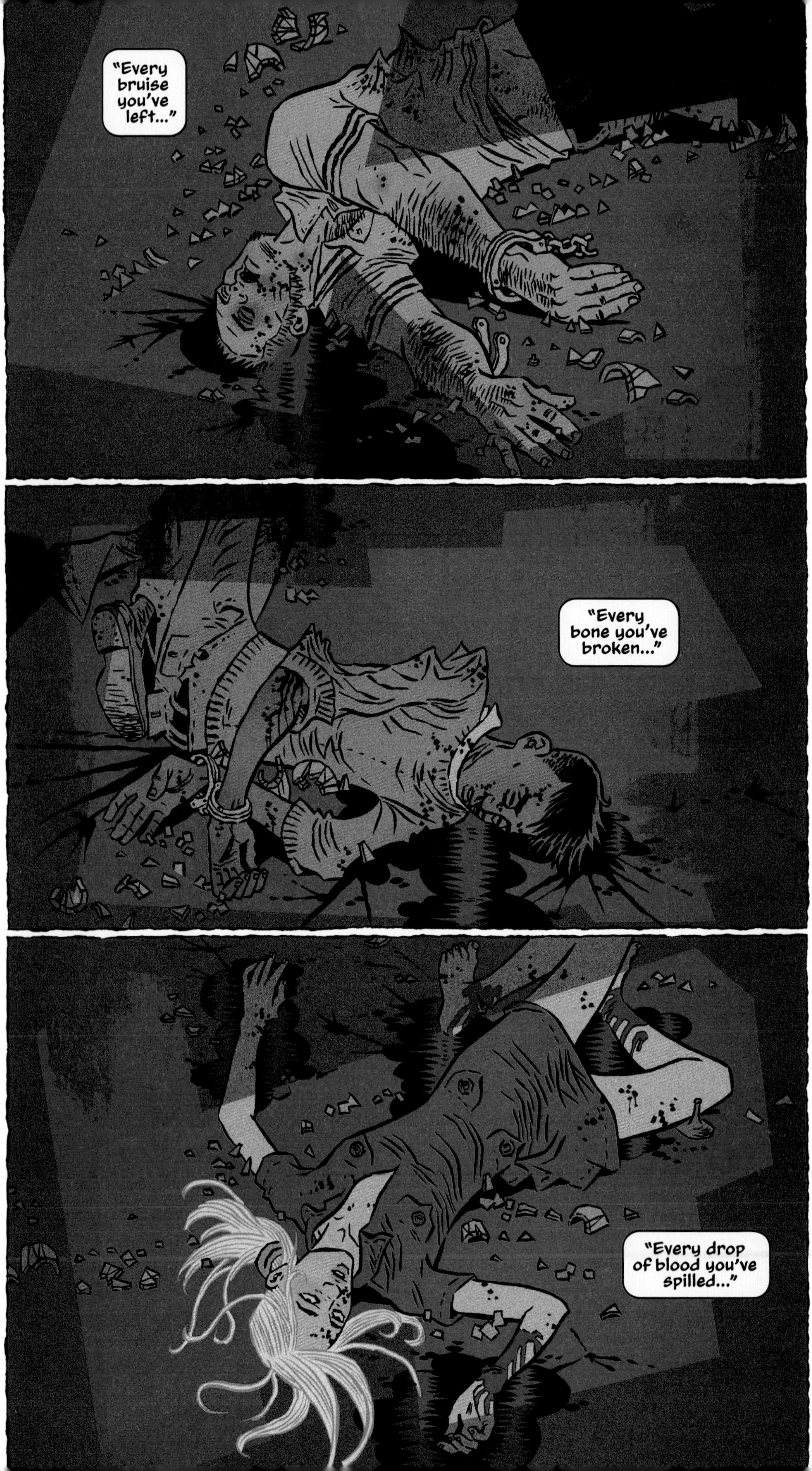
"Every bruise you've left..."
"Every bone you've broken..."
"Every drop of blood you've spilled..."

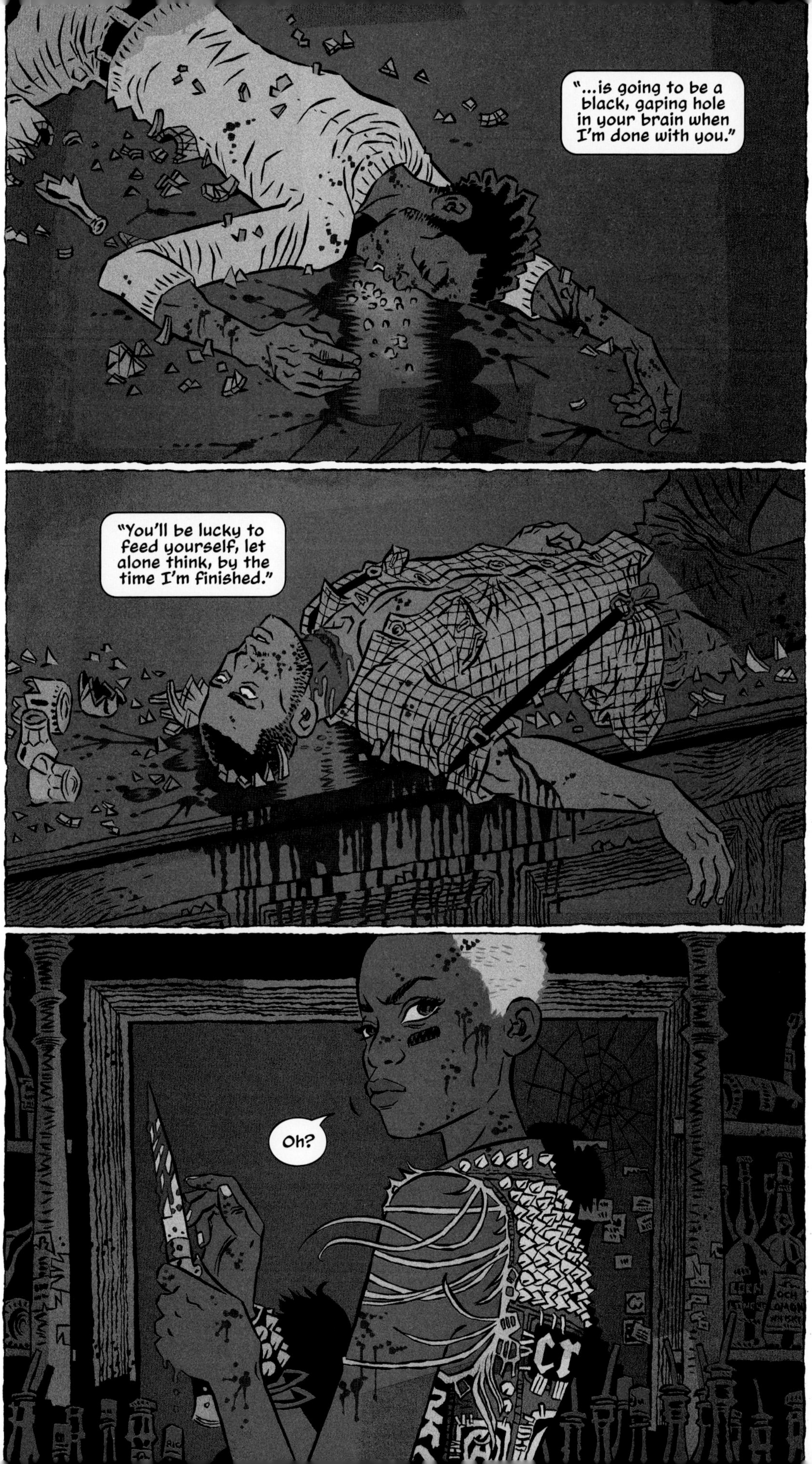
"...is going to be a black, gaping hole in your brain when I'm done with you."
"You'll be lucky to feed yourself, let alone think, by the time I'm finished."
Oh?

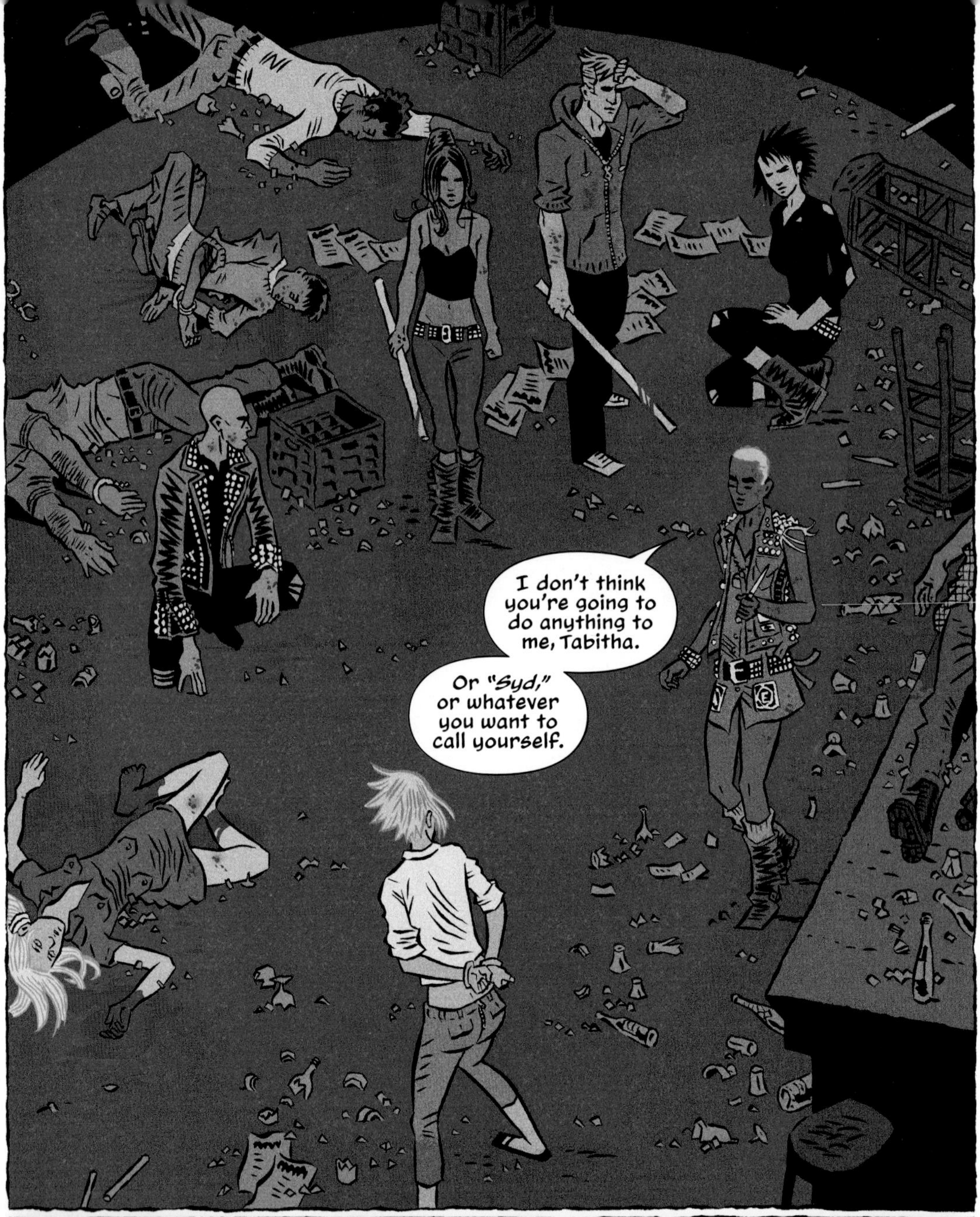
I don't think you're going to do anything to me, Tabitha.
Or "Syd," or whatever you want to call yourself.

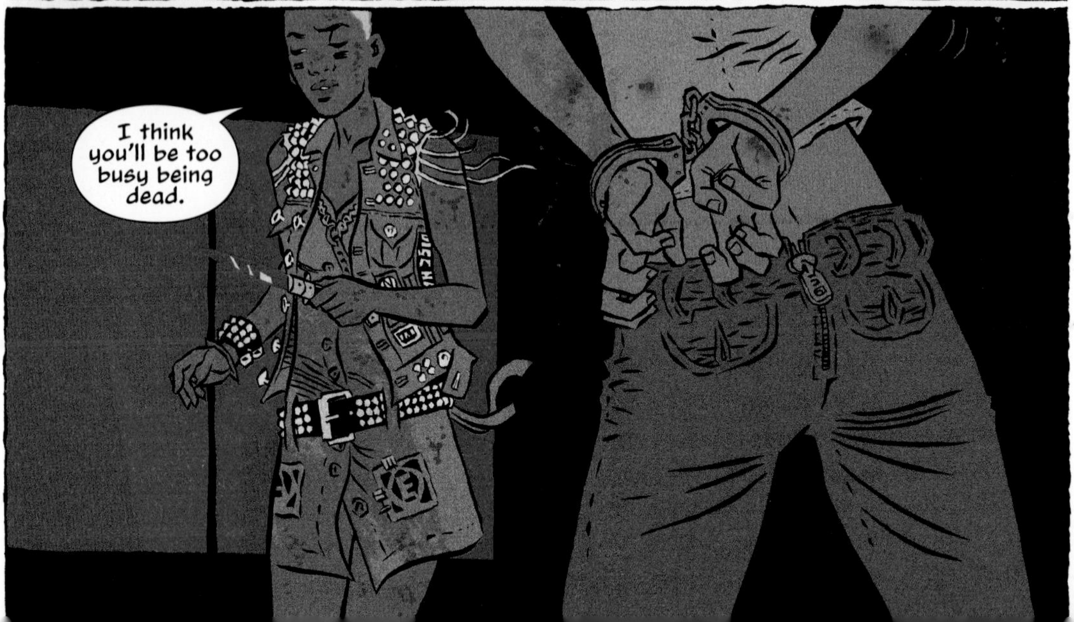
I think you'll be too busy being dead.

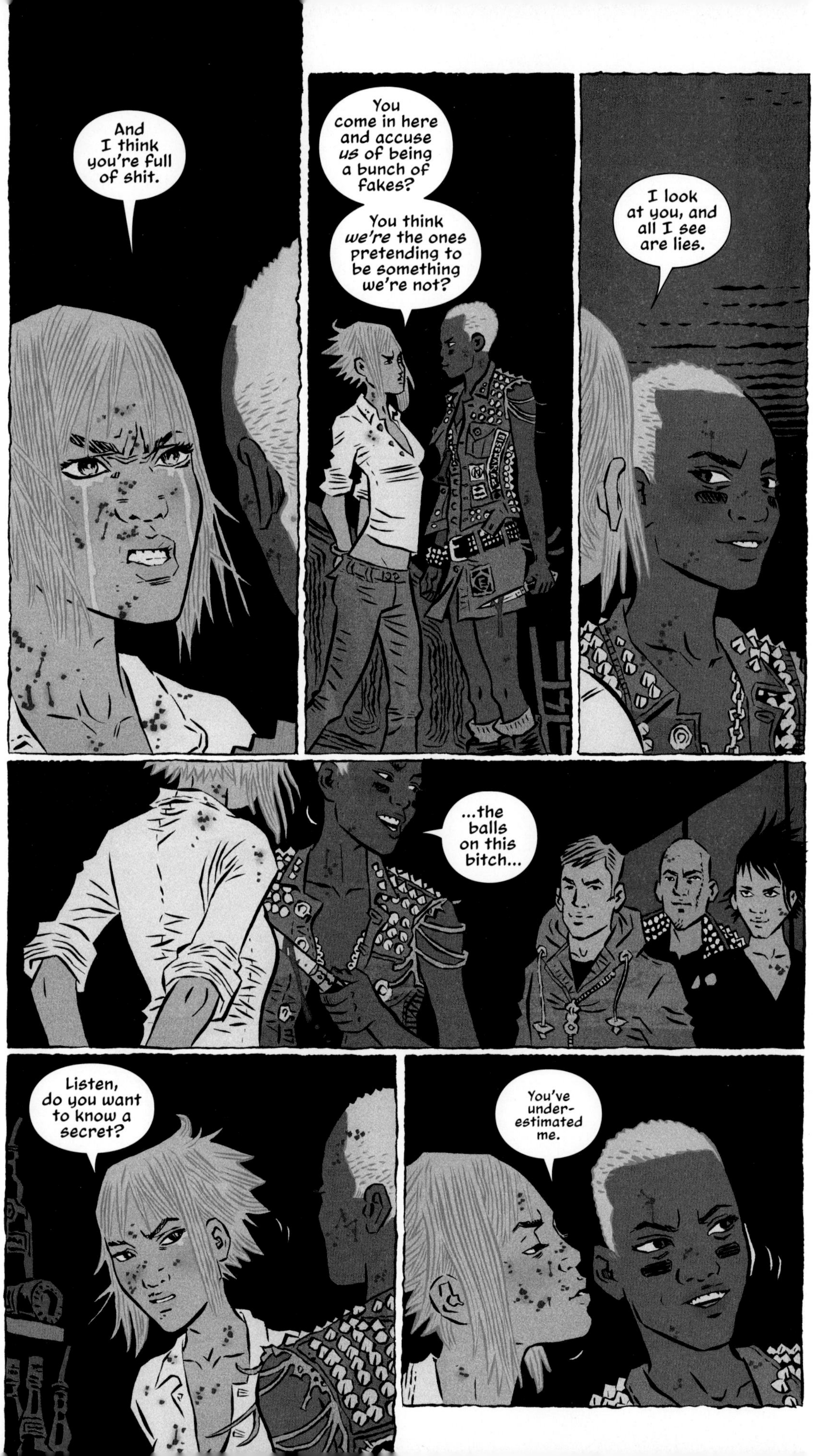
And I think you're full of shit.
You come in here and accuse us of being a bunch of fakes?
You think we're the ones pretending to be something we're not?
I look at you, and all I see are lies.
...the balls on this bitch...
Listen, do you want to know a secret?
You've under-estimated me.

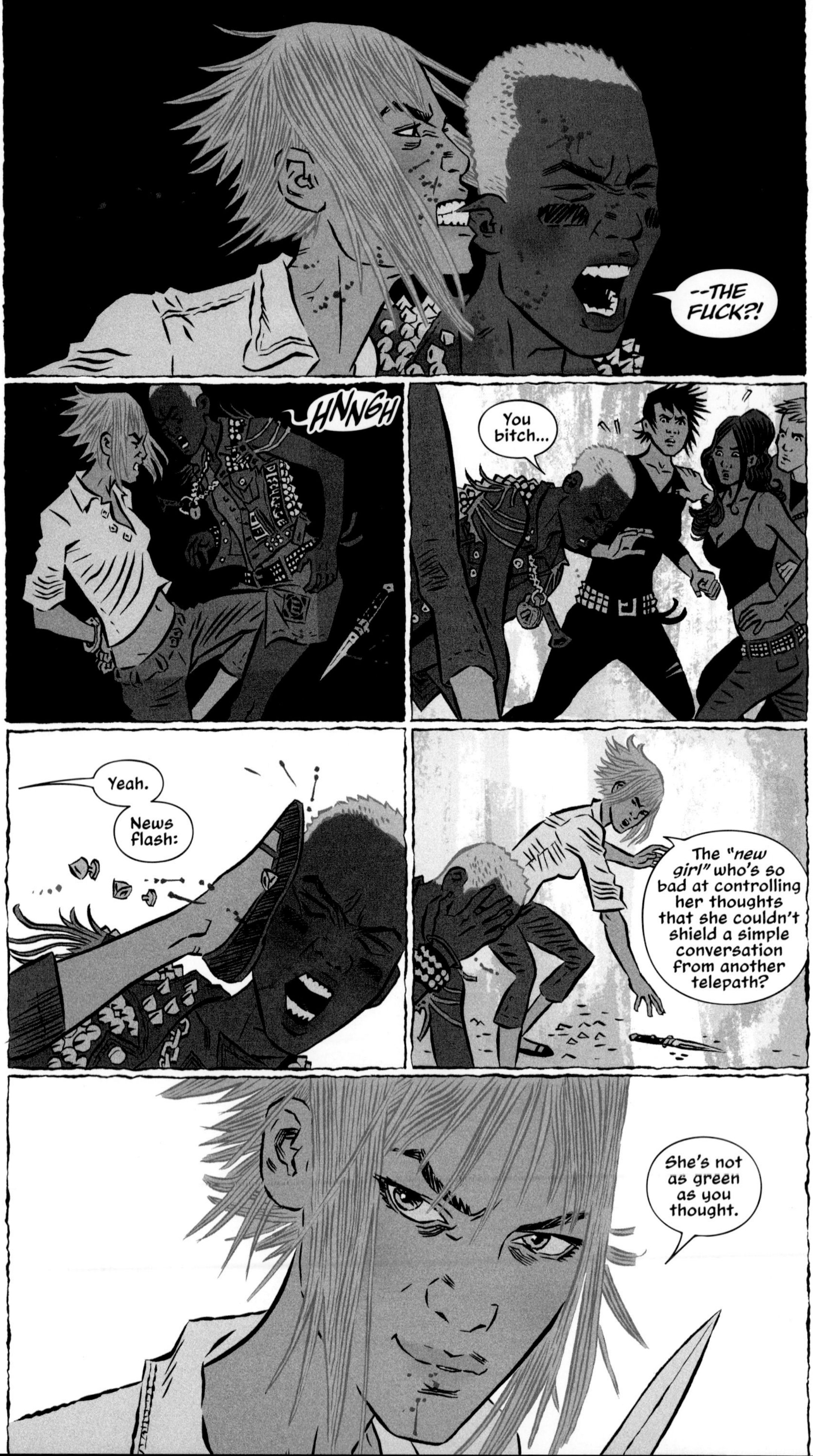
--THE FUCK?!
HNNGH
You bitch...
Yeah.
News flash:
The "new girl" who's so bad at controlling her thoughts that she couldn't shield a simple conversation from another telepath?
She's not as green as you thought.

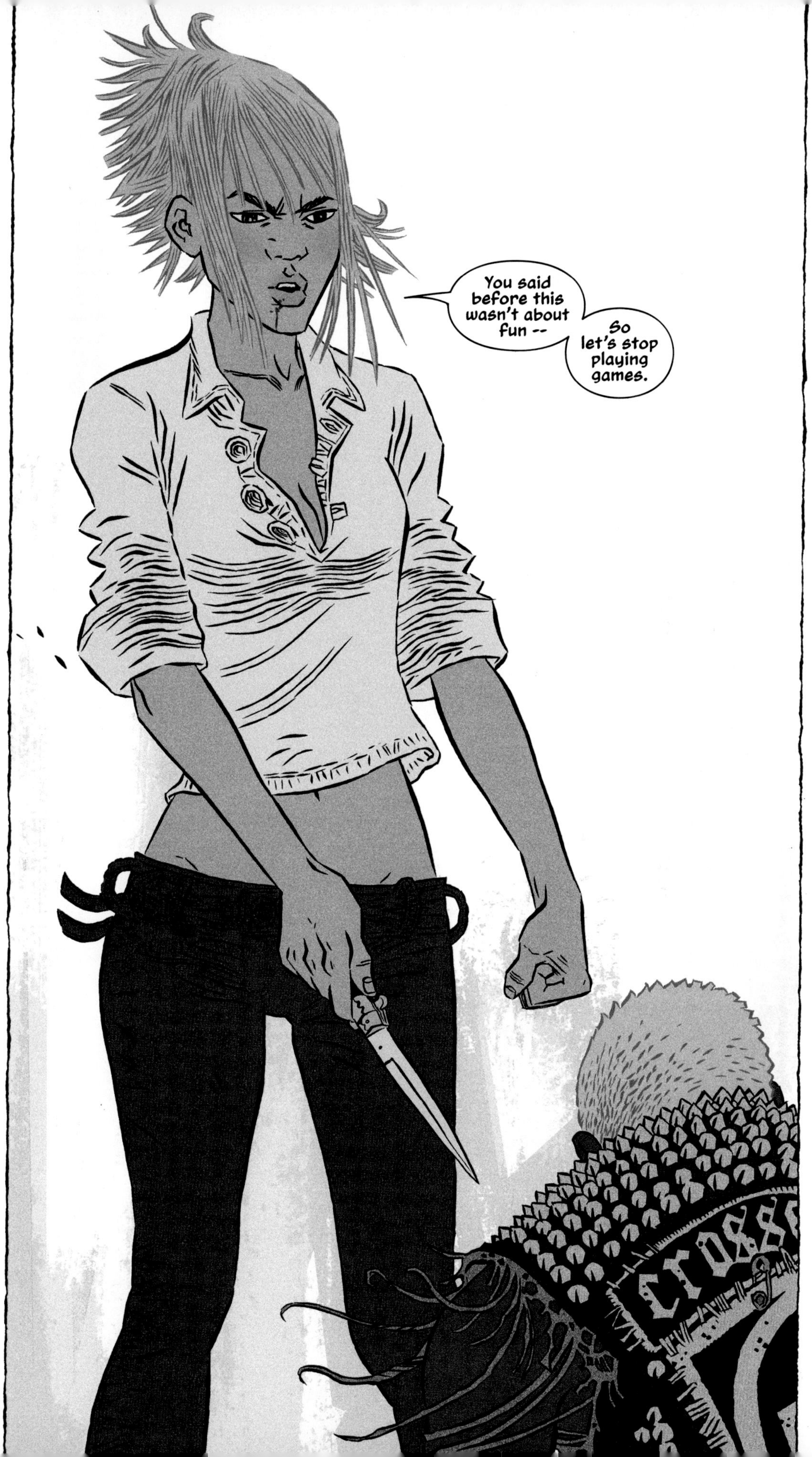
You said before this wasn't about fun --
So let's stop playing games.

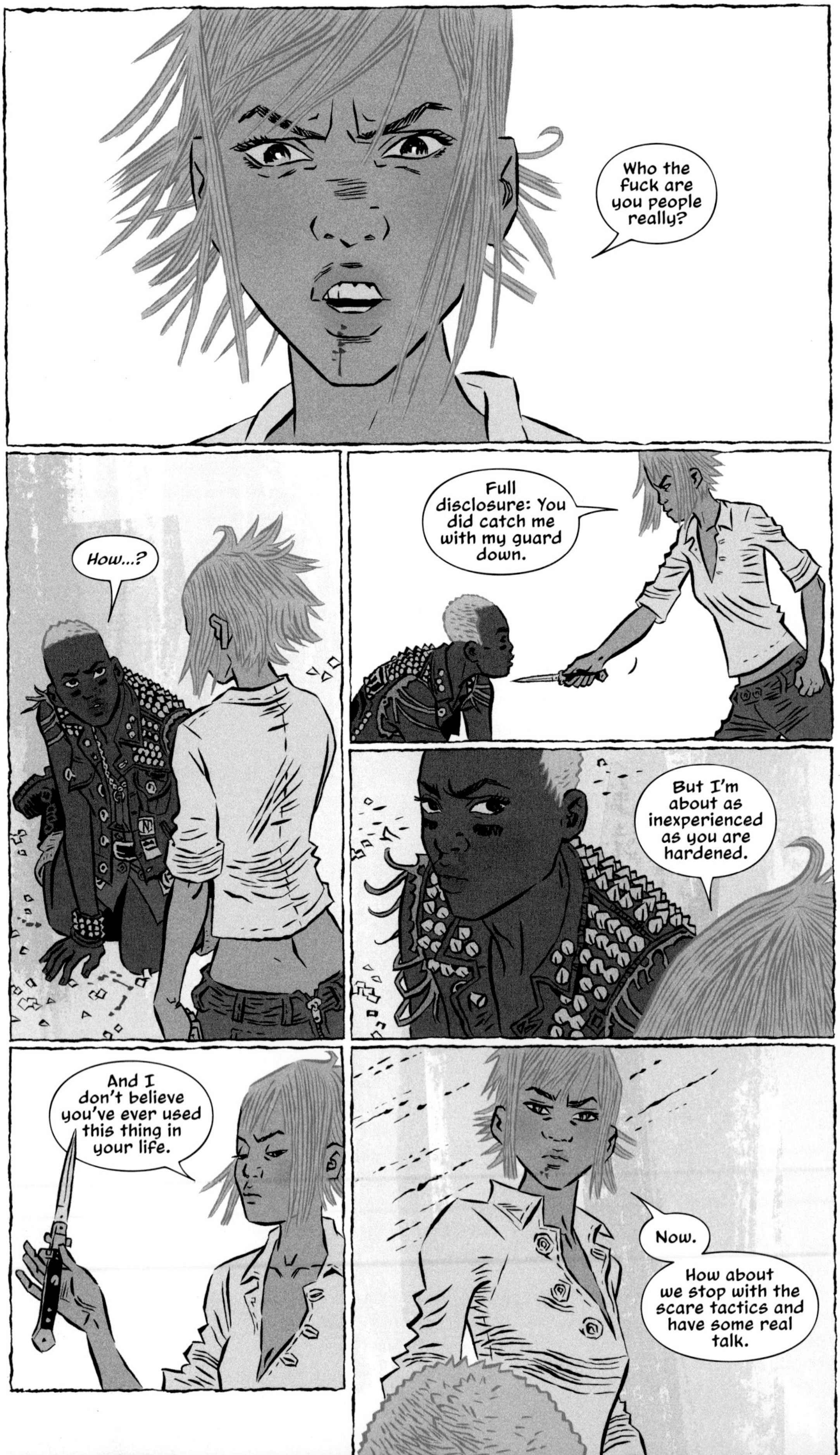
Who the fuck are you people really?
How...?
Full disclosure: You did catch me with my guard down.
But I'm about as inexperienced as you are hardened.
And I don't believe you've ever used this thing in your life.
Now.
How about we stop with the scare tactics and have some real talk.

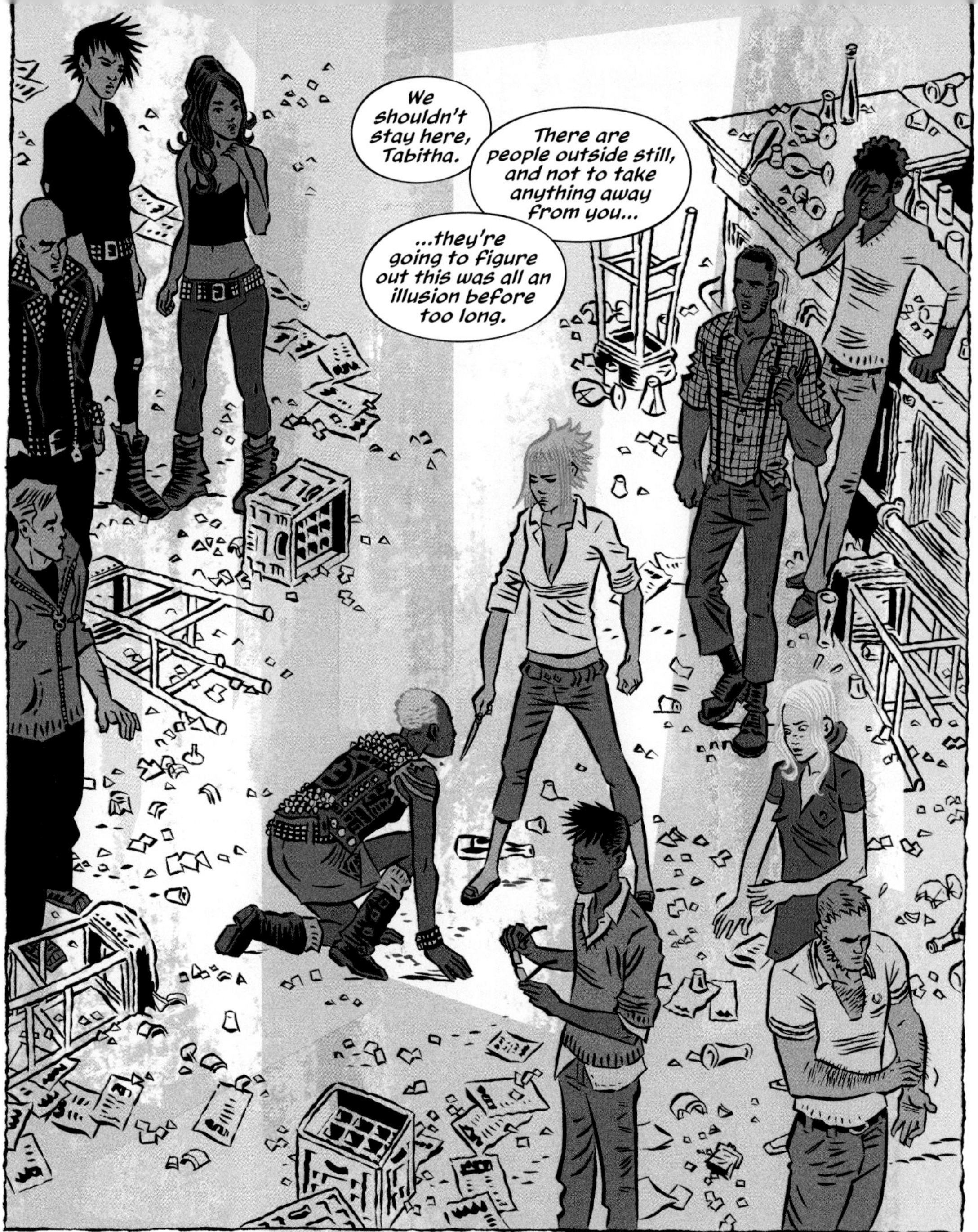
We shouldn't stay here, Tabitha.
There are people outside still, and not to take anything away from you...
...they're going to figure out this was all an illusion before too long.

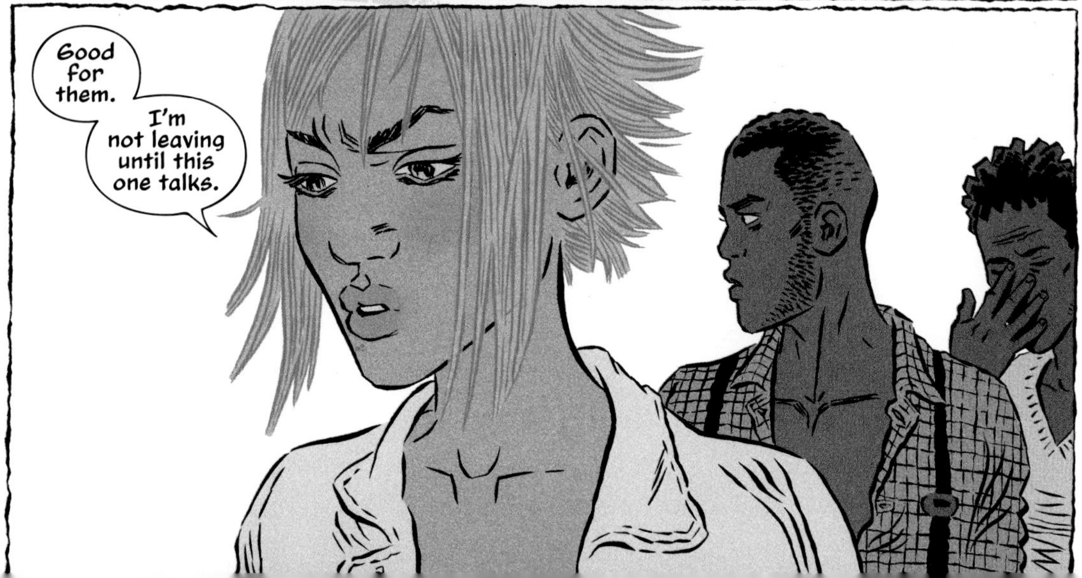
Good for them.
I'm not leaving until this one talks.

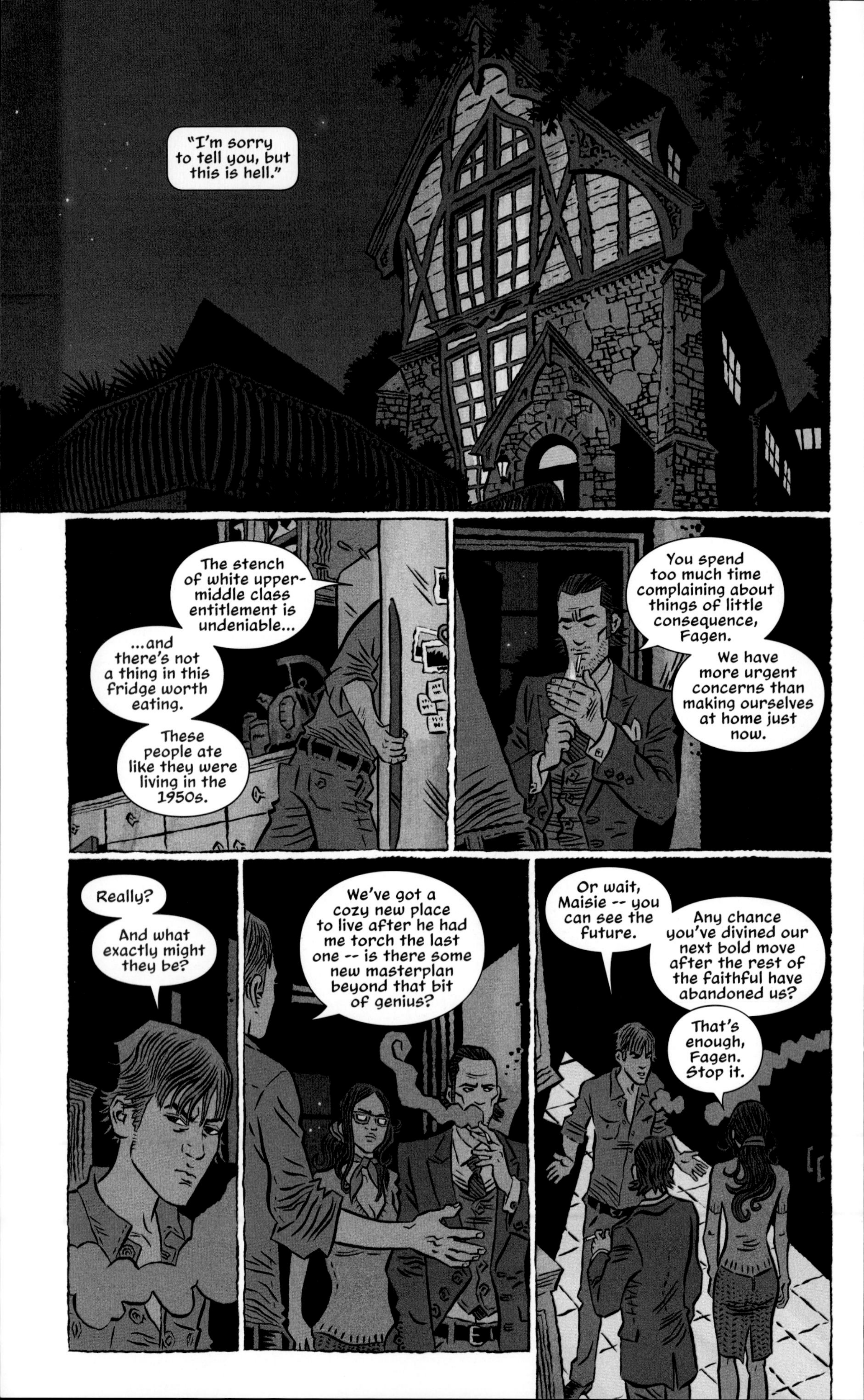
"I'm sorry to tell you, but this is hell."
The stench of white upper-middle class entitlement is undeniable...
...and there's not a thing in this fridge worth eating.
These people ate like they were living in the 1950s.
You spend too much time complaining about things of little consequence, Fagen.
We have more urgent concerns than making ourselves at home just now.
Really?
And what exactly might they be?
We've got a cozy new place to live after he had me torch the last one -- is there some new masterplan beyond that bit of genius?
Or wait, Maisie -- you can see the future.
Any chance you've divined our next bold move after the rest of the faithful have abandoned us?
That's enough, Fagen. Stop it.

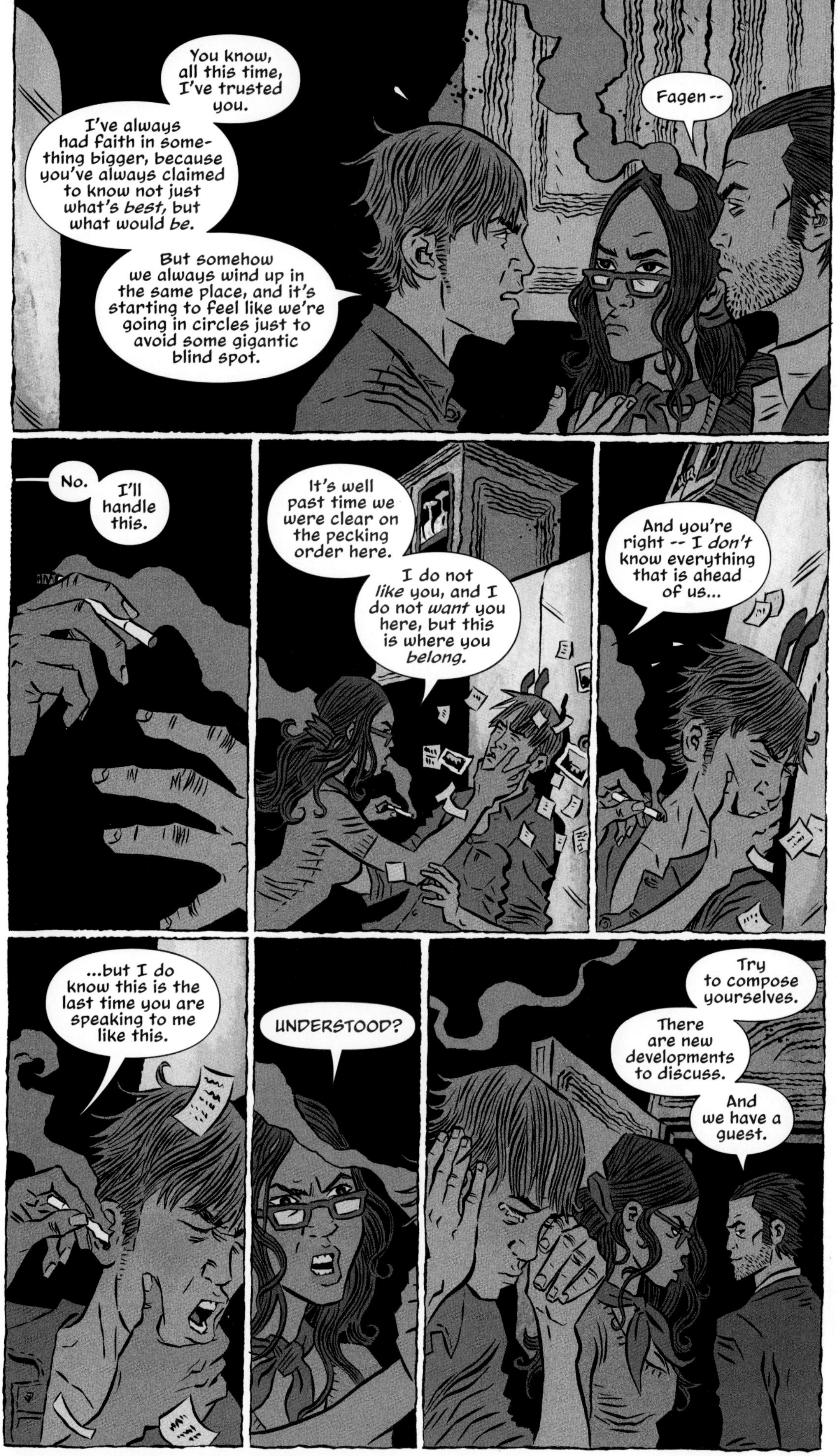
You know, all this time, I've trusted you.
I've always had faith in something bigger, because you've always claimed to know not just what's *best,* but what would *be.*
But somehow we always wind up in the same place, and it's starting to feel like we're going in circles just to avoid some gigantic blind spot.
Fagen --
No.
I'll handle this.
It's well past time we were clear on the pecking order here.
I do not *like* you, and I do not *want* you here, but this is where you *belong.*
And you're right -- I *don't* know everything that is ahead of us...
...but I do know this is the last time you are speaking to me like this.
UNDERSTOOD?
Try to compose yourselves.
There are new developments to discuss.
And we have a guest.

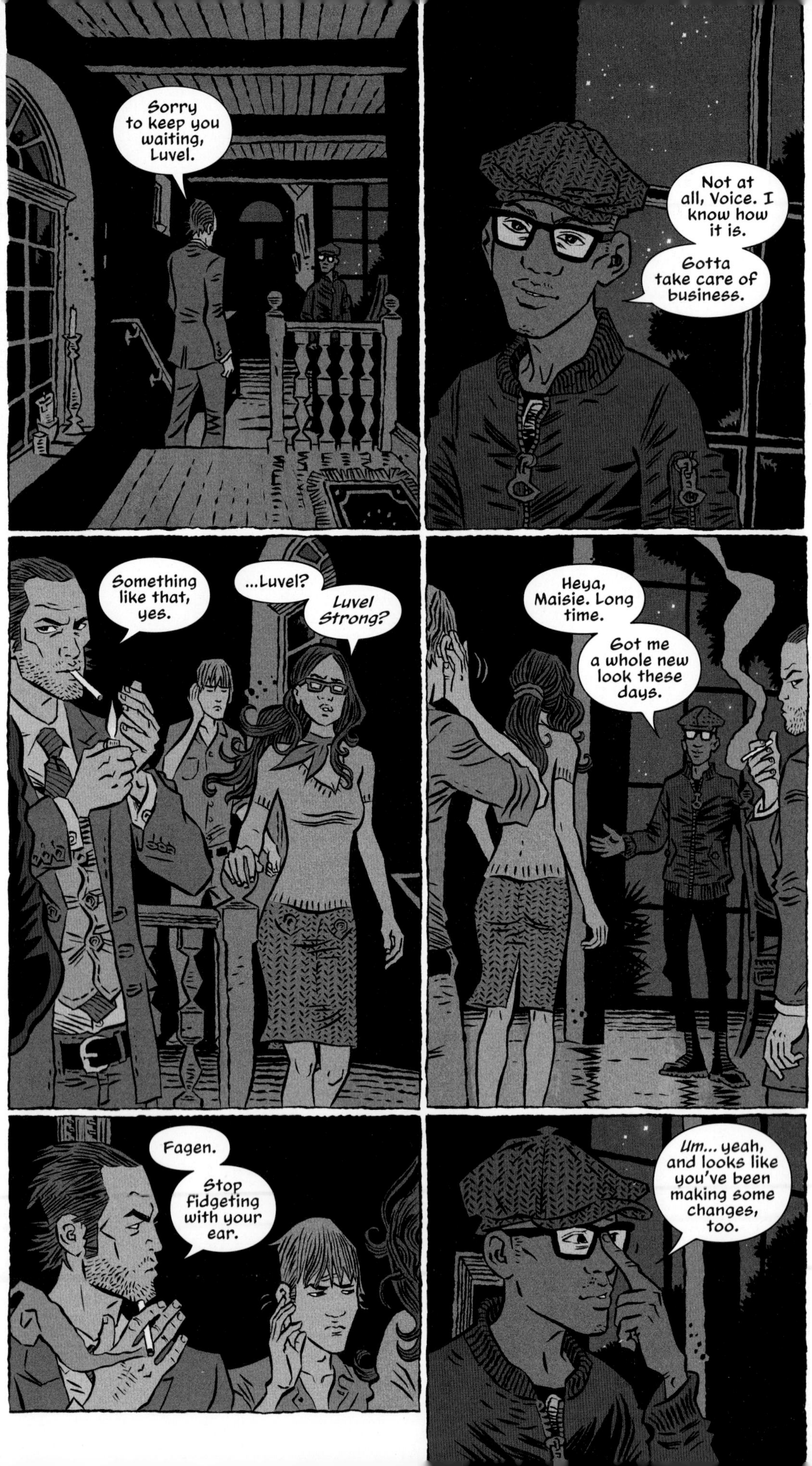
Sorry to keep you waiting, Luvel.
Not at all, Voice. I know how it is.
Gotta take care of business.
Something like that, yes.
...Luvel?
Luvel Strong?
Heya, Maisie. Long time.
Got me a whole new look these days.
Fagen.
Stop fidgeting with your ear.
Um... yeah, and looks like you've been making some changes, too.

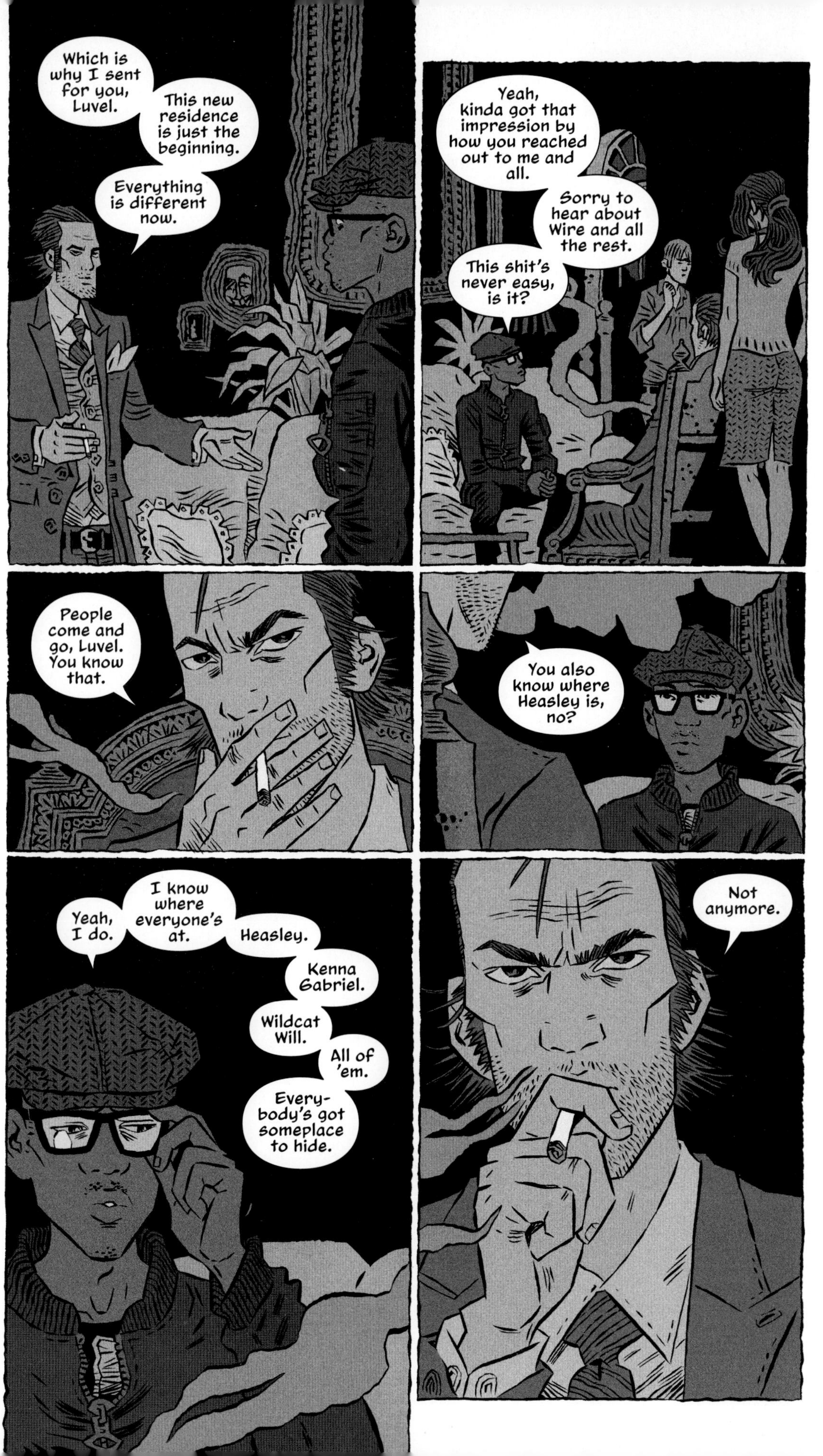
Which is why I sent for you, Luvel.
This new residence is just the beginning.
Everything is different now.
Yeah, kinda got that impression by how you reached out to me and all.
Sorry to hear about Wire and all the rest.
This shit's never easy, is it?
People come and go, Luvel. You know that.
You also know where Heasley is, no?
Yeah, I do.
I know where everyone's at.
Heasley.
Kenna Gabriel.
Wildcat Will.
All of 'em.
Every-body's got someplace to hide.
Not anymore.

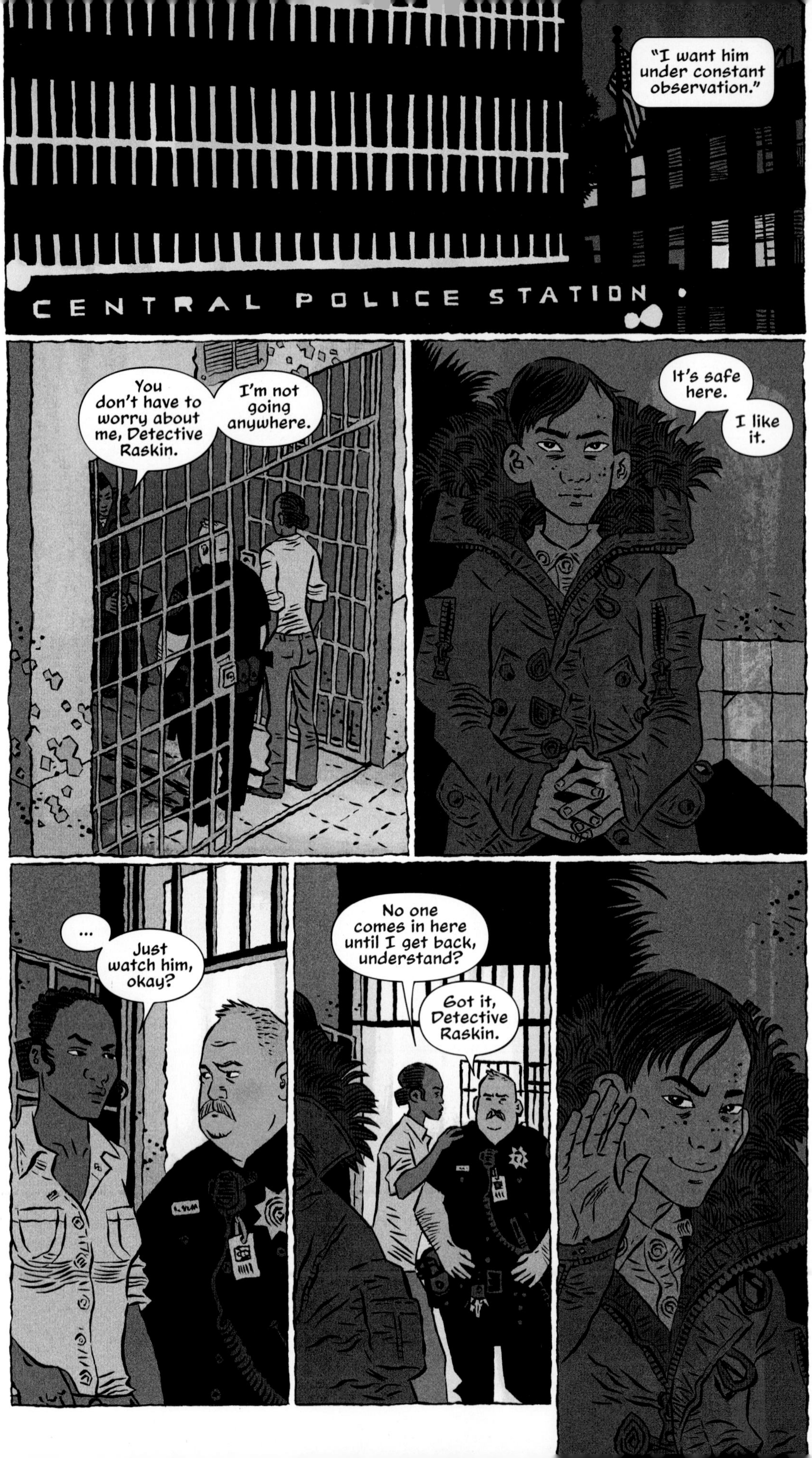
"I want him under constant observation."
CENTRAL POLICE STATION
You don't have to worry about me, Detective Raskin.
I'm not going anywhere.
It's safe here.
I like it.
...
Just watch him, okay?
No one comes in here until I get back, understand?
Got it, Detective Raskin.

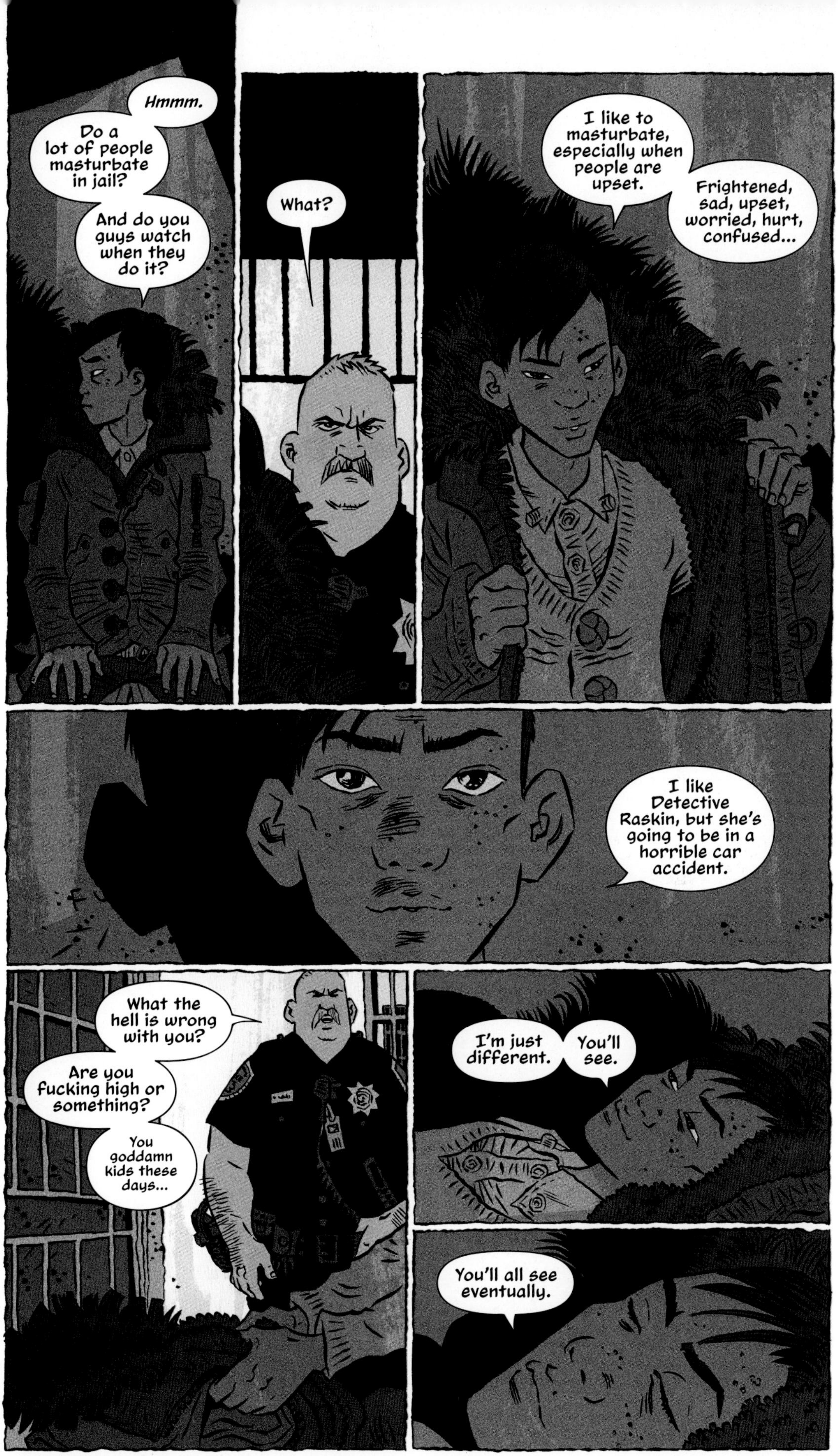
Hmmm.
Do a lot of people masturbate in jail?
And do you guys watch when they do it?
What?
I like to masturbate, especially when people are upset.
Frightened, sad, upset, worried, hurt, confused...
I like Detective Raskin, but she's going to be in a horrible car accident.
What the hell is wrong with you?
Are you fucking high or something?
You goddamn kids these days...
I'm just different.
You'll see.
You'll all see eventually.

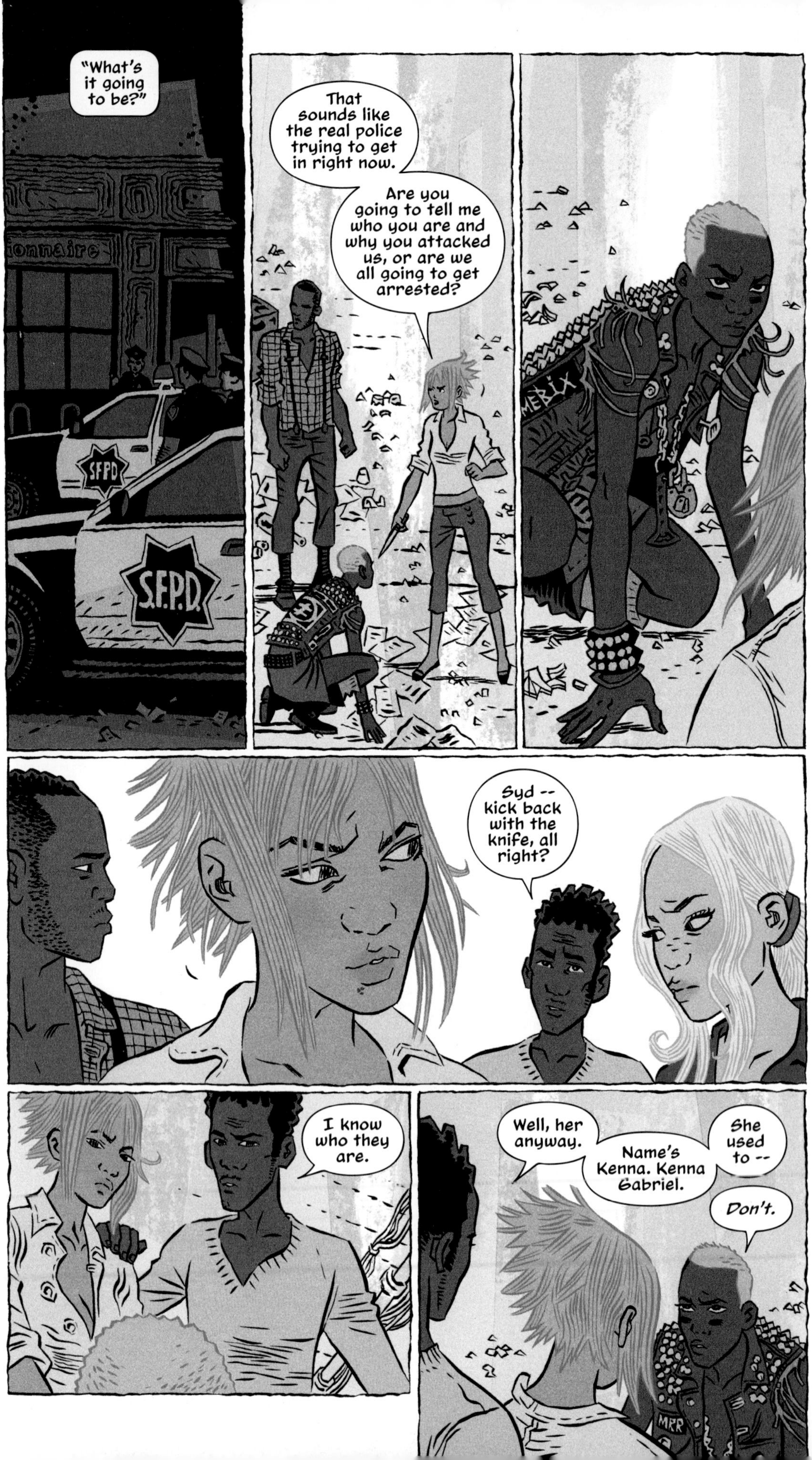
"What's it going to be?"
onnaire
S.F.P.D.
S.F.P.D.
That sounds like the real police trying to get in right now.
Are you going to tell me who you are and why you attacked us, or are we all going to get arrested?
Syd -- kick back with the knife, all right?
I know who they are.
Well, her anyway.
Name's Kenna. Kenna Gabriel.
She used to --
Don't.

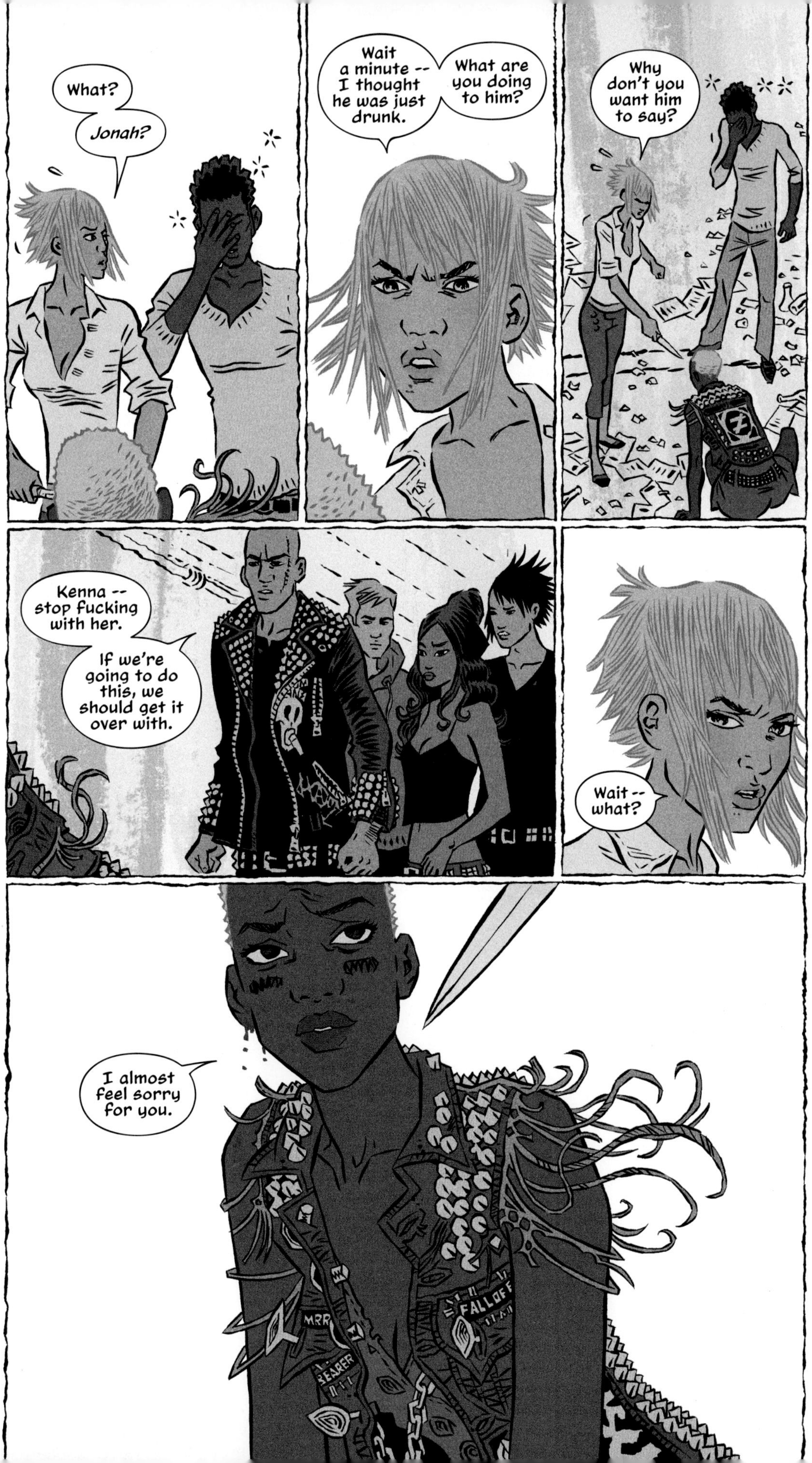
What?
Jonah?
Wait a minute -- I thought he was just drunk.
What are you doing to him?
Why don't you want him to say?
Kenna -- stop fucking with her.
If we're going to do this, we should get it over with.
Wait -- what?
I almost feel sorry for you.

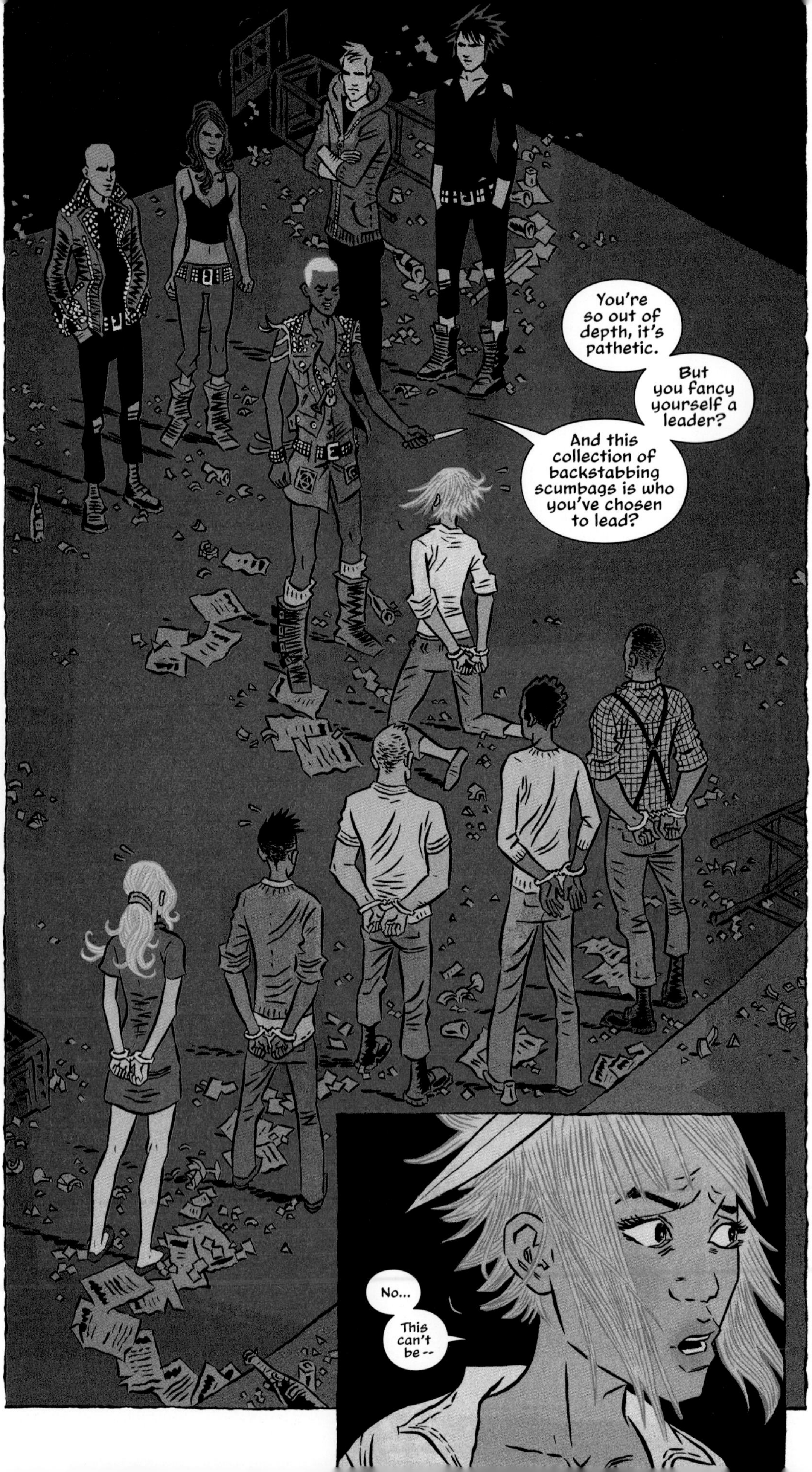

You're so out of depth, it's pathetic.
But you fancy yourself a leader?
And this collection of backstabbing scumbags is who you've chosen to lead?
No...
This can't be --

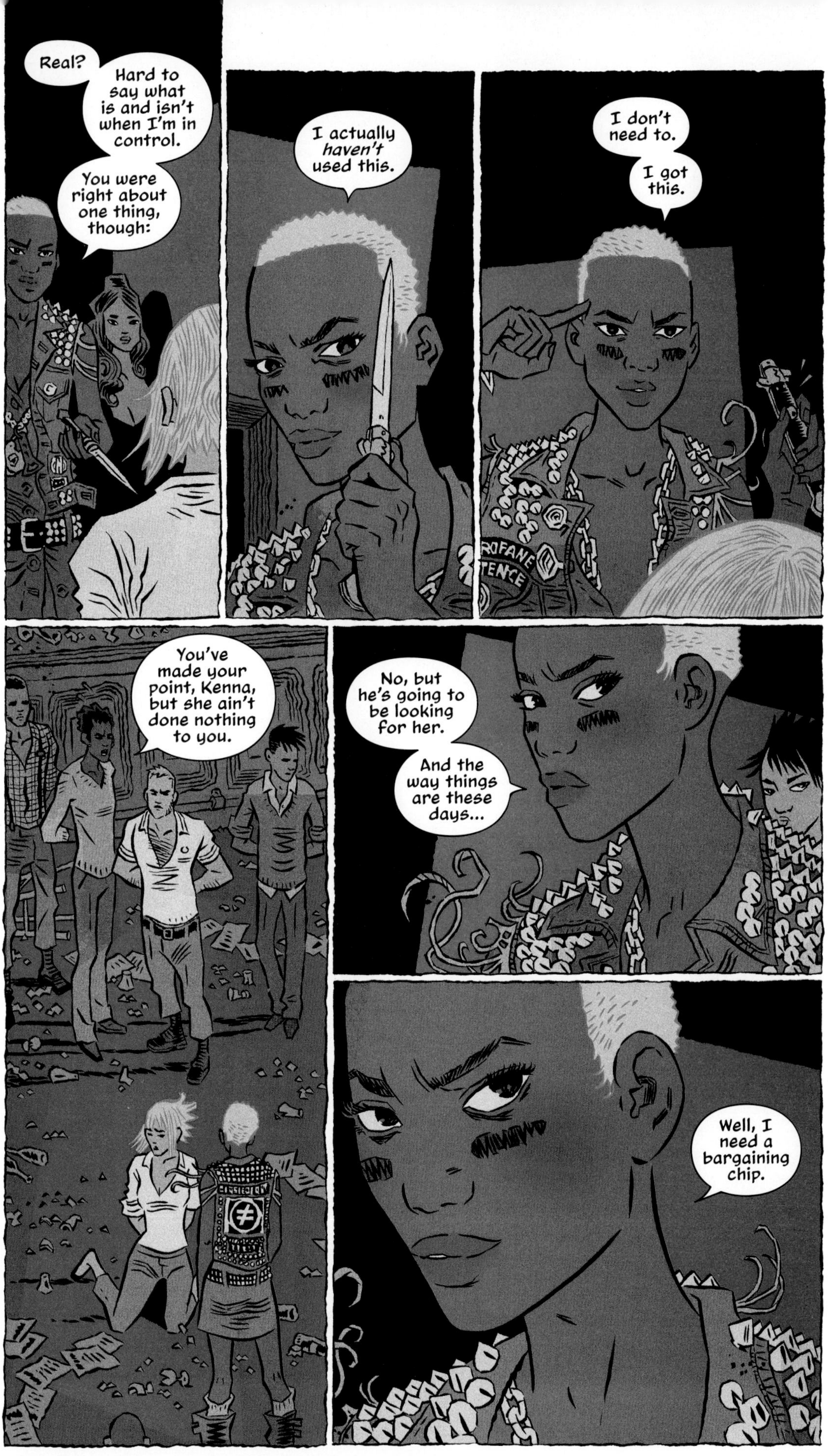
Real?
Hard to say what is and isn't when I'm in control.
You were right about one thing, though:
I actually *haven't* used this.
I don't need to.
I got this.
You've made your point, Kenna, but she ain't done nothing to you.
No, but he's going to be looking for her.
And the way things are these days...
Well, I need a bargaining chip.

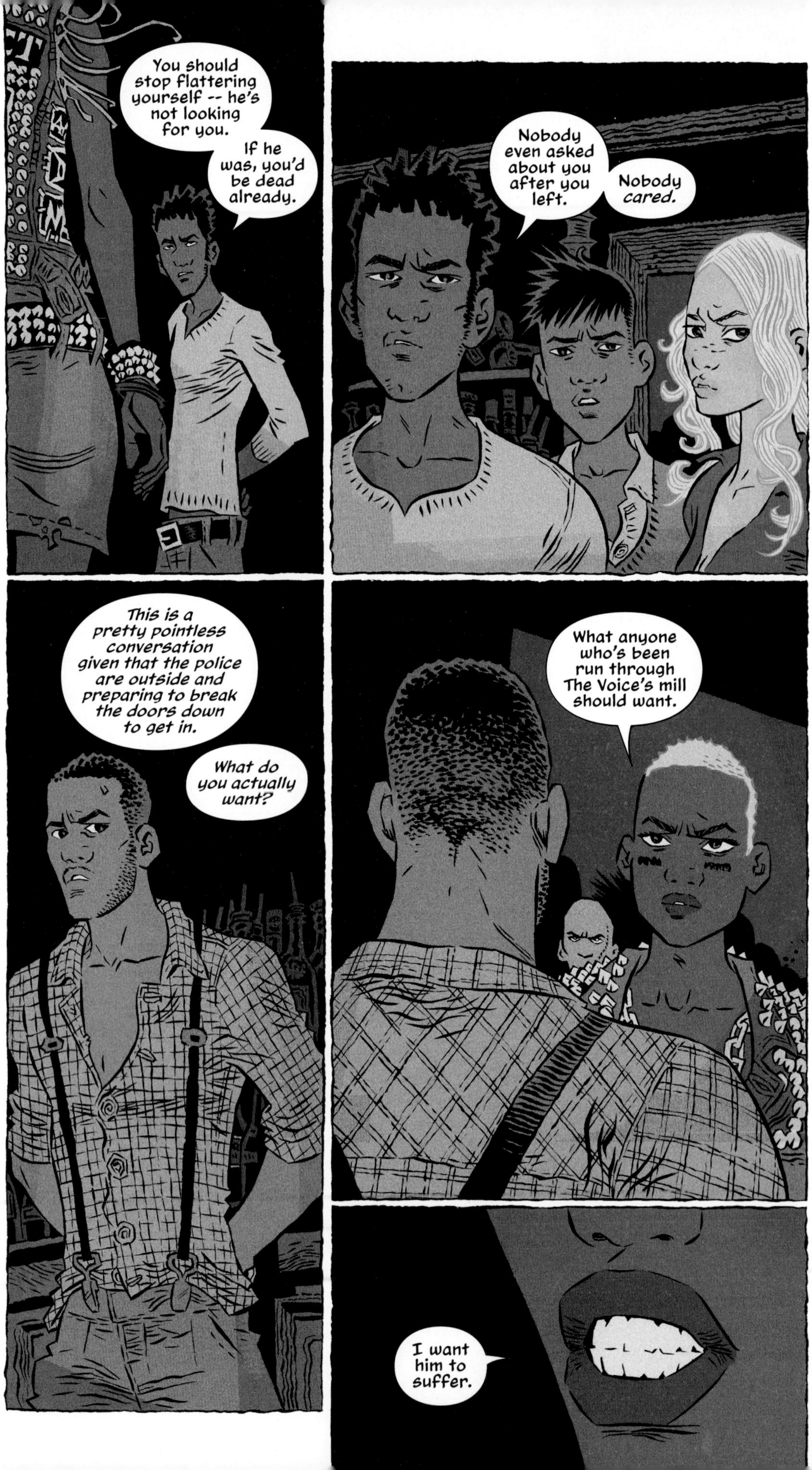
You should stop flattering yourself -- he's not looking for you.
If he was, you'd be dead already.
Nobody even asked about you after you left.
Nobody cared.
This is a pretty pointless conversation given that the police are outside and preparing to break the doors down to get in.
What do you actually want?
What anyone who's been run through The Voice's mill should want.
I want him to suffer.

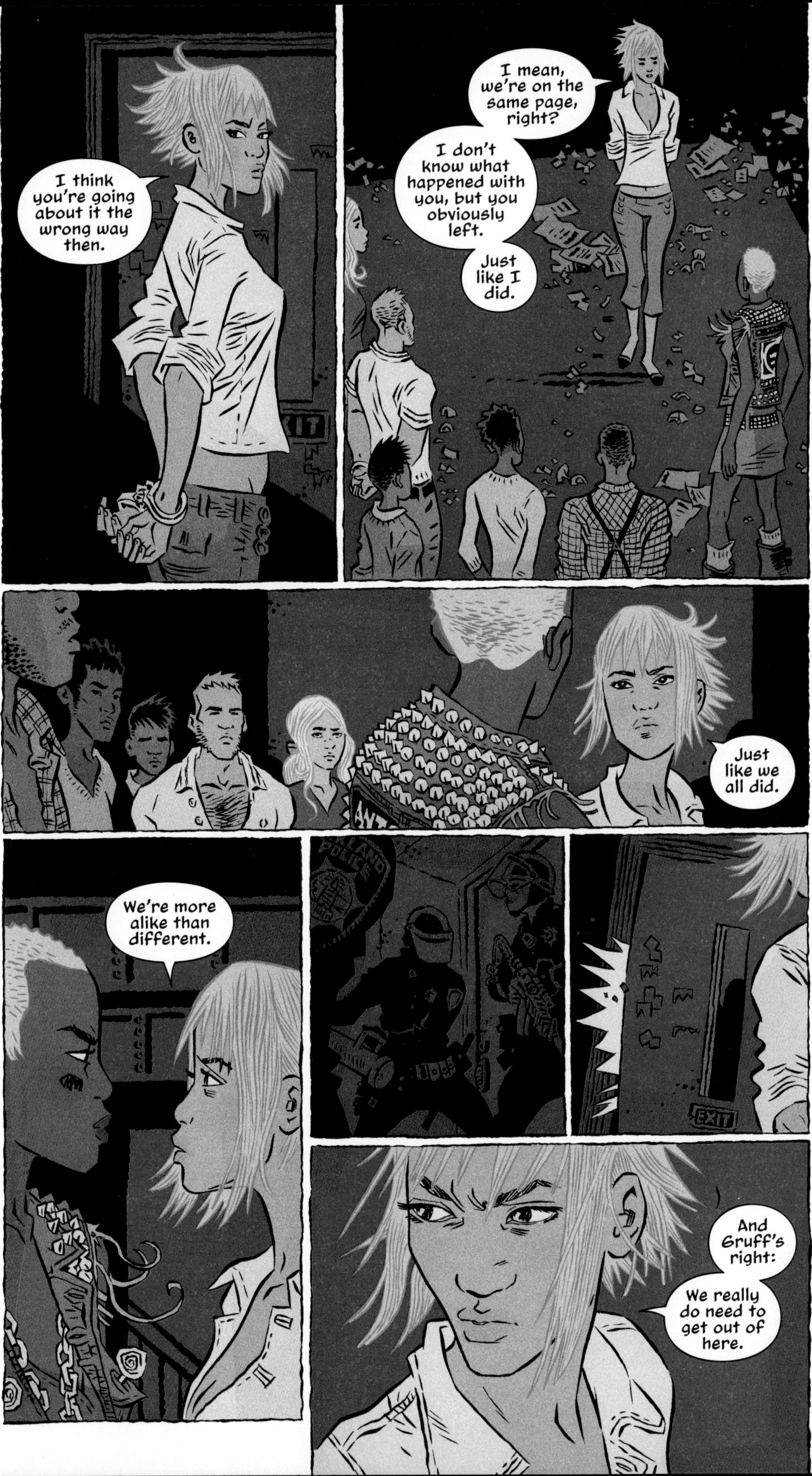
I think you're going about it the wrong way then.
I mean, we're on the same page, right?
I don't know what happened with you, but you obviously left.
Just like I did.
Just like we all did.
We're more alike than different.
And Gruff's right:
We really do need to get out of here.

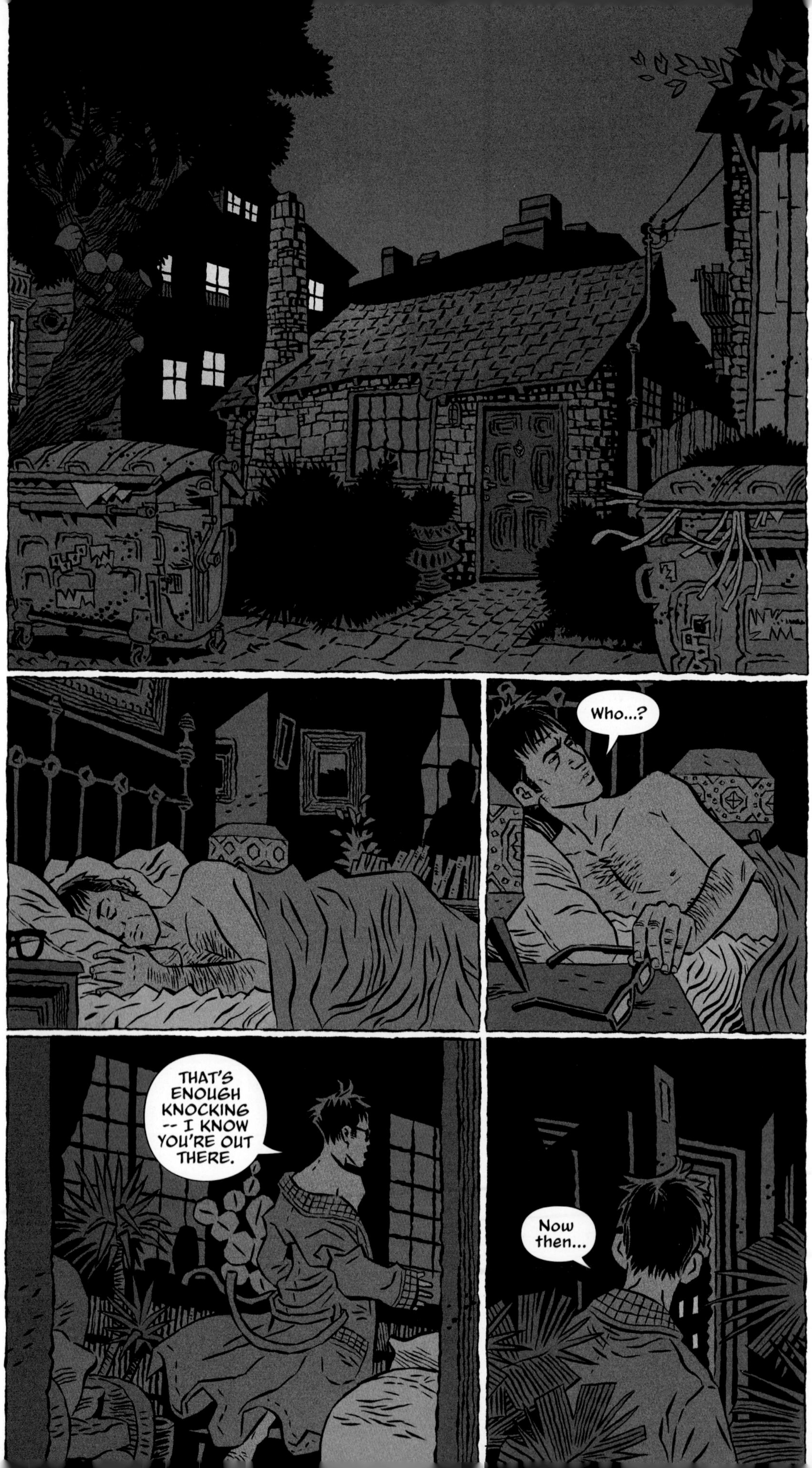
Who...?
THAT'S ENOUGH KNOCKING -- I KNOW YOU'RE OUT THERE.
Now then...

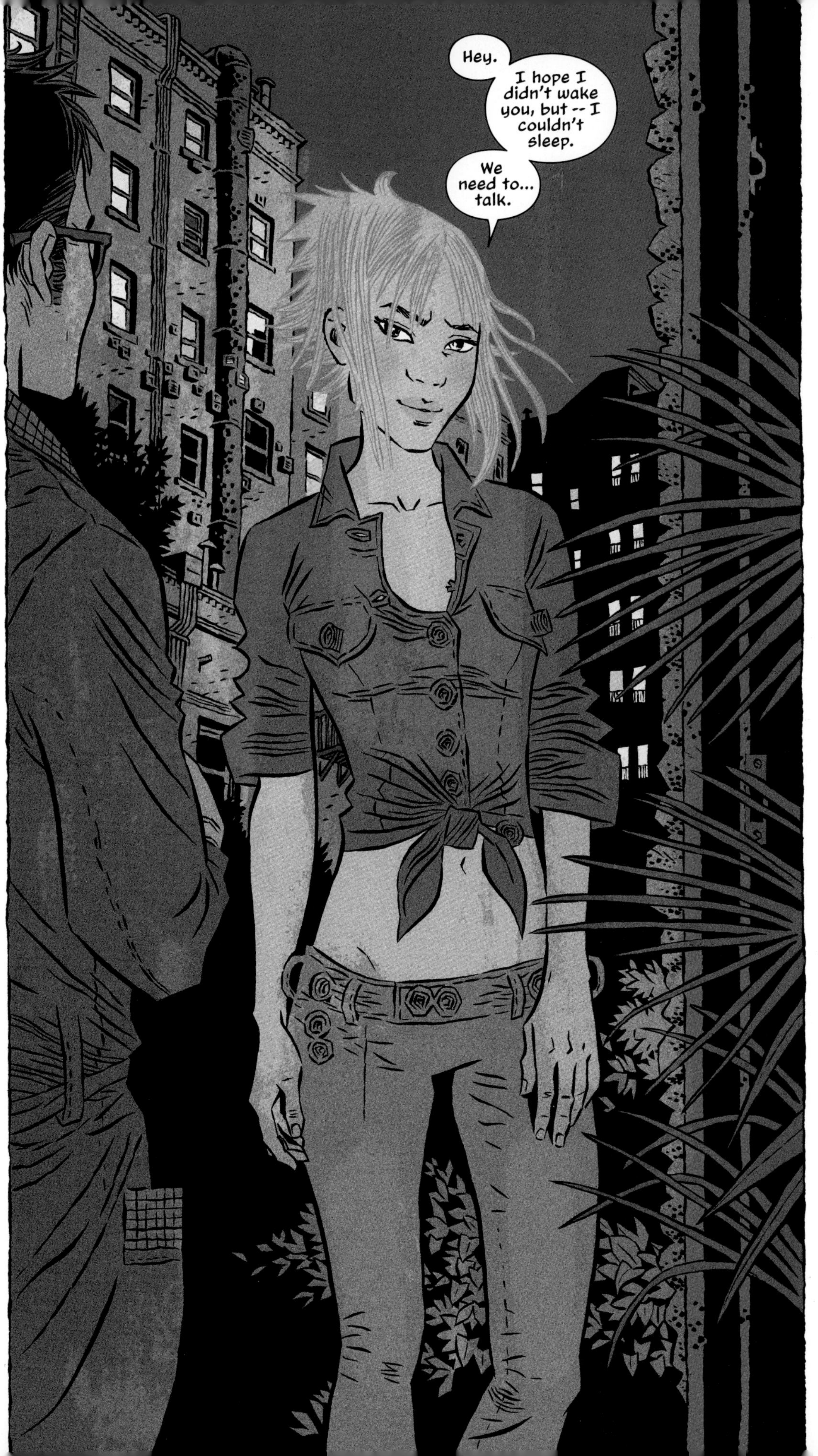
Hey.
I hope I didn't wake you, but -- I couldn't sleep.
We need to... talk.

YOU CAN
LAUGH AS IF
WE'RE STILL
TOGETHER,
BUT THIS
REALLY IS
THE END.

ALEX KAPRANOS

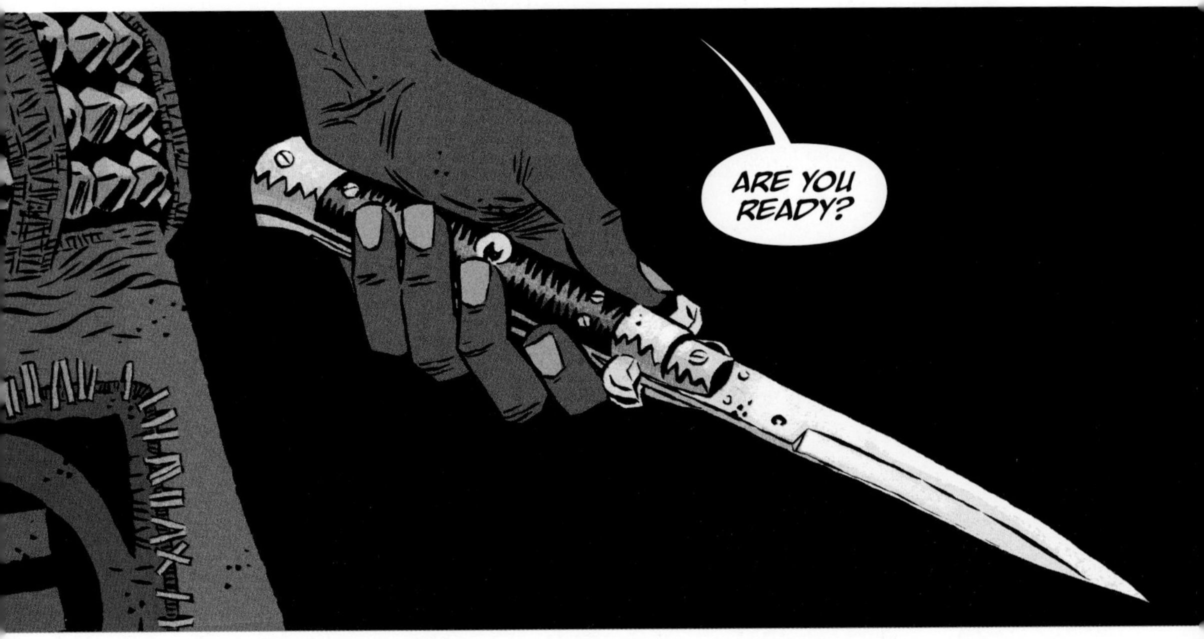
ARE YOU READY?

11: EVERYTHING HAS A PRICE TO PAY

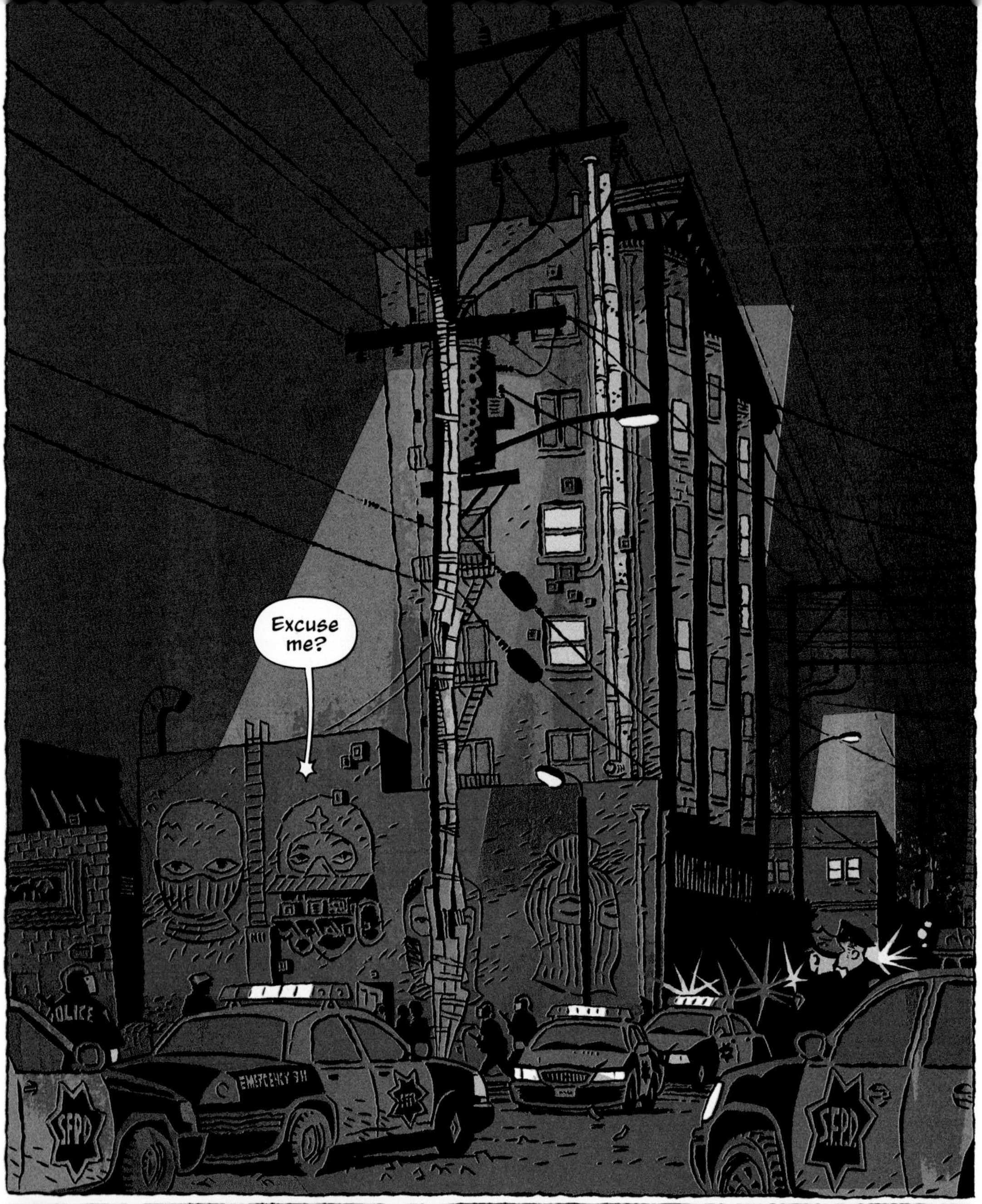
Excuse me?
EMERGENCY 911
SFPD
POLICE

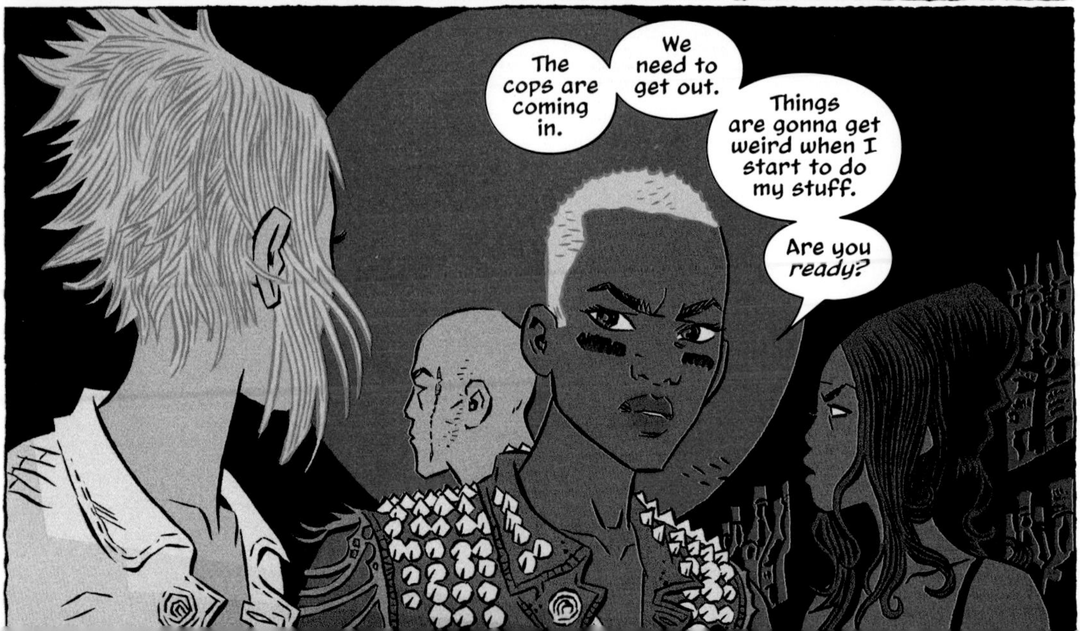
The cops are coming in.
We need to get out.
Things are gonna get weird when I start to do my stuff.
Are you *ready?*

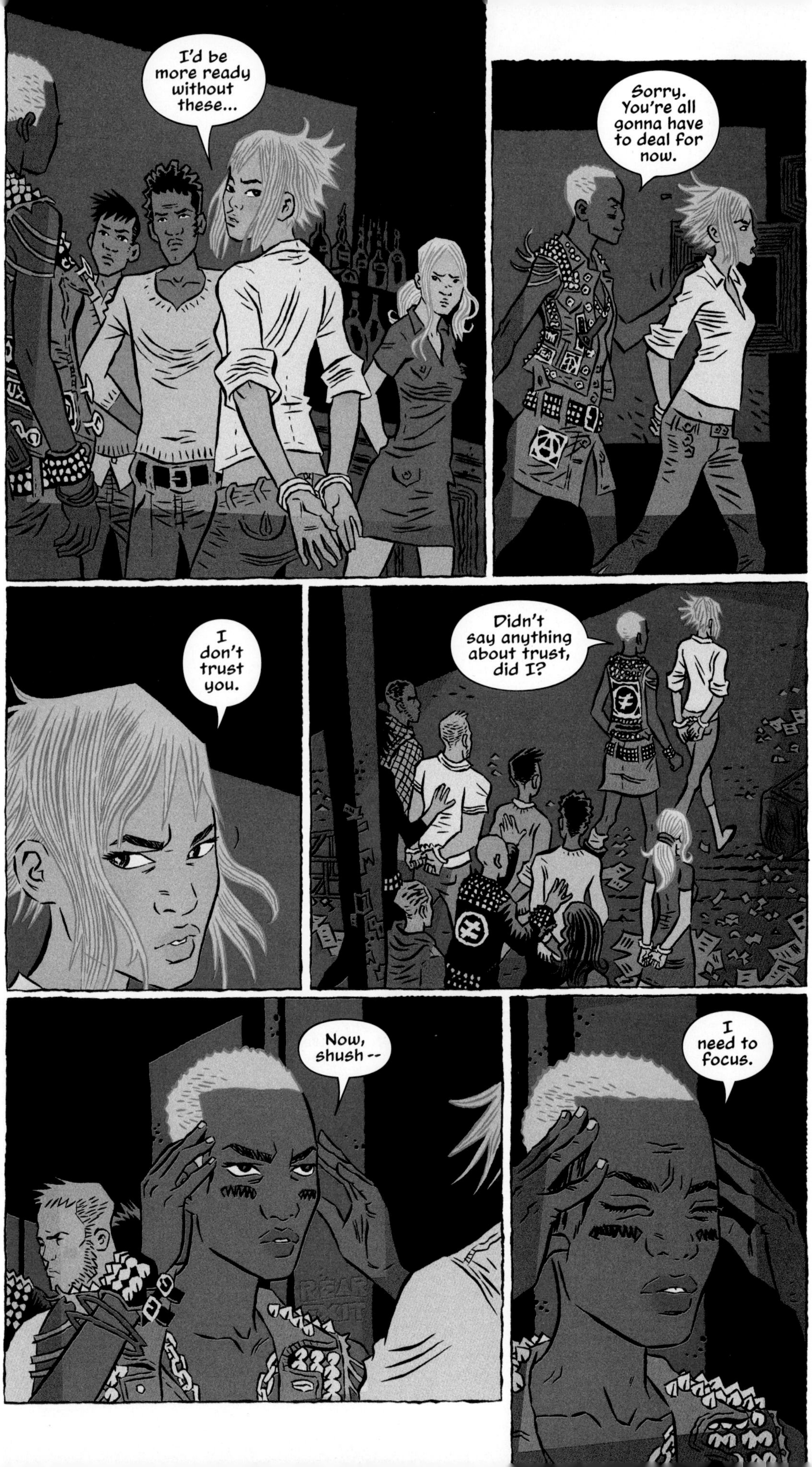
I'd be more ready without these...
Sorry. You're all gonna have to deal for now.
I don't trust you.
Didn't say anything about trust, did I?
Now, shush --
I need to focus.

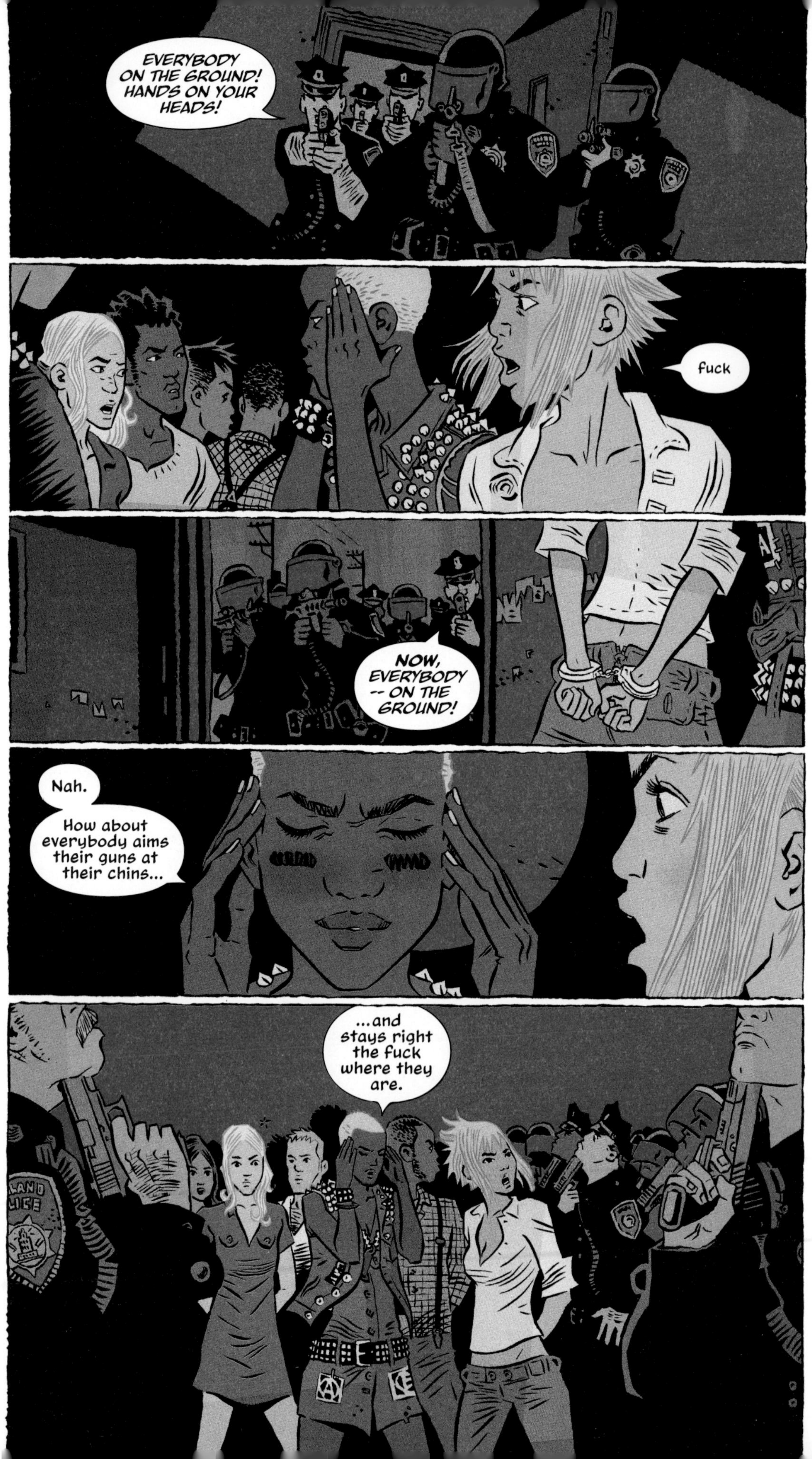
EVERYBODY ON THE GROUND! HANDS ON YOUR HEADS!
fuck
NOW, EVERYBODY -- ON THE GROUND!
Nah.
How about everybody aims their guns at their chins...
...and stays right the fuck where they are.

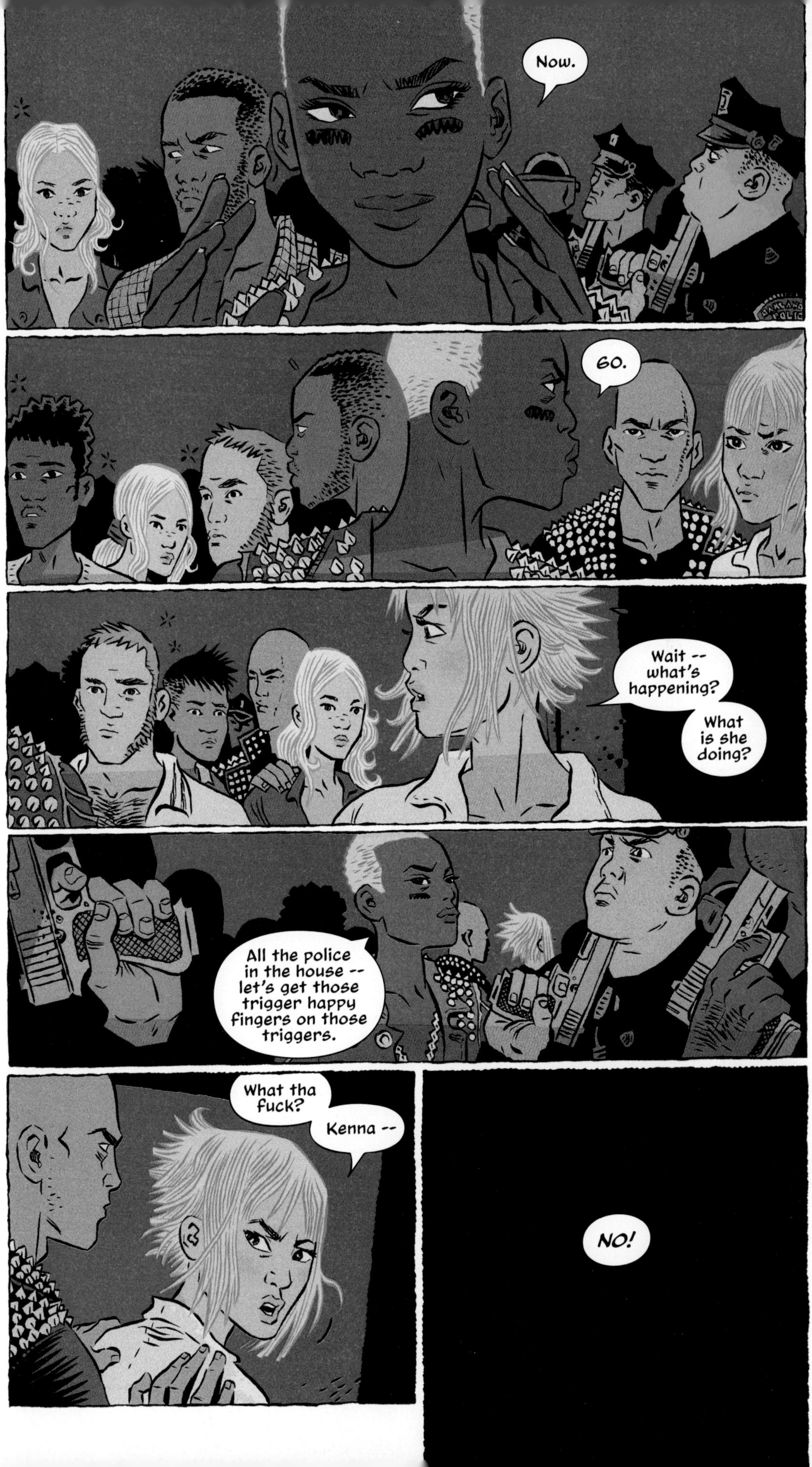
Now.
GO.
Wait -- what's happening?
What is she doing?
All the police in the house -- let's get those trigger happy fingers on those triggers.
What tha fuck?
Kenna --
NO!

A little piece
of advice.

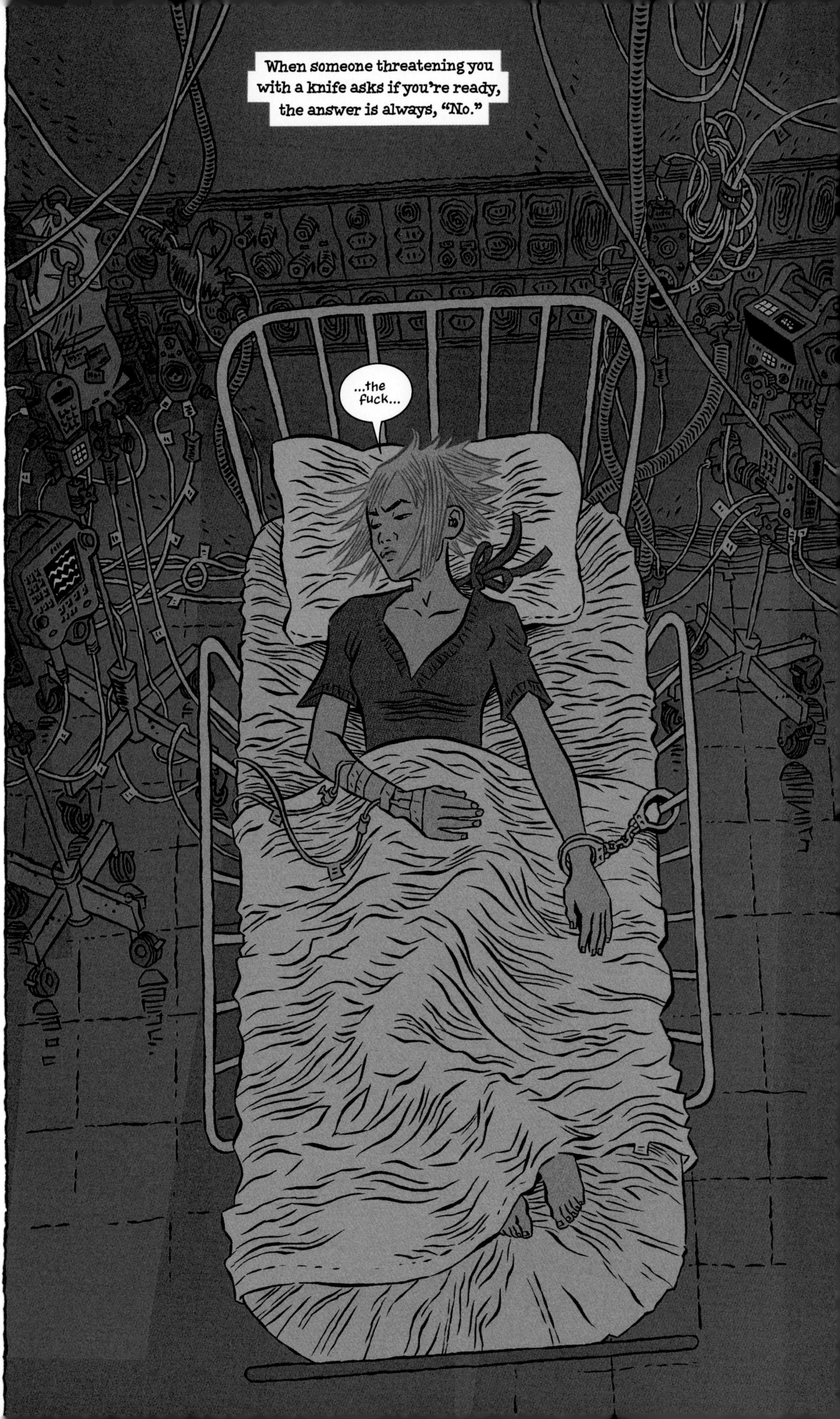
When someone threatening you with a knife asks if you're ready, the answer is always, "No."
...the fuck...

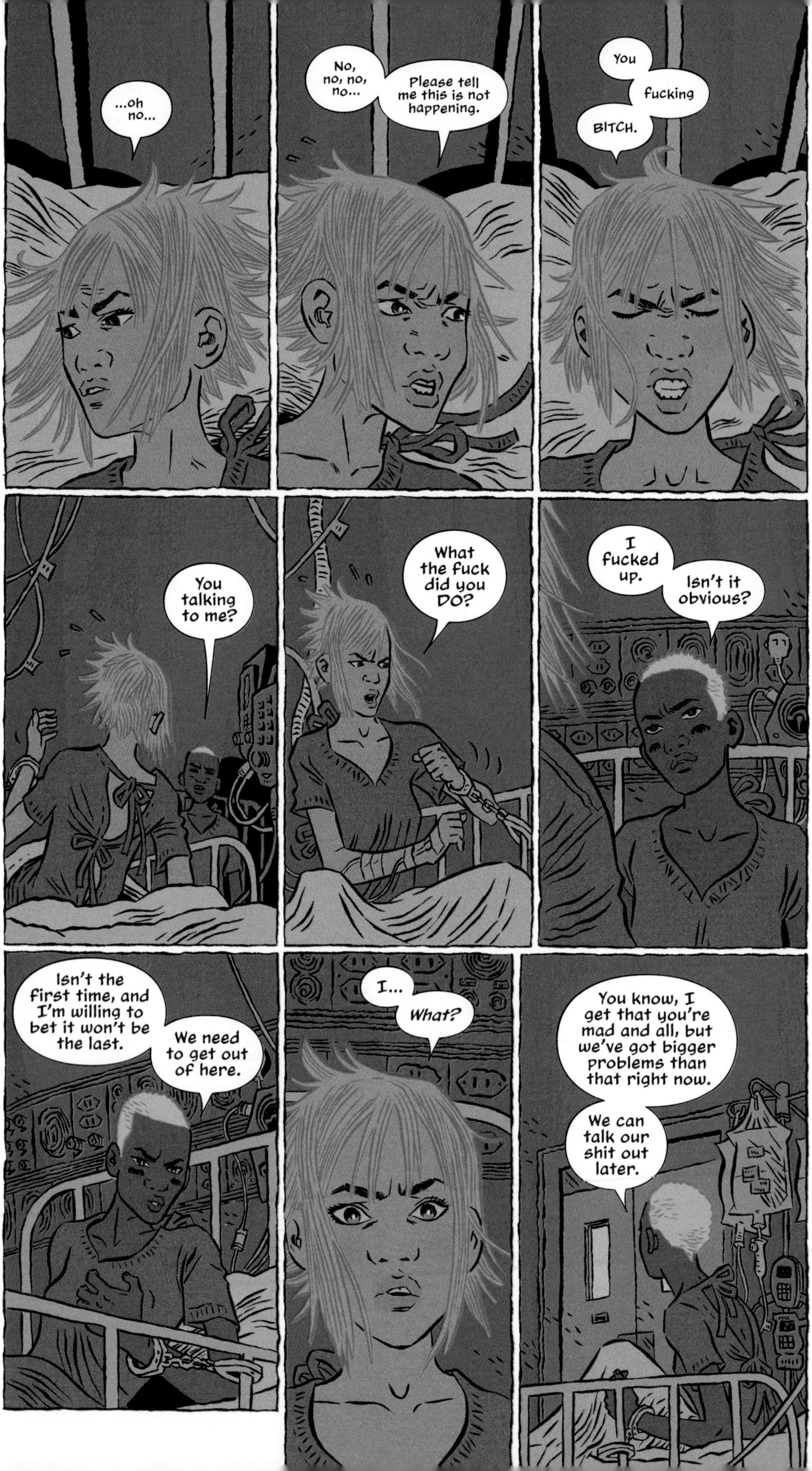

...oh no...
No, no, no, no...
Please tell me this is not happening.
You
fucking
BITCH.
You talking to me?
What the fuck did you DO?
I fucked up.
Isn't it obvious?
Isn't the first time, and I'm willing to bet it won't be the last.
We need to get out of here.
I...
What?
You know, I get that you're mad and all, but we've got bigger problems than that right now.
We can talk our shit out later.

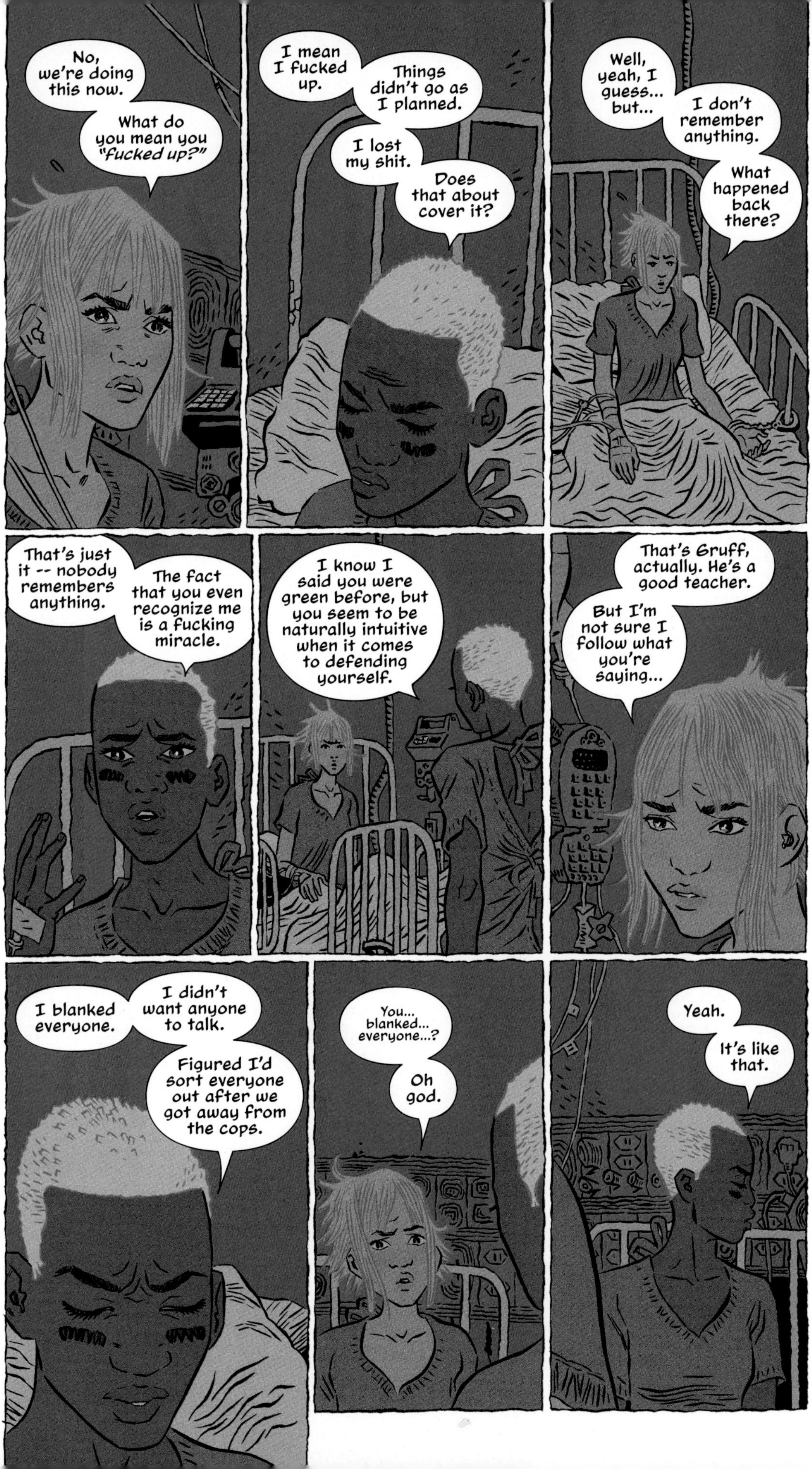
No, we're doing this now.
What do you mean you "fucked up?"
I mean I fucked up.
Things didn't go as I planned.
I lost my shit.
Does that about cover it?
Well, yeah, I guess... but...
I don't remember anything.
What happened back there?
That's just it -- nobody remembers anything.
The fact that you even recognize me is a fucking miracle.
I know I said you were green before, but you seem to be naturally intuitive when it comes to defending yourself.
That's Gruff, actually. He's a good teacher.
But I'm not sure I follow what you're saying...
I blanked everyone.
I didn't want anyone to talk.
Figured I'd sort everyone out after we got away from the cops.
You... blanked... everyone...?
Oh god.
Yeah.
It's like that.

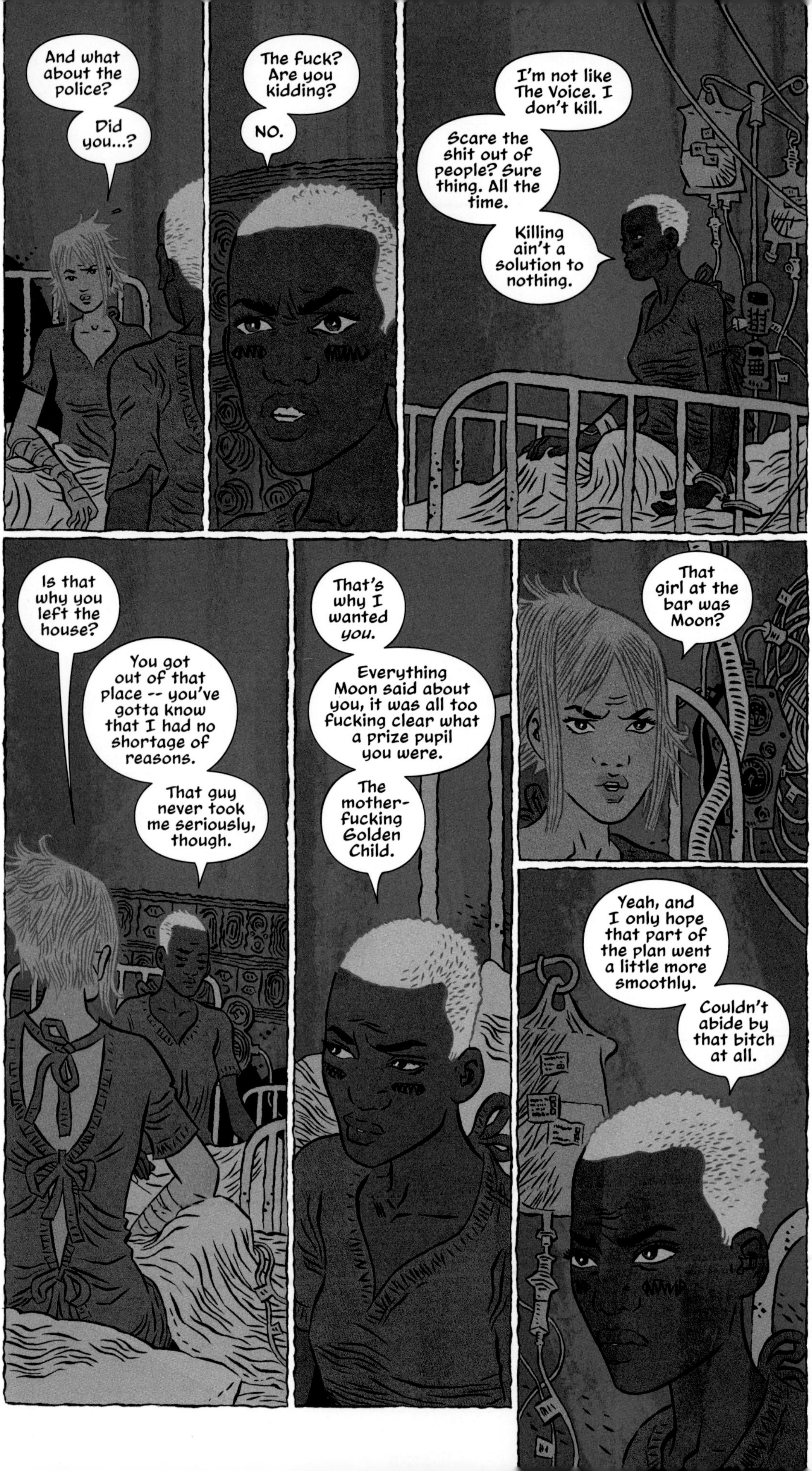
And what about the police?
Did you...?
The fuck? Are you kidding?
NO.
I'm not like The Voice. I don't kill.
Scare the shit out of people? Sure thing. All the time.
Killing ain't a solution to nothing.
Is that why you left the house?
You got out of that place -- you've gotta know that I had no shortage of reasons.
That guy never took me seriously, though.
That's why I wanted you.
Everything Moon said about you, it was all too fucking clear what a prize pupil you were.
The mother-fucking Golden Child.
That girl at the bar was Moon?
Yeah, and I only hope that part of the plan went a little more smoothly.
Couldn't abide by that bitch at all.

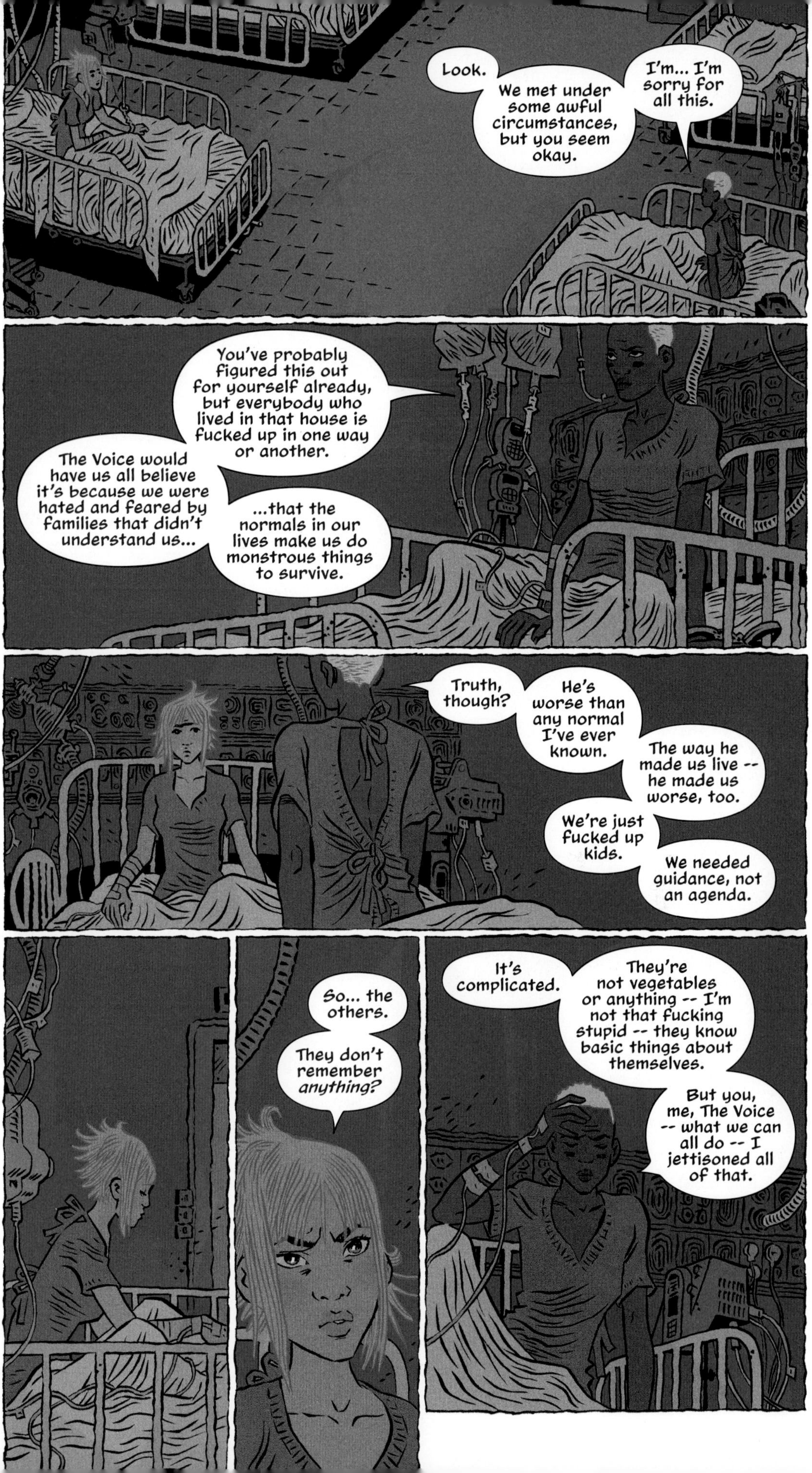
Look.
We met under some awful circumstances, but you seem okay.
I'm... I'm sorry for all this.
You've probably figured this out for yourself already, but everybody who lived in that house is fucked up in one way or another.
The Voice would have us all believe it's because we were hated and feared by families that didn't understand us...
...that the normals in our lives make us do monstrous things to survive.
Truth, though?
He's worse than any normal I've ever known.
The way he made us live -- he made us worse, too.
We're just fucked up kids.
We needed guidance, not an agenda.
So... the others.
They don't remember *anything?*
It's complicated.
They're not vegetables or anything -- I'm not that fucking stupid -- they know basic things about themselves.
But you, me, The Voice -- what we can all do -- I jettisoned all of that.

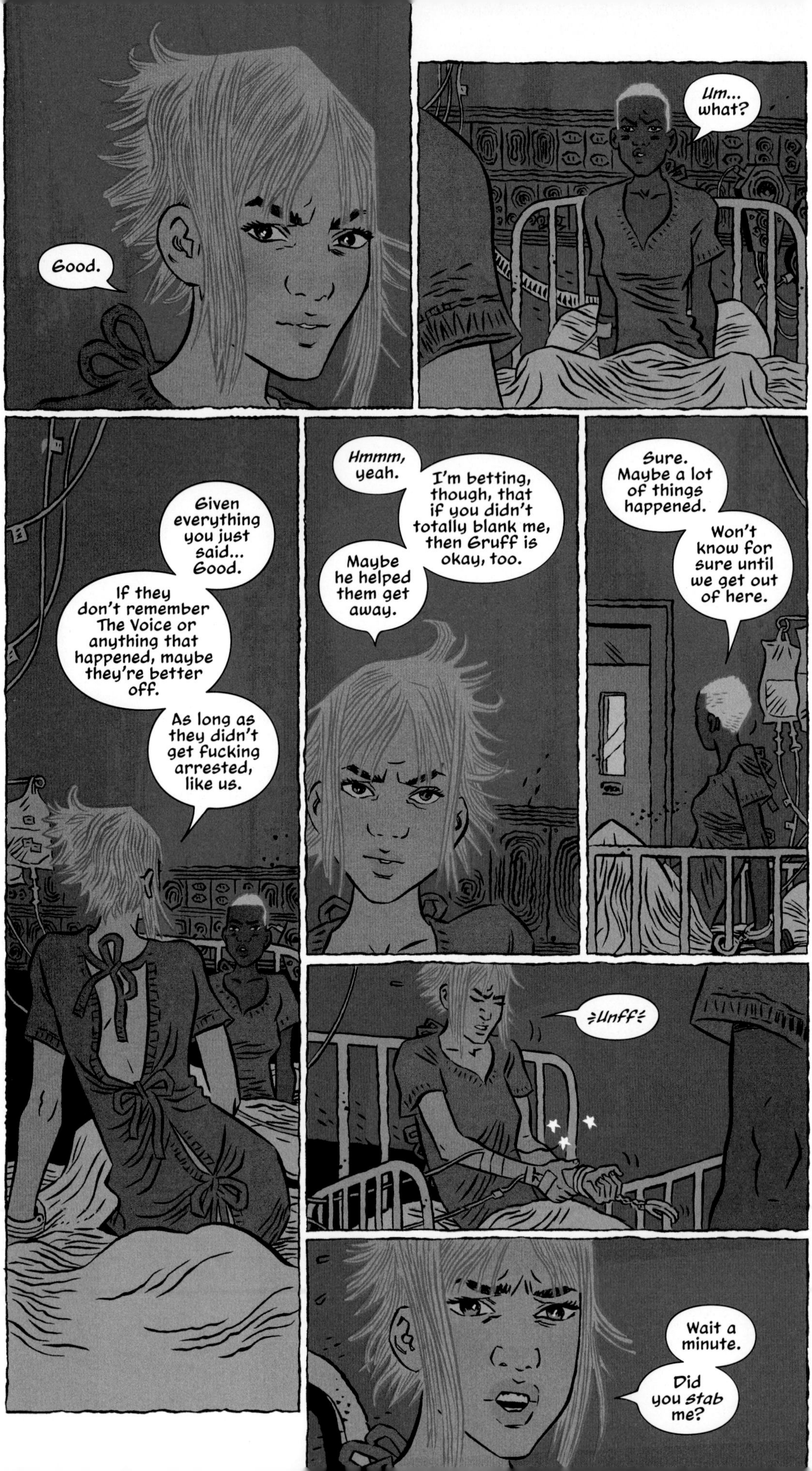
Good.
Um... what?
Given everything you just said... Good.
If they don't remember The Voice or anything that happened, maybe they're better off.
As long as they didn't get fucking arrested, like us.
Hmmm, yeah.
I'm betting, though, that if you didn't totally blank me, then Gruff is okay, too.
Maybe he helped them get away.
Sure. Maybe a lot of things happened.
Won't know for sure until we get out of here.
Unff
Wait a minute.
Did you stab me?

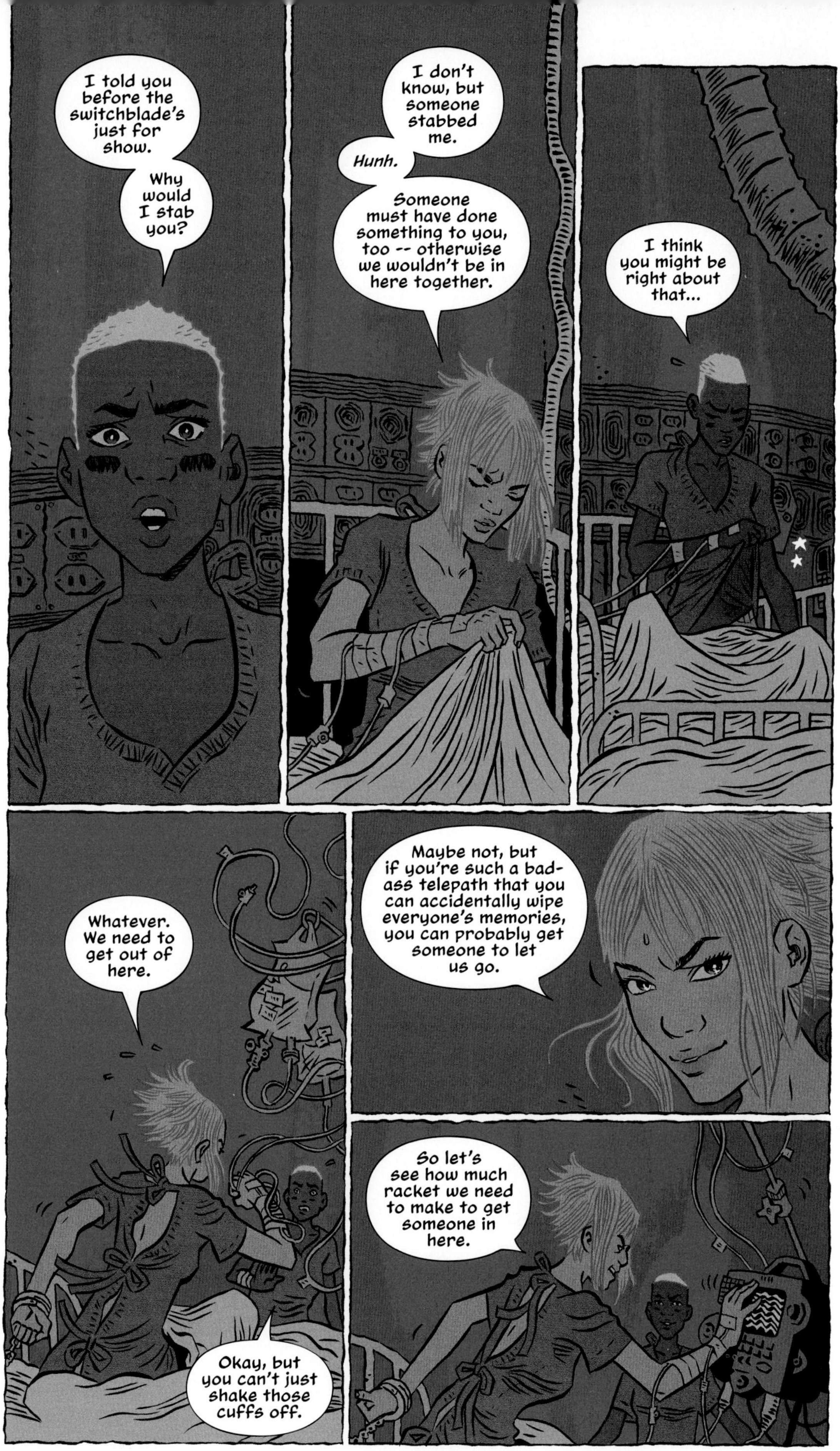
I told you before the switchblade's just for show.
Why would I stab you?
I don't know, but someone stabbed me.
Hunh.
Someone must have done something to you, too -- otherwise we wouldn't be in here together.
I think you might be right about that...
Whatever. We need to get out of here.
Okay, but you can't just shake those cuffs off.
Maybe not, but if you're such a bad-ass telepath that you can accidentally wipe everyone's memories, you can probably get someone to let us go.
So let's see how much racket we need to make to get someone in here.

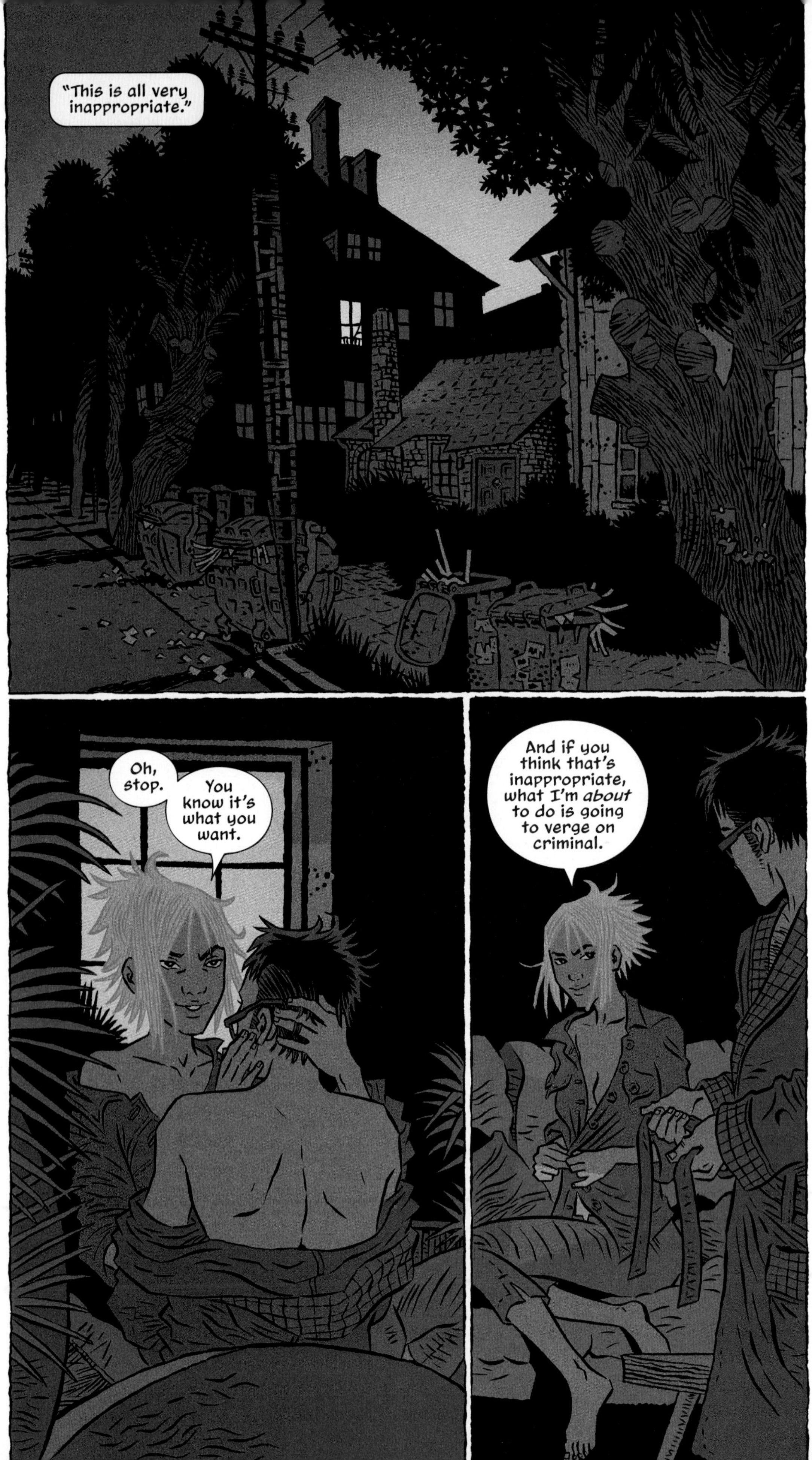
"This is all very inappropriate."
Oh, stop.
You know it's what you want.
And if you think that's inappropriate, what I'm *about* to do is going to verge on criminal.

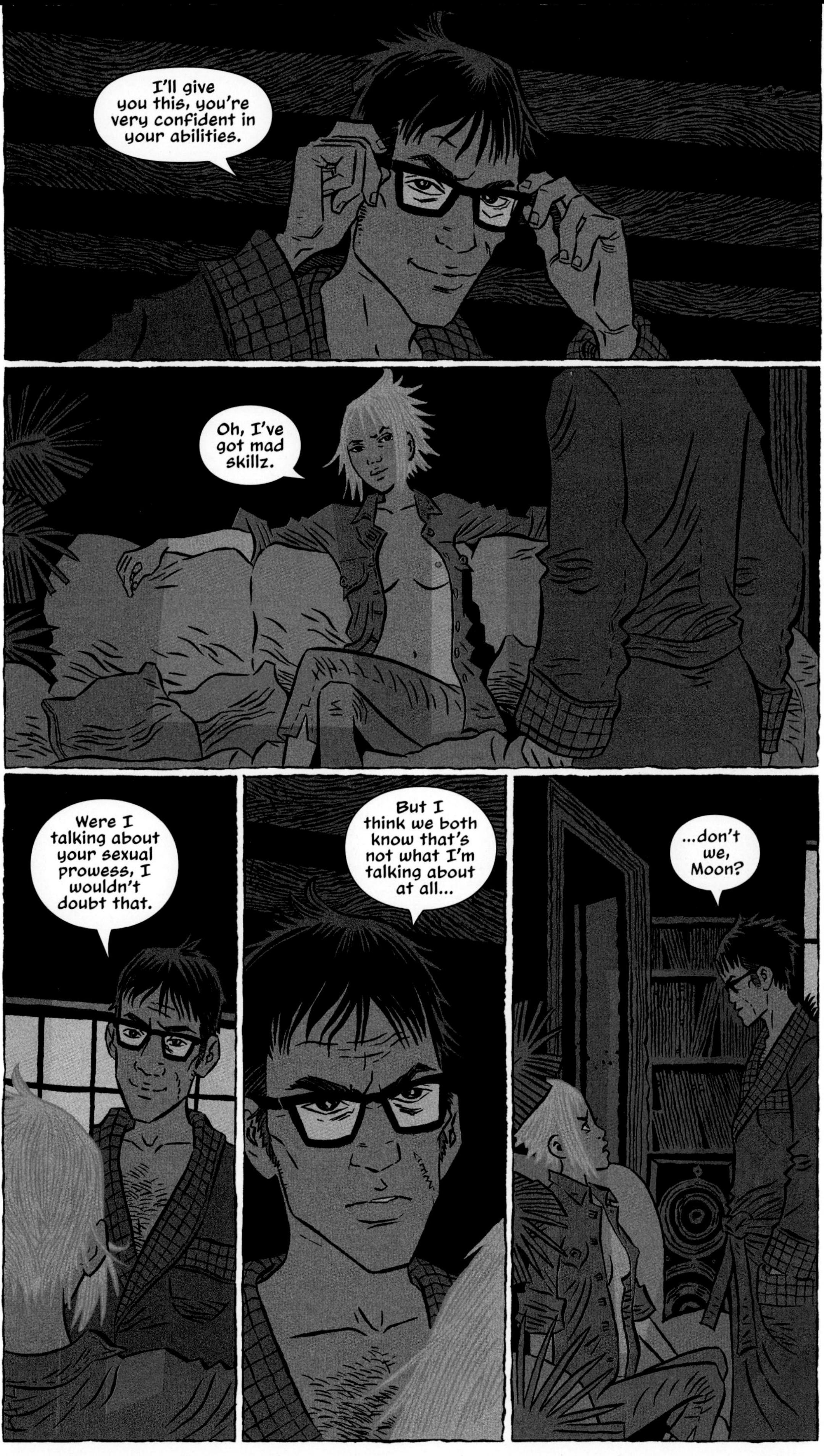
I'll give you this, you're very confident in your abilities.
Oh, I've got mad skillz.
Were I talking about your sexual prowess, I wouldn't doubt that.
But I think we both know that's not what I'm talking about at all...
...don't we, Moon?

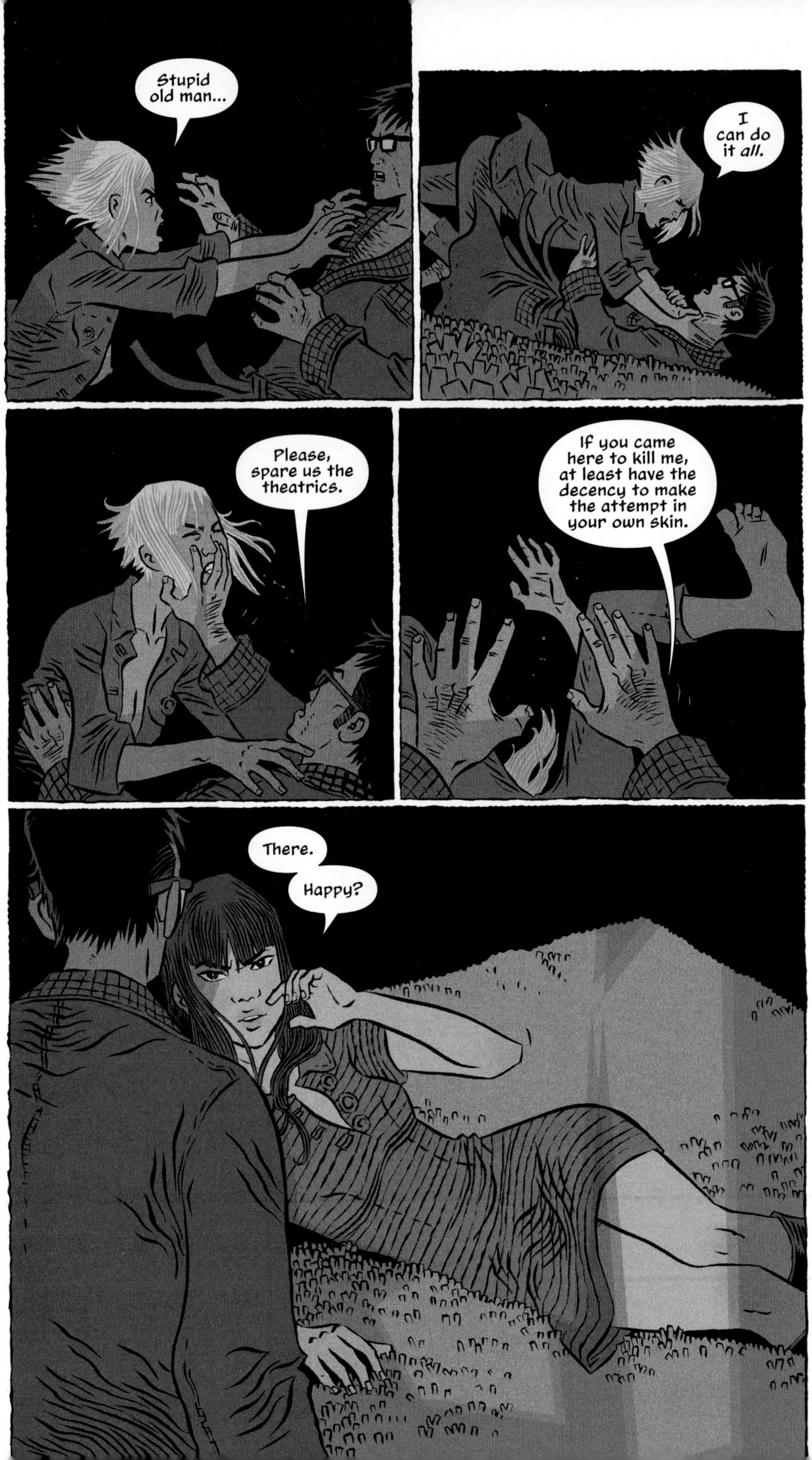
Stupid old man...
I can do it *all*.
Please, spare us the theatrics.
If you came here to kill me, at least have the decency to make the attempt in your own skin.
There.
Happy?

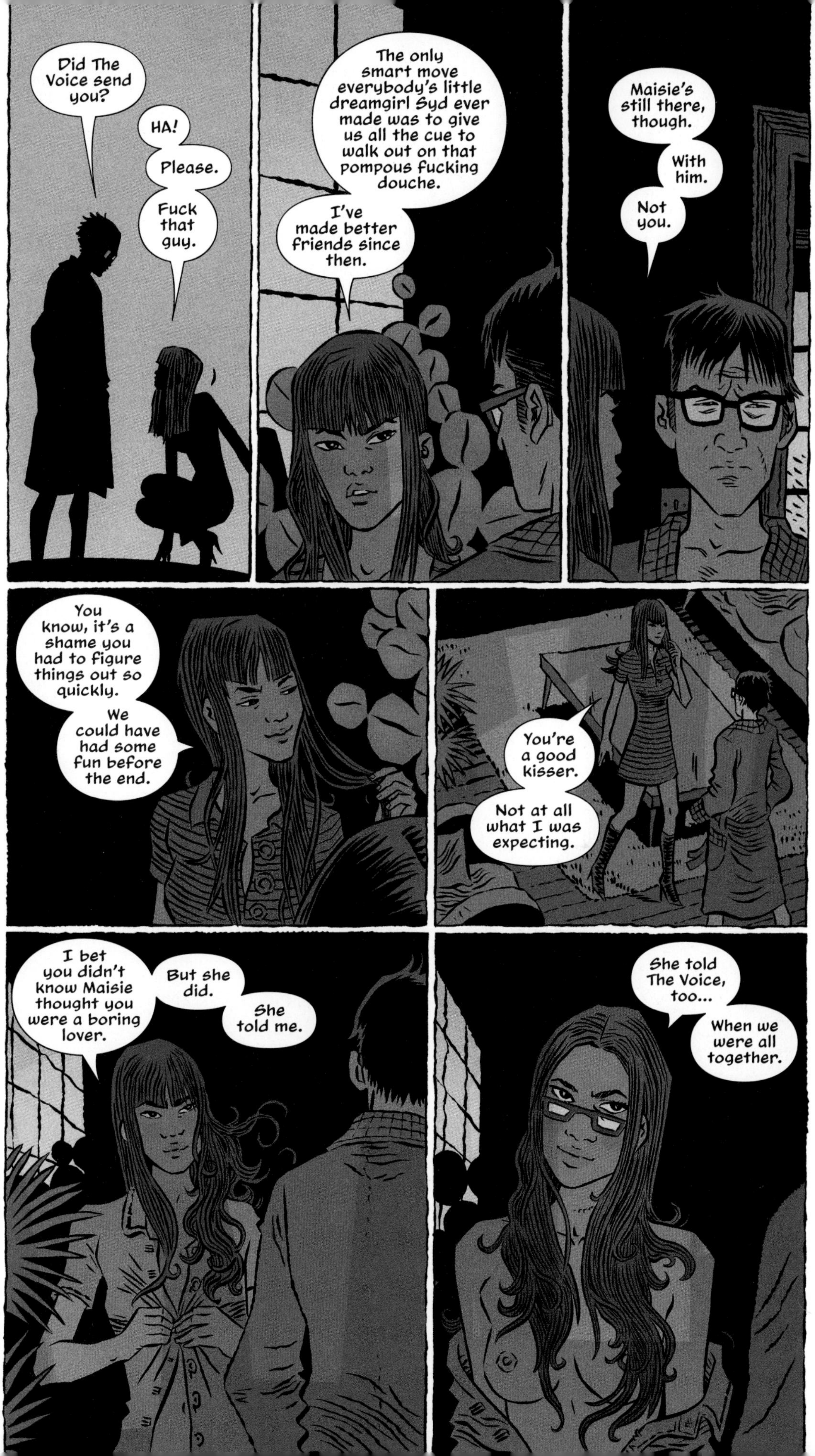
Did The Voice send you?
HA!
Please.
Fuck that guy.
The only smart move everybody's little dreamgirl Syd ever made was to give us all the cue to walk out on that pompous fucking douche.
I've made better friends since then.
Maisie's still there, though.
With him.
Not you.
You know, it's a shame you had to figure things out so quickly.
We could have had some fun before the end.
You're a good kisser.
Not at all what I was expecting.
I bet you didn't know Maisie thought you were a boring lover.
But she did.
She told me.
She told The Voice, too...
When we were all together.

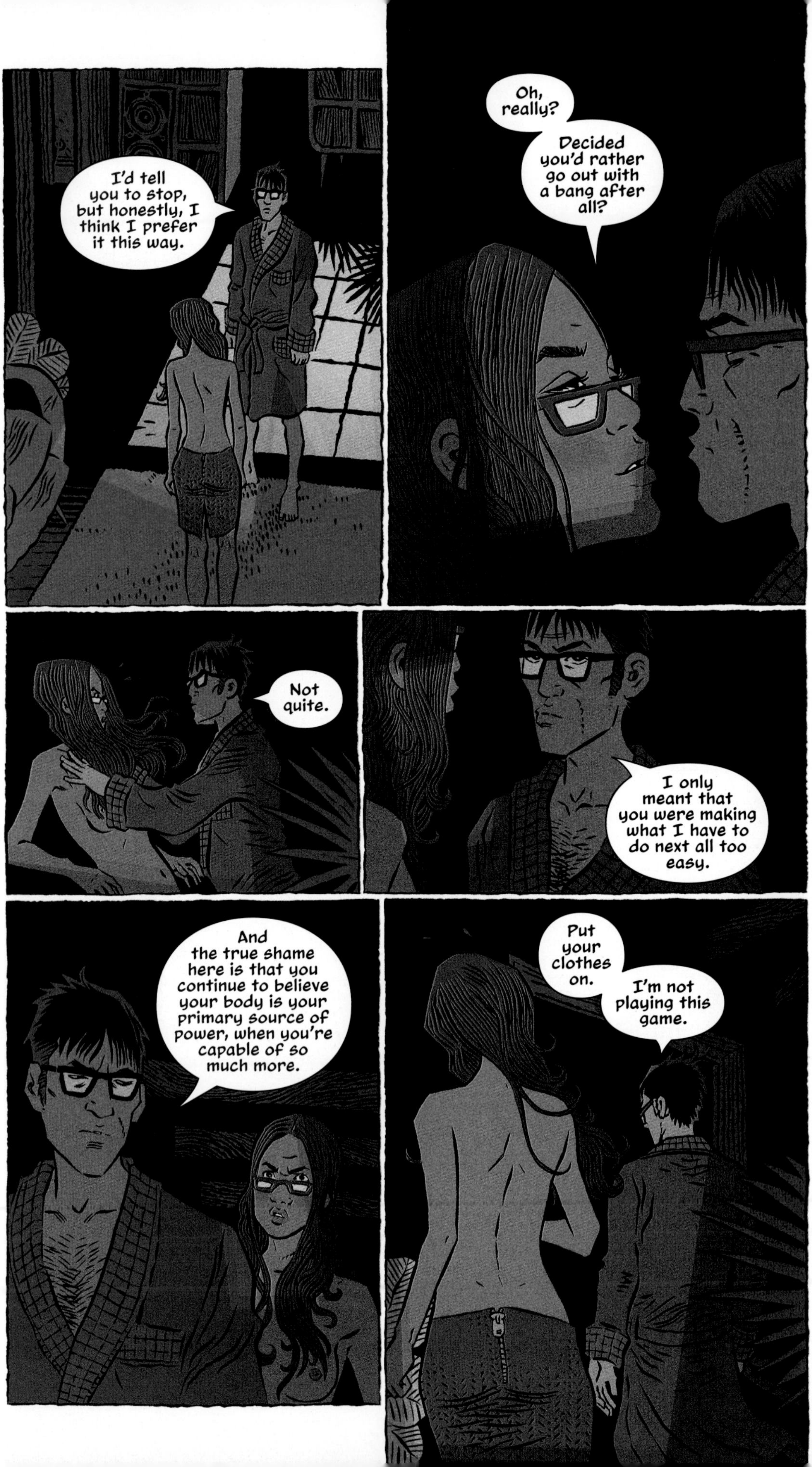
I'd tell you to stop, but honestly, I think I prefer it this way.
Oh, really?
Decided you'd rather go out with a bang after all?
Not quite.
I only meant that you were making what I have to do next all too easy.
And the true shame here is that you continue to believe your body is your primary source of power, when you're capable of so much more.
Put your clothes on.
I'm not playing this game.

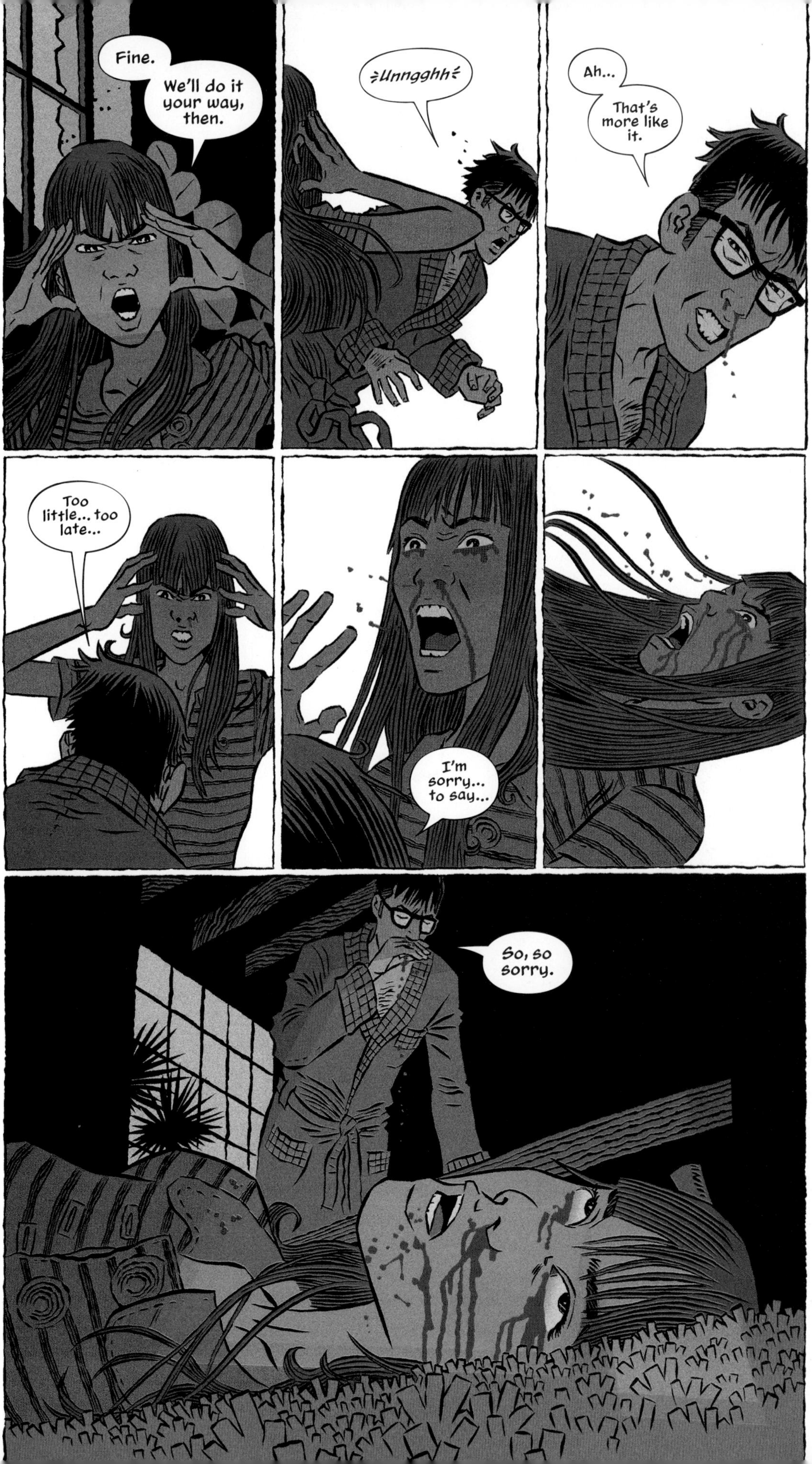

Fine.
We'll do it your way, then.
Unngghh
Ah...
That's more like it.
Too little... too late...
I'm sorry... to say...
So, so sorry.

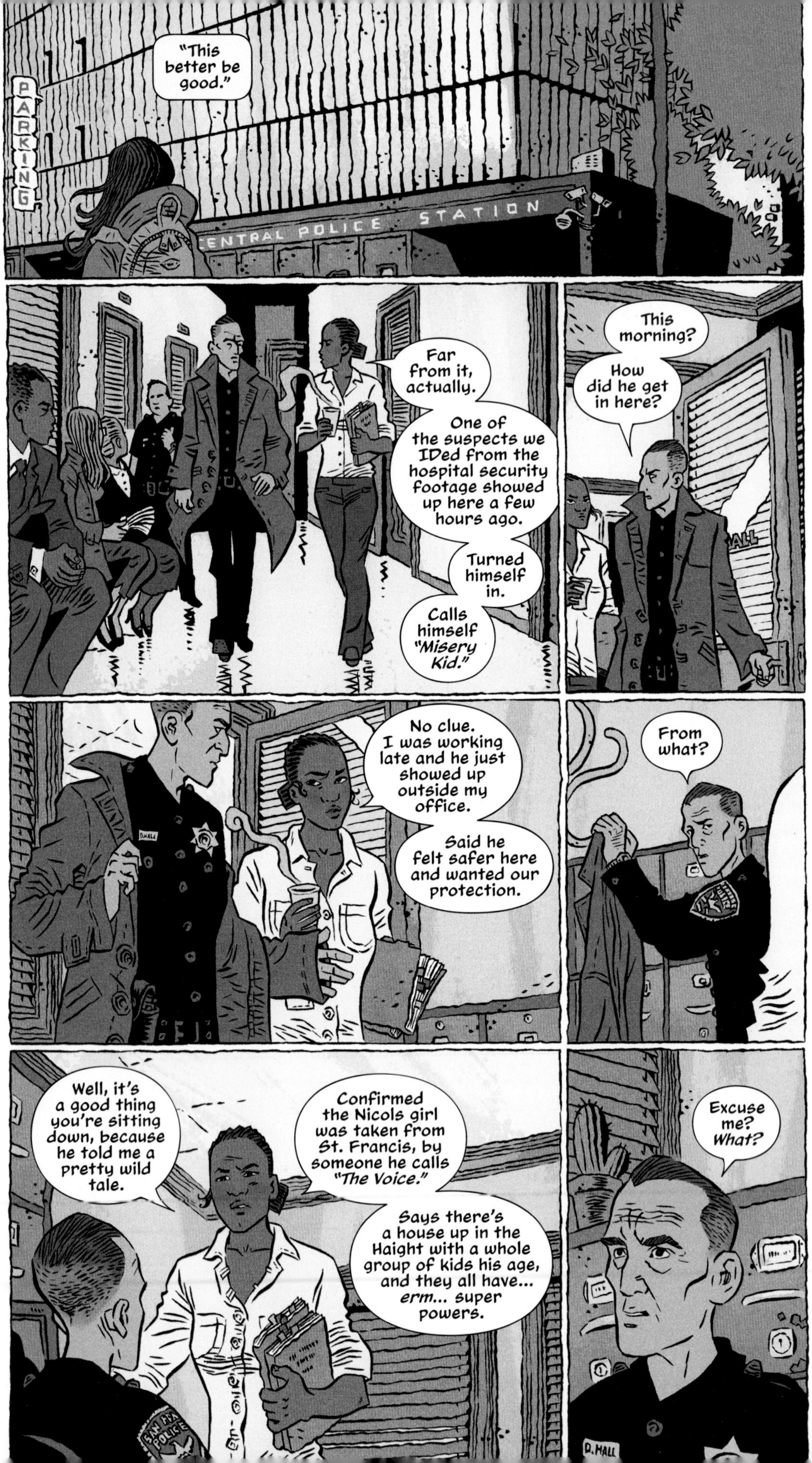
"This better be good."
PARKING
CENTRAL POLICE STATION
Far from it, actually.
One of the suspects we IDed from the hospital security footage showed up here a few hours ago.
Turned himself in.
Calls himself *"Misery Kid."*
This morning?
How did he get in here?
No clue. I was working late and he just showed up outside my office.
Said he felt safer here and wanted our protection.
From what?
Well, it's a good thing you're sitting down, because he told me a pretty wild tale.
Confirmed the Nicols girl was taken from St. Francis, by someone he calls *"The Voice."*
Says there's a house up in the Haight with a whole group of kids his age, and they all have... *erm*... super powers.
Excuse me? *What?*
D. HALL

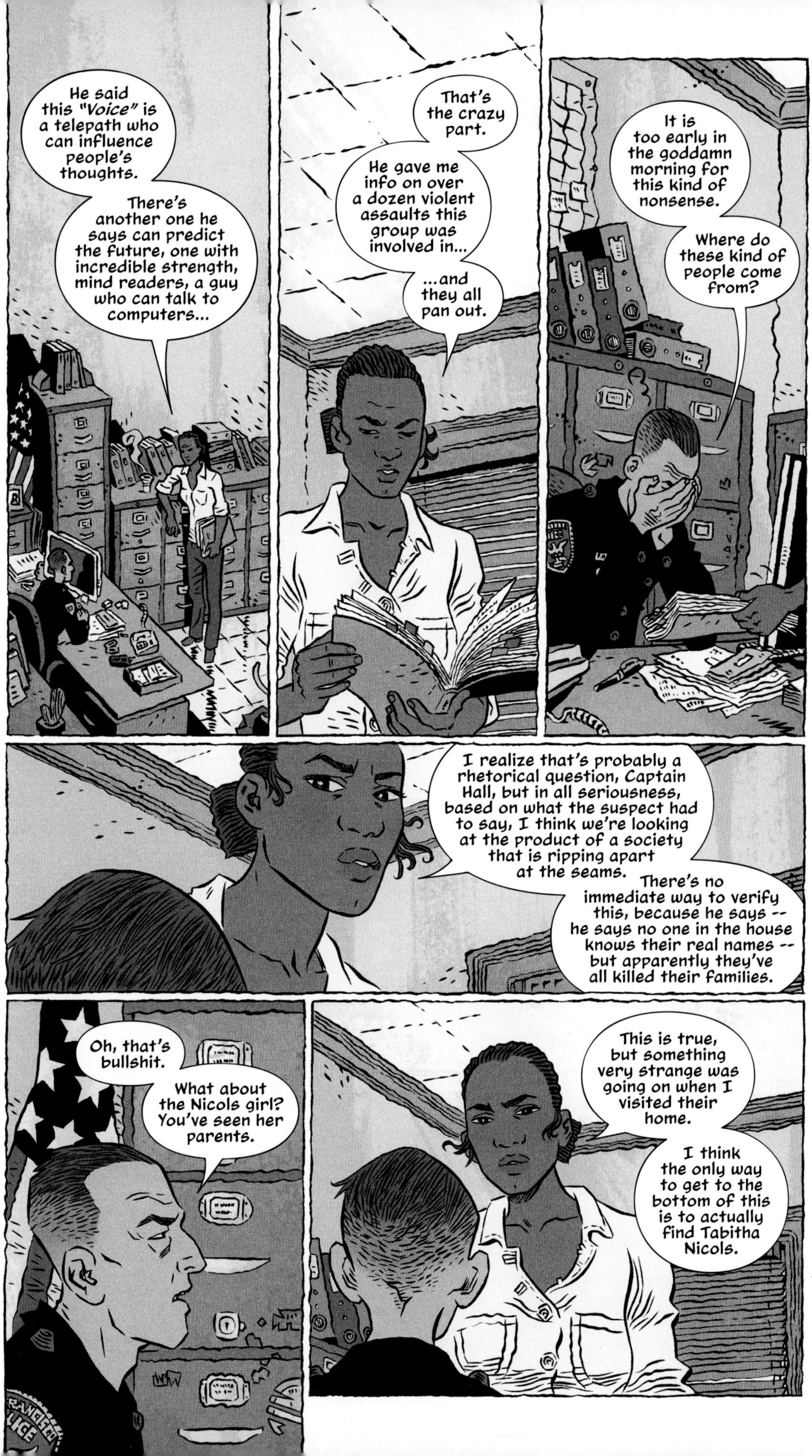

He said this "Voice" is a telepath who can influence people's thoughts.
There's another one he says can predict the future, one with incredible strength, mind readers, a guy who can talk to computers...
That's the crazy part.
He gave me info on over a dozen violent assaults this group was involved in...
...and they all pan out.
It is too early in the goddamn morning for this kind of nonsense.
Where do these kind of people come from?
I realize that's probably a rhetorical question, Captain Hall, but in all seriousness, based on what the suspect had to say, I think we're looking at the product of a society that is ripping apart at the seams.
There's no immediate way to verify this, because he says -- he says no one in the house knows their real names -- but apparently they've all killed their families.
Oh, that's bullshit.
What about the Nicols girl? You've seen her parents.
This is true, but something very strange was going on when I visited their home.
I think the only way to get to the bottom of this is to actually find Tabitha Nicols.

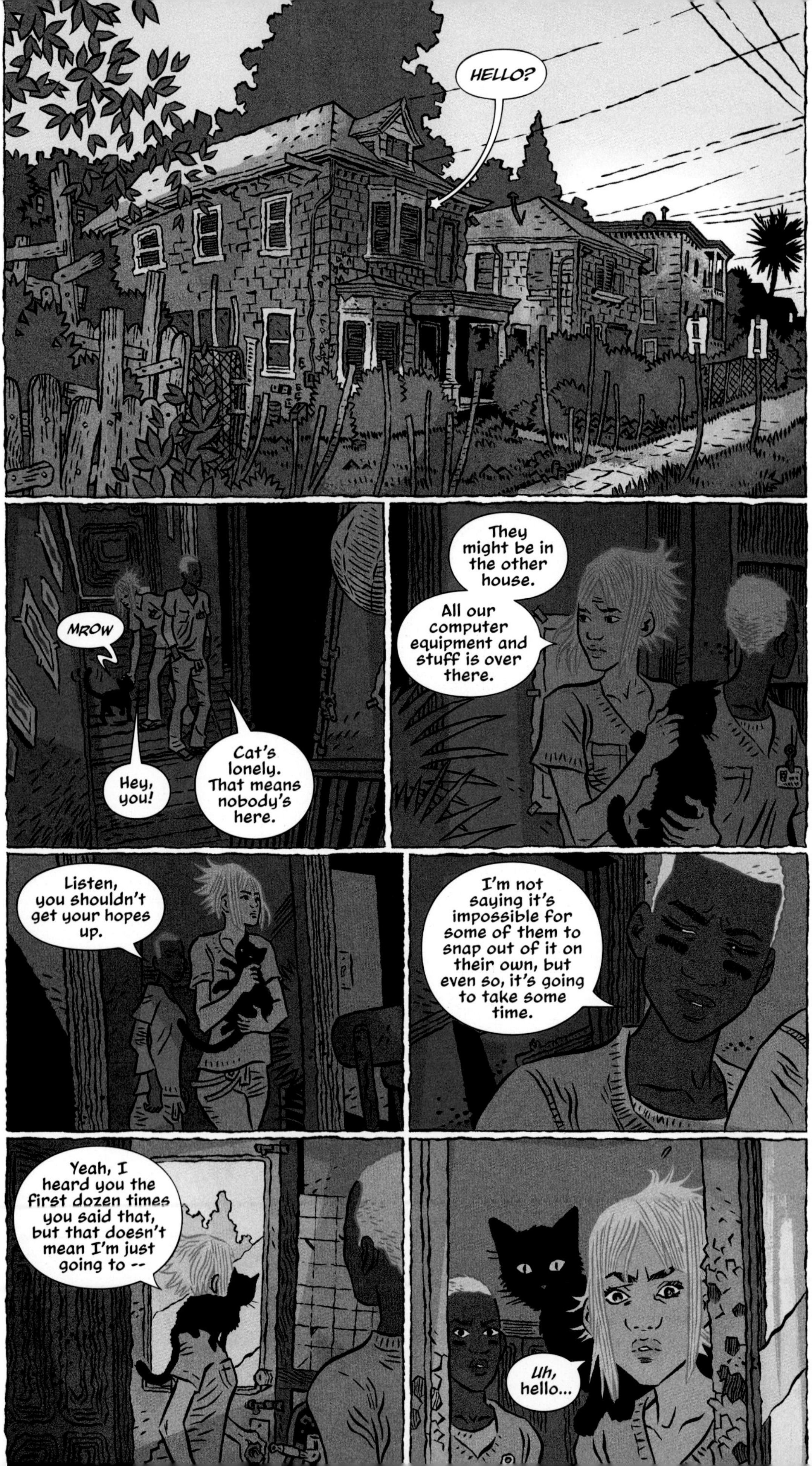
HELLO?
MROW
Hey, you!
Cat's lonely. That means nobody's here.
They might be in the other house.
All our computer equipment and stuff is over there.
Listen, you shouldn't get your hopes up.
I'm not saying it's impossible for some of them to snap out of it on their own, but even so, it's going to take some time.
Yeah, I heard you the first dozen times you said that, but that doesn't mean I'm just going to --
Uh, hello...

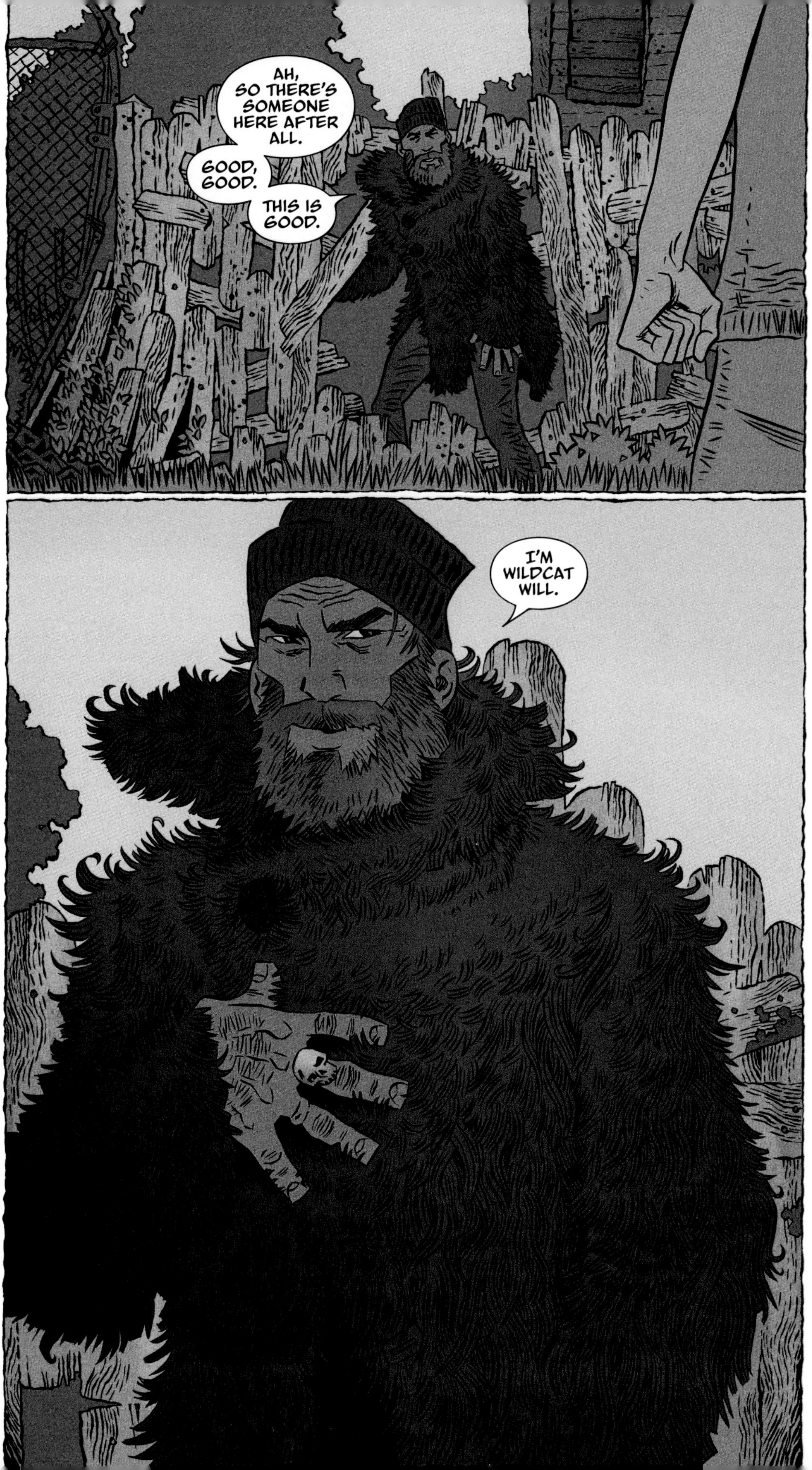
AH, SO THERE'S SOMEONE HERE AFTER ALL.
GOOD, GOOD.
THIS IS GOOD.
I'M WILDCAT WILL.

HATRED AND
FAILURE GO
PERFECTLY
TOGETHER,
LIKE THE
QUICK AND
THE SAND,
BEAUTIFUL
AND DAMNED.

NICK JONES

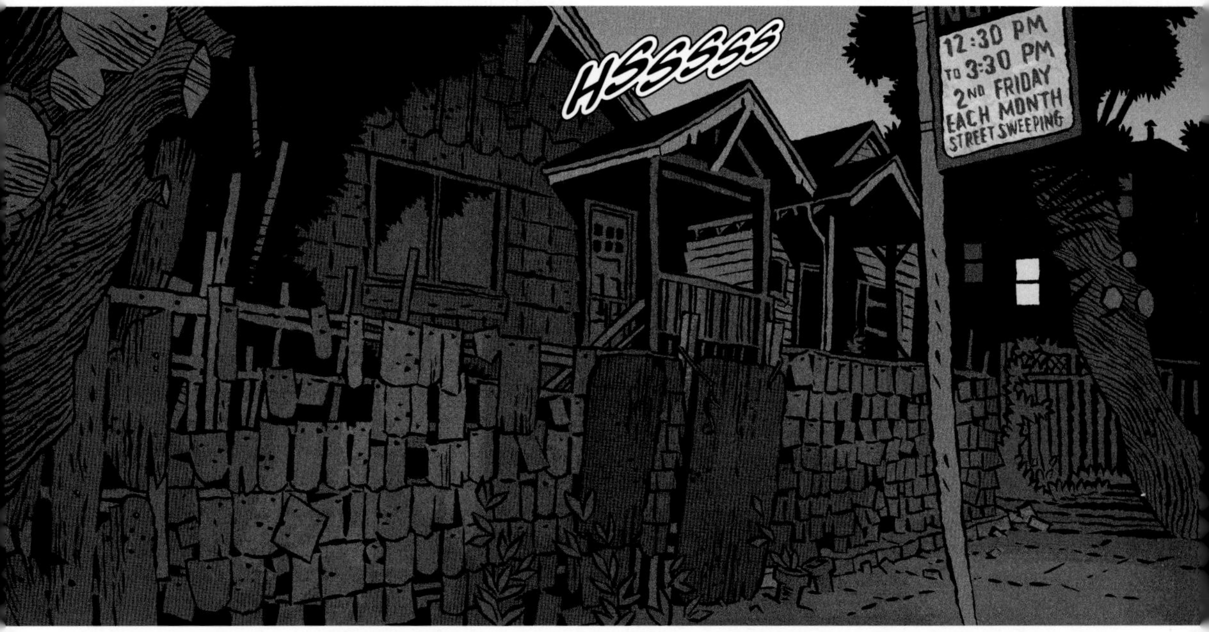
HSSSSS
12:30 PM
TO 3:30 PM
2ND FRIDAY
EACH MONTH
STREET SWEEPING

12: WHERE ARE WE NOW?

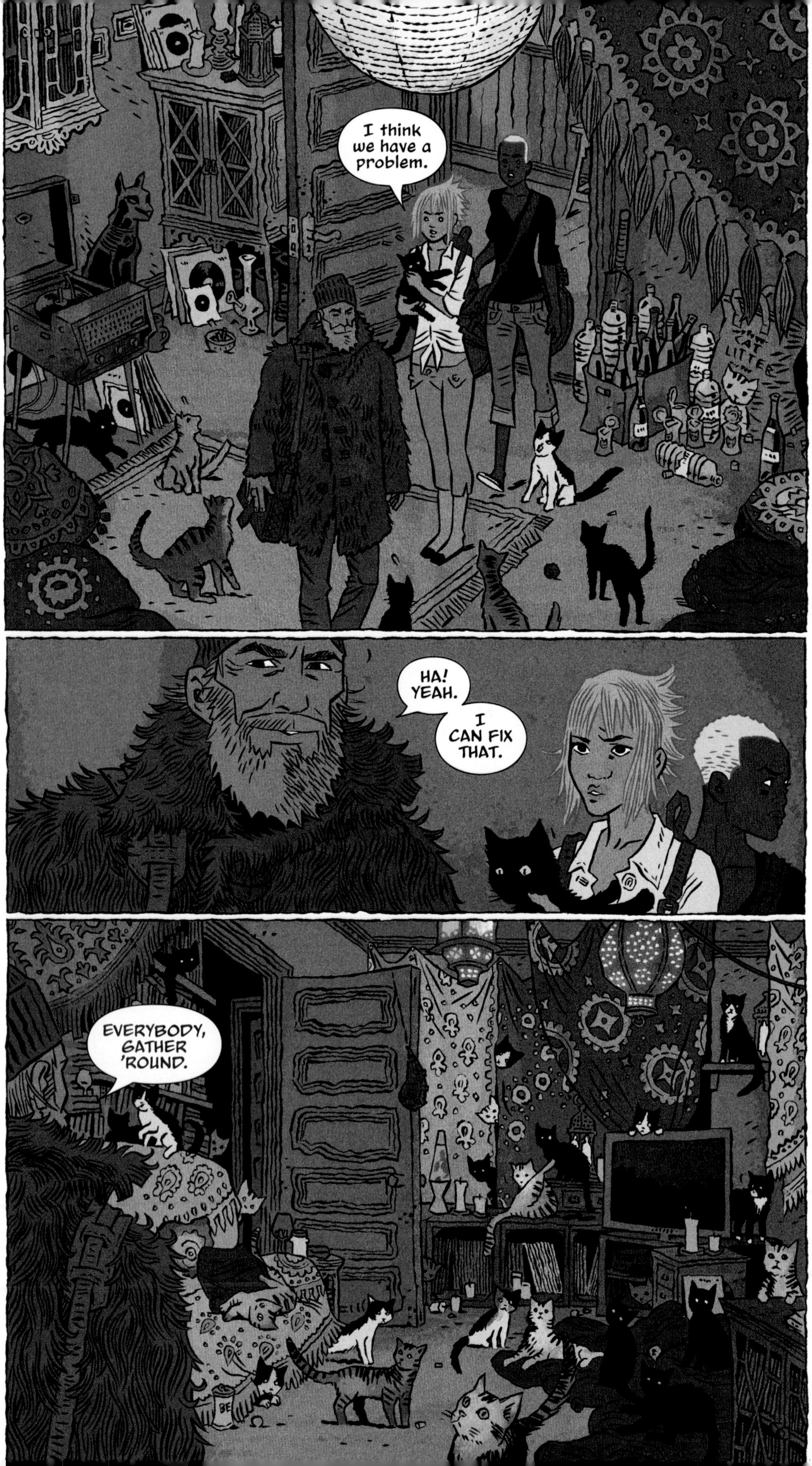
I think we have a problem.
HA! YEAH.
I CAN FIX THAT.
EVERYBODY, GATHER 'ROUND.

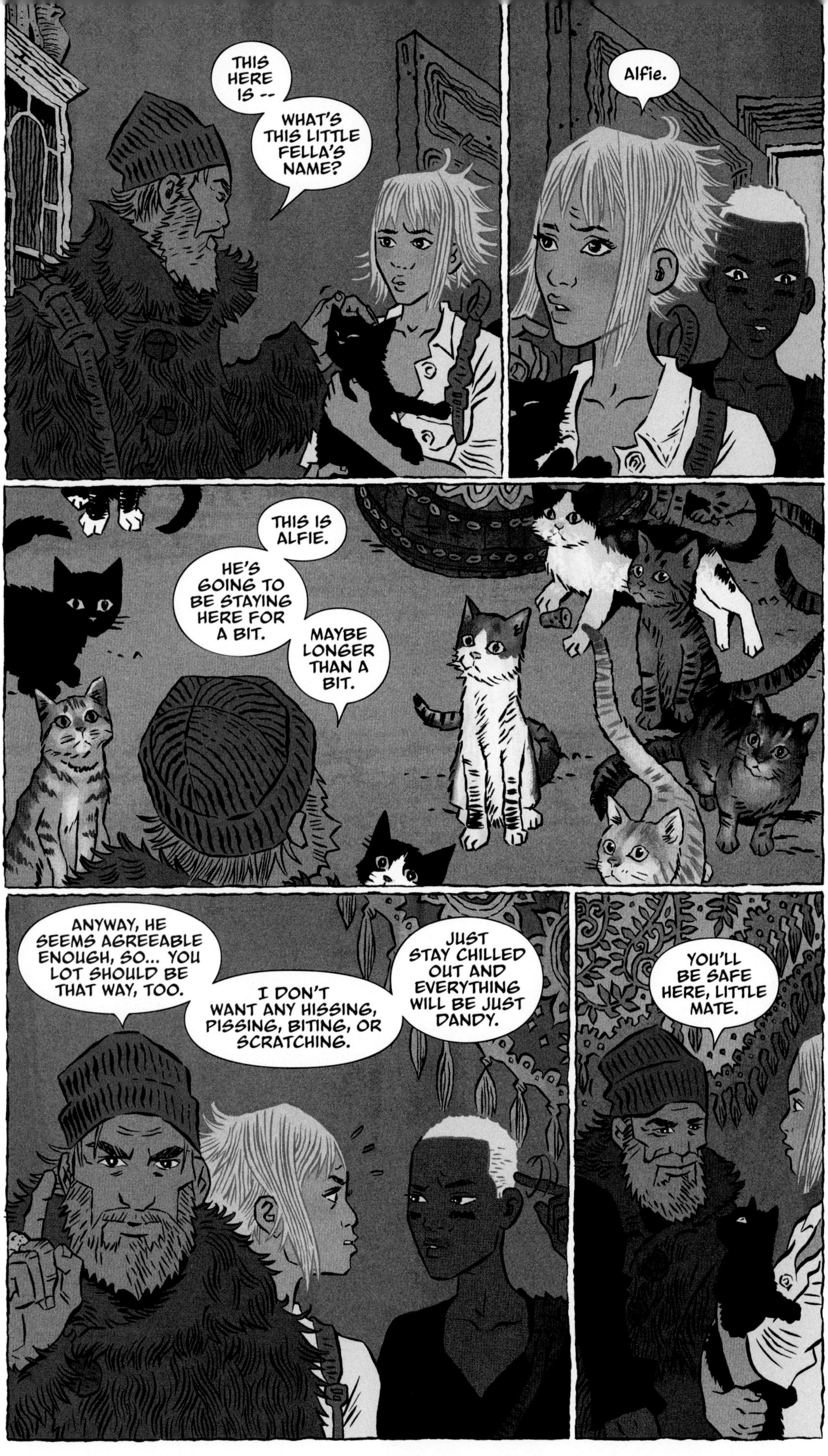
THIS HERE IS --
WHAT'S THIS LITTLE FELLA'S NAME?
Alfie.
THIS IS ALFIE.
HE'S GOING TO BE STAYING HERE FOR A BIT.
MAYBE LONGER THAN A BIT.
ANYWAY, HE SEEMS AGREEABLE ENOUGH, SO... YOU LOT SHOULD BE THAT WAY, TOO.
I DON'T WANT ANY HISSING, PISSING, BITING, OR SCRATCHING.
JUST STAY CHILLED OUT AND EVERYTHING WILL BE JUST DANDY.
YOU'LL BE SAFE HERE, LITTLE MATE.

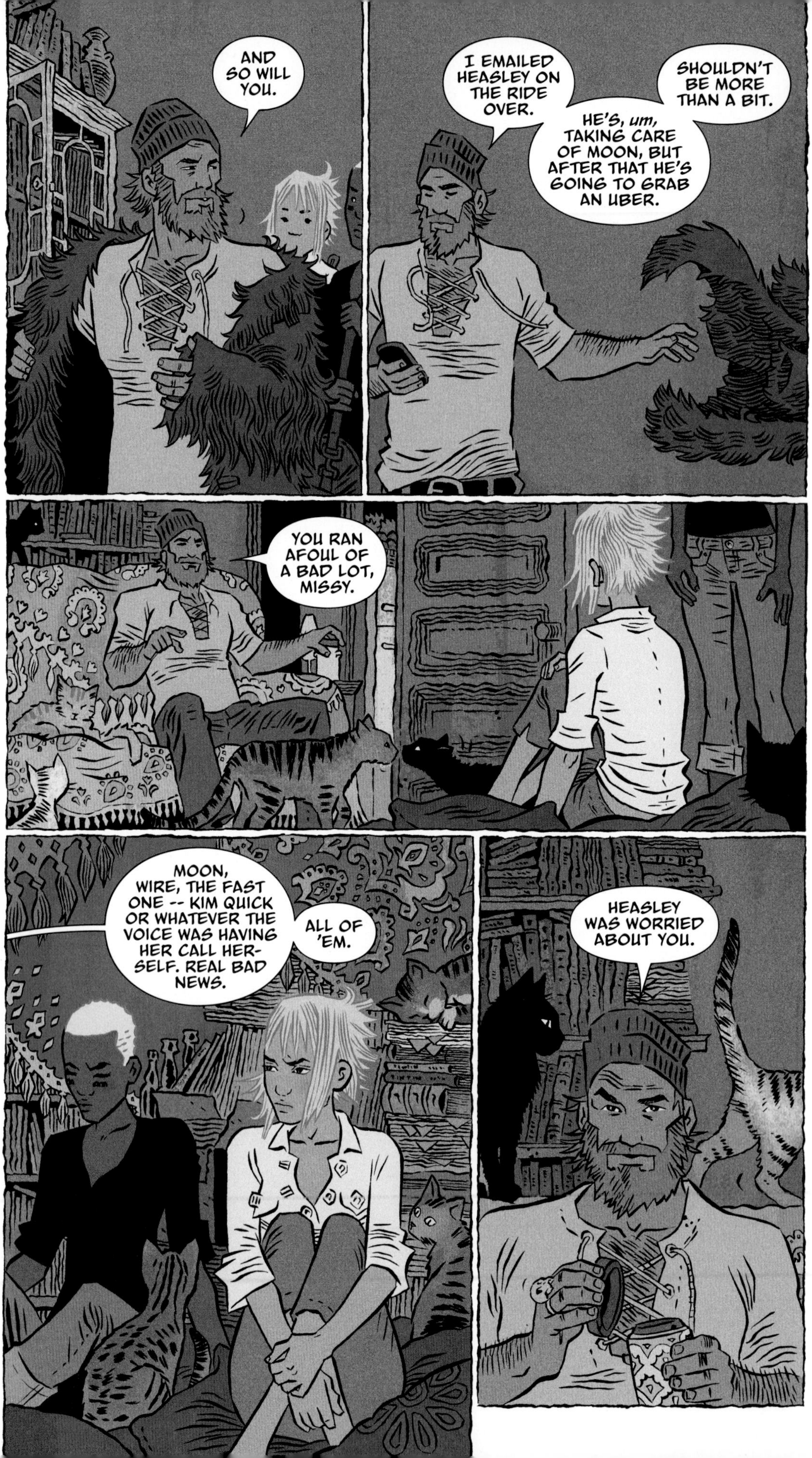
AND SO WILL YOU.
I EMAILED HEASLEY ON THE RIDE OVER.
HE'S, *um*, TAKING CARE OF MOON, BUT AFTER THAT HE'S GOING TO GRAB AN UBER.
SHOULDN'T BE MORE THAN A BIT.
YOU RAN AFOUL OF A BAD LOT, MISSY.
MOON, WIRE, THE FAST ONE -- KIM QUICK OR WHATEVER THE VOICE WAS HAVING HER CALL HER-SELF. REAL BAD NEWS.
ALL OF 'EM.
HEASLEY WAS WORRIED ABOUT YOU.

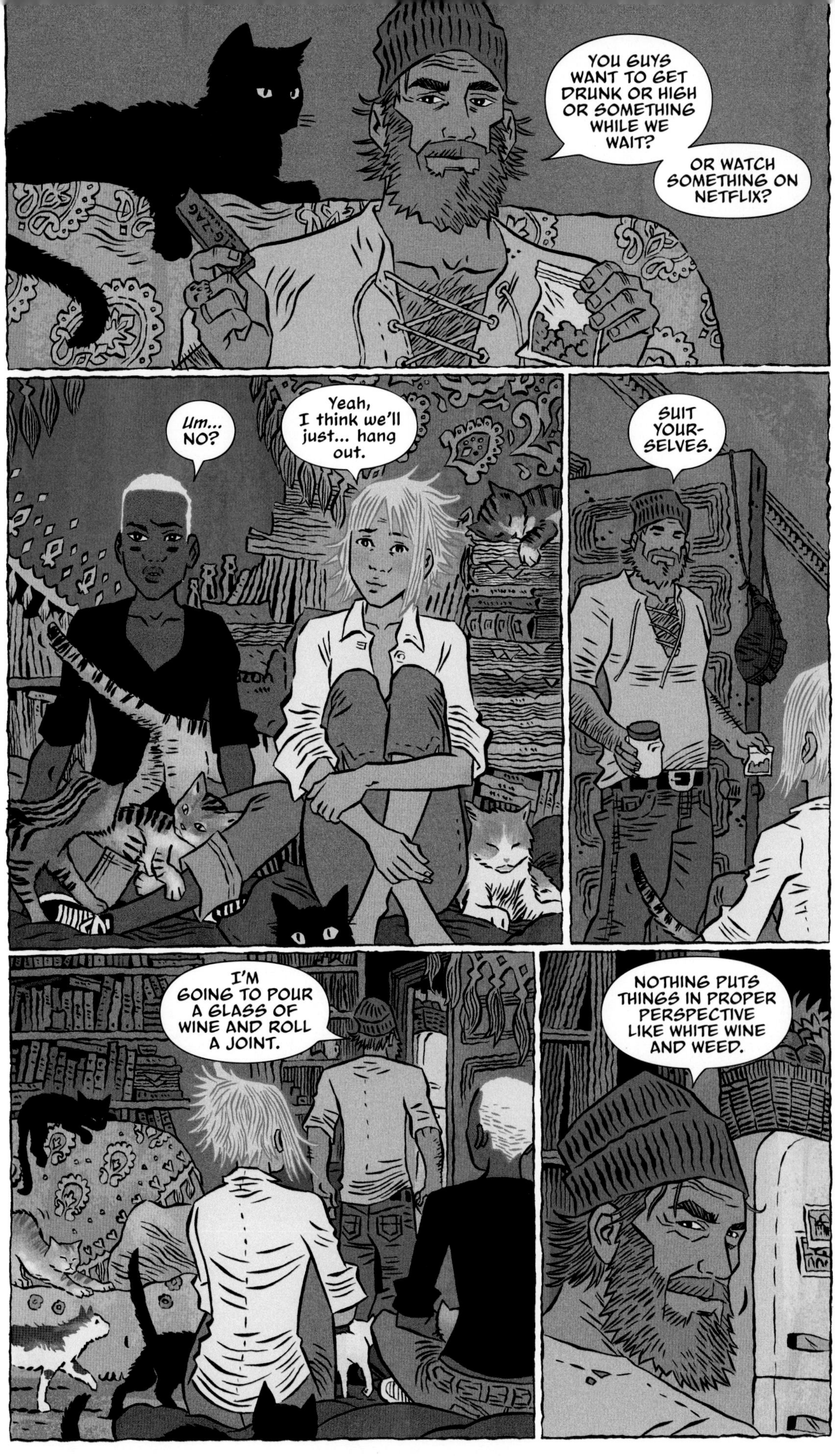
YOU GUYS WANT TO GET DRUNK OR HIGH OR SOMETHING WHILE WE WAIT?
OR WATCH SOMETHING ON NETFLIX?
Um... NO?
Yeah, I think we'll just... hang out.
SUIT YOUR-SELVES.
I'M GOING TO POUR A GLASS OF WINE AND ROLL A JOINT.
NOTHING PUTS THINGS IN PROPER PERSPECTIVE LIKE WHITE WINE AND WEED.

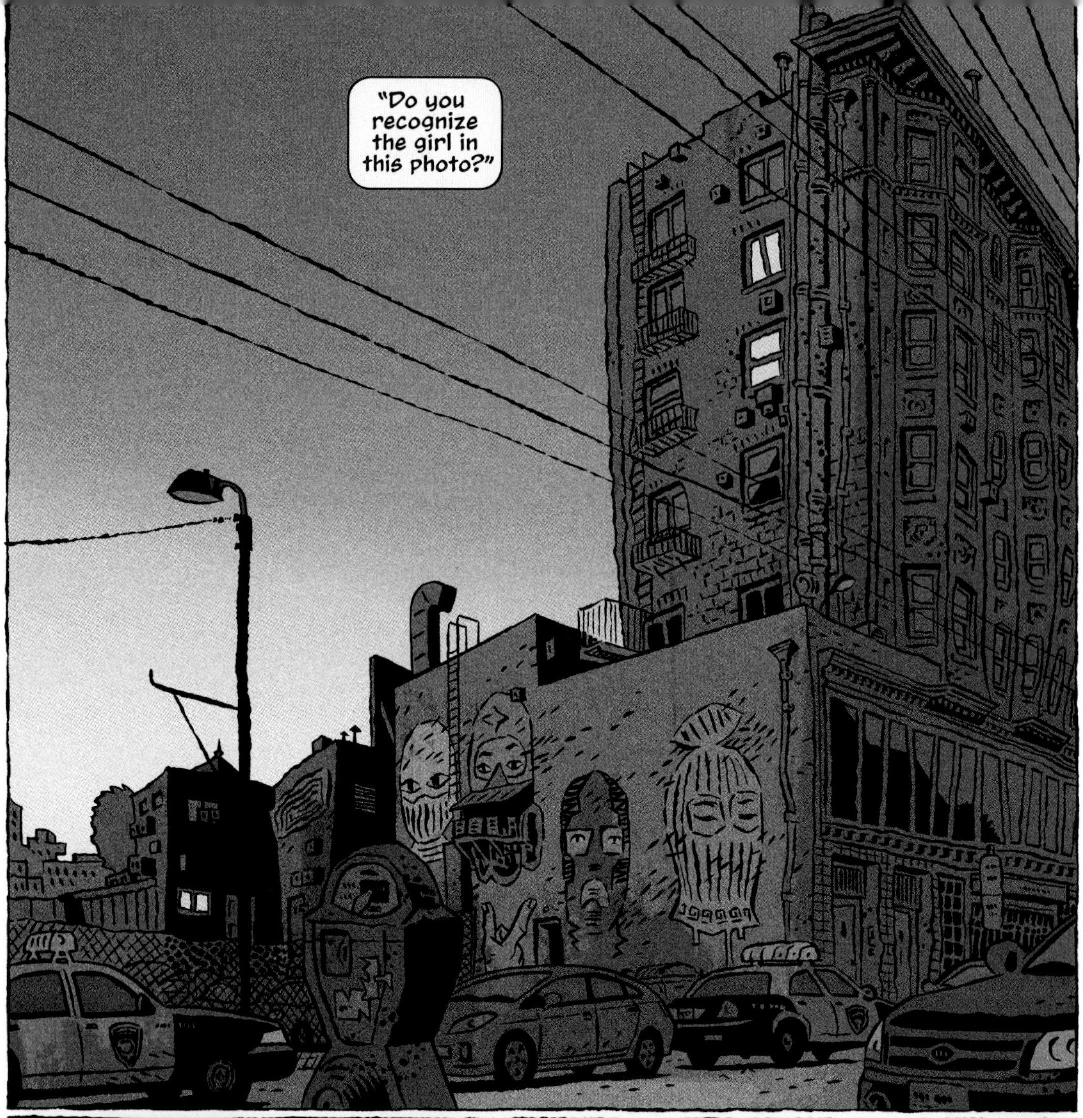
"Do you recognize the girl in this photo?"

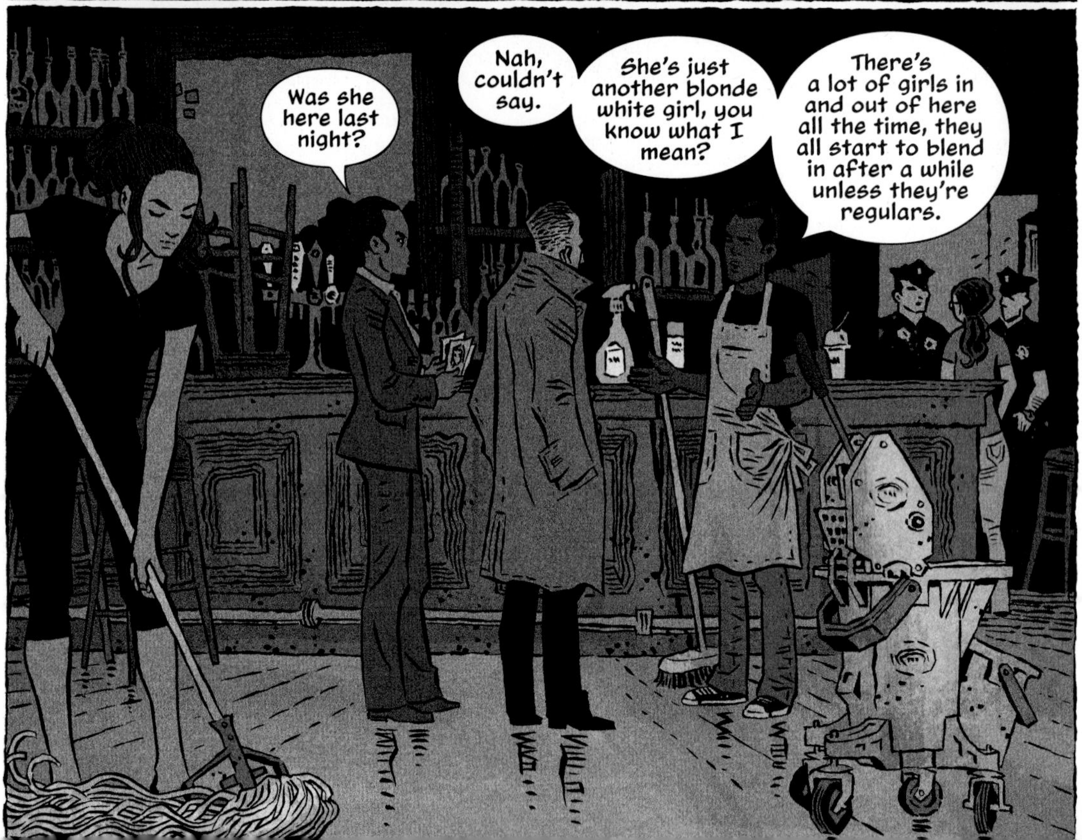
Was she here last night?
Nah, couldn't say.
She's just another blonde white girl, you know what I mean?
There's a lot of girls in and out of here all the time, they all start to blend in after a while unless they're regulars.

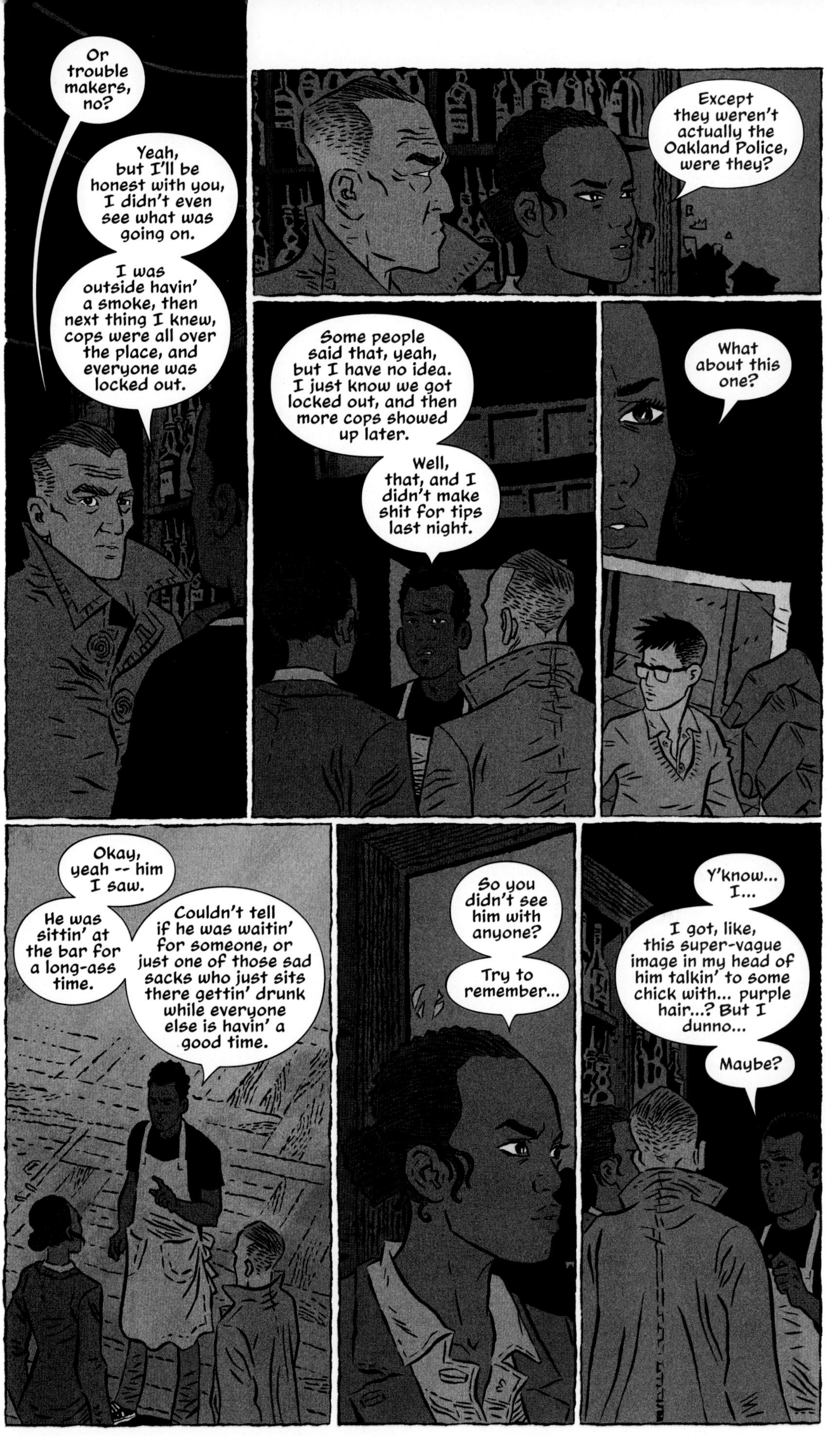
Or trouble makers, no?
Yeah, but I'll be honest with you, I didn't even see what was going on.
I was outside havin' a smoke, then next thing I knew, cops were all over the place, and everyone was locked out.
Except they weren't actually the Oakland Police, were they?
Some people said that, yeah, but I have no idea. I just know we got locked out, and then more cops showed up later.
Well, that, and I didn't make shit for tips last night.
What about this one?
Okay, yeah -- him I saw.
He was sittin' at the bar for a long-ass time.
Couldn't tell if he was waitin' for someone, or just one of those sad sacks who just sits there gettin' drunk while everyone else is havin' a good time.
So you didn't see him with anyone?
Try to remember...
Y'know... I...
I got, like, this super-vague image in my head of him talkin' to some chick with... purple hair...? But I dunno...
Maybe?

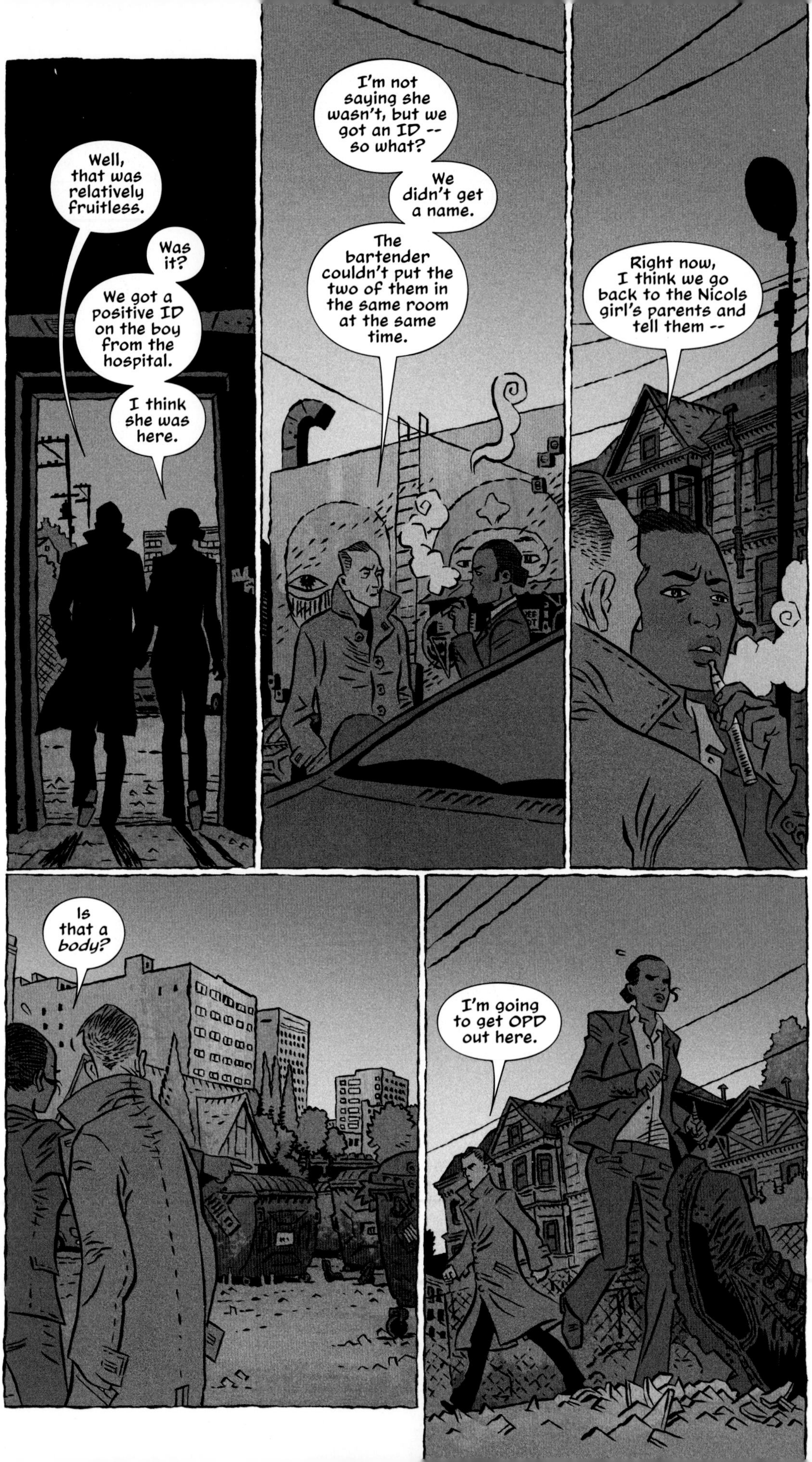
Well, that was relatively fruitless.
Was it?
We got a positive ID on the boy from the hospital.
I think she was here.
I'm not saying she wasn't, but we got an ID -- so what?
We didn't get a name.
The bartender couldn't put the two of them in the same room at the same time.
Right now, I think we go back to the Nicols girl's parents and tell them --
Is that a *body?*
I'm going to get OPD out here.

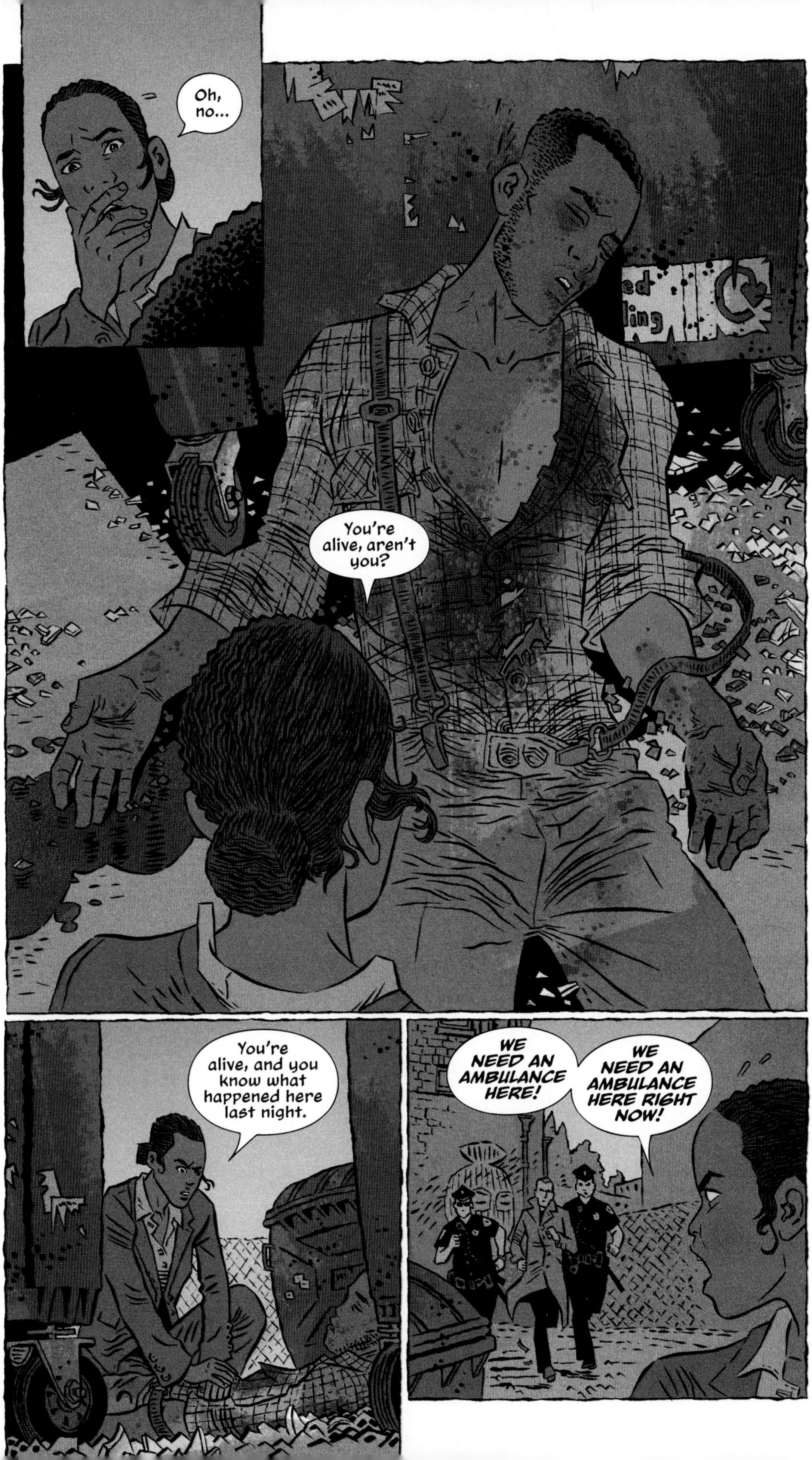
Oh, no...
You're alive, aren't you?
You're alive, and you know what happened here last night.
WE NEED AN AMBULANCE HERE!
WE NEED AN AMBULANCE HERE RIGHT NOW!

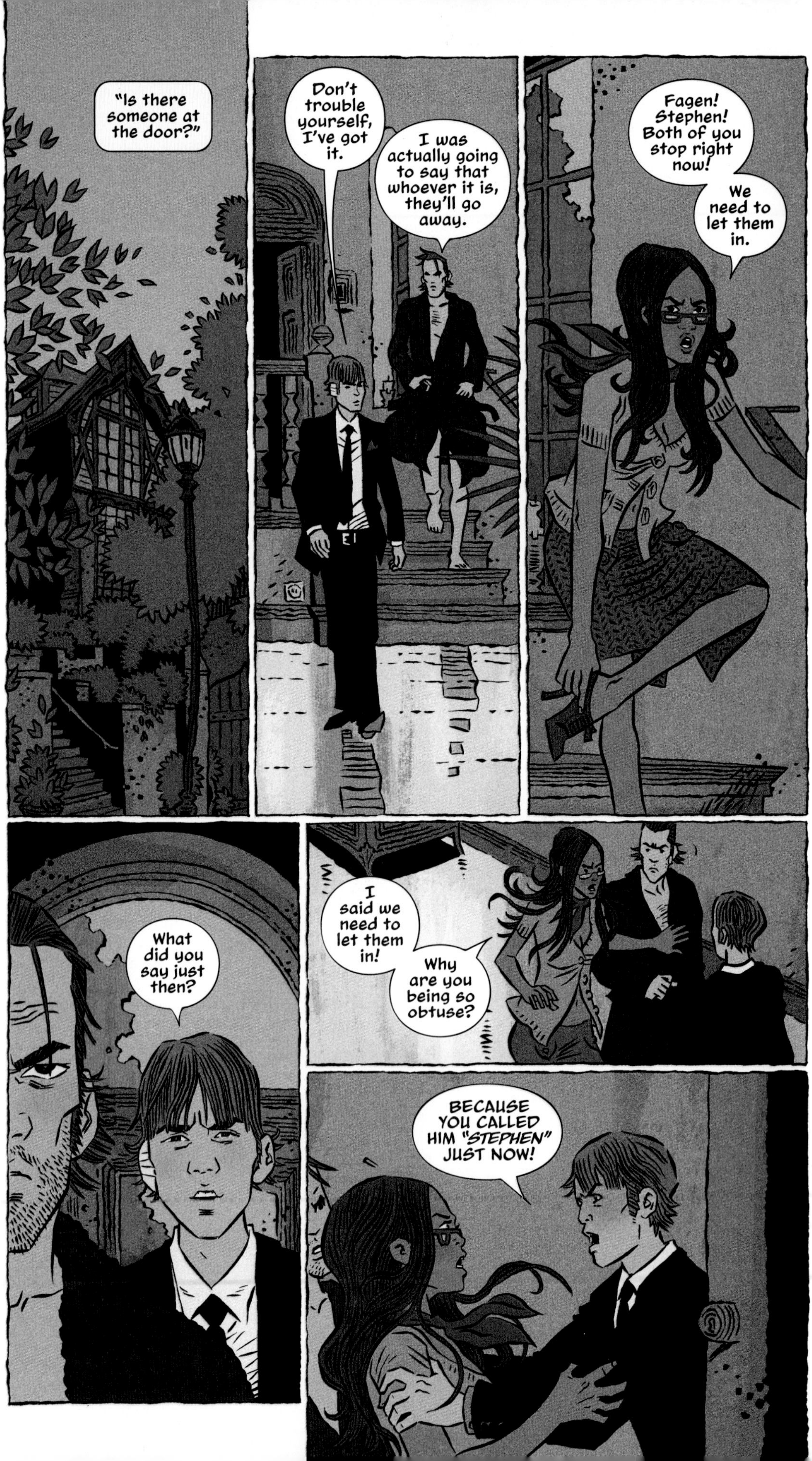
"Is there someone at the door?"
Don't trouble yourself, I've got it.
I was actually going to say that whoever it is, they'll go away.
Fagen! Stephen! Both of you stop right now!
We need to let them in.
What did you say just then?
I said we need to let them in!
Why are you being so obtuse?
BECAUSE YOU CALLED HIM "STEPHEN" JUST NOW!

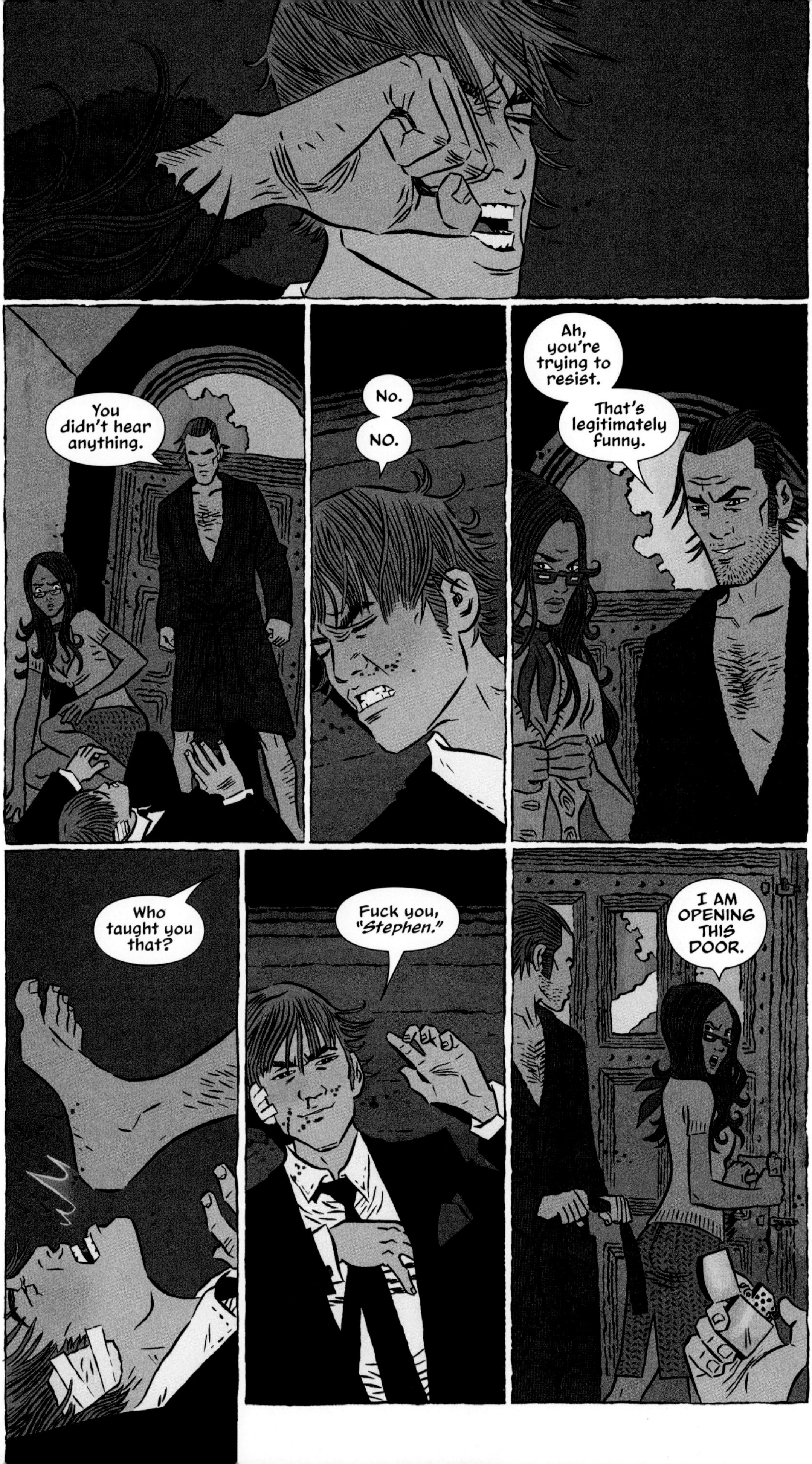
You didn't hear anything.
No.
NO.
Ah, you're trying to resist.
That's legitimately funny.
Who taught you that?
Fuck you, "Stephen."
I AM OPENING THIS DOOR.

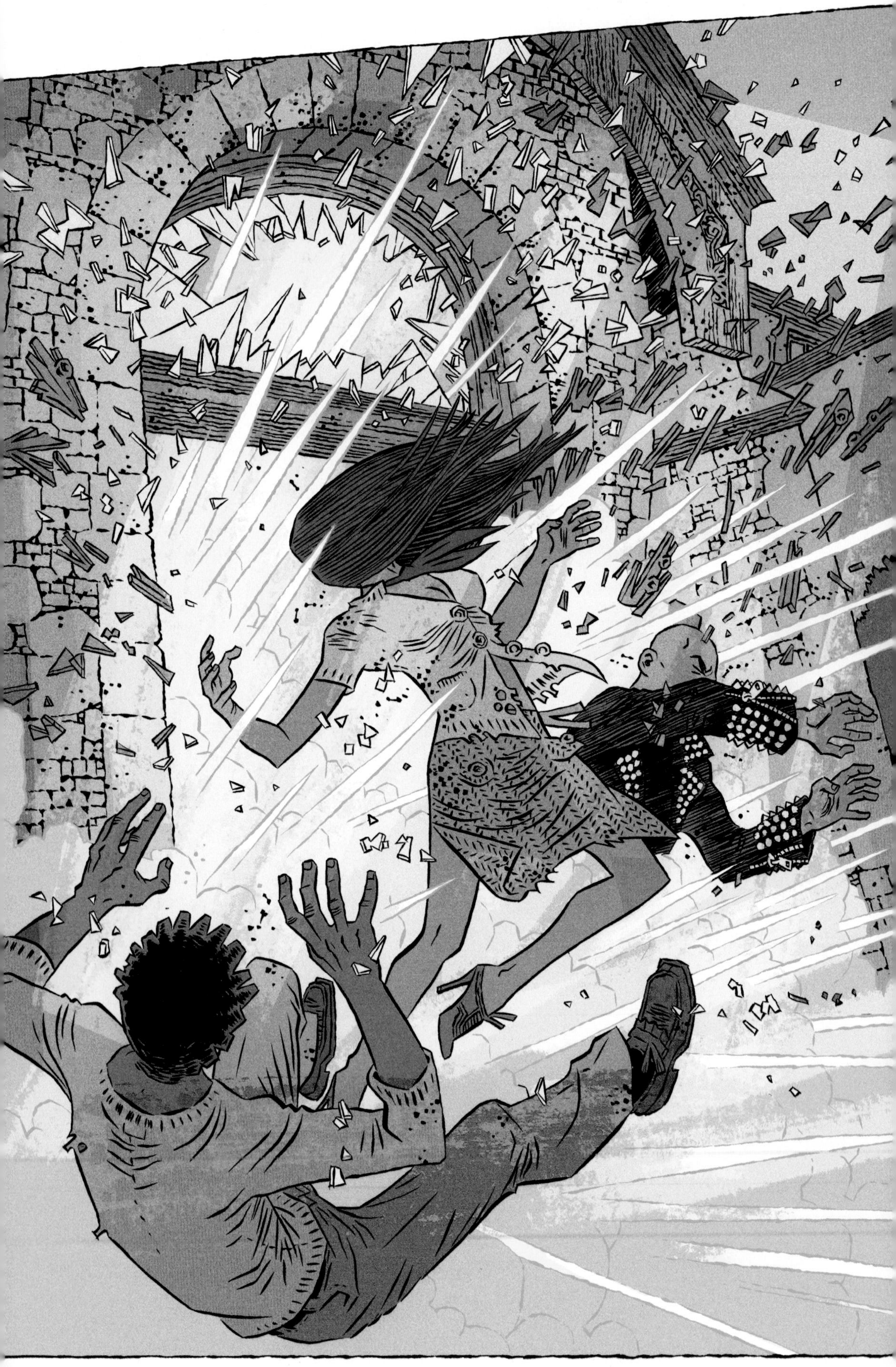

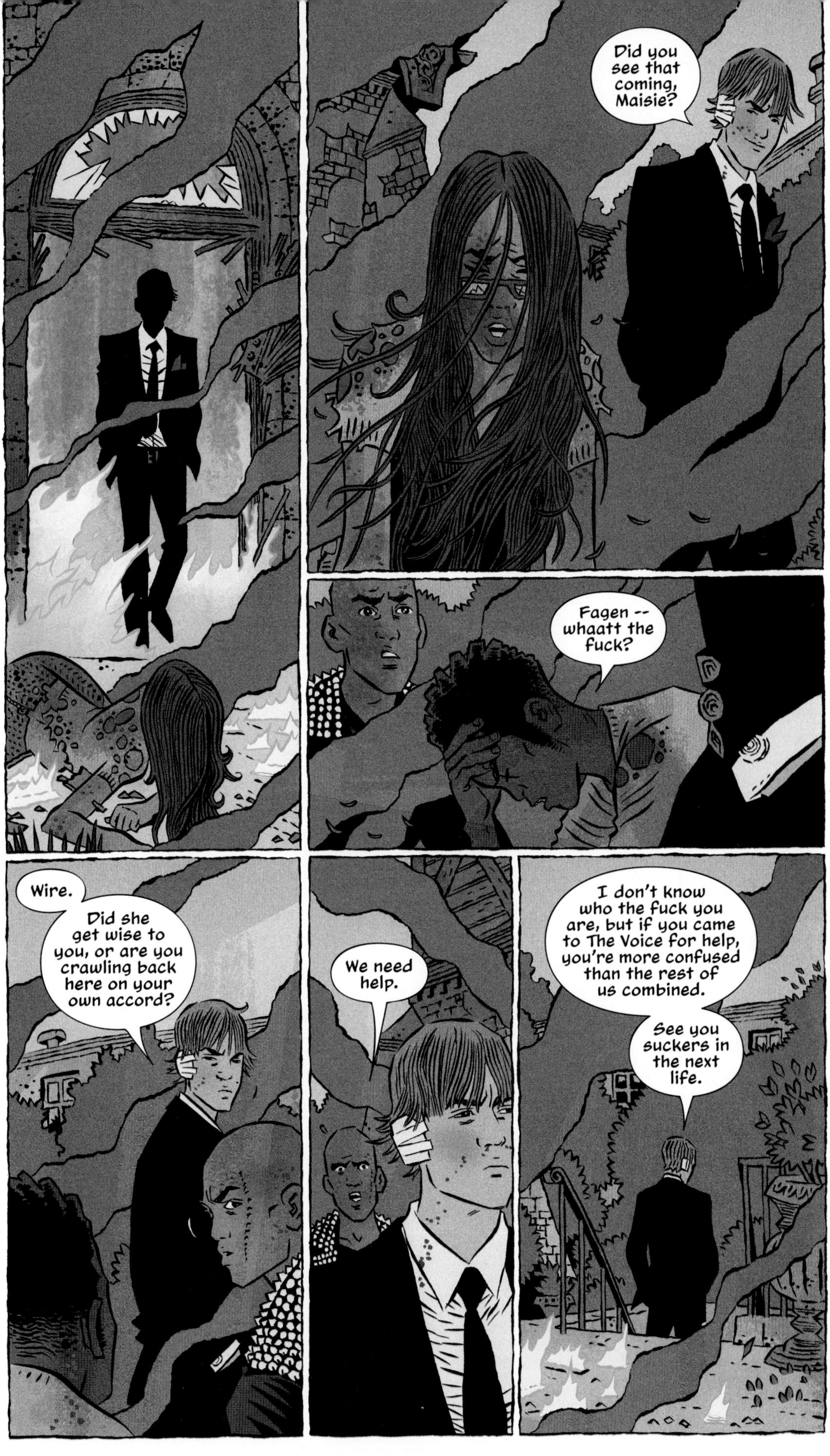
Did you see that coming, Maisie?
Fagen -- whaatt the fuck?
Wire.
Did she get wise to you, or are you crawling back here on your own accord?
We need help.
I don't know who the fuck you are, but if you came to The Voice for help, you're more confused than the rest of us combined.
See you suckers in the next life.

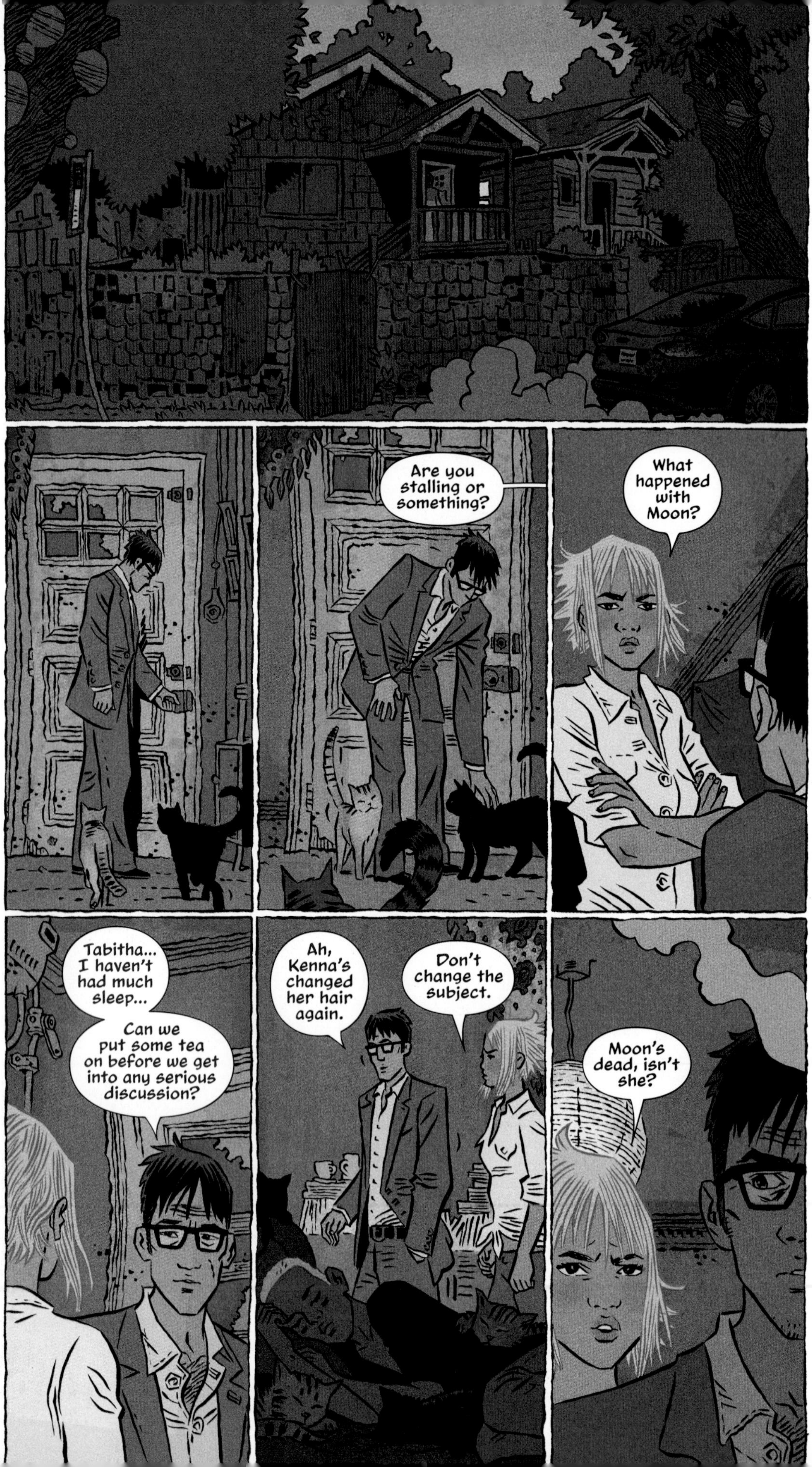
Are you stalling or something?
What happened with Moon?
Tabitha... I haven't had much sleep...
Can we put some tea on before we get into any serious discussion?
Ah, Kenna's changed her hair again.
Don't change the subject.
Moon's dead, isn't she?

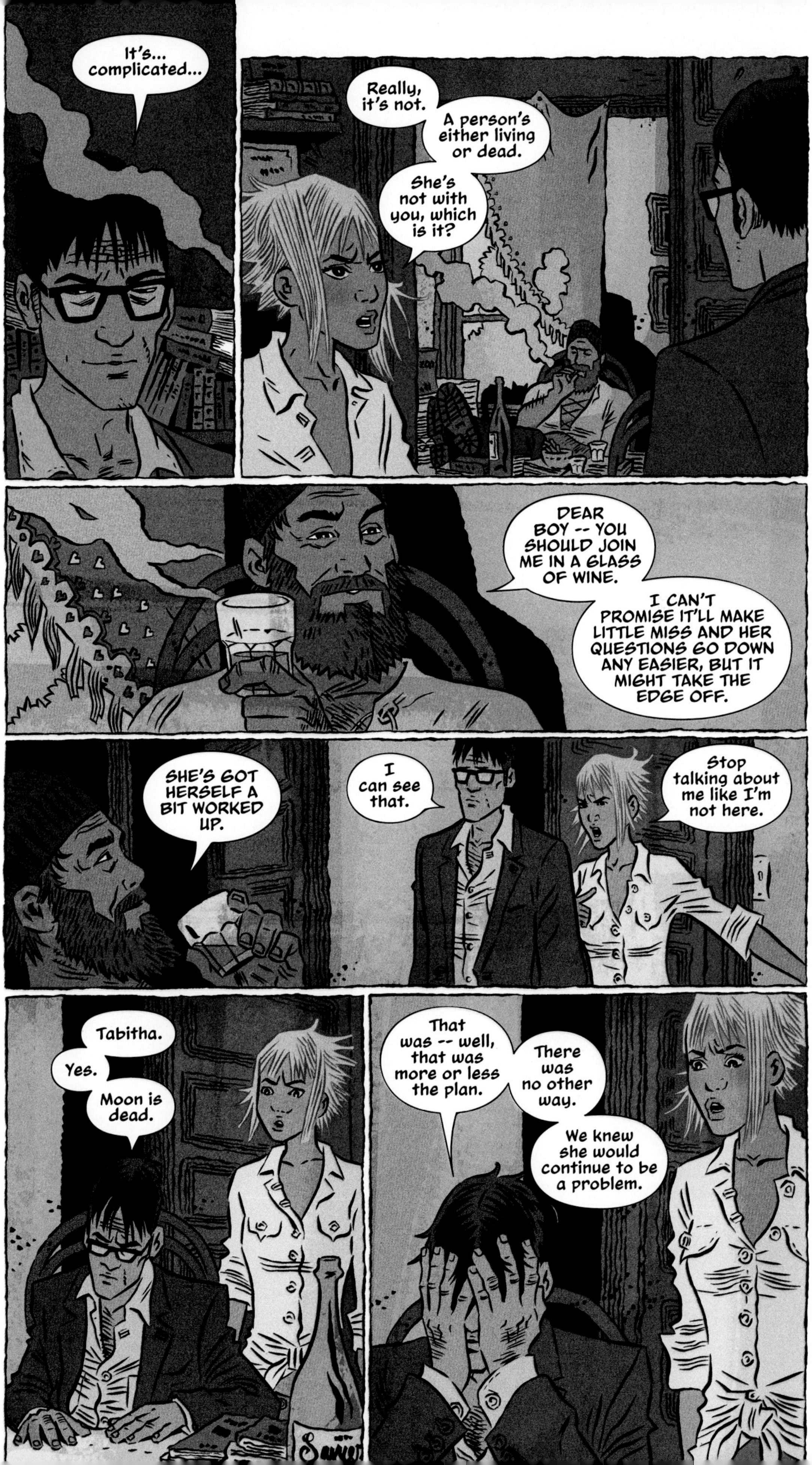

It's... complicated...
Really, it's not.
A person's either living or dead.
She's not with you, which is it?
DEAR BOY -- YOU SHOULD JOIN ME IN A GLASS OF WINE.
I CAN'T PROMISE IT'LL MAKE LITTLE MISS AND HER QUESTIONS GO DOWN ANY EASIER, BUT IT MIGHT TAKE THE EDGE OFF.
SHE'S GOT HERSELF A BIT WORKED UP.
I can see that.
Stop talking about me like I'm not here.
Tabitha.
Yes.
Moon is dead.
That was -- well, that was more or less the plan.
There was no other way.
We knew she would continue to be a problem.

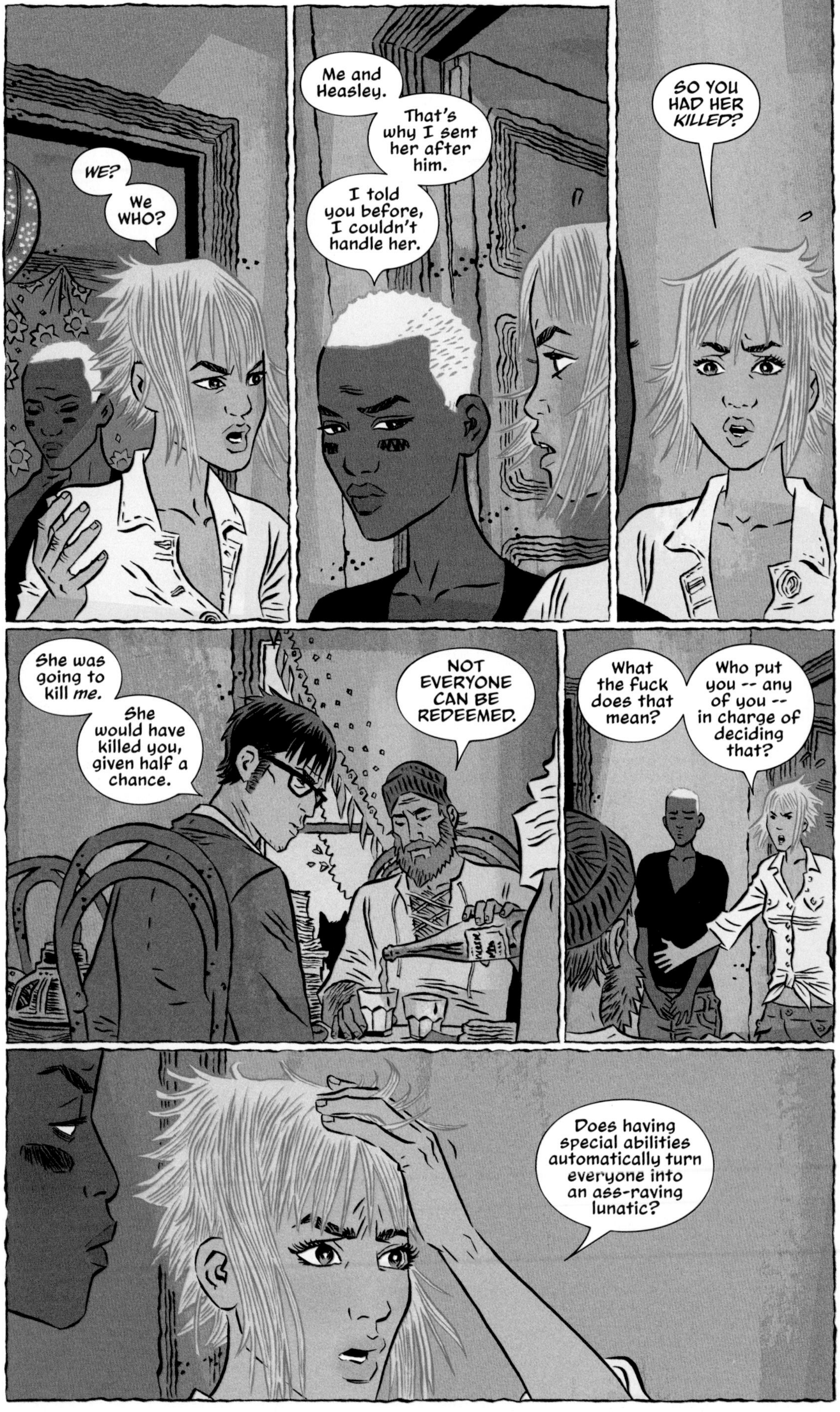
WE?
We WHO?
Me and Heasley.
That's why I sent her after him.
I told you before, I couldn't handle her.
SO YOU HAD HER KILLED?
She was going to kill *me.*
She would have killed you, given half a chance.
NOT EVERYONE CAN BE REDEEMED.
What the fuck does that mean?
Who put you -- any of you -- in charge of deciding that?
Does having special abilities automatically turn everyone into an ass-raving lunatic?

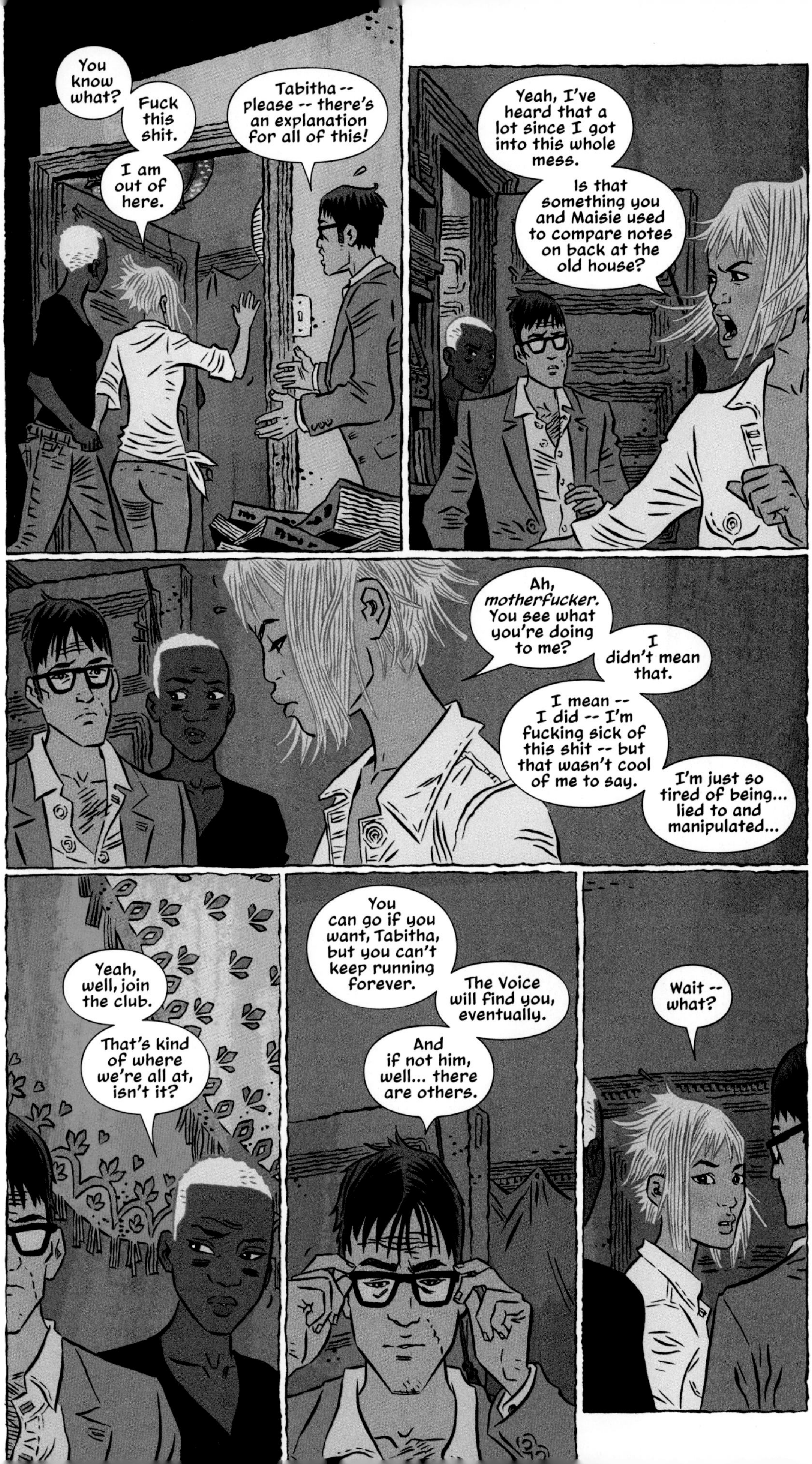
You know what?
Fuck this shit.
I am out of here.
Tabitha -- please -- there's an explanation for all of this!
Yeah, I've heard that a lot since I got into this whole mess.
Is that something you and Maisie used to compare notes on back at the old house?
Ah, *motherfucker.* You see what you're doing to me?
I didn't mean that.
I mean -- I did -- I'm fucking sick of this shit -- but that wasn't cool of me to say.
I'm just so tired of being... lied to and manipulated...
Yeah, well, join the club.
That's kind of where we're all at, isn't it?
You can go if you want, Tabitha, but you can't keep running forever.
The Voice will find you, eventually.
And if not him, well... there are others.
Wait -- what?

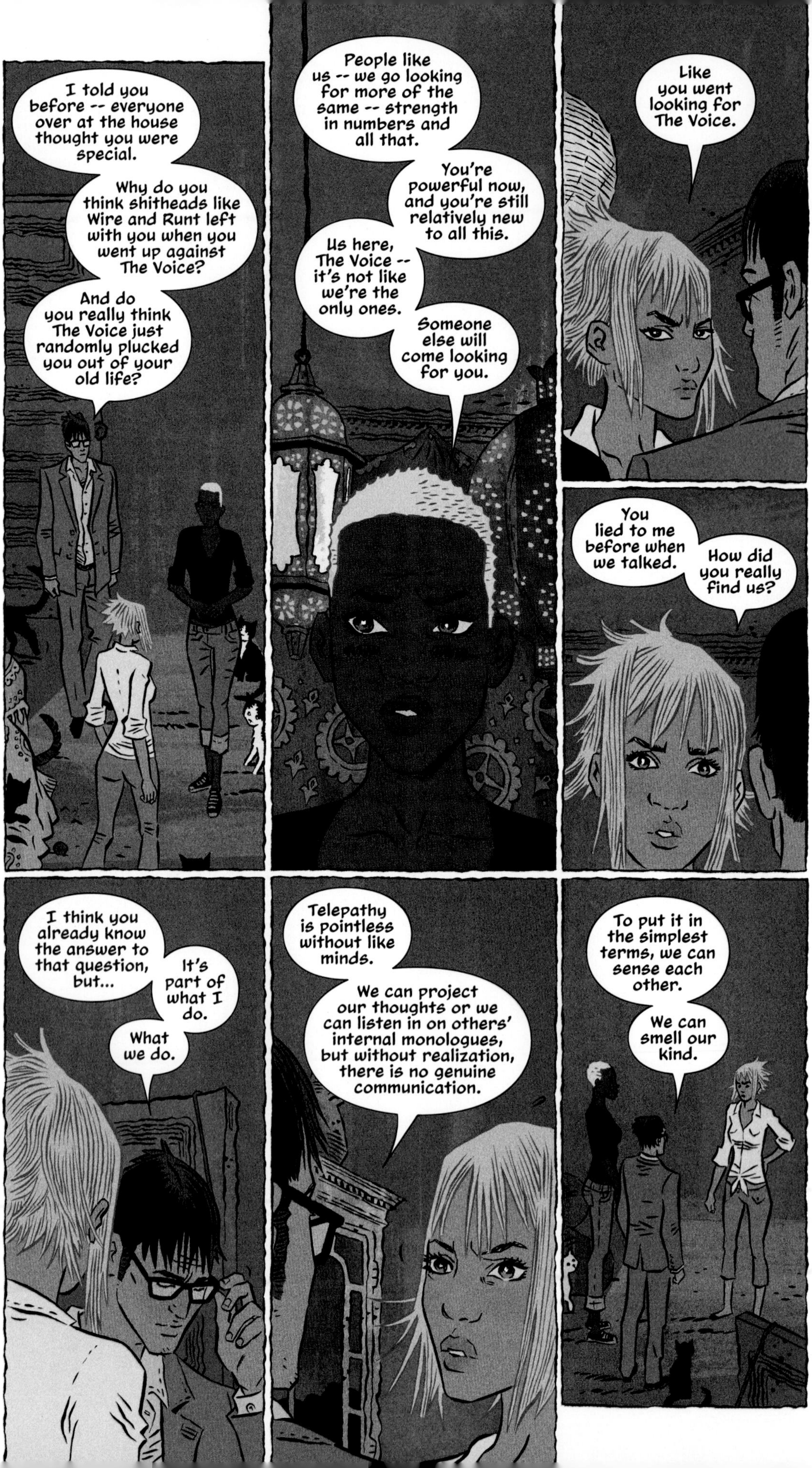
I told you before -- everyone over at the house thought you were special.
Why do you think shitheads like Wire and Runt left with you when you went up against The Voice?
And do you really think The Voice just randomly plucked you out of your old life?
People like us -- we go looking for more of the same -- strength in numbers and all that.
You're powerful now, and you're still relatively new to all this.
Us here, The Voice -- it's not like we're the only ones.
Someone else will come looking for you.
Like you went looking for The Voice.
You lied to me before when we talked.
How did you really find us?
I think you already know the answer to that question, but...
It's part of what I do.
What we do.
Telepathy is pointless without like minds.
We can project our thoughts or we can listen in on others' internal monologues, but without realization, there is no genuine communication.
To put it in the simplest terms, we can sense each other.
We can smell our kind.

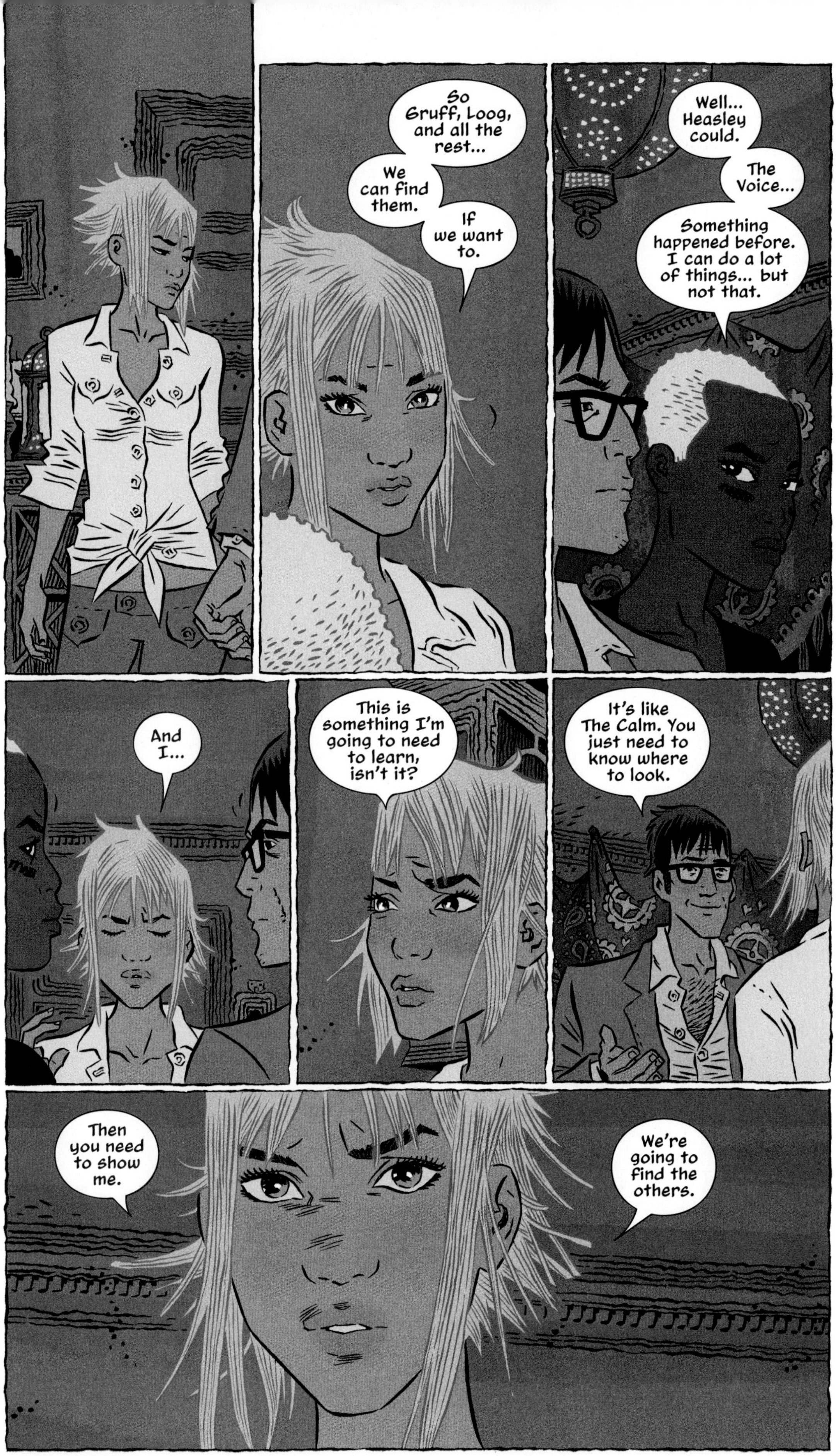
So Gruff, Loog, and all the rest...
We can find them.
If we want to.
Well... Heasley could.
The Voice...
Something happened before. I can do a lot of things... but not that.
And I...
This is something I'm going to need to learn, isn't it?
It's like The Calm. You just need to know where to look.
Then you need to show me.
We're going to find the others.

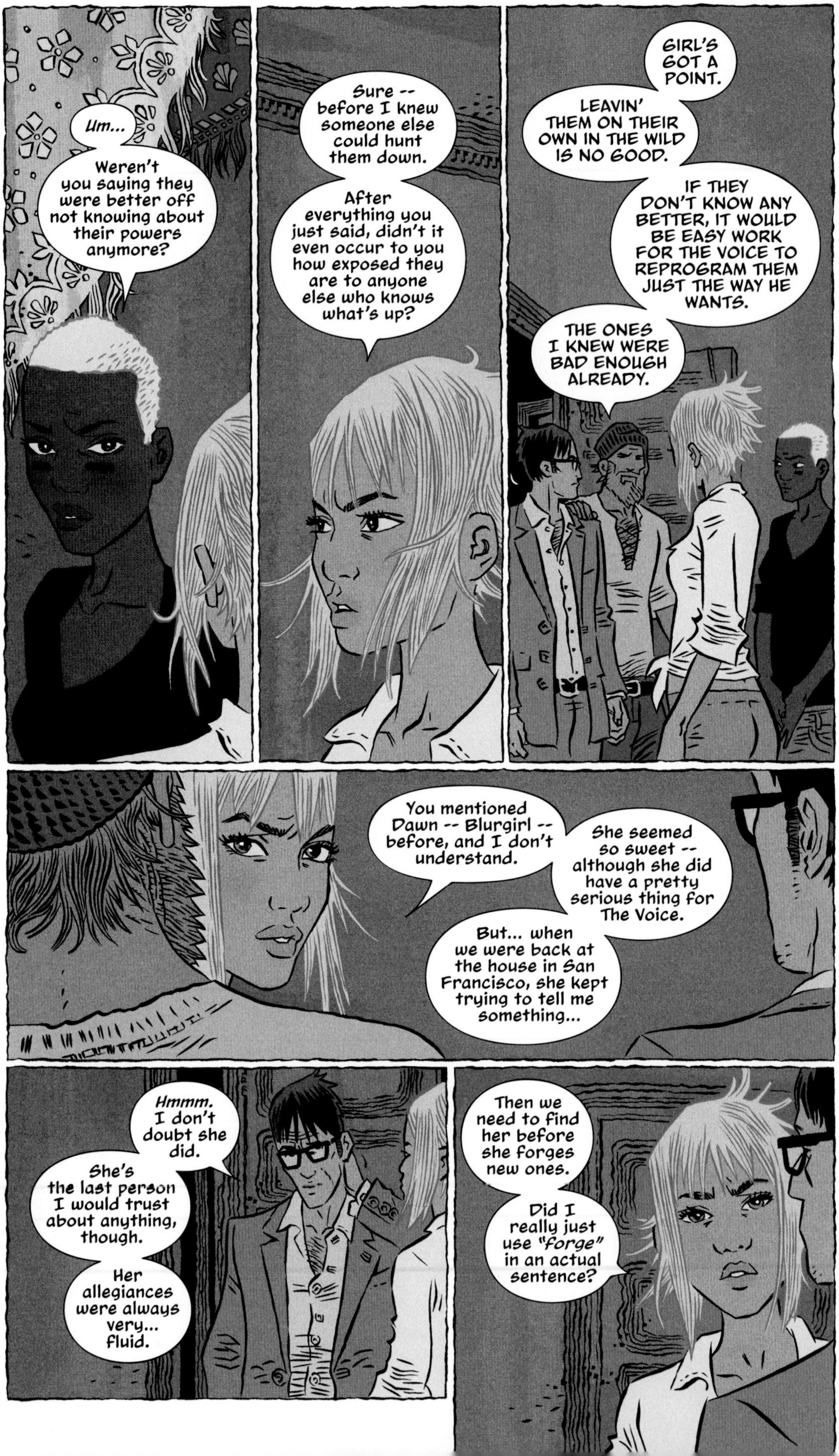
Um...
Weren't you saying they were better off not knowing about their powers anymore?
Sure -- before I knew someone else could hunt them down.
After everything you just said, didn't it even occur to you how exposed they are to anyone else who knows what's up?
GIRL'S GOT A POINT.
LEAVIN' THEM ON THEIR OWN IN THE WILD IS NO GOOD.
IF THEY DON'T KNOW ANY BETTER, IT WOULD BE EASY WORK FOR THE VOICE TO REPROGRAM THEM JUST THE WAY HE WANTS.
THE ONES I KNEW WERE BAD ENOUGH ALREADY.
You mentioned Dawn -- Blurgirl -- before, and I don't understand.
She seemed so sweet -- although she did have a pretty serious thing for The Voice.
But... when we were back at the house in San Francisco, she kept trying to tell me something...
Hmmm. I don't doubt she did.
She's the last person I would trust about anything, though.
Her allegiances were always very... fluid.
Then we need to find her before she forges new ones.
Did I really just use "forge" in an actual sentence?

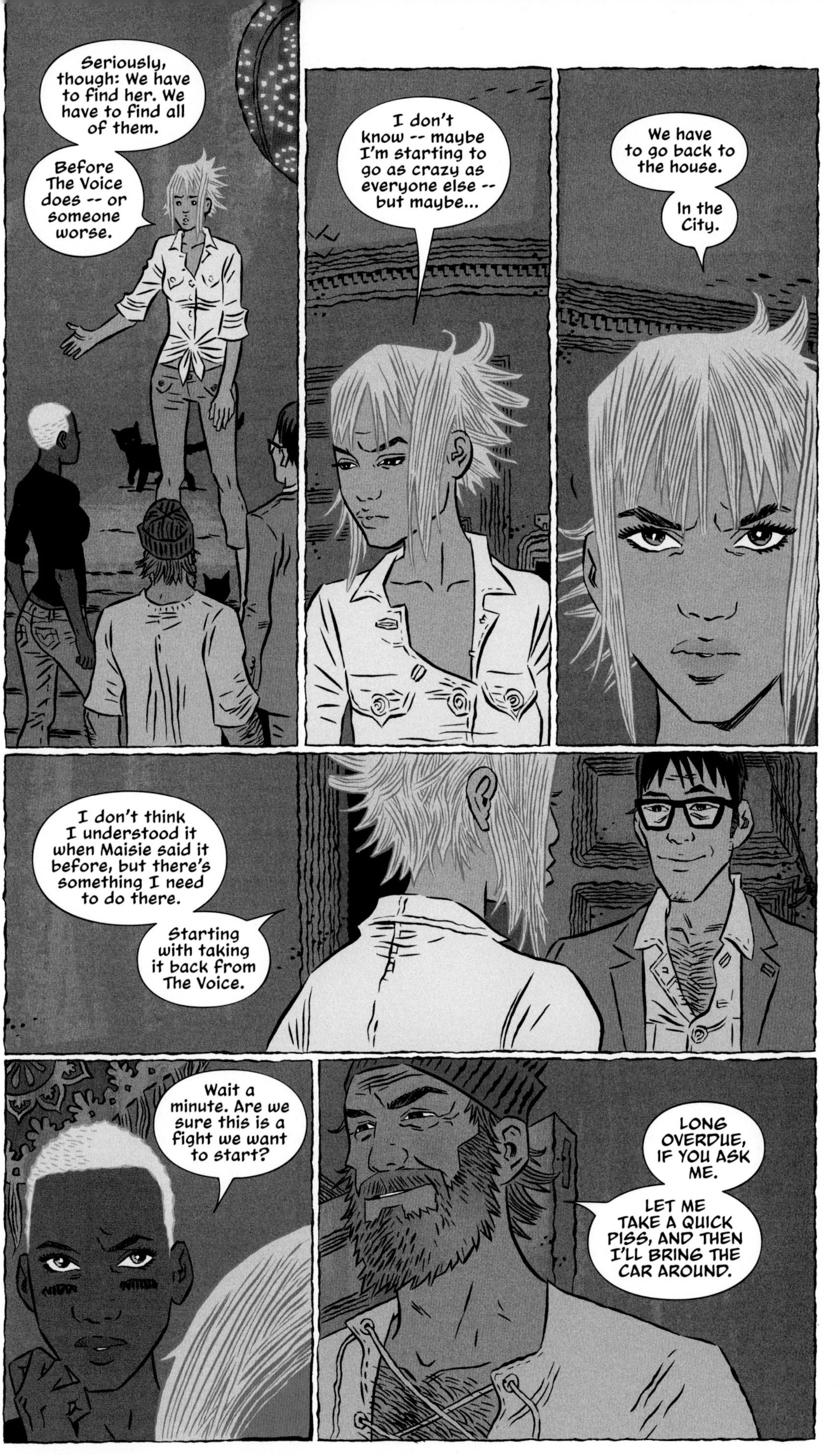
Seriously, though: We have to find her. We have to find all of them.
Before The Voice does -- or someone worse.
I don't know -- maybe I'm starting to go as crazy as everyone else -- but maybe...
We have to go back to the house.
In the City.
I don't think I understood it when Maisie said it before, but there's something I need to do there.
Starting with taking it back from The Voice.
Wait a minute. Are we sure this is a fight we want to start?
LONG OVERDUE, IF YOU ASK ME.
LET ME TAKE A QUICK PISS, AND THEN I'LL BRING THE CAR AROUND.

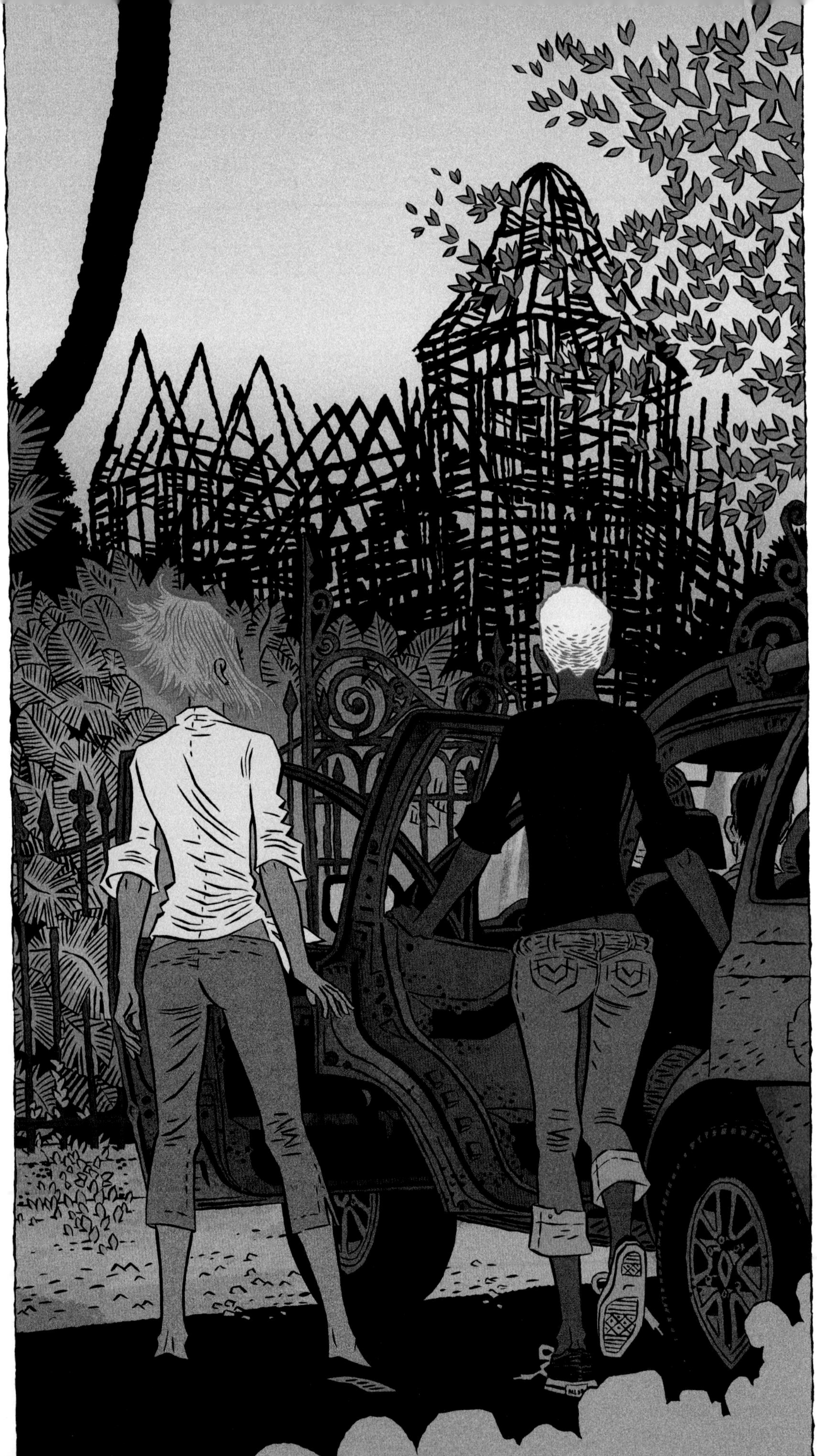

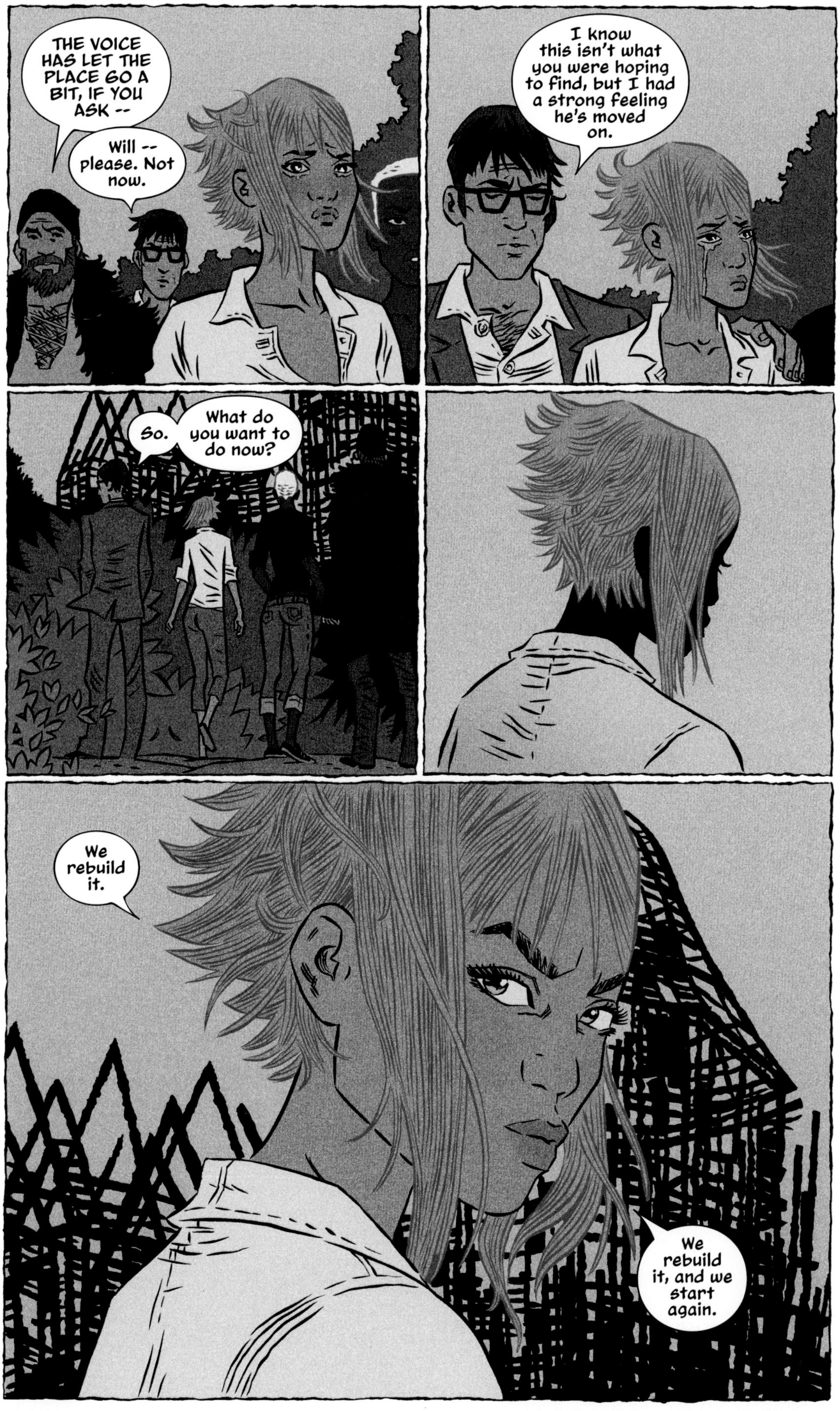
THE VOICE HAS LET THE PLACE GO A BIT, IF YOU ASK --
Will -- please. Not now.
I know this isn't what you were hoping to find, but I had a strong feeling he's moved on.
So.
What do you want to do now?
We rebuild it.
We rebuild it, and we start again.

REMEMBER IT'S TRUE, DIGNITY IS VALUABLE BUT OUR LIVES ARE VALUABLE TOO.

DAVID ROBERT JONES

SIMON GANE
THE ARTIST

Simon Gane draws things. Really, really well, as it turns out. The artist behind *Paris* and *The Vinyl Underground*, his other past credits include contributions to *Northlanders*, *Godzilla*, and *Graphic Classics*. Simon lives and works in Bristol, England, and when he's not drawing comics, he's basically on a never-ending quest to perfect a life of sheer awesomeness.

JORDIE BELLAIRE
THE COLORIST

Jordie Bellaire is the world's most beloved Eisner-winning colorist. It would be easier to list the books she hasn't worked on than the ones she has colored, but some of the highlights include *Injection*, *Pretty Deadly*, *The Manhattan Projects*, and *Nowhere Men*. Jordie makes her home in Dublin, Ireland, but don't let the red hair fool you, she's 100% American.

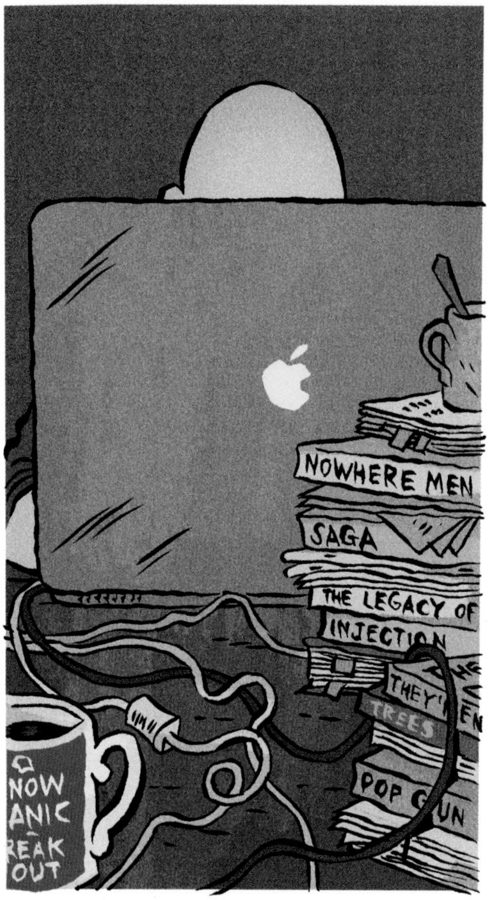
NOWHERE MEN
SAGA
THE LEGACY OF
INJECTION
TREES

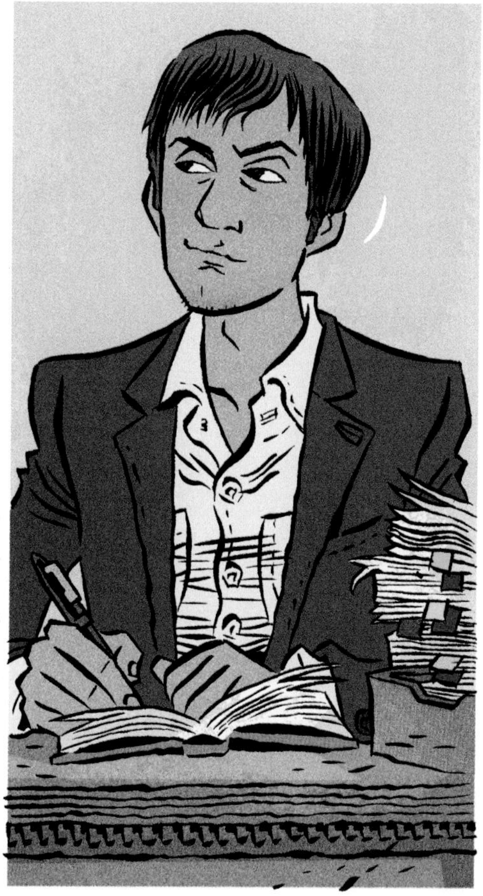

FONOGRAFIKS

THE DESIGNER

Fonografiks makes everything look its absolute best with some of the finest lettering and design in comics. From the *Luther Strode* trilogy to *Trees* to *Nowhere Men* to *Injection* to *Saga*, anything Fonografiks touches turns to, if not gold, something just as brilliant. The rich scenery of his native North East England is largely lost on him as he burns the midnight oil for his clients across the pond.

ERIC STEPHENSON

THE WRITER

Eric Stephenson has made a full-time occupation out of being utterly indebted to his beyond-amazing collaborators and eternally grateful for the tireless dedication of everyone at Image Comics. Eric is also writer and co-creator of the Eisner-nominated *Nowhere Men*, and generally speaking, he's fairly jealous of the rest of the *TNLU* team for living in the UK, even though Berkeley, California can be pretty nice, too.

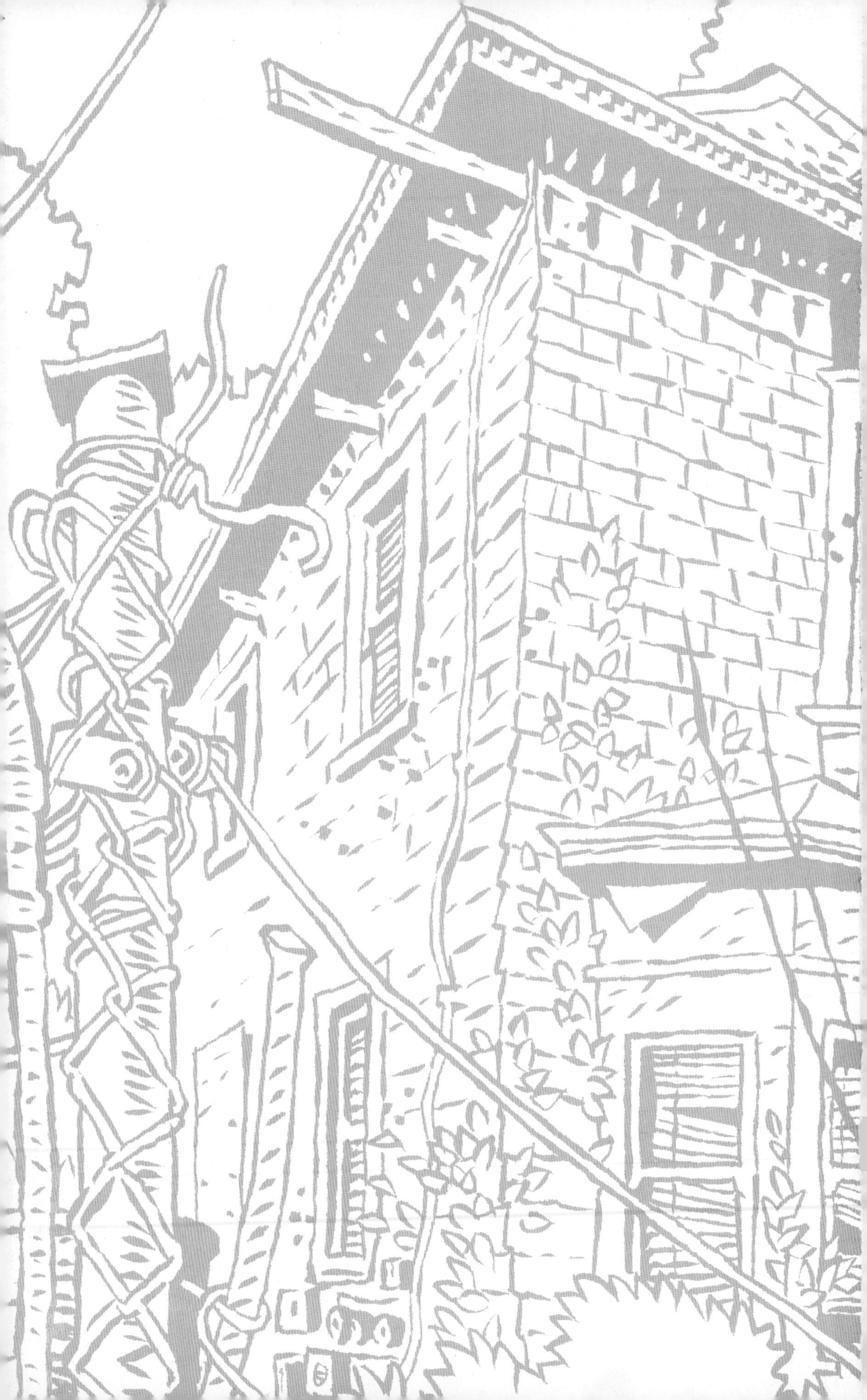